Mountains Can Move

PAUL MITCHELL

Mountains Can Move

DEDICATION

To my wife, Joan.
Thank-you for your patience, kindness, trust and hope.
Your support helped me persevere through this latest of the many journeys we have traveled together...

ACKNOWLEDGMENTS

Thank you to my friends and relatives who made their way through the early drafts and provided the encouragement I needed to see this project through.

Thank you Sarah T. Schawb of Cardinal Flix, INC for your consultation. Your unique vision helped bring my characters into focus.

Thank you Mary Kathleen Dougherty of Bootstrap Publishing who shepherded me along the self-publishing trail. Your calm guidance and expertise made the process interesting and enjoyable.

Thank you Scott Seifritz for being my editor, teacher, and honest critic. Your dedication to the craft of writing and your love for the art of writing are evident on every page of this story.

To the reader: Thank you for reading this book. No story is complete until it is shared with someone.

ONE

Of course they were late.

The green and white truck pulled into the driveway. It was the third lawn service he had hired this spring. The first was a nationally advertised outfit; the second was an old drunk and his stoner nephew. This one was supposedly local. The name, Lawn Order, tickled his fancy. He watched as a young guy dressed in a green jumpsuit walked head down, poking at his phone, to unload the zero-turn.

Albert was headed outside to give him a once–over when his phone rang. He lifted the avocado-green handset from the touch-tone phone. He knew it would be his daughter.

"Hi Dad, don't you have a doctor's appointment this week? I can take you. When is it?"

"It was yesterday. I had one of Bagger's grandsons to take me."

"Why didn't you ask me? I always take you. Are you hiding something from me?"

"I'm not hiding anything," Albert said. "It just worked out that he could take me."

He took another glance out the kitchen window as the kid donned a headset and started up the machine, too late now to give him instructions.

"Well, I don't like you hiding things from me. What did the doctor say?"

“Nobody sees doctors anymore, only providers," he said. "This was a guy, so I assume he was an assistant doctor and not some practicing nurse.”

“Dad, men can be NPs, and there's always a doctor available.”

“Well anyway, this one wasn't too bad. He actually closed his computer and looked at me when he talked.”

Bonnie waited for more information, but it didn't come. “What did he say about your dizziness?”

“Oh, it turns out he's not just a shill for Big Pharma. He told me I was over-medicated, so he stopped all my blood pressure pills. Since I cut down smoking and lost weight, I don’t need ‘em anymore."

“Did you tell him you're still smoking?”

“I told him I was down to three or four a day. He said at this point it probably won’t hurt me that much more. He thinks if it keeps me from being nervous, it's fine.”

“I doubt that's what he said. What about the shaking?”

“Well, that’s the best part. It’s definitely not Parkinson’s. He called it an 'essential tremor,' and like I told you, it goes away when I have a drink. So, it turns out smoking and drinking are actually good for my health. I love my new provider.”

"I looked it up on the internet," Bonnie said, "and that's what it said there too, so it must be true, and it runs in families, and..." She was just getting started.

Albert, however, was done talking. "Whatever," he said. "I gotta go and check on this yahoo ruining my lawn." He hung the receiver back in its cradle.

Albert considered his lawn an extension of his art. Its over two acres of Kentucky Bluegrass was an oasis in the desert of the neighboring neglected properties. The perimeter was bordered with a boxwood hedge and mulched with dark gravel set against a tall white fence.

He noticed the kid had started on the side instead of in the middle. There was no way the rows were going to match up. Albert always made even mowing tracks lined up like bowling alleys from north to south or diagonally making a green-on-green quilt of diamond patches. It wasn't like he couldn't mow the lawn himself. He just couldn't do it all at once anymore, and it took too much of his time. Hiring it out felt like desecration, but he was trying to get his priorities in order. It was one step on his new journey.

It would take some effort, but if he could get over this obsession, he might be able to make all the other changes he had in mind.

When the kid was done he pulled up in front of Albert. Albert checked the height. Not too bad -- short enough to look nice but long enough to support the roots. Still, he got great pleasure from harassing the kid and giving him a lesson on turf management. The young man waited out the haranguing patiently, hand twitching for his phone. He told the old man he would do his best to satisfy him.

After the kid left Albert sat on the bench by the lawn. He had been up early and was already getting tired, but it was too soon for his nap. He sat and looked at his lawn while he tried to light a cigarette. The tremor made him more likely to light his nose than the cigarette, so he gave up and went back to the house.

Albert leaned against the kitchen counter and took up the bottle waiting there. He left his glass sitting and carefully poured out a ration and drank it down. Soon the tremor subsided, and he made his way upstairs. Over the winter he had started sorting the contents of his house. He had taken several boxes of clothes to the local homeless shelter. He felt giving his jetsam to the flotsam of this capitalistic society was the least he could do. He had kept this on the sly so his two kids wouldn't notice. He had separated all the rest into piles.

His daughter's memorabilia made up one pile: baby pictures and high school yearbooks filled with pressed corsages and vows from classmates to never forget her. Brown newspaper clippings celebrating her short band career were mixed with post cards from around the country.

Another pile contained a worn blue jewelry box, a carton of porcelain figurines, a photo album, and a rubber-banded wad of unopened sympathy cards. There was an opened trash bag next to this pile. As much as he wanted to, he could not bring himself to discard these decades old memories of his wife. He left them there in limbo.

His son's pile was the largest. In it were photos of him dressed in his brown-shirt-like uniform of the Boy Scouts of America. Albert always thought the early exposure to this quasi-military cabal had laid the groundwork for his son's total buy-in to God, country, and the almighty dollar. There were scrapbooks of sports clippings and boxes of trophies and plaques. There was his scholarship offer from Princeton and a copy of his high school Valedictorian speech. He had urged his classmates to follow their dreams into the world of upward mobility. He never mentioned that most of them would live out their lives toiling for some rich guy only to be cast aside with a broken body and a meager social security check.

Albert worked until he had taped the boxes shut and piled them up. He looked at his own pile, still not sorted, and went back downstairs. He poured out the last of the bourbon to stave off the tremor so he could do the dishes and clean up the kitchen. He then read the local fish-wrapper until it was time for his three-o'clock nap on the broken-down living-room couch.

He slept soundly until fading sunlight slipped under the bottom of the pulled shades and soaked through his eye lids. He was then roused completely by a knock on the door. Albert pushed the shade aside and saw the dark, weathered face of his old friend, Bagger. He was holding the brown paper bag he knew contained this week's booze delivery. He pulled the door open, and Bagger handed him the bag.

"You ready?" Bagger asked.

"One sec," Albert said. He pulled out his wallet and paid Bagger for the bottle and a little extra for gas. He grabbed his union gimme hat and a Carhartt jacket then followed Bagger out to the old Ford Taurus. Soon they were on their way to The Backdoor Inn, just like every Thursday night for as long as Albert could remember.

They always ate at the bar. The bartender's name was Alice, but she would only answer to Mrs. Beasley.

"Want the usual, Al?" she asked after they sat down.

"No, this time give me a steak I don't need side cutters to get through."

Mrs. Beasley was in a lighthearted mood. She flipped her order pad open.

"Want fries with that, darlin'?"

Bagger gasped.

Albert slowly let his gaze rise from the glasses on a chain hanging over her drooping bosom, up past the fake pearl necklace, over the double chin to Mrs. Beasley's watery eyes and slapped a fifty-dollar bill on the bar.

He took his tone up a notch, "I haven't had a fry in two years, and you know it. Why do you always ask me?"

"Touchy tonight, eh Al?" teased Mrs. Beasley. "Would you gentleman care for a beverage?"

Albert spoke softly and slowly. "We've come here for thirty years. I always have a steak, no fries, whiskey, and a Genny Cream Ale chaser.

Why do we have to go through this every time?"

Mrs. Beasley clicked her pen and turned away.

"Jeez, Pablo, what's bitin' your butt?" Bagger asked.

Albert was quiet a minute. "I think I turned the corner Bagger. I can't stand it here anymore. I gotta move on. I really think I'm gonna do it."

Bagger quickly swiveled to face him. "Oh man. When'll you tell Bonnie and Andy?"

"Andrew will be making his quarterly guilt trip to see me next week. Bonnie will bring over supper one of the nights. After that, I'll call a realtor and get this thing moving. I might as well give up. The swine on the town board keep raising my taxes. They want me to sell out to their developer cronies, so they can all line their pockets."

Mrs. Beasley brought the whiskey and beer. They tapped their shot glasses on the bar and knocked them back together. Then they worked on their beers a bit.

Bagger gripped the rounded edge of the bar. His hands had the same patina as the worn wood. He looked straight ahead and said, "Pablo, I've known you for thirty-five years, and I never said nothin' about your painting. I only know it's important to you, but now, I gotta be honest. It ain't never brought you nothin' but trouble. It's your business alright, but maybe it's time you take a hard look at what you really want... or need."

Albert finished his beer and tapped the fifty. Mrs. Beasley caught the sign and delivered another round. Then she served the steaks. They ate in silence.

They had one more round and talked about the latest union guys that had died. It was hard to converse with Albert, he didn't own a TV and hadn't changed an opinion in sixty years. He kept up on local politics, but any discussion about them led to a red-faced rant, so Bagger avoided it. As the two old friends finished their last beer, Bagger's grandsons walked in on cue to drive them home.

Mrs. Beasley brought the change. "Was everything satisfactory?"

Albert left the bills on the bar and said. "You forgot my fries."

"You're a crock-get outta my bar."

"Love you too, Alice," Albert said and grinned.

When Albert got home, he went out on the back porch and lit a cigarette. He smoked in the dark and watched the jets come and go from the airport.

Andy put down his phone. It was the second time his wife had called since evening. A wave of exhaustion broke over him and he slumped back in his chair. He thought:

How did I let this happen again? Why am I so weak that I need pills to keep me normal? Three days without sleep this time. I just have to stay on them and not let this happen again. I've got to get home to my wife.

He pushed the intercom.

"Miss Ryan?"

"Yes, Mr. Martel?"

"Please call the driver. And Miss Ryan, thanks for staying late again. Call security to walk you out, and try not to miss me too much next week."

Andrew T. Martel, Esq. put some files and his laptop in his briefcase. He rode the elevator down alone. Out on Wall Street there was only one limo at the curb.

The limo was one of the best perks of being a partner, but he didn't fool himself; it also gave the firm another hour for him to work. But, not tonight. It was Thursday, and he wasn't going back to the office until a week from Monday. He fell asleep as soon as they hit the FDR and awoke at the first stop light in Chappaqua. After another ten minutes, the limo pulled around his driveway and came to a stop. The driver opened the door.

Andrew palmed him a hundred. "Thanks. See you in a week or so."

He unlocked the door and turned off lights as he made his way to the bedroom. His wife awoke as he eased in next to her.

"I'm home."

"Please try to sleep. We'll talk in the morning."

"I will. Good night."

TWO

Albert slept the sleep of most heavy drinkers. By 3:30 he was awake. He had to take a leak anyway, so he got up. There was a time when he would have gone to his studio and painted for a few hours then gone to work laying out and joining copper plumbing wherever the Union sent him. Sometimes it was to new residential work, other times to a gritty dank basement in an old commercial building.

This morning he got to thinking about what Bagger had said. *Everyone acted as though painting was something he could take or leave. They couldn't know that without painting, there would be no Albert Martel. Without painting, his demons would have nowhere to go. Without painting, his joys would wither unseen like flowers in a forest. They thought he sacrificed so much of his life to it. They could not know the pain of the sacrifices that took him away from it. But now, had he finally pickled his brain? Was his plan to sell everything and move away the delusion of an addled old man?*

Albert pulled out the file he had made. He looked at the numbers again. His pension and social security were not changing. The house insurance, utilities, and taxes were. He was in a spiral to deficit and had no options to selling. He had planned for this. Rather than investing in corporate America and the military industrial complex, he had bought land. He knew at some time he would have to sell it. The time had come.

≈

Lillian slowly slipped out of bed, trying not to awaken her husband. She put on her kimono and closed the door behind her. It was only seven in the morning. She hoped he would sleep in for once.

Down in the kitchen, remnants of her son's breakfast were in the sink. He had already left for the club driving range and then caddying for the day. She knew her daughter wouldn't make an appearance until mid-morning. She filled the French press and surveyed her kitchen.

Despite the best of intensions, the expanse of the granite island was cluttered with mail, leftover school papers, and magazines. Even though the refrigerator was enclosed with cabinet work, the outer doors were covered with calendars, schedules, and reminders. She had always said she wanted a home, not a show place.

Well, I got it, she thought to herself.

She took her coffee to the nook and sat on the window seat. Beyond the outdoor kitchen and the pool, the lawn was glistening from the overnight watering. She could see that the gardener had worked on the perennial beds yesterday.

Andy padded in, dressed in a sweat suit. His hair was wet from the shower.

"I thought you would sleep in," Lillian said.

"It's after eight, I didn't want to just lay there."

"What set you off this time?" Lillian asked.

"I'm still a little groggy, can we get into it later? I said I was sorry. I really am. I want to talk about it, but not right now."

"We can wait, but I'm telling you, you have to promise to get an appointment and figure this out."

"I promise. Aren't you working today?"

"Nope, I'm all yours, all day."

Andy poured some coffee. "Do we need to go shopping or something?"

"No, Andy, I thought we could spend the day together."

"I really hadn't thought about today. What do you have in mind?"

"We can wash your car, go for a hike, go to the club, or God forbid, just stay here at home. After three nights away I thought you would want to spend some time with me. I can go to work if you don't."

"Oh, right. How about I make omelets, and we can come up with a plan?"

Albert took a brochure out of the file. It was the color of a paper grocery bag and prominently stamped:

Made with 100% recycled paper. Ink is biodegradable. The front page said:

SUNADEW
Community
Caring
Creating
A home to be you.
A home for you to be.

Inside were the details describing an adult community that catered to artists of all kinds, free thinkers, and those wishing to live out their lives with minimal interference from the government, social mores, and expectations. It emphasized an atmosphere of self-expression and creativity. For an extra cost, studio space was available for any kind of art. The goal being to provide a communal experience of sharing and self-development.

The costs were a little hazy. They offered continuing care from independent to assisted living all the way to nursing home and hospice care. It stated the fees could only be discussed in person.

Albert believed this would be a place where, finally, he would be among like-minded people. People who would understand him. People he could actually discuss art and share ideas with. He had been an artist in the wilderness of a blue-collar world. Now he wanted to finish out his life and career amongst like-minded people.

An added benefit of Sunadew was that it was located in Vermont.

He would at last get out of the "Empire State" whose government existed of, by, and for the one-percenters – run by an inbred clan of career politicians, real estate moguls, and Wall Street billionaires. Typical New York voters display their Progressive virtues with a $40,000 Prius. They drive it to Star-Big-Bucks to buy their $5.00 lattes from a schlump making $7.00 an hour. They elect one limousine liberal after another to feel good about themselves while they grind their lives away for whatever corporation bought their souls.

Albert could feel the blood pulsing in his temples. He calmed himself down and tried to keep at the task at hand.

Albert knew he had to get organized before springing this on Andy. They had their differences, but Albert admired Andy for his intelligence and hard work. Unfortunately, he had run off to New York City and became a one-percenter himself; completely leaving his father and his working-class roots behind. Albert also knew, without his son's help, he wouldn't be able to navigate selling the property and moving.

Andy had mastered the omelet long ago. He made two in quick succession, each folded with a flick of a fork and served with a flourish.

Andy looked out the window. "This is nice. Good idea."

"Good omelet, hon."

Andy knew she was stalling. “To tell the truth," he said, "I'd like to stay here for most of the day. We can just putz around and talk.”

"Don't you want to get out? You've been cooped up in Manhattan, you should get outside. Is there stuff you have to do today? ”

“I don’t have that much to do. Monday is the final hearing on the Kowalski case. I have a few details to finish, and that’ll be the end of it. I'm not taking any more pro bono work this year.”

“Yeah, I've heard that before,” Lillian said.

“Really, I just can’t for a while. Then I need to do a little prep for the Wednesday meeting at the Albany office on my way to see Dad. I have a feeling he's worrying about the house. He knows he can’t stay there much longer."

“I just can’t imagine him in a little apartment, or worse, some kind of facility,” Lillian said.

“I think we could find an apartment with enough space for him to paint. He has money. It just isn’t going to last if he stays in the house."

“It'll have to be near his friends and his bar,” Lillian laughed.

“You’re right, he would never want to be far from either one. What I really dread is cleaning out the house and the junk over the garage. If he won't throw them out, we'll have to get a storage unit for his paintings.

When the coffee was gone, Lillian started picking up the kitchen. Andy began going through the mail scattered on the island. He made piles divided by addressee, recycling, and bills. He quickly scanned Jack's stack of graded school papers. He set aside a couple of B results to go over with his son later. Their daughter, Sophie – nicknamed Cookie as a child -- had conveniently left some information on studies in Paris along with a partially completed graduate school application.

Then he thought, *I'll get a jump on Lilly.*

"Hey, Lil, how about we go for a walk?"

"Or a run, if you think you can keep up," Lillian teased.

Andy worked out occasionally in his office gym or at the club. Lillian, however, was in marathon shape from her daily training regimen. Andy knew she would run him into the ground.

"I thought just a relaxing walk -- so we can have more time together."

"I'll get dressed fraidy cat," Lillian replied.

Lillian came down in Oiselle running tights. The matching top was fitted but modestly covered her bottom. It could not hide the long muscular legs, narrow hips, and high waist of a natural-born runner. Since she wasn't running today, she had chosen a sports bra that left some roundness on top. Her blonde ponytail hung below her shoulders through the back of her running hat.

Andy quickly changed out of his sweat suit and into his North Face hiking pants. He could still rock an Under Armour shirt, so he put on a fairly tight one and an unbuttoned light shirt. The town walking trail was just down the street. They hit that and found a comfortable walking stride together.

≈

Albert added a little more Jack Daniels to his coffee mug and filled it again. The task ahead of him was weighing him down. Most of the household contents could be thrown out. Not even the most desperate family would want the overstuffed green and gold couch. The matching armchair looked like a forlorn pile of fabric remnants. His brown Naugahyde Barcalounger had long ago listed to the right, and the footrest was stuck halfway down. The veneer on the dining room table was chipped and peeling. The padded chairs had not received much use but still looked worn and uninviting. In the kitchen the Formica table was shiny yellow with white showing through the scrubbed areas. There was brown filling peeking through the rips on the matching chrome and yellow vinyl chairs. He had no attachment to the knick-knacks and memorabilia covering every level surface. His kids could take what they want; the rest could go in a dumpster.

He carried his coffee into the garage, walking between his pickup and his now-abandoned zero-turn, then up the stairs to his studio. The north-facing windows and skylights filled the open ceiling with soft light; the earth tones glowed on the walls. He had always kept his studio clean and organized. Recently, he had cataloged all the loose sketches by subject and stored them in portfolios. The stretched canvases were in racks two deep, floor-to-ceiling against the west wall. The few that were framed were hung around the room. He had given away hundreds of sketches, portraits, and pastels. Rarely, if someone expressed interest, he would part with an oil. He had never sold a painting. He would be damned if one of his paintings ended up an accent piece in some bourgeois/yuppie/nouveau riche's latest "great room" color scheme.

Even though it was organized, the vast amount of material was unmanageable. He could not take it with him to Vermont. He wouldn't impose on anyone to store it. In an odd way, he really didn't care. Each painting had served its purpose. When he was done with one, he always moved on to a new project. He realized this hoard of canvas and paint held his life: it was him. For whatever its worth, maybe it should be kept somewhere. He would have to talk to Andy about it.

Andy and Lillian rounded off the street and onto their driveway. It had been a nice walk. Andy felt loosened up, the stiffness was gone from his neck and shoulders. As always, his wife was right. He just needed a few hours to get Manhattan and the last week behind him and get into life at home.

In the kitchen, Sophie was having breakfast, perched on a stool staring at her phone. When she saw Andy, she dropped her spoon and jumped off the stool.

"Hi, Daddy!"

"Hi, Cookie." Andy received her hug and kissed her forehead.

"Are you really home all next week?" Sophie asked.

“Mostly. I have to go see Grandpa though,” he said apologetically.

Sophie gave a little jump like she was a six-year-old. “Oh, Daddy, I have to go with you to see him.”

Andy was astonished. “Why ever would you want to do that?”

“I have to apologize to him.”

“What could you possibly have to apologize for?”

“He sent me a real letter with an envelope and stamp, and I never wrote back. At the end of the term I got an email telling me to come clean out my mailbox. Like, I forgot I had a mailbox. I feel just terrible. He went to all that trouble, and I never even let him know I got it. Who knew people still mailed letters?”

“What was the letter about?” Andy asked, forgetting he shouldn’t pry.

“He asked about my courses and what my main projects were. He wanted to know what my professors were like. He put in an amazing pencil sketch of his yard covered with a flock of crows. I've gotta go and thank him in person.”

"I'll think about it," Andy said.

"Daddy, I want to go," Sophie insisted.

Andy and Lillian puttered around the house most of the day catching up on some long-ignored tasks. In the afternoon Jack texted he could meet for dinner at the club at 4:30. At 4:15, Andy brought the Lexus out of the garage and up to the front where the ladies got in.

At the club, they entered through the bar. The duffers turned and shouted.

"Hey, Gunner, where you been?"

"Just working to pay your Social Security," Andy shot back.

"Keep it up, man, we appreciate it."

They got a table overlooking the18th green and settled in. The waiter approached.

"Good evening, welcome."

"Hey, hello Jorge, how'd your son's baseball team do?" Andy asked.

Jorge touched his heart. "You remembered. They lost in the state semi-finals. Manuel had two hits and a stolen base."

"Well, that's still a great season. Tell him congratulations for me." Andy glanced at Jack who took the cue.

"That's awesome, Mr. Perez! Tell Mannie hi for me, please."

"I will, thank you. What can I bring the ladies to drink?"

"I'll have a chardonnay," Lillian said blandly.

"I'll have a margarita." Sophie peeked at her father.

Lillian stared her down and waited.

Jorge broke in. "For Mr. Jack?"

"Are they making lemonade today?"

"Yes, it's fresh."

"Great. I'll have that."

Jorge turned to Andy, while trying to avoid Mrs. Martel's eyes. "And Mr. Martel?"

"Anything new on draft?" Andy asked.

"Broken Arrow has a new pale ale."

"Let's try it." Andy smiled at Jorge.

When the waiter had left Lillian looked at Sophie. "You should not be drinking at the club. People will notice."

"Yeah, like they notice their own kids vaping weed behind the caddy shack."

"Miss Sophie Alice, that's no way to talk! You will not have more than one drink." Lillian shot a blue-eyed dagger at Andy.

"Dad, can I go home with Gina after church Sunday?" Jack asked. "Her Dad wants me to go to the driving range with him in the afternoon."

Andy pulled at his chin. "Hmm, the girlfriend's father wants a golf lesson. Sounds like this relationship is getting serious. I guess I can give you up. Would you have time for a round with your father on Monday?"

"You mean it? We can play 18 here?"

"Sure, if you can fit it in," Andrew joked.

"I guess I have time to give you a lesson too," Jack said through his biggest smile.

After the margarita incident, the evening lightened up and they enjoyed being all together once again. Sophie nursed her drink. Andy had a couple more local brews. Lillian beamed at her healthy, happy, beautiful family and allowed herself a second chardonnay.

Back at home Andy let everyone out and took the car to the garage. As he came through the great room, Lillian said, "How about you start a fire? I'll bring you a fleece."

He went out to the patio and piled newspaper and kindling in the outdoor fireplace. Lillian joined him, and they cuddled up on the big rattan loveseat. She was quiet a minute then said, "Hon, can I ask you a question?"

"I know Lil, I know."

"It was three days again this time. Why did you stop taking the pills? You know your mood goes up and down without them."

"I'd been feeling so good I didn't think I needed them anymore... again. I promise I won't crash this time... I promise. I'm back on the meds. I feel better; am I acting OK?"

"You're acting fine, but I don't want you to act. I want you to feel well. I want you to be happy." Lillian's ice-blue eyes were misting.

Andy choked back tears. "Lillian, you've made my life so wonderful. I don't know where I'd be if it wasn't for you. I'm sorry I didn't come home. I don't know what happens; it's all a blur."

"Lillian said, "You have to listen to me when I tell you something's wrong. You need to trust people more."

"I trust you, Lil."

Andy added some wood to the fire, and they lost themselves in the flames.

THREE

Bonnie added some extra peppers to the vegan chili in hopes her father could taste it through his cigarettes and booze. Somehow, this had become her routine. Ever since he stopped driving two years ago she shopped for his groceries, did his laundry, and brought him dinner every Friday. It had progressed without much discussion.

When she was young she had felt trapped into caring for her father; this was different. After it was just her, Andy, and him she fell into the homemaker role. It didn't last. She felt guilty when she left. When she came back he wouldn't accept any help from her. Now they had come to a steady state where the crest of her guilt fell into his trough of resentment. She was happy with how things were going at the present. And who knows, maybe someday he will need her full time, and she can move back home.

≈

Albert took the bottle with him to the porch to prepare for his daughter's weekly visit. A few short ones and two cigarettes later, he heard Bonnie's beat-up Volvo grind to a stop in front of the garage. She came in bearing Tupperware and a Corelle casserole dish. Albert knew another vegan, gluten-free, non-GMO, fair-traded, organic meal was in store. He went out and carried in the groceries Bonnie had picked up for him.

His daughter was uniformed in Dead Head standard issue complete with a turquoise peasant blouse and a multi-colored layered cotton skirt. She had on one of the "healing crystal" necklaces she made. The pastel rubber bands listing her concerns du jour clashed with the silver bracelets coiled on her wrists. Her hair -- brown, with a touch of gray -- was in white-girl dreadlocks. She had tattoos of dancing bears, red roses, and skulls scattered about. She had been a pretty girl but disguised it well most of her life.

"Hi Dad, I just have to warm this up."

Bonnie opened the door of the Radar Range. She turned the dial to 10 minutes and pressed the start button.

"Before I forget, I talked to my herbalist and she said you should be taking valerian for your tremor. I got you some, so you can make tea with it. You should drink three cups every day."

She served her father dinner and began a discourse on the state of concert tours and how the cost of tickets was curtailing "real people" from attending. She had thought of peddling her candles, crystals, and brownies on the festival circuit again this summer but had decided against it. Albert agreed and again urged her to look for a steady job.

Other than the food, Albert enjoyed her visits. In her way, she was entertaining and had an unconcerned and joyous outlook on life.

They had dinner, and Bonnie mercifully packed up the leftovers to take home. They said goodnight, and Albert went back to the porch where the bourbon and cigarettes were waiting for him.

FOUR

Andy liked their church. It wasn’t a mega-church, but the Sunday service was in the contemporary style. It featured a band with guitars and drums. The worship songs were the usual three cords and nine clichés, but they were sung in earnest, and the musicians were quite good. He had no doubt God loved to hear them. The sermons were interesting and inspiring. Andy was glad he was committed to attending every week. He wished he could fit regular Bible study into his routine.

After the service, they met up with the Donatellis and made arrangements to get Jack back home after golf. Before Sophie could put her ear buds in, Andy asked, “Hey Cookie, would you help me clean my car this afternoon?”

“Sure, OK," she said without much conviction.

The Corvette was Andy’s indulgence when he made partner five years earlier. He had grown up watching the motorheads race their hotrods up and down Lake Avenue. In college his old Chevy Nova was an embarrassment next to the BMWs and Porches of his frat brothers. He had always coveted a '67 Vette and searched far and wide to find a black one with the 427 engine. The complete restoration included a Princeton orange air scoop.

He had put it away last fall, and now it was time to release it back to the road. He roused Sophie out of her room, and they went down to the garage. He really didn't need her help but wanted to talk to her about going with him to Rochester to check on his father.

After they pushed it out of the garage, they gathered up the dedicated plastic pails, the special soap, polishes, and wax and went to work. Sophie knew the drill: all jewelry had to come off, if you drop a cloth, you got a new one, and on and on.

"Cookie, are you sure you want to go up to Grandpa's with me?" Andy asked as he was rinsing for the second time.

"I have to, Dad. I can't live with myself having him think I ignored him."

"That's very mature of you. I'm proud. But I could explain it to him, and he'd understand. I have to stop in Albany for a couple hours for a meeting, so you'll have to wait there."

"I can always do some sketching or find a Starbucks. You really don't think I should see Grandpa, do you?" Sophie asked.

"You haven't seen him in a few years. He isn't real healthy, and he can be difficult at times. I don't want you to think he'll be all warm and fuzzy then be disappointed."

"He's always been nice to me. It's you he gets difficult with."

Andy flinched. "That's true, but it's always been like that for me. I just don't want you hurt."

Sophie giggled. "I'm used to grumpy old men. I live with *you*, don't I?"

Andy threw a wet sponge at her, but she was too fast to hit. Sophie finished up the interior and went back to the house.

Andy hooked up the battery and checked the tire pressure. The car started on the second try. The uneven grumble from the side pipes turned to a predatory growl then a roar when he touched the accelerator. The noise and vibration went right to his loins. He gave the hand-brake a pull and left it idling.

He shouted to Lillian who was out looking at the gardens.

"Hey Lil, I got the car started."

"Oh, really? I hadn't noticed," she said over the rumble.

"Let's go for a ride," he said ignoring her jab.

It was warm enough for shorts. Lillian caught her husband staring as she swung her legs across the black leather seat.

"Keep your eyes on the road, Gunner," Lillian said.

"And my hands on the wheel, right?" Andy was laughing.

It was a running joke that since Andy already had the blonde, he had to have a sports car.

She definitely dressed it up, he thought.

They cruised through town, turning heads as they went. Out in the country and heading into the mountains, he let it out a little. It surged from sixty to ninety before they could finish a breath. Lillian would never admit it to Andy, but she felt a quiver when the acceleration thrust her into the soft leather seat.

When they got back, Andy let the hot engine idle down and reached for his wife. She gave him a restrained kiss and pushed his hand away. "Andy Martel, what kind of girl do you think I am?" She laughed and folded her legs to get out of the cockpit.

Andy watched her walk away then backed the Vette into the garage. It was time to make his Sunday phone call to his father.

Albert poured a double into his coffee mug and headed to the studio. He had painted every Sunday morning for so long it was a ritual. He had finished layering up his painting in progress with brushes. He would be using the palette knife today and needed a rock steady hand. He uncovered the painting and loaded his palette. The next thing he knew it was after noon, and his hand was starting to shake. He never ceased to wonder where time went while he was painting.

He just got in the house when the phone rang.

“Hey, Dad.”

“Hi, Andrew. You still coming up this week? I have some stuff to go over with you.”

“Yeah, that's why I took time off. Cookie wants to come to see you too.” Andy waited while there was a pause at the other end.

“She wants to see me? Here at the house?”

“You know she's very interested in your painting and just wants to see you.” Andy didn't let on he knew about the letter.

“She won’t stay here will she?” Albert sounded concerned.

"No, we'll get a hotel over on Jefferson or somewhere. I need Wi-Fi to stay in touch with the office." Andy knew his Dad was embarrassed.

"It would be nice to see her. How are Lillian and Jack?" Albert tried to lighten up.

"They're doing well. I'm playing golf with Jack tomorrow. I hope he doesn't kick my butt. Lillian's business has taken off; she's listing some really nice properties. Maybe later this summer we can all come up, or you could come and visit us here."

Albert stiffened a little. "Well, we'll see, I've got a lot to do this summer. We can cook out on Thursday. Bonnie will be over on Friday, and we can all talk."

"I have to stop in Albany in the morning. We'll see you around three. You might have to cut your nap short. We can go out somewhere for dinner. Do you need anything?"

"Could you pick up some steaks for Thursday? Bonnie won't buy them for me. I'll pay you back."

Andy chuckled. "Sure, I'll pick up some nice ones. My treat."

"Great. See you Wednesday afternoon. Drive safe."

Andy could tell his Dad had reached his limit for talking on the phone. "All right, see you then."

Andy now knew for sure his father was making plans to sell. He would have to do a little footwork to prepare for that. He was even more apprehensive about Sophie going with him.

He thought, *it sounds like she'll be getting an education in grown up issues.*

Bagger had brought Albert some white hots for lunch, so Albert set to frying some onions and peppers in his cast iron pan. He thought about Andrew and how these white hot dogs had been his favorite when he was a kid. Back then they couldn't be bought much outside of Rochester. He supposed now, with enough money, anyone could get them. He took two out of the package and added them to the pan before sitting down at the table. He opened a beer and looked around the kitchen. The walls were stained with grease and nicotine; the countertop was dull with a filmy glaze. He swept and mopped the floor weekly, but it too carried the residue of neglect. He regretted not letting Bonnie help when she asked. Now it was beyond “tidying up;” it needed a major cleaning. He turned the hots over. They were partially blackened. Soon they split open, and he turned off the stove. He took the beans out of the microwave, made up his plate, and went out on the porch.

After lunch, Albert headed for the couch but knew he wouldn’t be able to sleep. He could see how decrepit he had become. He had to show Sophie *and* his son he could manage his affairs. He went back to the kitchen and poured a short one to settle the tremor. He searched through the junk mail by the door until he found the latest penny saver and spread it out on the table. After a bit of searching, an ad caught his eye:

OCD HOUSEKEEPING
We Clean Like Crazy
Routine cleaning to pre-sale prepping
Call for all your cleaning needs

He called the number. He was concerned because the woman said she could come tomorrow but decided to check her out anyway.

≈

That evening Lillian and Andy left the kids to fend for themselves and headed to the club for dinner. Right after the drinks arrived, a portly man wearing plaid pants approached the table. An unbuttoned purple golf shirt put his gold chains and white chest hair on display.

"Good evening Lillian. Hello Andy."

"Hello Frank," they both said.

"Lillian, are we still on for Thursday?"

"Frank, I told you those numbers you sent me were laughable. I don't see any sense in meeting if you can't show me something reasonable." Lillian took a sip of her wine.

Frank forced a salesman's smile. "I quoted you the market price. I just wanted to give you the first shot before I list it. I'm sure it'll sell in no time if you're not interested."

"I'm having dinner right now. If you want to talk seriously, give me call next week. Good evening." Lillian's glare turned him around and he walked away.

"Woah-oh, Mrs. Heinig-Martel, where did that come from?" Andy asked.

"I get so sick of these guys and their bullshit. He thinks I don't know he's under-water on that property. He would never try that with any of the male developers in town." Lillian took a drink of water and swallowed hard.

Andy wasn't sure what to say. "They're all just looking for any advantage they think they can get away with."

Lillian didn't lighten up.

"No, they think I'm a ditz, just playing with your money. I want to sit down this week and go over a few things. I'm getting in a position to make some moves, and I want to run them by you."

"How about tomorrow after I golf with Jack?"

"That'll be fine. Come by my office. I have the numbers there. Sorry. I got worked up. What are you going to order?"

FIVE

Monday-morning light filtered into the bedroom. Lillian pushed Andy away and got out of bed. She hadn't put her lingerie back on after last night.

"You got enough this weekend. Come on and run with me, then take a cold shower. That'll settle you down."

Andy looked at his wife silhouetted against the window and sighed. "Baby, you know I can't get enough of you."

Lillian didn't turn around.

"Remember that the next time you leave me alone for three nights."

"Oh, now that's a low blow."

"Come on, hurry up. I want to get a quick five miles in this morning."

Lillian surprised him and ran at a pace he could almost maintain. She kept up a steady monologue about the kids, club gossip, and his upcoming trip. Andy managed to make short replies and grunts. By the time they walked back up the driveway her breathing was completely normal. As Andy tried to walk off his leg cramps and catch his breath, he pledged to himself he was going to get back in shape.

≈

Albert was finishing up his breakfast when the doorbell rang. At the door was a tall woman, very thin. Her hair was covered with a blue bandana. She appeared to be in her late thirties, but it was hard to tell. She reached out with a slender hand.

"Hello, I'm Vivian. You called about some house cleanin'?"

"Yes," Albert replied. "Thanks for coming so soon. Come on in and take a look at what you're up against."

Vivian had seen worse. Typical of these situations, a man could keep up with washing dishes and minding messes as they occurred but didn't do any routine heavy cleaning. It needed to be gutted and remodeled, but he was obviously looking for a quick fix.

She finished her tour, and Albert invited her to have a seat in the kitchen. She looked at the chairs.

"I've been sittin' all day."

"Are you just getting your business started?" Albert asked.

Vivian took a moment before she replied. "I'll be honest with ya; I'm sorta startin' over. I got a eatin' problem. I got sick and needed to go in the hospital, then to a treatment center. While I was gone, one of my workers stoled most of my clients. I've picked up a couple a houses to clean, but still need more work."

"Well, I'd like this room and the downstairs bathroom cleaned, but I need it done by Wednesday. My son and granddaughter are coming."

Vivian stood akimbo. "The dirt'll come off like a prom dress, but it won't look much better unless the walls are painted and the floors waxed."

"Can you do all that?"

"That's what I do. I'll prolly get some help with the paintin', if I can find someone." She peeked in the bathroom. "So, I'll wash everythin' down, paint the ceilings and walls. The bathroom floor is bad, but I'll wax both floors. Be the resta today, all tomorrow and maybe havta finish up Wednesday morning. Call it two solid days, make it an even five hundred. You buy the paint. You plannin' on sellin' the place?"

"Yeah, I'm going to list it soon."

"You might consider havin' me quote preppin' the entire house. I'll do as much or as little as ya want."

"Let's get this part done, then we'll talk. So, what's up with your company name?"

"If I'm not cleanin' someone else's house, I'm just home cleanin' mine over and over. I figured I might as well get paid for it."

Vivian brought in a ladder, pails and two totes of cleaning supplies. She sat a travel mug and a large thermos on the table.

"I'll be needin' that paint tomorrow."

Albert sighed. "I guess I'll have to call my daughter."

"You don't drive?" Vivian asked.

"No, I don't. I'll call her," Albert said. "She doesn't know I'm selling – please don't mention anything about that."

≈

After breakfast with Lillian, Andy headed into Chappaqua for the Kowalski hearing. This pro bono case had dragged out for over a year. An overzealous bank officer had called in a mortgage and put his bank in a tough spot. The hearing with the judge went very well. He ruled in favor of Mr. Kowalski, and the foreclosure was averted. Mrs. Kowalski thanked Andy and promised to bring him perogies then broke down in tears. Mr. Kowalski gripped Andy hard with a calloused hand and said he would never forget this. The bank lawyer was a club member; he and Andy chatted about golf on the way back to their cars.

Andy drove out of town to the country club and met Jack outside the locker rooms and picked up the cart. On the first nine holes, Jack and Andy engaged in the usual golf banter. By the twelfth, it was just an occasional, “nice shot” or “that'll play.” After the fifteenth, there was no talking. Jack still had honors.

Andy could not fathom how or when his barely post-pubescent son had learned to shape shots both ways – turning around dog legs and avoiding traps. Jack was consistently hitting one -- sometimes two -- clubs higher than him. He had a touch around the greens that only confident, relaxed golfers can find. He was hitting flop shots, running chips, and soft pitches as needed. His putting stroke was smooth and solid.

Andy Martel -- Gunner -- the former club champion -- did not like to lose. It was obvious that on this day he was going to lose to his seventeen-year-old son. And it wasn’t because Andy was rusty. He had never made some of the shots Jack was making. Maybe, if he really bore down, he could rattle the kid and make a run at the end. He could sense Jack was embarrassed for him, and that made it worse. Neither one backed down. Jack didn't get rattled. On the 18th hole they took off their hats and shook hands. Andy grabbed his son and didn't hesitate to hug him right there in the open and said, "Great match, thanks for playing with me."

Jack looked down. "I had some lucky shots."

Back at the clubhouse they had iced tea and nachos.

"Do you have a coach I don't know about?" Andy asked.

"No, just Mr. Bradley at school," Jack replied, wiping cheese from his mouth.

"Good match today. I hope we can get together more." Andy said.

"That would be great." Jack replied.

Andy left Jack at the club and drove to Lillian's office. Her office was situated between a liquor store and a consignment shop in the middle of a small strip mall just outside of town. The formerly rundown mall was the first property she ever bought and refurbished. Now it was full of busy stores. Her low rent and high-quality remodeling cut into her profit margin, but she had lured several stores from the nearby property Frank owned. Now that property was failing and coming on the market. Andy went into the office and before he could sit down Lillian asked.

"How did it go?"

"I had no idea how good he is. More than I could handle today."

"Don't tell me. You lost?" Lillian asked.

"Yes, Lillian. Jack beat me."

"Oh wow. What'd he say?"

"What do you mean? He said, 'Good game.'"

Lillian couldn't let it go.

"He must've been thrilled! What'd you say to him?"

"What's to say? It was just a golf game."

"There's no such thing as 'just a golf game' to you. How do you feel?"

"Well, my wife ran me into the ground this morning, then my kid beat me at golf. At least I managed to win against a backstreet lawyer this morning."

"I just can't believe it. I have to text Jack."

"Could we just do what I came here for?"

"Oh, come on, this is a big day for Jack. You should be happy for him." Lillian opened a file on her computer.

"He's really good. I need to pay attention and get him competing more, maybe a coach. But it was just one match. I'll be ready for him next time. What did you want to show me?

Lillian printed out a file. "I want you to see my balance sheets and net-worth statement."

Andy took a quick look at the spreadsheets.

"You have a fair amount of capital for emergencies and upkeep. You're drawing a reasonable salary, plus you make money on commissions. Your rental income from the duplexes is good, and you don't have any debt. I would say you're in a really good position."

Lillian pulled her chair around to the side of the desk.

“But I do have debt, a lot of it. All my original capital came from our personal account –your money.”

“Lillian, please. What we have, we earned together. You worked while I went to law school and supported both of us. You manage the house and do all the work there and raised the kids almost on your own. It's taken both of us to get where we are. It's our money, not my money.”

Lillian rearranged the papers.

“I know in my head that's true, but I just don’t feel like I've accomplished anything on my own. I want to sell off some property and repay our account. I'll still have some capital and equity to keep growing.”

“We'll take a beating on our taxes,” Andy warned. “People do this all the time. We have money invested that would have just been taxed out of our pockets.”

“I know, but I just want to be free and clear of our personal money. It got me where I am, but I want to keep going on my own.”

Andy took a deep breath. “Would you at least talk to Bryan and find a way to minimize the tax hit? You can go down with me someday – meet with him and have a day in Manhattan."

“I can do that. It makes sense.”

“Do you want his number, or should I set it up?”

“I’ll call him,” Lillian said quickly.

Andy didn’t wait for a kiss. "All right, I’ll text it. See you at home.”

≈

Bonnie was so startled when her landline rang, she knocked over the stack of little white boxes she was using to ship her necklace orders. The only person who called on that phone was her father, and that wasn't very often.

"Dad, what's wrong?"

Albert cleared his throat. "I was wondering if you had time to take me to Home Depot today."

Bonnie's heart slowed down.

"Oh, I thought you were hurt or something. What do you need there?"

"I need some paint."

Now Bonnie was ticked off.

"Mind telling me what's happenin'?"

"I've got a woman here doing a little cleaning and she wants to paint the kitchen and bathroom. I have to buy the paint. Could you help me pick a color?"

"I'll come over and see what's going on. See you in a couple minutes."

Bonnie didn't knock. She entered the kitchen and saw a skinny woman rummaging through the kitchen cupboards.

"Hello, I'm Bonnie... Albert's daughter."

Vivian took off a glove and extended her hand.

"I'm Vivian. Your dad hired me to do some cleanin'."

Bonnie briefly gripped her hand from the bottom.

"My Dad is kinda old and doesn't always make the best decisions. How'd you meet him?"

Vivian slowly took off her other glove.

"He called me. I'm a professional cleaner. I can give references if you like."

Bonnie looked at all the equipment. "It's just weird, after all these years, he decided to clean the place now. You know what I'm sayin'?"

"He mentioned something about his son and granddaughter coming to visit."

Bonnie stepped back a bit. "Oh, OK. I'll talk to him."

Albert came in. He looked at Vivian then looked at Bonnie.

"You two have met?"

Vivian nodded. "I'm going to check out the bathroom and see where to start on that."

"Were you going to tell me Golden Boy and the Princess were coming?"

Albert lowered his voice. "Andrew always comes about this time. I found out about Sophie yesterday. I don't want her to see the place like this."

Bonnie leaned against the counter and crossed her arms. "When will this blessed homecoming occur?"

Albert had to sit down on the chair. "Wednesday afternoon."

"No doubt you'll be killing a fatted calf."

Albert pondered this. "Oh, very funny. Yeah, Andrew is bringing steaks for Thursday. You can bring supper Friday. We're going out on Wednesday. You're welcome to join us."

Bonnie raised her voice. "Oh, thank you, thank you for allowing me to bring you supper. And wash your clothes, and get your groceries, and anything else you need or won't do for yourself. Thank you so much. I'm sick of being treated like a servant while your son comes a couple times a year and gets treated like a king. I won't be going out with any of you."

Albert tried to look her in the eyes.

"I appreciate your help. You'll get paid back when I'm gone. It's only right we have some fun when Andrew does come home."

Bonnie felt her tension rising as she gripped the edge of the countertop. She closed her eyes and started Ujjayi breathing, letting her breaths slow while making a low rushing sound in her throat. After just a few moments she opened her eyes and went out of the kitchen to look for Vivian.

"I'm sorry about that. I lost it for a minute. Lots of old heavy trips in this house. All of this freaked me out."

"No worries, been there myself. He seems like a tough old bird."

"He's a strange ranger for sure," Bonnie said. "He pretty much has it together except for this house. He's really let it go. How can I help you get this done?"

Vivian looked around the bathroom. "I'm just puttin' lipstick on a pig here, but that's what he wants. Once I get everythin' wiped down, I'll paint. You need to pick colors and get the paint. I have everythin' else.

"I've done quite a bit of painting in my house. I'll help if you want."

Vivian looked at Bonnie's trim figure and decided she could get on a ladder without busting her ass.

"Sure, OK, I'll pay ya."

Bonnie returned to the kitchen.

"C'mon," she called to her father. "I'll take you to Home Depot. We'll look at colors there."

≈

Jack decided not to hang around the caddy shack on a Monday afternoon. He was still stoked from the match with his father. When he got home, Sophie was making a salad and made some for him. He added a couple leftover hot dogs and some salsa.

Sophie gagged. "You're so gross."

"It's like a garbage plate Dad talks about. It's good," Jack said through a mouthful of food. "I beat him at golf today."

Sophie jerked her head around.

"No way."

Jack swallowed. "I had a really good day, and he hasn't played in a while."

"He must have let you win."

"Yeah right. He wouldn't let me win at Candy Land. He sure isn't going to let me win at golf."

"How'd he take it?"

"Didn't say much, probably kinda weird for him. Do you think things are OK between him and Mom?"

"Why would you ask? What's been going on?"

Jack put down his fork. "Well, Dad left for three days. Mom is running more than ever and working a lot. Neither one of them is home very much. I mean, they seem normal around each other most of the time, but Mom was mad for a while when Dad was gone. I wonder if all my school stuff is too much for them."

Sophie leaned toward Jack. "You know, Dad has done this before. It used to be worse. It hasn't happened in a long time."

"What's it about? Why does he do it?"

"He really can't help it. Like, he gets going and can't stop. Sometimes he's really grouchy when it's over. I don't think there's anything bad going on with him and Mom. I'm sure my situation is stressing them out too. I'm done with college and still don't have a clue what I'm going to do. I can't stay here forever. Anyway, I can't wait to get on Dad about losing to you."

"I wouldn't push him much. You've got to ride to Rochester with him," Jack said.

Sophie gave a little giggle. "I know, that's going to be so awkward. He hasn't been stuck alone with me for years. I'm going to make him talk the whole way."

Jack laughed. "You love to torment him."

Sophie giggled again. "It's just so easy."

Lillian decided to leave the office early so she could make dinner since everyone would be there. She came home to balloons in the kitchen and a decorated cake that read: *"Congratulations Jack #1 Golfer."*

"Where's Dad?" Sophie asked.

"I'm not sure he's going to be in the mood for this," Lillian said. "He texted me he went to the club to work out and catch up with some of the guys."

"Oh, he'll be fine with it. Can you believe Jack beat him?"

"It may seem funny to you and me, but it's a big deal to him. Just go easy."

They heard Andy's car pull into the driveway. Sophie hit the intercom.

"Jack, hurry up, he's coming. Don't come in the kitchen until you hear the music."

Andy was surprised to see Lillian's Audi in the driveway. He parked behind it and came in the front door and around to the kitchen.

He saw the balloons and wondered if he had missed someone's birthday, then noticed the cake. "Oh, very funny you two."

"It wasn't me," Lillian said, turning her hands up.

"Alexa, play Rocky's Theme!"

Jack came in as the music started to play and waited to see his father's reaction. Andy shook his head but couldn't help smiling. "You got me fair and square today, but you better believe there will be other days."

Jack walked over and gave his Dad a high five and chest bump.

"I can't wait."

Sophie hugged her Dad and he jostled her hair. She could smell beer on his breath.

"You're a real piece of work, Cookie. What'd you make for supper?"

"How about we make a pitcher of margaritas and order pizza?"

Sophie watched her parents carefully. She noticed they hadn't said hello with their usual quick kiss, and they seemed to be avoiding each other.

She thought, *maybe it was because her father had been drinking with his club friends or something. Anyway, this is fun. Being home for a little while won't be totally lame.*

SIX

Tuesday morning came with a rainstorm. Andy was awakened by Lillian's hair dryer through her open bathroom door. He got up and went into his bathroom to shave and shower. Jack heard the rain and went back to sleep. Sophie didn't hear anything.

Lillian finished her daily devotional and prayed for guidance and patience. She heard Andy coming into the kitchen.

"I'll make omelets," he said.

She met him with a hug. "Good morning, I'd love an omelet."

Lillian was accustomed to Andy and his omelets. He once told her he had made them since childhood. This man, who otherwise never ventured beyond a grill to cook, could produce perfect French omelets anytime, anywhere, as long as he had his old pan.

They sat at the island to eat. Lillian broke the silence.

"Have you thought about my idea?"

Andy remained quiet. Lillian waited him out. Finally, he said, "I can't help feeling you want to be independent in case something happens to us... or happens to me. Do you think I'm going to go over the edge or something?"

"Andy, this has nothing to do with us or with you, it's about me. I don't think it's selfish to want my own career and make my business grow."

"We'll lose thirty, forty percent in taxes."

"That isn't what this is about, and you know it. You feel threatened in some way. What's up with that?"

"I'm not threatened. I just don't understand why we can't be a team, like we've always been."

Lillian tried to stay calm. "You have your own career. I don't help you with your work. I have a degree; I have experience, and I know what I'm doing. I guess I'm being prideful, but I just want to be recognized for what I do. If I can always fall back on your income, I'm playing, not working. I don't think it's unreasonable."

Andy refilled his coffee. "I can't say I understand it, but you're determined. I guess that's that. When are you meeting Stan?"

"Andy, come on. I can't believe you're being such a chauvinist. Why is it so hard to accept I want my own business?"

Andy stood up behind the island. "You have your own business. We invested in it and now we're making a profit. It's the way this stuff works. To just throw away money because you feel guilty or something makes no sense. I'm not telling you what to do. I just don't agree with it. If that makes me a chauvinist, then so be it. You can have your business, and I'll have my work. If you want your own account for your salary and commissions that's fine with me too. We can talk more later. I have to go over some files for tomorrow."

Lillian cleaned up the kitchen with a little more vigor than it needed; the plates clanked into the dish washer. She wiped out Andy's precious omelet pan, daring not let soap touch its sacred seasoned surface. She left Sophie and Jack a lengthy and detailed list of chores and went to her first showing of the day.

Andy got back from a late afternoon workout at the club. He was amazed to see Jack vacuuming the great room. Sophie was in the kitchen working on dinner. The island was clear except for the day's mail. It looked like the patio had been blown off as well.

"Hey kids, the place looks great. What're you cooking?"

Sophie laid on her best British accent, "We're preparing the castle and fixing a repast for our Lord and Lady, kind sir."

Andy gave a repartee with an accent as well.

"Carry on. I shall dress for dinner."

Lillian argued with herself all the way home from her office. She knew how she felt, but Andy was right about the taxes. Still, she was sure there was more to it than that for Andy. She was surprised and angry he didn't like her becoming independent from him. She tried to put it away for now.

I don't want the kids to see us argue.

She almost cried when she got home. The house looked beautiful. The aroma of Sophie's famous lasagna filled the air, and the table was set and decorated with flowers from the garden.

How blessed I am, she thought.

Andy came back down into the kitchen. He gave Lillian a kiss and asked, "I'm making a gin and tonic, anyone else want one?"

Both women said they would. He mixed up three, one light on the gin. He gave that one to Sophie and left the other for Lillian. He carried his out to the patio where Jack was stacking firewood.

"Would you like a Coke or anything?" Andy asked

"No, I'm good," Jack replied.

"I called a fraternity brother of mine. He's a golf coach at Cornell. He said he could fit you into his summer camp if you want to go."

"I would go to Cornell for it and have to stay there?"

"Yeah, you would play golf every day and get individual lessons too."

Jack came and sat on the counter next to the grill. "That would be OK I guess, but what about my job?"

"I'm sure Mr. O'Shaugnessy will understand. Jack, you have the potential to be a really good golfer. Is it something you're interested in?"

"I don't know. I like playing by myself or just with the other caddies."

Andy put his hand on Jack's back. "Bud, you'll do fine at the camp. It'll just be guys like you, and Coach Andrews is a friend of mine, so he 'll know who you are.

"OK, cool, does Mom know?"

"We can tell her at dinner."

The ladies had dinner on the table. Andy said grace, then opened a nice Amarone he knew would go well with the lasagna.

"Now, business first," he said. "Cookie, we have to be on the road at seven tomorrow morning. We're only staying until Sunday - you don't need an entire wardrobe. So, pack a bag tonight, set your alarm, and be ready to go. If you want to go into the office with me, wear something appropriate."

"I thought your meeting was at eleven," Sophie said.

"It is, but I want to show up early and rattle their chains a little. Hopefully we can get done and get going. Just be in the car at seven."

"Yes, Mr. Martel," Sophie said and rolled her eyes to her mother.

"So now, Jack, tell Mom about your plans."

Lillian perked up.

"Dad wants me to go to a golf camp."

Lillian glanced at Andy.

"Do you remember Dustin Andrews?" Andy asked.

"Is he still a professor at Cornell?"

"Still is," Andy replied. "He also works part-time with the golf team. They have a summer camp, and he can make room for Jack."

"He's a real nice guy," Lillian said nodding. "Sounds good to me."

"If it isn't a hassle, I'd like to try it," Jack said.

Lillian and the kids continued bantering about Jack beating Andy and talking about the upcoming week. After dinner, the kids partially picked up then retreated to their rooms. Andy refilled his wine glass and noticed Lillian hadn't finished her first glass. "Don't you like the wine?"

No, it's too dry, and it gave me a headache. I'm going to bed."

"Can't we talk some more?" Andy asked. "We're not supposed to go to bed angry."

"I don't want to talk now. I'm tired and tomorrow will be a busy day. Goodnight."

So much for a romantic send off, Andy thought. He finished cleaning the kitchen and watched the Yankees lose again. Lillian didn't move when he got into bed.

SEVEN

Wednesday morning was chaos, as Andy expected. Lillian had an early showing. Jack was out the door for the club. Sophie struggled down the stairs with two suitcases and a backpack, but in time to have breakfast.

Andy turned to Lillian. “I'll check in with you on the details for the golf camp, it should work out. Good luck with your showing.”

Lillian gave Sophie a once over and nodded her approval.

“You look nice. Put your hair back when you get there.”

Sophie had chosen a spring-green A-line dress. It came just above her knees and had a modest scoop neck. Her genes came from Andy's side – darker and more voluptuous than Lillian. Her brown eyes were set off by her creamy tan complexion and long black hair. She had on mascara and subtle eye shadow. Her lips were colored pale rose. It was almost unfair that, even with her full hips, she inherited Lillian's leggedness. Just like discovering Jack was now fully a young man, seeing his little Cookie as a striking woman was disconcerting to Andy at the least.

Andy came to Lillian. "I don't want to leave with you mad at me. I'll think things over and we can talk when I get back. Please? They embraced and had a lingering kiss.

Sophie looked up from her phone. "Gaagh, stop that, I'm trying to eat here."

Andy had already loaded his bags in the car. He picked up Sophie's two suitcases and she followed him with the rest.

Sophie had a plan, but she wanted to wait until a little later to start quizzing her Dad. She had been worried by Jack saying something was wrong; it sure didn't seem like it this morning. It was gross that they couldn't keep their hands off each other at their age. She had been wondering: *How does falling in love work? How do people know who to marry?* She had been on dates with boys in college and let a couple kiss her. They always wanted more, so she mostly went out with a group. She heard all the stories of what some girls did on dates and knew that wasn't for her. Her mother believed in regularly having "the talk" and had drilled into her about boys and what they want – even Christian boys. She said they really can't think straight around girls. But, how was she supposed to meet someone? How did that all work? She was hoping to get some information from her father and get him to talk about him and her mother.

Albert was awakened by voices in the kitchen and the smell of coffee. Vivian and Bonnie had been chatting like old friends while they pulled the blue painter's tape off the walls. Because of Bonnie's help, there wasn't much left to do. She had bought a tablecloth and some matching chair pads for the kitchen table. She was hanging new curtains when Albert came in.

It wasn't that he couldn't remember it looking this good. In fact, he felt transported back years. He seemed absent for a minute but quickly broke into a forced smile.

"Good morning ladies, did I wake up in the wrong house? The place has never looked so good."

"Did the best we could," Vivian said. "Can't make a silk purse, ya know, from a sow's ear."

Bonnie smiled. "I hope it's good enough for the royal visit. Do you like the curtains?"

Albert shakily poured a half cup of coffee and kept his back turned as he topped it with bourbon and immediately took a sip, then another.

"I like it all. The colors are nice. Maybe Sophie won't think I'm such a slob when she sees this."

The two women started loading the supplies and equipment into Vivian's minivan. Albert went upstairs and came back with a large worn leather wallet on a chain.

"How much extra for Bonnie?"

"Five hundred -- that's what I want," Vivian said. "A deal's a deal."

Albert pulled six one-hundred-dollar bills and tapped the edges quickly on the table. Vivian took them without counting. He saw Bonnie was still outside.

"Thanks so much for getting this done. I know it was ridiculous, but I feel better about them coming now. Stop by next week sometime and we can discuss the rest."

After they both left Albert went to the porch and sat down and fell into his thoughts. His old companion was tempting him into the darkness, not as a malady, but as an escape. He thought of the familiar comfort of dispassionate lethargy. *So easy, so easy to float on that morose lake where memories soften like dead trees on a fog-shrouded shoreline -- where the future slips into the cold depths and lies there... forgotten. What did Kierkegaard call it? "...A cowardly craving of depression."*

He stood up and threw the rest of his coffee on the lawn and headed for his studio. He forced himself up the stairs. The sharp smell of oil paint cleared his mind like smelling salts; the rich, warm light lifted his mood. He uncovered the painting, opened the paint tubes and squeezed out lines of deep-saturated color onto his palette.

After a short time, the traffic evened out and Andy set the cruise control. He was thinking about what to say to the new associates. The senior lawyers at the Albany office had been begging for more help. Andy approved hiring some sub-Ivy-League graduates. They were relatively cheap and could take some drudgery off the older guys, so it was like a bonus to them. He wanted to welcome the new hires to the company and set some expectations.

Sophie finished texting her college roommate and looked up. "So, how did you and Mom meet?"

Andy was jolted out of his thoughts.

"We met at Princeton. You know that."

"I know where, but how did it happen?"

"What's this all about? You've never asked about it before."

Sophie turned in her seat.

"I just want to know some history... like, how things happened in the old days. Did you ask her out or what?"

Andy had to admit she had her mother's sense of humor and sarcasm.

"It wasn't the *old days.* We were both there on sports scholarships. In our junior year, we had to attend a meeting about rules and regulations. I'd seen her before at fraternity parties but didn't give her much thought. Every rich guy on campus was after her, so I never considered even talking to her. That day it was just us jocks there, so I got up enough nerve to talk to her."

"Did you say something lame?"

"Why do you think I'm such a goof? I said something about her last track season and that I'd heard she did great."

"Did she talk to you?"

Andy thought for a moment. "She said thanks and asked if I ran track. I told her I was on the basketball team. I do remember she said, 'Oh really? I go to all the games. I've never seen you.'"

Sophie laughed out loud. "I can just hear Mom saying that. What a put-down. What'd you do?"

"I was a little ticked. I told her I wasn't getting any floor time yet. I was just trying to hang on to my scholarship and hoping for a better year. Then one of her friends came -- like it was her job to rescue her -- and they both left."

Sophie went into a giggling fit.

"You mean Mom had a wingman to keep the boys away? That's hilarious, so you made the first move? Now it's mostly the girls who make the first move."

"Is that what you do?" Andy asked.

"We're talking about you; no changing the subject. So, how'd you get together?"

"I found out when she did her workouts in the gym and went every time I could when she was there. I just kept saying hi and trying to talk to her. Eventually she was overcome by my magnificent body and charming personality."

"Oh Dad, I'm sure. Did she finally just give in and go out with you?"

"We talked at some parties and finally went for dinner."

Andy didn't give many details. He didn't go into how after two years most guys had given up pursuing Lillian, who had by then earned the unfortunate nickname "Ice Princess." The old-money chaps moved on to the debutantes pursuing their MRS degrees, and the Long Island preppies went for the easy conquests. That left the scholarship guys who were too intimidated by her looks and reputation to make a move.

"I always thought Mom was so obsessed with running she didn't do much of anything else. She must have missed out on a lot of college stuff."

"She was a great runner, really world class. She was working toward the Olympic Team, don't forget. " Andy said.

"I know she loves it," Sophie said. "Are you and Mom disappointed I didn't do sports?"

"It's not for everyone. You had your plays and art."

"Yeah, and besides my hair gets frizzy when I sweat, and I sure wouldn't want a big scar on my knee like Mom."

"Your mother is a strong, beautiful woman. A little scar doesn't change that."

"I know, but she can't wear short skirts in public. I couldn't handle that."

They crossed the Hudson, went through the E-Zpass, down the expressway and into the Capital district. We're almost there. Do you want to come in? I think there's a Starbucks just a couple of blocks down."

"I'll come in first then decide."

Andy pulled into the underground parking garage. He took his suit coat off the hanger and picked up his briefcase. Sophie rummaged through her backpack and pulled out a hair clip and brush. She brushed her hair and brought the sides to the back and slipped on the clasp. She went from looking cute to professional in fifteen seconds.

Where do women learn this stuff? Andy wondered.

They stopped at the security guard and Andy showed him his ID and introduced Sophie. The guard clicked open the door. As they approached the receptionist she stood up.

"Good morning Mr. Martel. We weren't expecting you until eleven."

"No problem; we got an early start, so I hoped to get things going sooner. This is my daughter, Sophie."

"Nice to meet you. Would you mind having a seat? I'll have Mr. Vrooman's assistant take you upstairs."

Andy sat on one of the leather couches. Sophie inspected some paintings on the wall. He saw a group of young men in the security area talking to the guard. They looked his way and quickly walked to the elevators. Andy noticed one take a second glance at Sophie.

In place of his assistant, the principle lawyer at the office, Peter Vrooman, came to greet Andrew himself. He was tall, and looked to be a healthy early sixties with a full head of silver-gray hair. He walked with a long steady stride toward Andy.

"Good morning Andrew. It's so great to see you. We've been looking forward to your visit. And is this Sophie?"

Andy gave a brief handshake and said, "Good morning Pete. Sophie meet Mr. Vrooman."

Sophie took his hand. "Pleased to meet you Mr. Vrooman."

"We're traveling on to Rochester after our time here," Andy explained, "so, she's stuck with me today. She might go look for a Starbucks or something."

Mr. Vrooman said, "Why doesn't she come with us? We have a coffee bar upstairs and a very nice lounge. What do you think Miss Martel?"

"Thank you," Sophie said. "I won't be hurt if you need me to leave when you're discussing business."

They entered the elevator. Peter pressed a button and turned to Andy. "We have everything just about ready for you. We can have some coffee then get started."

"Let's meet the new associates first," Andy said. "Was that them just coming in now?"

Mr. Vrooman's ears went a little red. "I think they were here late last night, so they may have stopped for breakfast."

As they got off the elevator Andy could see into the glass-walled conference room. Several people were taking papers off printers and clipping them into files. Others were busily working at laptops. Mr. Vrooman directed them towards the lounge.

Andy stopped. "We can have coffee later. Let's meet the new associates in the conference room now. Then I have some questions on the Boardwell account, and I'd like an update on the GE account as well. Then we can quickly look at the others we talked about."

Mr. Vrooman's easy familiarity vanished. "We can pull those two files. I didn't know you had questions about them."

Sophie felt the tension in the air. "I'll get some coffee and wait in the lounge."

Mr. Vrooman spoke to his assistant while Andy went into the conference room. Sophie watched through the big windows. Everyone in the room stopped what they were doing and stood up. She half expected them to bow. Soon, four young men dressed in loose-fitting gray suits filed into the room. Everyone else left, leaving stacks of paper and folders on the table. Mr. Vrooman came in and made introductions. They all sat down except her father. Sophie thought about how imposing he must seem to the young men shrinking before him. He was dressed in a tailored suit that shifted like skin on a cat as he moved around the room. Although she constantly picked on him, she admired his tall athletic build and chiseled face. He was a big handsome man, and he seemed to fill the room. This was a side of her father she had never seen. He was intimidating and totally in control of the situation.

She felt sorry for the other people; he seemed to be purposely stressing them out. She took a sketch pad out of her backpack and recorded the scene, drank some coffee, and chatted with a paper salesman waiting to be seen. All the while, men and women came and went from the conference room giving papers to her father and answering questions as he looked them over. After about an hour, a group of them came into the lounge with Andy. They all exchanged pleasantries for a few minutes, then he followed Mr. Vrooman into his office. Thirty minutes later, he emerged, and Sophie could see the older man rub his forehead, slide his hand along his scalp, and briefly rub his neck before he came out. Mr. Vrooman escorted the two of them down the elevator and to the door.

"Thanks so much for coming to see us out here on the frontier," he said. "It's always great to see you. I'll get back to you on the information you asked for."

"Thanks for your time," Andy said. "I'll report to Robert, and one of us will touch base with you. Say hello to Elaine for me. Lillian and I are hoping to make it out for the year-end party."

"Will do. Hope to see you then. Drive safe. Nice to meet you Miss Martell. Please come again."

Andy and Sophie went back to the car. "Are we going to get some lunch?" Sophie asked.

"Yeah, there's a great little diner on the way to the Thruway. We can stop there."

Sophie whined. “Can’t we go to a real restaurant? Your diners are always so lame. Aren’t we a bit overdressed anyway?”

“I don’t want to wait all day for a sandwich. This is a really good place. We’ll go out tonight.”

Sophie caught up on her texting and tweeting until Andy pulled off the expressway and into a place called Mike’s.

“Mike’s -- that sounds just great,” she said, shaking her head.

They sat in a booth. “So, what was that about back at the office? All this 'Yes, Mr. Martel,' “No, Mr. Martel,' 'Certainly, Mr. Martel. 'They were practically groveling, and you stressed them out even more. I mean, like, they were almost afraid of you.”

Andy put down the menu.

“Not really fear, it's respect. One of my responsibilities is overseeing that entire office. I'm all of their boss. To tell the truth, I was pissed. They've known for a week I was coming today. They should've had everything ready days ago. Then, I see those kids coming to work at nine o’clock, it set me off. When I was a junior associate I practically lived at my desk; nobody beat me into the office. It was embarrassing that I got in earlier than they did. That's not the way it works, and I let them know it.”

“Mr. Vrooman seemed nervous too,” Sophie added.

“He thinks he can just take up space until he retires in a year or so. His billing is going down; the office isn't hitting their numbers. I needed to shake things up and get them back in the game. I made it clear he may get cut if things don’t improve. I wouldn't be surprised if the managing partner gives him a call. In the end, what goes on there reflects on me. If things don't go well, I'll hear it from my bosses"

"I thought you were an equal partner."

Andy chuckled. "That's true, but some partners are more equal than others."

"Oh my, you've read Orwell."

"Yes, my dear, I did take some lit classes, along with pre-law – *at Princeton University* –back in the day."

"But Animal Farm was so recently published way back then," Sophie deadpanned, "I'm surprised it was being taught already."

"You know," Andy said, "for someone living on my dime, you're kinda cheeky."

Sophie batted her eyelashes at him.

"Oh Daddy, you'll always take care of me."

Sophie ordered a chicken club sandwich and a small salad. Andy studied the menu like he was memorizing it.

It's always the same; he's so lame, Sophie thought.

"Dad, you know what you're going to order."

"Yeah, I guess I'll have a ham-and-Swiss-cheese omelet."

"Home fries with that?" the waitress asked.

Sophie was surprised to hear him say, "No not today, just one piece of rye toast."

Andy put down his fork. Sophie thought, *Wait... wait... here it comes.*

"That was pretty good," Andy said, "but I like mine better."

How Sophie wished her mother was there. They could have rolled their eyes at each other.

Andy left two twenties on the table, and they got back in the car.

Sophie took her hair down and put it in a ponytail. She got lost catching up on what she missed on Twitter in the last half hour. They got back on the Thruway. It was a straight three-hour shot to Rochester. The big SUV settled in at 75 and rode like a jet in smooth air. Andy hit the Eagles station on Sirius and reclined the seat a bit.

"Eeew," Sophie snickered. "What is this? Country music?"

"Just listen," Andy said, "maybe you'll learn something."

Lillian headed back to her office after meeting with the buyers at the property. She was very pleased. They put in a good offer. It could be one of her biggest commissions ever. She was starting to list properties that only the big brokers generally get. She knew they would soon be either courting her or bad-mouthing her. If she continued to discount her commissions just one percent and give personal attention to every client, they couldn't stop her.

She had decided to wait until afternoon to call the accountant in Manhattan. The conflict was tearing her up--not only between Andy and her, but between her vision of a Christian wife and her own sense of worth. She hated that money was impacting her marriage. On the other hand, the issue wasn't really money; she just could not get Andy to understand that. It was about much more than money. She knew she wasn't seeking adulation or recognition. She truly felt it was about fulfilling her inner drive. For now, the plan they had agreed on was she would meet with their accountant. So, that's what she was preparing to do while continuing to pray over her decision.

Sophie, unused to getting up so early, put her seat back. Soon she fell asleep to Glen Frey's voice singing *Lyin' Eyes*.

Sophie thought, *Just another cheatin' song. What did that girl expect if she only married for money?*

One of Andy's favorite pastimes was to drive a fine automobile down a highway, listening to music. He liked to drive in the most efficient manner he could-not aggressively, but smartly. He made a game of stereotyping people by the cars they drove. Old sports driving Mini Coopers, bargain hunters on safari in their Range Rovers, Saturday-night cowboys in chromed-out Silverado's. There were Prius drivers signaling virtue and the ostentatious, like himself, in oversized SUVs. He reserved disdain only for the Beemer wannabes weaving between lanes in their Nissan Altima's.

The Mohawk Valley rolled along. Andy wanted to wake Sophie and show her where the Erie Canal, the New York Central railroad, and the Thruway all ran side-by-side, but he doubted she'd appreciate it. Soon it was time for a pit stop, and the next plaza had a Starbucks. Sophie woke up as Andy pulled into the parking space.

After performing the Starbucks ritual, they headed off again.

"So, Cookie... about seeing your Grandpa. There's some stuff going on you need to know. First of all, you haven't seen him in a while. He has some health problems, so he may not look all that good. Also, he... can tend to drink a lot. He doesn't ever appear very drunk, but sometimes after a while, he'll say things that can be embarrassing."

Sophie was quiet for a moment. "Is he an alcoholic?"

"I guess, technically," Andy replied. "He's lost his driver's license. I doubt he could go a day without drinking."

"Shouldn't he get some help. Can't you do anything about it?"

"He's eighty-some years old, there's no changing him. He doesn't see it as a problem. We just have to deal with it as best we can."

Sophie was appalled. "Well, that's no way to deal with it. We need to talk to him and get him treatment."

"That's exactly what I'm talking about. You can't bring up things like that. He'll get irritable. He's fine as long as no one tries to interfere with anything he does. That's what I'm trying to tell you."

Andy waited for her to absorb some of this.

"Also, there's a good chance he's going to talk about selling his house. He may or may not talk about it when you're around. I don't know."

"I was looking forward to a nice visit," Sophie said. "This sounds really awkward."

"It will be nice. He's fine most of the time, and he's really looking forward to seeing you."

Albert added a few yellow highlights and decided the painting didn't have anything more to say. It was finished. As he cleaned and reshaped the brushes his tremor worsened. He set the well-used brushes up to dry and took another look at the painting. It was a move away from the more pictorial work he was doing last year which was a last-gasp homage to draftsmanship before the tremor took that away forever. The current project was a salute to his glory days of Abstract Expressionism. All-in-all, he was pleased with the work and this latest addition especially.

Lillian hung up the phone after talking to the accountant. Now, she wasn't sure if she was more ditzy for using Andy's money or for wanting to pay it back. It had been as she expected; the accountant asked, "Do you and Andy need more money? Don't you want to expand your real estate holdings? Do you understand you'll be taxed as regular income?"

She told him, yes, she understood all of that and would explain more when they met. She had no more appointments and was fairly well caught up in the office. She went home.

The house was quiet. Andy and Sophie were away, and she could feel their absence. Jack wouldn't be home from the club until after dark. She had a few uninterrupted hours to herself, so she decided to reseal the kitchen floor. Physical work was her cure for a brain that couldn't rest. The grout was dirty, and the tiles were dull. She had bought all the supplies weeks ago. Today was the day to get it done. She changed into some old clothes and made coffee. She found a Mercy Me CD and put it on the stereo. The whole house filled with guitars and four-part harmony.

She had scrubbed partway across the worst of the grout between the sink and island when the doorbell rang. She took off her gloves, hit mute on the remote, and went out to the foyer. Standing under the portico was a middle-aged woman, much shorter than Lillian and round. She was wearing an olive-green dress with a black shawl across her shoulders. Lillian flashed back to ladies at Mass in her church back home. The woman looked up at Lillian through blue-faded-to-gray eyes and said, "Hello, my name is Dorota Kowalski. You are Mrs. Martel?"

"Yes," Lillian replied. She noticed the woman was holding an aluminum cooking pot.

"Mr. Martel, he save my husband and me from losing home. He is great man. We could not pay him. I bring perogies -- only as appreciation. I know it does not pay him."

The woman seemed to shrink even more as she looked down and rounded her shoulders.

"Please, come in."

"No, no, I'll not disturb you. Take perogies, please." The woman began to tremble.

"At least come in while I put them in another dish, so you can have yours back."

"No, I wait here. I no want disturb lady."

"Mrs. Kowalski, you're welcome in my home. Please come in. I'll make tea. It's so kind of you to do this. Please excuse my mess. I'm cleaning the kitchen floor."

"What mean you "cleaning floor?" You watch housekeeper to do good job?"

Lillian laughed. "I don't have a housekeeper. I let the floor get stained; now I have to clean and reseal it."

Mrs. Kowalski straightened up. "I will see kitchen."

Lillian took the pot from the woman. She saw her hands were red up to her wrists, the skin was peeled off her fingertips. Lillian turned; the woman bustled behind her, so she picked up her pace.

Mrs. Kowalski surveyed the kitchen and saw the brushes, the cleaners, and the can of sealant. She took off her shawl and said, "I'm cleaner at school. I know how to seal tile floor. I clean and seal floor. You read magazine, sit by pool until done. Why Mr. Martel not get housekeeper for you?"

It took a moment for Lillian to react. "Mrs. Kowloski, you do not need to clean my floor. My mother worked full time, took care of my father and four kids. She never had a housekeeper.

I work part-time; my kids are mostly grown. I can take care of my own house."

"Not right lady like you to clean floor. My husband ashamed he could not pay for lawyer. He would be more ashamed if I did not clean floor, as way to show appreciation. I clean your floor."

With that the woman got on her knees, hiked up her dress, and tied it in front of her, leaving her slip partially covering thick brown stockings. Lillian was startled to inaction. She stood holding the still-warm pot and stared. The woman's upper arms flapped as she worked the brush along the grout lines. Her dress strained over broad shoulders and buttocks rolling back and forth.

"Mrs. Kowalski, please get up. I don't want you cleaning my floor."

Lillian waited for a reply. None came.

"Mrs. Kowalski..."

"Put perogies in refrigerator. They will get sticky," the woman said without looking up.

Lillian tried one more time. "I insist you stop. I do not want you cleaning my floor."

The woman pulled herself up with one hand on the island. She seemed taller and looked Lillian in the eyes. "Mrs. Martel, my husband have to swallow pride and accept help from your husband. He not rich, but he is good man. He never asked for anything. He does best he can. I help too. We are team. He will feel better I do this. I do for him, not for you. Please."

Lillian started to cry. The woman stepped forward and took Lillian's hands.

"What is matter, my dear? It's just floor."

"Oh, Mrs. Kowalski, God bless you. Clean my floor if that's what you want."

Lillian went outside to compose herself. When her voice was back to normal, she went up to Andy's office and left a message with the accountant's secretary. She wouldn't be needing the appointment.

Andy turned off the cruise control and let the Lexus slow down to exit the Thruway. He circled around to the expressway then off into the stop-and-go traffic of suburban Rochester. In his youth, rich farmland was just starting to yield to new housing developments. Now, the congestion had expanded with shopping malls, chain restaurants, and strip malls with faux colonial facades.

Behind the big-box stores, the tree-lined streets of old neighborhoods remained. The homes still had front porches with flower boxes -- some tended, others not. They were separated by pock-marked driveways. Netless basketball hoops drooped over the fronts of garages. There were no bicycles blocking the doors. He turned down his street. Near the end, on the right, there was a wall, making a gap in the houses, like missing teeth in a mouth. Then on the corner was his home -- his father's house. The paved driveway ended at a two-bay garage, offset behind the house. The garage had a hoop attached, but this one had a glass backboard and a spring-mounted rim. Andy had shoveled sidewalks and mowed lawns to buy it. He put it up at the end of his freshman year of high school. The garage had a Dutch colonial second story with a dormer.

Sophie popped her seatbelt off and opened the door. Andy sat with his hands on the wheel.

"Are you coming?" Sophie asked.

Andy took a deep breath. "We'll see what kind of shape he's in. Let's go."

Albert met them on the back porch. He was wearing his signature blue Dickie's shirt and pants. The fabric was worn to a thin chamois, but clean. His Red Wing boots were laced halfway up.

"How was the trip? Which way'd you come? What kind of mileage do you get on that thing?"

"It was good," Andy answered. "Came up the Thruway."

"Hi Grandpa!" Sophie said as she flung her arms around Albert and kissed him on the cheek. He brought his arms up slightly and opened his hands then let them drop loosely to his side until she released him. He smelled of tobacco, whisky, and turpentine just as she remembered.

"It's so great to see you," she said, stepping back. "I'm excited to see your new paintings. I haven't been here in so long."

Andy was almost shocked; his father looked pretty good. There was some color in his face, he was moving smoothly, and his voice was steady and strong. He didn't appear to be drunk.

"Come on in," Albert said. "We can sit in the kitchen and have coffee or something."

The kitchen was a small island of cleanliness in an ocean of clutter, dust, and moldering furniture that lapped up to the doorway. The new seat cushions slid precariously over the worn vinyl chairs, but the bright tablecloth and curtains lent a shadow of cheeriness to the newly painted walls.

They all sat down at the table.

"How do you like the kitchen?" Albert asked. "I thought it needed freshening up. I had the bathroom done too."

Sophie was aghast at the overall condition of the place, but at least they had a clean place to sit. She was glad to hear about the bathroom. She had to pee but had not wanted to risk seeing what the bathroom might be like. She excused herself and found her way down the short hall.

"Dad, you look good. How're you feeling?"

Albert put his hands under the table. "I've been getting better. I got off a bunch of pills, and since then I feel good. Still can't mow the lawn but taking care of myself mostly."

"If there's anything you need done while I'm here let me know."

Sophie returned and sat next to Albert.

"So, Grandpa, I came here to apologize. I didn't see the wonderful letter you sent last winter until the end of school. I feel awful that you thought I ignored you. I love hearing from you, and I'm so sorry."

"I just figured you were busy."

"No, it wasn't that; I would have written if I had known. Grandpa, I'm really sorry. Will you forgive me?"

"Sophie, there's no need, don't worry. Do you want some coffee or a beer or pop or anything?"

"Actually," Andy said, "if we want to get to dinner, we should get checked in and change clothes. We're staying at the Hilton over by Strong, so it won't take long. I just wanted to check in. I didn't know if you'd answer the phone."

"Bonnie calls more now," Albert said," so I try to answer. Why don't you give her a call? Maybe she'll come to dinner with us."

"That would be nice," Andy replied, "I'll do it from the hotel."

Andy escorted the bellhop and Sophie to her hotel room, and then went to his room to make his calls. First, he called his fraternity brother, Dustin Andrews, in Ithaca. The plans to enroll Jack in the golf camp were working out well. Jack had to be there a week from Saturday, so Andy and Lillian could take him and not miss any work.

He then called Lillian.

"Oh, Andy, I wish you were here."

"Why, what's the matter? Is Jack OK?"

"Mrs. Kowalski cleaned the kitchen floor."

Andy felt like he had fallen down the rabbit hole after Alice.

"What are you talking about? Why would Mrs. Kowalski clean our kitchen floor?"

"To pay you back for helping them. Well, really she did it because it would make her husband feel better. She did it because they work together as a team. I cancelled my appointment with the accountant."

Andy took some deep breaths. He was determined to remain patient, despite Lillian's apparent loss of her faculties. *Maybe she had been into her chardonnay. She could get silly after a couple glasses.*

"I'm not sure I understand all this," he said, "but it sounds like we should talk about it face-to-face."

Lillian started talking about perogies, aluminum pots, Mrs. Kowalski tying her dress in front of her, and her refusal to stop scrubbing the floor with her red hands. She kept going about marriage and working together and having tea with Mrs. Kowloski and how she wished she could hold him right now.

"Lill, it sounds like this was all a good thing. Do you think we should wait and talk more when I get home?"

"Oh, Andy, I know it's a lot, and I can't really explain it all. Anyway, I cancelled my appointment with Stan. I'm not going to transfer any money to our account. Are you happy about that?"

"I think that's a great idea as long as it's what you want to do. Can we talk about Jack's golf camp?"

"It is. I know it's right," Lillian said. "I understand now. Mrs. Kowalski is amazing. She's so joyful and in love with the Lord. We're going to have tea together again soon."

"You're right," Andy said. "They're a wonderful couple. Jack has to be there next Saturday."

"That's great. I'll tell Jack. I can't wait for you to get home."

"We'll talk more later. Glad you had a good day. I love you."

Andy could tell his wife was crying.

"I love you too," she said. "Come home as soon as you can."

Bonnie wasn't surprised when she heard Andy's voice.

"Hi, "she said, "Are you in town?"

"Yeah, we just got in. I stopped quick at Dad's. We're going out for dinner, can you come?"

"I don't want to intrude," Bonnie replied. "I'll catch up with you later in the week."

It's always the same, Andy thought. If I don't beg her to come, later she'll say we excluded her.

Andy tried not to sound annoyed. "Bonnie, you're not intruding. It will be nice to all get together. Where would be a good place?"

"Well, if you really want me to. I'll meet you at Dad's. I'll get reservations at a nice place."

Andy changed and went to get Sophie. She was wearing skin-tight jeans and a blue blouse. It, of course, required a new makeup job which Andy had interrupted.

"Cookie, we're just going out for dinner."

Sophie continued looking in the mirror. "Yeah, but like, how will you ever marry me off if I don't look nice?"

"Fat chance of that. No man your age could afford your upkeep."

"I'll just find a rich guy. See? I was listening to your hillbilly music."

Andy had no answer. "Come on, we'll be late."

The restaurant Bonnie suggested was in the hipster district on Park Avenue. As Andy feared, it served neither Genesee Cream Ale nor liquor. This made for an ominous start for Albert, but he settled for a Rohrbach's Scotch Ale. The menu was mostly vegetarian/vegan with a few entree's reserved for the unenlightened. In the end, however, it was quite good.

When they were done, the waitress, asked, "Can I interest anyone in dessert and coffee?"

"Does anyone want to share a piece of cake?" Sophie asked.

"They have a delicious vegan carrot cake." Bonnie replied. "I'll have a few bites of that if you want."

When the waitress brought the check, Bonnie started poking through her big striped bag as Albert pulled some folded bills out of his pocket.

"I'll get mine and Bonnie's," he said. "How much is it?"

Andy closed his eyes and shook his head. *Some things never change.* "Let me treat. I'm just so glad to see you two."

Back at his house, with his family settled around him, Albert decided tonight would be as good a time as any to introduce his plan to sell the property. He poured some bourbon for himself and Andy. Bonnie made gin and tonics for herself and Sophie. They all settled around the kitchen table.

"The kitchen sure looks better," Andy said. "Almost like it used to."

"Vivian is really good," Bonnie said. "I did most of the painting. She said if she gets busy enough, she might want some part-time help."

"That would be a good job for you," Andy said.

"We connected. Like, she's on the same part of a trip as me. You know what I mean? I'll have to chill and see if her kismet runs into mine. The best would be if we just kept going here -- get the living room done next."

"I'm not sure how much I want to put into this place right now," Albert said. "It's getting harder to take care of. I already had to hire the lawn done because I can't keep up."

"Oh Dad," Bonnie said, "if you'd just let me, I could help even more than I already do. You don't want to leave here."

"You know I can't stay here forever. I've got to at least start thinking about it."

"That won't be for a long time," Bonnie assured him. "You're doing much better after I searched all over and found the new doctor. And you're eating better since I do all your shopping now. And at least your clothes are clean now that I do your laundry."

Andy could see where this was going. Better to leave it for now and let Bonnie absorb this much. "We don't have to get into this right now," he said.

"Right," Sophie agreed. "Grandpa, tell me about your new paintings."

Andy started to zone out as the three of them started speaking a language foreign to him -- about projects and artistic influences and techniques. Bonnie was trying to keep up and interjected about her jewelry. It was all too artsy for him. He went out on the porch and looked at the yard.

The lawn had long been a repository of resentment he held toward his father. The lawn was off limits. No running after balls, no bike riding, no rolling in the grass. It was to be respected; it was above the mundane. Most of all, it was to be cared for like a treasure. One day, when he was fourteen, Andy thought he would do his father a favor and mow the grass as a surprise. An unreasonable tantrum would have been easier to take than the dispassionate reaction he received.

"It'll take me the rest of the summer to fix it. Don't ever touch the mower again, and stay off my lawn." He remembered that as a turning point. He knew for certain this man he lived with would never be a story-book father to him. He accepted it as a fact and from that day forward, he looked for encouragement elsewhere.

Despite his resentment, Andy felt yoked by filial obligation. Lillian and the kids saw Albert only as an eccentric, harmless old man, so he had to keep up a pretense of concern.

Even right now, Dad's in there playing his suffering artist act, he thought. Sophie will be eating it up. Her romantic eyes won't see the old plumber who wasted a life in his "studio" over the garage. Oh, well, no need to think about all that. It's only Wednesday. Maybe I can get a realtor here before we leave. Andy walked slowly around the perimeter of the lawn. He could see the wooden fence was breaking down.

Lillian took her glass of chardonnay over to the nook and admired the kitchen floor. She had sealed it a couple times in the past, but it had not looked this good since it was new. She felt at peace. She had peace of mind and peace in her marriage, and it all came from peace in the Lord. This whole episode with her money had strengthened her faith. She had been praying for wisdom and guidance, and God sent it in the form of a little Polish woman. Her only regret was being so flighty when she last talked to Andy.

He must think I've completely lost it, she thought. The landline rang. She knew it was him even before she answered.

Andy put his phone on the bedside table. It was nice to hear Lillian so happy. He wished his faith could be as personal as hers. She was convinced she received a message from God through Mrs. Kowalski, and that's why she no longer wanted to give the money back. It had something to do with their marriage and pride and trust. He needed to ask her more about that sometime. Anyway, God was obviously a good accountant and saved him a boatload in taxes.

He figured Cookie wouldn't be ready until lunchtime tomorrow, so he decided to wait and go through emails in the morning. He called the front desk and requested a late checkout and then caught the end of the Yankee's game and fell asleep.

EIGHT

Sophie surprised Andy and was ready to go by midmorning. After a stop at Starbucks for a mocha and pastry, they arrived at Albert's. The driveway was blocked by the lawn service truck. The kid unloading the mower actually let his jaw drop as he watched Sophie walk up. She caught him looking and shot him a sideways glance and a half smile. His eyes followed her as she passed by, but then he noticed Andy at the end of the trailer and quickly got back to loosening the tie-downs.

Andy noticed the kid didn't look strung out like so many laborers his age. In fact, he was fairly good looking, not quite as tall as him but with an athletic build. Andy pressed up close and said, "Good morning, I see you're enjoying your work. I'm Mr. Martel's son. That was his granddaughter."

The kid reddened and choked out, "Yes, sir, hello, sir. I do enjoy working on a nice lawn like this one. This is just my second time here. I'm hoping your father will be satisfied this time."

"Fat chance of that. Keep your mind on your job and not my daughter."

Albert was heading out to intercept the mower. Sophie almost tackled him with a hug. Albert patted her shoulder this time, like a wrestler tapping out. She kissed his cheek and let him go. Albert had completed a detailed diagram of how he wanted the mowing done and set on the kid with instructions.

The landscaper had been mowing for years, but he listened patiently and folded the diagram into his pocket.

After Albert supervised the mowing for a few passes he met Andy on the back porch.

"I see the storm door is still on," Andy said. "Do you want me to get the screen?"

"That would help. I have a hell of a time with a screwdriver anymore. We'll need the grill for later too, if you can get that."

Sophie joined them. "Can we go up to your studio now and look at your new painting?"

Sophie followed Albert through the dim garage and up the stairs to the studio. After seeing the house, she expected to see a jumbled, dirty mess. Albert unlocked the door and they went in. She was enveloped in a warm light reflecting off the walls. She felt transported into an alternate world -- an open, light-filled place of inspiration and creation. She looked at her grandfather. His face had the same warm glow as the walls. What she had thought was an unmovable melancholy visage had come off like a mask. His tight lips were now full, his usually V-shaped brows were quizzically raised, making his eyes wide. They were bright and highlighted by the window's cross-hatched reflection. Sophie had sudden overwhelming understanding that this is where her grandfather lived. The world beyond these walls was a purgatory from which he escaped only by rising up the steps and into the luminance behind the locked door.

Every artist is an observer, but Albert wasn't sure if he saw pity or understanding in his granddaughter's eyes. He knew her face well, because it was the same as his mother's. Maybe that's why he always had a soft spot for Sophie. She also seemed to have the same strength and independent streak that brought so much trouble to his mother.

Times are different now, he thought. *Both traits will serve this young woman well.* He was jolted out of his reverie.

"Grandpa, this is beautiful! I never would have guessed. It's the most awesome studio I've ever seen. The light is perfect."

Sophie started to walk around the studio. On the left were racks and racks of stored paintings along the entire length of the room. On the right were shelves with neatly organized mixing pots, boxes of paint, and a collection of colored powders. There was a separate section of various solvents and chemicals; some she recognized, others she didn't. There were boxes of brushes and palate knives and all the sundry tools of painting and drawing. There was a large worktable -- clear except for some brushes drying in a rack. The floor had areas of splattered paint. In the far back right was an alcove formed by bookshelves with a small table, club chair, couch, and floor lamp.

On the walls were a few framed paintings and drawings. One caught her eye. It wasn't large, but it was filled with bold strokes of an abstract human face.

"That looks like a Willem de Kooning. Did you do it?"

Albert came over behind her. "You have a good eye. Actually, it's by his wife, Elaine. It's a portrait of me."

"You knew the de Koonings?" "Really?".

"Well, I like to think they knew me."

Sophie studied the painting. "I had no idea... How did that come about? He died about twenty years ago, didn't he?"

Albert was surprised. "I knew them when I lived in New York City. That was a long time ago. You seem to know a lot about him."

"I took mostly modern art for my art criticism electives. You have to tell me about your time in New York."

"Like I said, it was a long time ago. Maybe someday we can talk about it. Do you want to see my painting?"

"I'll hold you to that. Yeah, let's look."

Albert pulled the paint-stained cloth off the easel. Sophie took a sharp breath and sighed it out slowly. She stood completely still and quiet for several minutes.

To Sophie the painting was an overpowering composition of darkness giving way to lighter tones toward the top of the canvass. The strength of the brush strokes and the action of the color combinations gave it a dynamic feeling. At first it appeared to be a complete abstraction, but with concentration an overpainted figure emerged in the central portion. The figure was amorphous, floating through the colors - definitely feminine.

"Well, what do you think?" Albert finally asked.

Sophie looked at Albert. She had tears in her eyes.

“Grandpa, I had no idea. How can this be? How can you paint like this? Doesn’t anyone know?”

Albert looked at the painting. “No, you're the first person in years that's seen this kind of thing. I haven’t done anything like it in a long time.”

"This isn’t like the landscapes you’ve shown me before. I've never seen anything – anywhere--that made me feel this way before.”

Sophie looked at the painting again. “Grandpa, I'm so sorry. I'm so confused. I’m sorry. I don’t understand. I have to be alone. I’m sorry.”

Sophie went down the stairs and out to the lawn. The lawn guy was still there. Her father was on the porch. She went down the driveway and onto the sidewalk and started walking down the uneven concrete. She was feeling unnamed emotions but some combination of regret, guilt, and anger. But there was more. The image burning in her eyes touched some place deep and dark that she had not known existed. She wasn't sure she wanted to go there.

She thought of the skill and mastery of the media it would take to produce that painting. She thought of how he transferred emotion onto the surface. Then she thought, *How can it be no one knows any of this? He's a treasure who has been ignored by his family and the world. He's a sad old man. He’s suffered in darkness and solitude. He’s put all of that onto a canvass that no one sees, that no one cares about.*

After she had walked several blocks, anger rose up, and washed out all her other emotions. *How could her father not know this? How could he not even know who his father is? Why did her father treat her grandfather like a burden?*

≈

Andy could have found the screen in the dark. It was stored in the specially made rack under the stairs. The replacement screws were taped to the frame. The Yankee screwdriver that fascinated him as a boy was in its designated drawer under the bench. He could hear Sophie and his father upstairs. He was no doubt regaling her with tales of his glory days in New York.

Hopefully, it won't be embarrassing for her to look at his painting, he thought. She's learned enough about art to know the difference between real art and amateurish stuff done over a garage. He was adjusting the door closer when Albert came onto the porch.

"Well, what did Sophie think? Where is she?"

"I don't know. Didn't you see her?"

Andy stood up. "What happened? Did you say something to her?"

"No, I didn't say anything. She was looking at my painting and seemed upset. She said she had to be alone. I don't know what was the matter."

Andy thought, *Must be the painting was so bad she couldn't face him. She must be really disappointed.*

"She has to be around here somewhere," he said. "Maybe she just went for a walk."

Sophie turned around and looked at the row of little old houses fronted by the broken-up sidewalks tilted by the roots of the big trees that remained. This was where her father grew up. Being here made her feel older. Thinking about her father as a boy and talking to her grandfather made time stretch out beyond her little world. So much time had passed, yet there was so much ahead. Where did she fit in all this?

I need to slow down and think. I won't cause a scene with Dad with Grandpa around. I'll pick my time, but he's going to hear from me.

When Sophie got back, her father and grandfather were on the porch drinking beer.

"Kinda early isn't it?" she asked.

Andy looked at her. "Are you all right? Where'd you go?"

"I guess I felt a little closed in up in the studio. I needed some fresh air. Grandpa's painting is -- I don't know what to say -- it's unbelievable. I want to look at it some more. Do you guys want some lunch?"

Andy never knew what Sophie would do. Most of the time she was needy and high maintenance, then other times she was considerate and semi-domesticated. He was glad she was being tactful about the painting.

"Sure," Albert said. "Look in the fridge. Do whatever you want."

Andy and Albert were reminiscing about how Albert made the big lot he had. His neighbors thought he had completely lost his mind when he bought the house next door only to tear it down. He had worked for months taking it apart piece by piece to salvage the lumber. How they would complain, when he was banging hammers and running saws in the middle of the night. Then he did it again when the next house on the block came up for sale. Looking back, Albert said, it was kind of crazy, but seemed like a good idea at the time.

They were interrupted by Sophie shouting from the kitchen. "Is there something wrong with these hot dogs? Are they spoiled or what?"

Albert yelled back, "No, they're supposed to be white. Don't you remember having white hots when you came to visit?"

"No, hot dogs are red at home. How old is this potato salad?"

"I just got it. There's some beans there too."

They heard pans rattling and clanking from the kitchen. Then Sophie yelled out, "You know, these aluminum pans will give you Alzheimer's."

"What pans?" Albert yelled back.

"Very funny. What a bunch of junk."

"There's a good one in the oven."

There, in the oven, was a frying pan just like her father's. Black and so shiny a white band reflected off the broad inside curve.

As Sophie was bringing out the food, the kid disengaged the mower blades and motored over to the driveway. He left the machine idling and came up to the porch.

"Would you like to take a look? See if the height and everything is right?" he said to Albert.

Albert went with the kid and surveyed the lawn. "Not too bad. It takes some practice to keep it lined up. See you next week."

"Yes sir, I'll keep working at it. Have a good day." The kid was careful to avert his eyes as he passed by Sophie.

Albert got out the TV trays he kept on the porch and clipped them together. They all settled back with their white hots, beans and potato salad. After the Lawn Order truck had backed out, Andy opened two more beers, handed one to Albert and said. "Well, we should stop beating around the bush. Have you decided to sell this place?"

Albert set the beer down. "I guess I have. I can't afford it, and I can't keep it up. It's past time I got rid of it. I've been avoiding it because it's going to be such a pain in the ass to go through the process. Sorry, Sophie."

Andy let that thought ripen a bit. "Do you want me to help with getting it sold and cleaned out?"

Albert looked at Sophie, then at Andy. "I know I can't do it alone. I'd be beholden but grateful if you could do that."

"I'm sure it's hard to give it up, but it's the right thing to do," Andy said. "I can take care of everything and make it as easy as possible."

Albert took a long pull on his beer and finished up the salad. Andy stayed quiet and leaned back with his beer.

"Grandpa, would you let me snoop around your studio a little and look at some other paintings?"

"Go ahead; we've gotta figure out what to do with all that canvas anyway."

“Do you remember Geoffrey Connors?” Andy asked his father after Sophie had left. “I graduated high school with him.”

“No, I really don’t.”

“Anyway, he's a lawyer here in Rochester. He does real estate closings, wills -- little stuff like that. We still exchange Christmas cards. I was thinking I could call him for some names of a good realtor, and maybe Geoff could handle the closing. With his help there’s an outside chance of getting it listed before we have to go home.”

“So, you're not surprised about this, are you?”

“Dad, you’ve been hinting at it for a while, and it's the common-sense thing to do. I'm not surprised.”

“Are you at all sad to see it go?”

"I left a long time ago.”

“I guess that’s right.”

“Do you want to sleep on it, or are you ready to do it?”

Albert took a deep breath and looked at Andy. “Let’s get it done.”

Geoffrey called back in less than an hour. Andy knew the lawyer would want to get in on this deal. Geoff was going to come over to visit and bring a relator tomorrow.

Must be this was meant to be, Andy thought.

Sophie went back into the studio. She wanted to take a more objective look at the painting. She knew it was emotionally charged, but how did he do it? She started by standing farther away this time. The composition was evident and obviously thought out but didn't distract from taking in the entire image at once. It had movement, but the eye was drawn back to the center and the hidden image. The colors were dark, but distinct, a very technically difficult effect. There was no muddiness in the colors. The female figure was haunting, but how did he hide it, and why could it not be ignored?

She went up closer, now the brush strokes became more evident. They were confident -- full of paint with sharp edges. Most were long and powerful, some short jabs and slashes. The impasto was mostly medium, some heavy, and expertly done with a knife. She went in closer to examine the figure. Up close it could not be distinguished from the colors. It could only be seen at about five feet from the surface. As she came closer, it disappeared. As she stepped back, it reappeared. At about three feet, she could start to see -- the figure wasn't overpainted or under-painted. It was formed by the direction of the strokes and very careful changes in color and impasto. She had never seen anything like it.

She wasn't sure why, but she was trying to convince herself that this was a technically excellent painting. Perhaps because she had always thought of her grandfather as an amateur -- a hobbyist. Now, she felt inadequate to even comment on such a painting. She knew this would be classified as from the New York School and Abstract Expressionism of the fifties. He was obviously influenced by the de Koonings, both Willem and Elaine. But he had taken that to a different place.

Now, she was even more confused than when she first saw it. How could this be happening? It was like something out of a movie or a novel. An undiscovered genius from the hinterlands, who had worked in obscurity for sixty years, only to be discovered by his granddaughter, who just happened to have a BFA with a minor in gallery management. She was suddenly struck by a thought.

Is this a God thing? Is there more going on? Am I supposed to be doing something here? She didn't believe in coincidence. I just have to keep my eyes open and look for the connections. Too much, too much to think about. Dad isn't going to understand any of this.

Sophie pulled a few more paintings out of the first rack. They were similar to the new one, all of them technically superb. She felt herself getting overwhelmed again. She put the paintings back and headed down the stairs. Her father was coming into the garage.

"Grandpa is taking an early nap," he said. "I'm just going to drag the grill out for tonight and head back to the hotel. Do you want to go with me or stay here?"

"I'll ride back with you."

Andy found the grill. It was a Weber, but the bottom of the kettle had been reinforced and the original flimsy legs replaced with black pipe. It had heavy rubber wheels where the cheap plastic ones usually were. It weighed a ton but wheeled easily out the side door and over to the driveway. It was the only grill Andy remembered.

Sophie was waiting in the car while Andy finished up. She was quiet as they headed out of the residential area and onto Jefferson Avenue.

Andy finally broke the silence. "Thanks for lunch; that was nice of you."

Sophie looked at the chain stores and franchise restaurants lined up like a Lego town. Every city she had been in had a strip like this. They were a different reality from where she had been in her grandfather's studio.

"You're welcome. Have you seen any of Grandpa's paintings lately?"

"No, I've never looked at many of them. Some of them are recognizable places or people; a lot of them are just random colors splashed on. They look like what you did when you were five years old. Why do you ask?"

Sophie turned to look at Andy. "You don't have any idea who or what he is, do you? You've never taken the time to understand him."

Andy stared straight ahead. "I figured he was filling you full of stardust. You're innocent enough to fall for it. Don't make a hero out of him. He isn't one."

"Do you think I learned anything in school?"

"I hope you did, and hopefully you can make something out of it. Have you got the grad school stuff together yet?"

Sophie gripped the arm rest tightly.

"Well, I learned what makes a painting good and special and true. Grandpa's paintings represent all those things."

"You know what those paintings represent to me? They represent every basketball game he never saw me play. They represent every merit badge and Eagle Scout step he never helped with. They represent my lost childhood and my lost... Anyway, he puts on an act around you. You don't know anything about him."

Andy was surprised he had lost control. He looked over at Sophie. "I'm sorry, you didn't need to hear that. Just believe me and don't make a big deal about his painting. Cleaning out above the garage is going to be the biggest pain of this whole deal. He'll probably want to keep all the crap up there."

Sophie spoke through a set jaw. "You're my father, but I can tell you, you're completely wrong. He has not told me anything about himself or about his paintings. And no matter what else he's done to you, there is no doubt he's an important artist-- his paintings are important. They don't need to be stored; they need to be seen."

"That's up to him," Andy said. "All I know is I'm going to get that place sold and get him moved somewhere he can afford for a while. And that's only because there is no use in even talking about a facility. He would never do it right now."

Andy pulled into the hotel lot and parked. Sophie got out of the car and walked into the hotel alone. She had been mad at her father in the past for the usual things: enforcing arbitrary rules, limiting who she could see and where she could go, dictating what clothes she could wear. He'd been constantly on her about grades and plans and setting priorities. She was a little girl when she found out he wasn't a superhero capable of fixing every hurt and drying every tear. This was different. On this trip she had encountered a part of him she never thought could exist. It started at the meeting in Albany. He was ruthless and had no guilt about using his position to intimidate people. He had even used his size to overpower those young lawyers, like he was playing basketball. He seemed to enjoy making people cower. She saw him with the poor guy mowing the lawn. He was kind of cute, and all he did was look at her a little. Now to hear him talk about her grandfather like that -- to hear almost contempt in his voice--maybe he wasn't the man she thought he was.

How can he be so wrong about Grandpa's painting? She wondered. He's totally ignorant about that part of his father's life. Even if Grandpa did hurt him, what about forgiveness? Is he a hypocrite on top of everything else? He knows he has to forgive if he claims to be a Christian.

Andy changed into a warmup suit and went down to the gym. He got on a rowing machine and hoped to empty his mind. No such luck.

It's just like Dad to turn Sophie against me, he thought. He's just using her to stroke his ego and play the ignored-artist card -- something he knows she'll sympathize with. He's trying to make me look like an ungrateful son on top of all my other failings. She has no idea how close I've come to just washing my hands of him completely. I would, except I can't let my kids see me do something like that.

Sophie spent some time in prayer asking for guidance and direction. She asked God to soften her father's heart and give her patience until he did. She knew at this point there was no use talking to her father anymore about the paintings or even her grandfather. Her phone buzzed with a text from her father:

Leaving in 30. Need to stop @ Wegmans.

She texted back: K.

They rode in icy silence to the grocery store where they efficiently gathered what they needed, including a small chocolate cake that caught Sophies' eye.

They remained quiet on the way back to Albert's. Each had decided to ignore their previous blowup for now. Andy was focused on his task at hand. Sophie knew she had to bide her time, and she wanted to look at more of the paintings.

When they pulled in front of Albert's garage, he was sitting on the porch with a drink in his hand. They all went into the kitchen, and Andy took charge. "I'll salt the steaks and let them warm up. Sophie, you can get the potatoes started. Dad and I can get going on the fire."

Albert walked over to the countertop. "That's some nice looking porterhouse. How much do I owe you?"

"I told you it's my treat," Andy said. "We have a really good market in Chappaqua. They have dry-aged steaks all the time."

"Guess I couldn't afford them anyway," Albert said and headed outside.

Andy went in the garage and got the chimney starter and some newspaper. He crumpled the newspaper into the bottom and poured the charcoal into the top.

"Where did you get the briquettes?"

"At Wegmans where I got the rest of the stuff," Andy replied.

"Yeah," Albert said, "It's hard to find the good ones anymore. We can always add more if we have to."

Andy wondered, *Is every old man like this, or does my father have a special knack for the put down? Just let it go, it's almost half time of this game. Soon I'll have some plays in place, and it'll be over.*

Just as they were getting back on the porch, Bagger drove up in his Taurus. Andy watched as he swung his legs out and grabbed both sides of the door frame. He rocked twice and pulled himself upright. Andy went out to greet him.

"Mr. Bagwell, it's been too long. You look good."

"Oh, don't you be joshin' me. I'm this side of the grass; that's about it. Good to see you too Mr. Andrew. How you gettin' on?"

"Other than putting up with my miserable old man, I'm doing well."

"Sure don't envy you none havin' to put up with him. I know I can barely stand it."

Albert came down the driveway.

"Well, the both of you can get out of my business. I sure don't need a senile old man and a yuppie taking care of me."

"You old souse," Bagger said, "you'd go into DTs and starve to death if we all didn't take care of you. You should be obliged."

"Well that ain't nobody's business but mine. You want a beer?"

"Wouldn't mind a Genny if you got one to spare." Sophie heard the exchange and brought a beer out for Bagger.

"Is this Miss Sophie? Oh my, it's been too long. You're all grown up. You probably don't even remember me."

"I remember you, Mr. Bagwell. I'm pleased to see you again."

Bagger took her hand. "It'll be nice to have dinner with a beautiful young lady, instead of the fossils down at the Back Door."

"I'm looking forward to hearing some stories about Grandpa."

"I've got a bushel of those, but he won't like the tellin'."

Sophie made a gin and tonic and went out on the porch. The three men were grunting over the fire. She checked her phone and posted a picture of the three guys on Instagram for a laugh. She messaged it to her mother as well.

After a while, Andy headed back up to the house.

"Have the elders made any momentous decisions?" Sophie asked.

"Yeah, they think we should start the meat soon. I'll make the salad. Could you set the table?"

"Sure, I can do both if you want"

"Thanks, you always make a nice salad."

Finally, after much poking, laying on of hands, and a final flip, the three grill masters arrived at a consensus and the meat came off the fire.

When they all sat down, Andy said, "You're outnumbered, Dad. Mr. Bagwell would you offer grace?"

"I would be honored. Dear Lord, thank you for this food and this time together. Please watch over us and bless us with your grace. In your Precious Son's name, Jesus. Amen."

Albert was able to chew the meat easily. It had a deep and complex flavor. He didn't think he would ever order steak at the Back Door again; it would be too disappointing. He could tell Bagger had never had anything like it either. He was quiet for once.

"So, Mr. Bagwell, Dad has some news."

Bagger looked up at Andy then over at Albert. "You finally made up your mind to unload this place? You sure been talking about it long enough."

Albert looked up a little. "I am. Andrew is going to take care of everything and find me a place to live."

Albert and Bagger locked eyes, Albert gave an almost imperceptible shake of his head. "I think that's a fine plan," Bagger said. "You don't need the consternation of all this property and big house. I'm sure there's plenty of good places right here where Bonnie can keep an eye on you. That's what I think."

"We have a realtor coming tomorrow," Andy said. "We'll hire somebody to start cleaning out the house once we get it listed."

"Well now," Bagger said, "if you need help carrying things or any heavy work, I can send my grandsons over. They're old enough to drive now."

"We can throw everything out for all I care," Albert said. "It's nothing but junk. We should just get a dumpster and start hauling it all out. Maybe I'll hire your boys; they've helped before. They aren't as lazy as most kids these days."

"Those boys'll give you an honest day's work or hear it from me," Bagger exclaimed.

Sophie jumped in. "The paintings will have to be boxed for storage. That will take some time."

"What would we need, a carpenter?" Andy asked.

"No, you make boxes out of Styrofoam and cardboard. I did it a lot during my internship. It's easy but takes time."

Andy looked at his father. "Dad, is that something you could do?"

Albert looked at his hands. "I'm not very safe with a utility knife anymore. I might be able to help someone else."

Andy thought a minute. "Maybe Sophie could teach the boys before we leave, and they could do it. It sounds easy enough."

"Those boys are good workers, but they got the attention span of a squirrel. They need bull work, nothing requiring any delicacy. I'd hate to see them put a foot through one of Pablo's masterpieces."

"We'll figure something out," Andy said. "It's not a priority right now."

"It will need to be done sooner or later," Sophie said, "and like I said, it'll take a long time. You guys finish your beers. I'll start picking up and get the cake."

"I don't eat cake," Albert said. "I think I'll have a little bourbon to settle my stomach."

“I can’t have any cake,” Bagger said. "I’m going to need an extra shot tonight as it is, after the beer and potato, but much obliged for the offer.”

Albert got a bottle and two glasses out of the cupboard and the two old men went out the back door.

Albert poured a couple fingers of bourbon and handed the bottle to Bagger to pour his own. They sat in silence for a while until Bagger said quietly, “I’m glad you gave up that hare-brained idea to move to Vermont.”

Albert took a sip. “I haven’t changed my mind. I just don’t want to tell them yet. I’m waiting for the right time.”

Bagger snorted. “There ain’t no right time to tell them. It’s a stupid idea.”

"Just drink my liquor," Albert said. "You talk too much."

Bagger finished his drink and went into the kitchen. “I gotta get home and take my sugar shot or I’ll be in trouble.”

Andy and Sophie were sitting at the table having coffee and cake. Andy got up when Bagger came in.

“Thank you two very much. “It was great food but better company. I hope I can see you again real soon. I’m glad you're getting him outta here. It’s been a worry on his mind for quite a spell.”

“We appreciate everything you do for Dad,” Andy said. “You've been a real friend to him. I have your number. I'll be in touch if we need your grandsons.”

Andy and Bagger shook hands.

“Good evening, Miss Sophie.”

"It was so nice to see you again, Mr. Bagwell. Don't forget you promised me some stories about Grandpa."

Bagger smiled. "I'll come up with some good ones for the next time I see you."

On his way out he saw Albert cleaning the grill. "I'll stop in Sunday to see if you need anything. Thanks for the drinks."

"See you then," Albert said.

Albert came back in the house. Andy could see he had not needed that last drink. He was slow and holding on to the table as he sat down. He almost slipped off with the chair pad but caught himself.

"Well, that was nice," he said, "but all that food made me drowsy. Guess I'll turn in a little early tonight."

"It's been quite a day," Andy said. "We'll head back to the hotel. Geoff is coming after lunch and the realtor will be here around three. What time does Bonnie come with dinner?"

"Usually about five. We'll have to get her up to speed with all this. I don't think she has a clue."

"Wouldn't be the first time," Andy laughed.

"Oh, she's alright. Gets by mostly."

"OK, Cookie, let's head back. See you tomorrow, Dad."

Sophie helped Albert out of the chair and gave him a little hug.

"Sleep well. I'll come back and look at some more paintings."

After a quiet ride back to the hotel Andy said, "I know it's early, but I'm tired, so I think I'm going to call your Mom and maybe watch a game until I fall asleep."

"Whatever," Sophie said. "I'm going to my room."

Sophie had to be alone; she needed to think and to pray. Something had changed, and she wasn't sure what. One thing was for sure: she needed to grow up. She wasn't Daddy's little girl anymore, and she needed to stop acting like one. She had spent her whole life living up to his expectations; now he wasn't even who she thought he was. Until now, she had been directed by him. Sure, she chose to go to Carnegie, but he insisted she take business courses along with the art courses. He "highly suggested" she do an internship at a gallery. She had wanted to go to France and study art. Now he wanted her to go to grad school and start on an MBA.

Well, maybe I don't want an MBA, she thought. Maybe I won't have a "successful career." Maybe I'll paint and be poor. Anyway, right now, I'm being led to be with Grandpa and do something with his paintings. I need to make a plan. I need to ask God for guidance.

NINE

Despite lying awake much of the night, Sophie awoke early, got dressed and went down to the lobby for the free breakfast. She had decided to go back to her grandfather's studio and get a good look at everything. She got a second cup of coffee and texted her father: *Going to uber to grandpas.*

She didn't hear anything back, so she pulled up the Uber app on her phone and requested a ride.

Albert was in the driveway cleaning the grill when she arrived. He was startled to see his granddaughter get out of a strange car.

"Where's your dad?"

"He's still at the hotel. I wanted to get an early start, so I got an Uber here.

I want to go through your paintings and see what's what. I have a couple ideas."

Andy finished his work out and checked his phone. He immediately texted Sophie: *Where are you?*

Sophie's phone buzzed. *That didn't take long,* she thought.

She texted back: *Grandpas cu when you get here bye.* She hoped he wouldn't text back.

No such luck.

Should have checked with me first.

I texted.U didn't get back.

Be there with lunch.

Sophie put her phone in her pocket and turned to her grandfather. "Have you numbered your paintings or kept an index?"

"No. When I'm done with one, I put it in the racks."

"Do you have any idea how many are up there?"

Albert thought for a moment. "Well, there haven't been many months in the last fifty or so years that I haven't finished at least one oil. Some years more, some less. Plus, the drawings and pastels. Then there's the stuff I did in New York."

Sophie looked up at the studio. "There could be way over six hundred pieces up there!"

She thought back to her internship. She worked with another person, and they could pack two -- maybe three -- paintings an hour. Doing it alone would take more than double that time. It could easily take over two months just to pack everything working forty hours a week. They should all be labeled, photographed, and cataloged. Realistically, it would take four months or more.

"Grandpa, let's go have a cup of coffee."

"OK. I'll finish the grill later."

Albert made the coffee and they sat down.

"What's on your mind?" he asked.

“I've been doing some thinking. First, you need to know what's going on with me. My plan-- or really my Dad's plan-- is for me to go back to school and get a graduate degree in business or marketing. That would get me a really good job, but I've decided I just don’t want to go to school anymore right now. That means I have to find a job. I also want to be able to concentrate on painting. So, I have kind of a crazy idea to run by you. You need the studio cleaned out, and the paintings have to be boxed to get moved. I know how to do it. And... I need a job. Is there any way you can afford to pay me to get your paintings ready to store? I obviously haven’t worked out all the details, but I have to know if it's even possible first.”

Albert pushed himself back up in the chair.

“Damn these cushions. Sorry. Where would you live if you don’t go home?”

“I haven’t thought everything through. If I don’t go to school, I have to get a job. Plus, I want to move out on my own as soon as I can. I need to grow up and be responsible for myself. I’m just asking if this is even feasible.”

“I'm sure your father wouldn't be happy. I don’t want him blaming me. He'll think I put you up to it. Although I'm glad you don’t want to get sucked into the capitalist machine like he did.”

“I know he'll flip out. I'm not going to grad school in any case, so he'll be mad at me no matter what. It can’t be helped. I'll make sure he understands you didn’t have anything to do with it.”

"You won't be living like you do now on what I could pay you. Though, I'm sure your father will make sure you're taken care of."

Sophie stood up. "That's the point. I need to be on my own. I don't want to depend on him or Mom. Dad always says, 'Every right comes with a responsibility.' I have a right to live on my own, but that makes me responsible for myself. I have to find a way to make something work. What could you afford to pay me?"

Albert finished his coffee. *Everybody has to make their own way, he thought. What they do is who they are. She wants to do this, but Andrew will be furious and might not help me sell the place. For some reason, I can't let her down. She's so much like my mother was. Soft on the outside, like iron pipe inside.*

"Right now, I have an extra two hundred a week I could pay you," he said. "Plus we'll need the materials. After the place is sold, I could give you more."

Sophie leaned against the counter. "I need to look at your paintings some more and think about it. Can I go up to the studio?"

"Go ahead."

Sophie felt an immediate sense of calm and centeredness when she passed through the studio door. The walls were saturated with her Grandfather's countless hours of inspiration and concentration.

Sophie started with the stacks closest to the wall. There were portfolios full of sketches and pastels. She pulled oils out randomly. Some were fully representational landscapes and scenes of men working in factories. Others were in various degrees of abstraction. She continued back and found some obvious studies and other highly imitative works of Impressionists; Picasso, Cezanne, and others. She went back to the front and studied several of the abstractions with hidden figures. They all had "push and pull" -- the quality that was exalted in every art class she had ever taken. The direction and density of the brush strokes made them dynamic -- drawing her in, then launching her out. At the same time, her eyes were moved around the surface by the colors. But these paintings had the added element of the disguised figure. It came and went with her degree of intention and seemed to change each time she found it. It was a part of the painting but also existed on its own. The effect was disquieting. It was like reading a poem: the meaning was there but entangled in the verse. It had to be absorbed, not understood.

She continued her exploration and went all the way back to the little room with the bookshelves. She sat in the leather chair. It made her feel small and embraced her the way she wished her grandfather could. She melted like wax in the cast his body had molded. She soaked in that feeling for quite some time then got up to look at the bookshelves.

On one side was a collection of large art books: several on Cezanne, the rest covering the Great Masters, Impressionists, Surrealists, and the Cubists. There were several gallery catalogs and torn out magazine articles.

On the other side were rows of books arranged by author: Sartre, Camus, Nietzsche, Kierkegaard, and Beckett. There was a shelf just for Jung and Joseph Campbell. Hemingway, Dostoevsky, Fitzgerald, and others were lined up shoulder to shoulder. She had cocktail-chatter knowledge of many; some she had never encountered. She was shocked again at how wrong her father and everyone else was about her grandfather. What the world saw of him outside his studio was blind to his mind, heart, and soul. She was awestruck that he had invited her beyond that locked door. She felt exalted by what God was doing with her life. Who she was and all she had done had brought her to this place – at this time – to love this man.

Albert poured his mid-morning dose of bourbon to calm his tremor and finished cleaning and oiling the grill. He went back on the porch to finish his drink and thought of Sophie up in his studio. *No one had ever shown any interest in his paintings. It was just as well; no one he knew had anything in common with his life up there. Sophie was young -- but smart -- and seemed to have actually learned something in college. She was complicating his plans, however. Her offer to pack the paintings took him by surprise. He had assumed Andrew would get a truck and stack them up in a storage shed somewhere.*

This will be better for the paintings, he thought, *but Andrew is going to blame me for her refusal to go to graduate school. Hopefully, he'll want to get me out of here enough to keep helping. I'll tell him and Bonnie about Sunadew tonight. He'll have his doubts but go along because then he won't have to find a place for me. Bonnie will be upset because she gets a good part of her income from helping me out. She'll be more troubled about selling the house. She's hinted that she'd like to take it over and move in, "when the time comes." Of course, she has no idea what it costs to keep this place or how much work it needs.*

Albert watched as Sophie came out of the garage. She was beyond a resemblance to her great-grandmother. It was as if his mother were being given a second chance. Like Sophie, she had been beautiful, smart, talented, and full of life. His father had quelled any chance for those qualities to flower. Now with Sophie, he might see what could have been, if Andrew didn't nip her in the bud.

Sophie sat next to her grandfather. "I looked at some more of your paintings. Sometime soon I need to go through them with you and have you tell me about them. I need to know where you studied and so many other things. Right now, I'm sure I'm doing the right thing to stay and get them packed. At least the oils. Maybe we can just wrap most of the rest of them. I'll just have to tell Mom and Dad and take what comes. Maybe they'll understand, but I doubt it. I know it's the right thing to do, and I have faith it'll work out."

Albert finished his drink. "You have to do what's true for you. That's the only way it will work out."

By the time Andy had finished exercising, taken a sauna, cleaned up, and checked in with the office, it was eleven o'clock. He gave Lillian a quick update and headed out. He was feeling good after his workout and thought, *Today should be a good day. We might even get a contract signed. Having Geoff should make it easier. He was never the most ambitious guy; he didn't make it past third string on the ball team, but he should be able to handle this deal. It'll probably be a nice billing for him.*

He remembered there was a car wash just a block or two off Jefferson. He took time to run the Lexus through. He wanted to be sure it looked nice for Geoff.

Albert and Sophie watched as Andy pulled in and turned the big SUV around and backed it up to the garage.

Andy came onto the porch. "Well, good morning, Miss Independent. You couldn't wait and come back with me?"

"I knew you would putz around all morning. I wanted to get back here. It's not like I need you for everything. I managed on my own at school without problems."

"It would have been good if you talked to me first, is all. I've got lunch."

After lunch, Andy put the grill back and took an inventory of the garage. The tools were arranged like a museum exhibit. They looked old and worn but probably still had value to someone. The zero-turn and the walk-behind mower looked brand new. There were edgers and blowers as well. All of it would be a bargain to someone needing them. Then there was the truck. It was hard to believe it was now over thirty years old. With the exception of the crumpled corner of the passenger-side, it only had a few minor nicks and dings. It still had the side-mounted toolboxes and the base for a vise welded to the inside of the tailgate. He remembered when his father bought the truck. He was at Princeton working in the off-season washing cars at a Chevy dealership. It would probably bring a couple thousand from a kid or someone wanting to restore it. As he was looking at the odometer, he heard a car drive up.

Geoff pulled his Outback up to the shining Lexus, and thought, *That's got to be Gunner's. He saw Andy coming out of the garage. Unbelievable, he looks like he could still dunk. I've got to get back to the gym.*

"Andy, my man. How long's it been?"

Andy reached out his hand.

"I guess since the last class reunion, whenever that was, I've lost count. You look great. Thanks for clearing your schedule to do this. I really appreciate it."

Geoff gave Andy a firm shake and grabbed his elbow.

"I was so glad you called. I try to keep Fridays light so I can get home early at least once a week. I still have kids in school to deal with."

"I want to hear all about it. Come on up and say hi to Dad and meet my daughter."

Sophie watched the two men walk up. Her father's friend wasn't a small man, but her father seemed to tower above him. His shoulders were rounded, and he had a noticeable paunch which made him look even shorter. He was wearing an obviously off-the-shelf plaid dress shirt. The pocket didn't even match up. She wondered if she would always compare every man to her father.

“Sophie, this is Mr. Connors. We're high school friends and played ball together. He’s going to help us sell the house.”

“Please call me Geoff. Your father is being kind. We didn’t play together. I sat on the bench and watched him play.”

“Hey man,” Andy protested, “we were all on the team. Those were good times. And do you remember my father, Albert?”

Geoff shook Albert’s hand.

“We met many years ago. It's nice to see you again. Andy tells me you want to make some changes"

“Not so much want to," Albert replied. " I need to. It’s not easy getting old. I don’t recommend it.” Albert replied.

"I always say, we have to consider the alternative."

“Are you allowed a beer on duty?” Andy asked.

“Hey, it’s Friday. Why not?”

Andy headed towards the door. “Dad, do you want one?”

“You know me. I wouldn’t want to be unsociable.”

“Mr. Connors," Sophie asked. "I've always wanted to know: how did my father get his nickname, Gunner?”

Geoff laughed.

“Well, shall we say, your father was slow to develop his passing skills. In junior high and JV, his idea of teamwork was for someone to pass him the ball so he could take a shot. Fortunately, for the rest of us, he scored about forty percent of the time, so if we wanted to win, he was our best option. He played varsity his sophomore year, and it wasn't long before he was getting double-teamed. They had a losing season mainly because he wouldn’t pass. Something happened over that summer. In his junior year he led the league in scoring and assists. By then, the rest of us were on varsity and won sectionals two years in a row. The nickname stuck all these years."

"I heard you talking about me," Andy said as he handed out the beers. "Don't believe everything he says. It wasn't my fault those other guys never got open."

"Let's just leave it at that," Geoff said. "I don't want to disillusion your adoring daughter."

"I'm afraid it's too late for that."

Andy and Geoff compared family photos and their busy schedules. Andy could see that Geoff's priorities were his kids and family life. He had married a classmate and stayed in Rochester close to their families. His children knew their grandparents on both sides. He coached sports with his kids and was still involved with Boy Scouts. He had done well financially, by Rochester standards, but obviously didn't push his career. Sophie took it all in and tried to pry more history about her father from the two of them.

During a lull in the conversation Geoff said, "Before I forget – I run into Jack Armstrong once in a while. He still shows up at Scout events. He's doing great and still loves to reminisce about the old days."

"It's funny you mention him. I thought about him when I passed the church coming in."

It wasn't long before a white BMW 3 series oozed into the driveway. A fit, but stocky, man got out and put on his suit coat and picked up a briefcase. He made a study of the house and yard while Andy and Geoff came off the porch to greet him.

"Andy, this is Don Washington.

"Afternoon, Don. Come up and meet my father. He owns the place."

The three went onto the porch. Don offered his hand to Albert.

"A pleasure to meet you, Mr. Martel. This is a beautiful property – really unusual for this area."

"It was at one time."

"And this is my daughter, Sophie," Andy said. "She came with me from Chappaqua where we live."

"Welcome to Rochester, Sophie. I hope you enjoy your stay."

"Thanks. I hope to see more of it while I'm here."

Andy morphed into lawyer mode and made it clear it was he with whom they would be dealing. He was professional but tried not to come across too Wall Street. He was a quick judge of men and sensed both to be honest. He was sure Geoff wouldn't lead him astray. Don had prepared a standard ninety-day exclusive contract with the usual seven-percent commission.

"I wasn't expecting this much property and street frontage. I admit I'll have to do some research before recommending an asking price," Don said.

Andy looked at his father. "Just so you know Dad, if you sign the contract, Don is the only one who can sell the property. You have to negotiate in good faith if he brings an offer. From here on, you can't change your mind about selling for ninety days.

Also, Geoff will be representing you and helping with negotiations. He'll also manage the closing when that time comes. He'll be charging a normal fee. Does this sound like what you had in mind?"

Albert, who'd been silent up until this point, responded. "Just put whatever money is left over in my bank account."

Don went over the contract again and Albert took up the pen. He signed in all the places Don showed him, then they shook hands.

"Mr. Martel, we'll make this as easy as possible for you. I've seen this situation many times. There are always concerns, but I've never had anyone regret simplifying their lives. If you have any questions you can call me any time. You're fortunate to have a son like Andy to be here for you. We'll all do what's best for you."

"We all do what's best for each of us," Albert said. "Sometimes it works out. I'm going up to my studio."

"Sorry about my Dad," Andy said once his father was gone. "He can be gruff at times."

"Please, don't apologize." Don said. "This is a hard time for folks. I sure would hate to be giving up everything I worked for, then have strangers come in and take over. Believe me, it can be much worse when they don't have family to help. I meant it Andy. He's fortunate to have you."

"When he sees what you can get for this place, I think he'll feel pretty good."

"Maybe, maybe not," Don replied. "Do you mind if I walk around a bit?"

"I'll show you around. The house is a mess and needs some repairs. Do you really think it'll be a factor in the sale?"

"I doubt it. Most likely this will go to some kind of developer. They won't want the house in the way. We can just look outside for now."

Sophie was struck by how cavalier her father was about his boyhood home. She followed Albert up to his studio.

Andy took Geoff and Don to the back of the lawn where it ended at the rear of a strip mall then along the outside as it followed a residential street.

"So how do you two know each other?" he asked.

"Our sons are friends, and we coached travel teams together all through school," Geoff replied.

"Plus, we work together on real estate quite a bit," Don added. "Geoff really knows how to do it right the first time.

Sophie found Albert sitting in his leather chair. She sat down on the couch across from him. Albert kept his eyes closed. "I just needed some time," he said. "Those young guys were too intense, too sure of themselves."

"Is this what you expected?" Sophie asked.

"I knew it would be like this. I was hoping I would die before I needed to go through it."

"Grandpa, you spend too much time thinking about dying."

Albert looked at his granddaughter. "You can't live free if you don't expect to die."

"I don't know what that means."

"Just as well," Albert sighed. "Sophie, I've been thinking, you should do what your parents want you to do. You don't want to get stuck here, and you don't want to disappoint them. You think you want freedom, but freedom is hard."

"I'm tired of taking the easy way out. I have to start my own life. Anyway, I know in my heart this is what I should do."

"I don't know. I want to take a nap up here today. I'll see you later."

Sophie was getting used to her grandfather's abrupt ways and left him alone. She saw her father sitting on the porch talking on his phone.

"That was your mother. We got it all set for Jack to go to golf camp. She can take him next Friday, and then we'll go back and pick him up the next week."

"That's nice for Jack. He'll do fine."

"Maybe he'll like Cornell," Andy said. "He needs to be looking at colleges. It's not Princeton but wouldn't hurt to look."

"How far is Cornell from here?" Sophie asked.

"Two hours, maybe less, why?"

"If Mom is going to be that close, I should stay here and work on packing up Grandpa's paintings. She could just come this way and pick me up. It would be good to get started on that soon. I was thinking I could talk to Aunt Bonnie tonight. Maybe I could teach her to do it. I can do all the grad school stuff online at Starbucks or some place."

Andy thought for a few moments.

"What if you went through all the paintings and picked out just the ones he definitely wants to have packed? Maybe we could kind of wrap up all the rest or something. If you did that,

I bet you and Bonnie could be done in a week. I'll pay Bonnie for her time."

That's a great idea, Daddy. I never thought of that. It's amazing how good you are at solving problems."

"Thanks, Cookie. Maybe this can work. There're some hotels closer to here that I could move you into. They would have Wi-Fi so you can finish the applications. I don't think your mother would mind. That way she could see Dad too."

Sophie was feeling worse by the minute. She wasn't only lying, now she was shamelessly manipulating her father as well. She prayed that eventually he'd see what she was doing was right and forgive her.

"I guess I won't get as early a start tomorrow as I'd hoped," Andy said, "but that's OK. This has been quite a day all ready. I need to clear my head. I think I'll walk around the neighborhood before Bonnie gets here. Do you want to come with me?"

"No thanks. I'll stay here."

"I'll call your Mom and see if this'll work for her."

Andy walked along the houses. The front doors were lined up like a cell block sentineled by the scarred maple trees standing beyond the moat of broken sidewalk. Some of the houses were in their third reincarnation complete with new roof, siding, and vinyl windows. Others were slumping toward abandonment.

He was long past nostalgia for this place. Selling his father's property would be the final turn in his prolonged escape from his childhood bounds. He had made his future away from this place and had no desire to look back. He heard the hum of traffic before he came to a wrought iron fence that marked the boundary of the church standing at the end of his street. It was there he attended services in the airy sanctuary. He went to Sunday School and Boy Scout meetings in the low-ceiling basement.

He noticed a man trimming bushes along the red-bricked wall of the church. Andy thought, *How odd is this? It's Jack Armstrong. Geoff and I were just talking about him. Lillian would say, "There are no coincidences."*

Andy went through the side gate and across the lawn. He found where two extension cords were joined and unplugged them. He watched as Jack inspected the trimmer, turned it on and off several times, then looked along the cord to where Andy was standing. His mentor and friend smiled and walked toward him. His limp looked worse than Andy remembered. His trademark boonie hat covered a shock of white hair. He remained barrel-chested but thicker in the waist than the last time Andy saw him. He still had his booming voice.

"Look who's in the neighborhood. I figured you couldn't find your way back anymore. What're you doing here?"

"You won't believe it," Andy said as they shook hands, "but Geoff Connors and I were just talking about you. I'm here to arrange selling my dad's place. Geoff is handling some of the details."

"Do you have time to visit? We can go downstairs where it's cooler. I'd love to hear how you're doing."

"Sure," Andy said. "I have time."

They went through a back door and down a flight of concrete stairs. The long room smelled of the last scalloped-potato-and-ham dinner, crayons, and musty construction paper. The brown folding tables still had the same gray metal chairs surrounding them. The Boy Scout Oath and the Pledge of Allegiance were enshrined on one wall behind a wooden desk flanked by the American flag and the troop flag.

"We'll sneak a couple bottles of pop from the Scouts," Jack said and went into the kitchen.

Andy felt transported back to the many times he had walked from his father's house to this place of refuge. It was here that Jack Armstrong gave him the attention and support he did not get at home. They grew closer as adults, and Jack counseled Andy through college and beyond. He remembered how they sealed their bond when Andy announced his son would carry on Jack's name.

Jack returned with two Cokes. "This is so great. How's your family doing? How is my guy, Jack?"

"He's super -- finished his junior year. He's become quite the golfer. Sophie is here with me. She graduated from college this year. She'll be starting grad school in the fall. Lilly is fantastic. With everything else she does, she's managed to get her real estate license and is doing really well at that. You look the same. How are you?"

"I had to fully retire last year. I'm doing a lot of stuff here at the church. I bother the Scout leaders any chance I get. Helen doesn't get out much. I can leave her for a few hours at a time, but she needs me a lot."

"Sorry to hear about Helen. Are you getting any help with her?"

"No, I mostly manage. She's getting worse though. I have some church friends that will sit with her if I have to go somewhere. What about your dad?"

"He's actually getting better. He's fairly sharp and steady on his feet most of the time. Still up in the garage painting most days. He can't manage the yard and house anymore. He wants to sell it and move into an apartment nearby."

"That'll be hard on him. I dread the thought of ever having to move. He must be upset over it."

"You know him," Andy said. "It's hard to tell what he's thinking. Some things never change."

"I've often thought of going to visit him, but I wasn't sure how he'd take it. He never took kindly to my interfering in your life."

"Jack, I've told you before, I never would've survived without you. I hope you know how much you mean to me. I'm truly sorry I haven't stayed in touch better."

"I get that's how it goes. We all have to move on and not live in the past. It's a blessing you stopped in today. How long will you be home?"

"I'm leaving in the morning, but I'll be back soon to check on things. We have to arrange to get the house and garage cleaned out. Bonnie is coming over with dinner soon, so I have to get back for that. I'll make time to get you out for dinner the next time I come."

Jack took Andy's hand. "That's something to look forward to. I'd really appreciate it."

Jack and Andy went outside. They hugged and slapped each other's back.

Andy crossed the street and walked back on the other side. He thought about Jack and how comforting it was to see him.

Albert closed the studio door behind him and carefully made his way down the stairs. He saw Sophie sitting on the porch staring into her phone.

"What are you looking at?"

Sophie looked up. "Just doing a little research on de Kooning – trying to refresh my mind about him."

"I have some books about him."

Sophie laughed. "No, no need. I just Googled him."

Albert shook his head and went into the kitchen. He poured a double and went back to the porch.

"So, Grandpa, I'm not telling Dad my whole plan yet. I still need to think about it and figure out a way to tell him. I told him I'm staying here for a week until Mom comes to pick me up."

"Where'll you be staying?

"Dad said he would pay for a hotel room. Once you start paying me, I'll come up with something else. Do you think Bonnie would want to help pack the paintings?"

"She always has a lot going on, but she might be interested. There she is now."

Bonnie eased her Volvo into the driveway. Sophie came out to meet her and picked up one of the totes from the back seat.

"What's for supper?" Sophie asked.

"I thought we could have a picnic, so I made some vegan burgers and potato salad. Are there any salad greens here?"

"That sounds good," Sophie said. "There's plenty of salad left from last night."

Even Albert admitted the burgers were edible and the potato salad was good. It had plenty of onion and a little mustard, just the way he liked it. They ate at the picnic table on the edge of the lawn. Andy and Bonnie laughed over some well-worn stories from high school. Sophie tried to pry more family history out of them but was met with diversions and changes of subject. She could sense a gap in their history. After dinner Andy and Bonnie cleaned up the kitchen.

"Hey, Bon, can you stay for a bit? We need to go over some plans Dad's made."

"I take it he's thinking about selling the house. He's been funny about it for a few months."

They went out on the porch and interrupted an obviously deep discussion between Sophie and her grandfather.

"Well, that's not what I read," Sophie said.

"I don't care what you read. I was there, dearie." Albert was nearly jovial.

"Hey, you two," Andy called. "Can you take up whatever you're talking about some other time? We need to discuss some things. Dad, do you want Sophie to stay?"

"I guess she's in the middle of it now. She might as well stay."

Bonnie sat down across from Albert. "It sounds like I'm the only one not in the middle of it... as usual," she said.

Albert looked at his son. "Andy, why don't you explain things."

"Bonnie, as you said, Dad's been considering selling the house and getting into some place easier to take care of. Actually, even if he wanted to stay here, he can't afford it. I came this week just for my regular visit, but now he's asked me to help get the place sold."

Bonnie looked to her father. "Well I'm glad we can at least talk it over. We should look at the whole scene and see how all the circles come together. Maybe by really getting into it, some way to keep you here will show itself. If we put all our energy together something righteous will flow out."

"I signed the papers to sell it this afternoon," Albert said.

Bonnie stood up then dropped back into the chair. "I don't fucking believe it! How could you two just sell it out from under me? You don't think I care about this place? Why would you do this without asking me first? Andy, do you think you can just come in here and move Dad out? I've been taking care of him for years. You don't do shit unless there's a buck to be made. Hell, you could afford to keep him here, but no, you would never consider that."

Albert stood up. “I don’t want his money. I wouldn’t take it if he offered. He knows that. In fact, I don’t need either of you.” The screen door screeched as he threw it open and went into the house.

“Look Bonnie," Andy said. "I wish it could have happened slower. Nothing you say will change his mind. We don’t have to make this a fight. He doesn’t have any choice."

“You're wrong. There's always more than one way to do things. It’ll kill him to leave here. You know that don’t you?”

“I didn't convince him to do it. I certainly don’t want to get involved any more than I have to. You know that. Just calm down, you’re making this harder than it has to be.”

Albert came back out with a file folder.

“I've been thinking about this longer than either of you know. The last time the swine downtown raised my taxes I knew I had to leave. I have all the numbers in this file. If I could just die in the next few months, none of this would matter. But if I don’t, I'll be screwed if I stay here. As long as I'm alive, all I really care about is painting. So, any plans I make have to include being able to paint. The second thing I want is to not burden either one of you. I want to make sure you don’t have to do anything more for me... ever. Here's where I'm going after this place is sold.”

He had two copies of the brochure for Sunadew. He handed one to Andy and one to Bonnie.

Bonnie spoke first. “Vermont? You want to move to Vermont and leave me here?”

Andy studied the entire brochure.

"This looks like a scam to me," he said. "It doesn't even say how much it costs."

Albert was prepared.

"What I want is someplace that will take care of me until I die. That's what this place does. I pay up front and no matter what I need I can get it there. They'll even have me cremated and shipped wherever I want – all included. For once I'll be around other painters--people who understand what I do. You two won't have to worry yourselves about me. It says they have to see me before they can give any details on the cost."

"I don't see why we can't figure out a way for you to stay here," Bonnie said. "That way I can still help you, and you get to keep the house."

"I don't want the house, and I don't want anyone to help me."

Andy was sure the more they argued the more entrenched his father would become.

"Let's go step by step. We just got it listed, so it will be several months before all that's done. We can hold off worrying about where you'll go for a while. It won't hurt to look at other options even if you still decide on Vermont."

Albert knew his lawyer son was trying to mollify him. He could play that game too.

"That's right, we can look around, but I want to get out of here. I've been stuck in this hole most of my life. I'm sick to death of it."

Bonnie started to cry.

"That's an awful thing to say, Dad. Do you think I wanted to stay here? I stayed because you need someone to take care of you, and no one else would."

"I don't know why you stayed. That's your business. I stayed because I was too damn lazy to move. Now I'm finally being real and doing what I need to do to finish up my miserable life with some semblance of freedom."

Bonnie was sobbing now. "Why don't you just say it? You've had a miserable life because of me. You got stuck here because of me. You hated being my father."

"My life is the way it is because of the choices I made. I was in the middle of the scene in New York. I could've been something. I could've kept drinking and working and whoring around. I could have been like those other cowards in New York and killed myself. Or, like the irresponsible bastards that left their wives. Your mother could have had an abortion, like other women were doing. But no, we came back here. I took care of you two as best I could. Then your mother craps out, and I'm left alone. Maybe I wasn't the greatest father in history, but it was the best I could manage."

Andy could see Sophie was wide-eyed and looking at him. "Sophie, why don't you wait in the car. I'll be just a couple of minutes. Try not to be upset."

Sophie nodded to her father and silently walked to the car.

"We can make this easy or we can make it hard," Andy said. "I don't expect it to be milk and honey, but can we at least not drag up stuff from the past? We have to play where it landed and move forward."

Bonnie was standing against the porch post.

"It doesn't hurt to get our feelings out sometime," she said. "It's the only way to open up our chakras."

"The time isn't in front of Sophie."

"She's not your little princess anymore. She has to know the truth sometime."

"It would have been better if I could have chosen the time, now she's going to ask questions. I really don't have time for that now. I have to move her to a different hotel in the morning. I'll come back here after that. She's going to stay for a week and get started on the paintings. If you want to help, Sophie can teach you how to wrap the pictures."

Bonnie stopped at the kitchen door.

"I still have to get used to all this. I don't know what I'm going to do."

"Please tell Sophie I'm sorry," Albert said.

"Tell her yourself. She's in the car over there."

Albert looked toward the driveway. "I wouldn't know what to say."

Andy started down the steps. "I should be here in the morning by ten at least. Good night."

Sophie was quiet on the way to the hotel.

"It's early," Andy said. "Do you want to stop for a drink or coffee and dessert?"

"Some wine would be good," she replied.

"The bar at the hotel will be as good as any."

When they arrived at the hotel, the bar was filling up with the evening crowd.

"I guess I better put on a jacket," Andy said. "You can change, but please, you don't need a makeover."

Sophie decided she wouldn't go frumpy just because she was with her father at an old-folk's bar. She found the little white cami she got at the Gap and tried the jacket over it. She buttoned the bottom buttons, so it hugged her waist and flared around on top. Then she thought, what the heck, and slithered into the stretchy black pencil skirt she had thrown in at the last minute. She brushed out her hair and added a touch of smoky eye shadow just as her father knocked on the door.

"I don't think I've seen that outfit before," Andy said when Sophie opened the door. "I take it your mom didn't go with you that day."

"Oh this is just some old stuff I had. I didn't bring much with me. Do I look all right?"

"You're a beautiful woman, Cookie. You make everything look nice."

"Fiddle dee dee, you say that to all the girls."

The hotel lounge was typical Rochester: designed on the dull side to avoid any hint of pretension. As they walked through the high tables Andy wasn't surprised to see the men take a glance, but the women followed them with squinty eyes too. They found a small table beyond the pale of the bar lights.

"Hi, my name is Brittinee, I'll be your server. Would you like a drink before looking at the menu?"

"We're just here for drinks." Andy said. "I'll take a Manhattan."

Brittinee surveyed Sophie. Her voice went up a half octave.

"Love your jacket. What kind is it?"

"It's by Paige. I couldn't find one I liked at Penney's. You can bring me a glass of merlot."

"Oh, no wonder it fits you so nice." She gave Andy a once-over. "I'll be right back with your drinks."

"What was that all about?" Andy asked. "Weren't you a little catty?"

"She thinks I'm an escort."

"What do you know about escorts? Why would she think that?"

"There were girls at school who went out with men so they could buy nice clothes. It happens everywhere. That witch knew this is a designer jacket, and like, I'm here drinking with an old guy. Anyway, I want to talk about Grandpa and Bonnie."

"I'm sorry you had to see that tonight. Bonnie loves drama and can only see how things affect her. She's always been like that. You also saw what your grandfather is like. He doesn't see why anything he says or does should affect anyone else. He lives in his own little world. He thinks everyone behaves that same way except the rest of us won't admit it."

Brittinee arrived with their drinks.

"I hope this will be a nice start to your evening," she said.

Sophie tried to give the skinny, green-haired waitress a look of condescension but came off only as annoyed.

She sipped her wine. She was trying to like dry wine. She knew it was more sophisticated than the sweet kind she usually had, but her mouth felt parched. The merlot was a little smoother than most though.

The Manhattan came neat. *I could settle in with a couple of these,* Andy thought.

Sophie looked into her glass of garnet wine. The surface was shimmering. She swirled it the way she had seen other people do.

"Dad, you have to tell me about your mother. I can only guess something bad happened to her. Why was Grandpa talking about abortions and people committing suicide? What did he mean about your mother 'crapping out?'"

Andy knew he could not conceal that part of the family history any longer. He wished Lillian was with him.

"My mother and father got married in New York City. He was going to art school at the time and she was working. Mother got pregnant with Bonnie, and they couldn't afford to live there. Dad had to leave school and move back here. He got in the union and went to work as a plumber. From what I know, Mother always had mental problems. After Bonnie was born, she became much worse and never really recovered. Then she had me. Back then, there wasn't much treatment, and people mostly hid it. She never left the house. I remember her sleeping much of the time. At times she tried to take care of us. She cooked breakfast some days. I loved her French omelets. Bonnie and Dad did most of the other housework. She was drinking at night. She also took sleeping pills and had gotten into diet pills when she was in New York. Anyway, she just got worse and worse. Dad would take her to the hospital, but she always got out in a few days. Then one morning, when I was fourteen, Bonnie found her dead in the bedroom."

Sophie's eyes welled up.

"Where was Grandpa?"

Andy looked away. "He had slept in his studio that night."

"That's the most horrible thing I've ever heard. It must have been so hard on everyone. Poor Grandpa. He must've felt terrible."

"I don't know what he felt. It was hard on the rest of us. Maybe you can see why Bonnie is like she is."

Andy could not look away from his daughter's searching eyes as she reached across and touched his hand. "I can see why you're like you are too."

"I have my problems, that's for sure. I know I'm not always the easiest to get along with. But, I can promise, I would never do anything to hurt you. I love you Sophie. I guess this trip has been good for us – for me. Times are changing, and it's hard. I just want to protect you, but I can't and probably shouldn't try so hard. I just feel like you lost some innocence today."

Sophie was filled with guilt again.

"Daddy, you know no matter what happens I want to make you proud of me, don't you?"

Just then Brittinee approached.

"Can I get you and the young lady another drink?"

"I've heard chocolate goes good with merlot," Sophie said. "Do you have any cake?"

The emotions of the day had exhausted them both, so they fell into small talk and general plans for the upcoming week. Sophie enjoyed the chocolate and wine and learned to appreciate the interplay of acid and sugar on her tongue. For

Andy, the second Manhattan was like a timeout. He took himself out of the game for the rest of the night. He wondered why a drink that brought on a mellow mood was named after the most frenetic place he knew.

"By the way, this is my daughter, Sophie," Andy announced to Brittinee when she brought the check.

"We get a lot of daughters in here," she said, her purple eyelids at half-mast.

Andy signed the bill and didn't add a tip. In the elevator he said, "I'd like to check out by nine. We can find you a place closer to Dad's and get you settled then go over there."

Sophie laid her head against her father's chest and hugged him hard.

"I love you, Daddy. Thank you for everything."

With all the emotion and alcohol he had on board, Andy's eyes watered.

"I love you too, Cookie. You're my little girl."

TEN

In the morning Sophie packed for her move to the new hotel. She hadn’t specifically brought clothes to wear for something like working in the studio. She put on the T-shirt and boyfriend jeans again. She was tightening up the T-shirt with a knot when Andy and a bellhop showed up with a luggage cart. The men loaded up the cart and they all went out to the Lexus.

Andy pulled out of the parking lot.

“Dad, I need some other clothes.”

“You need bubble wrap and stuff too don’t you? We can get everything at Walmart.”

"Walmart? We've never gone to a Walmart."

"You'll survive. I won't tell anyone."

Andy parked at the empty end of the lot and they walked in under the big blue sign.

This isn't as lame as the Internet makes it out to be, Sophie thought upon entering. *The people seem normal enough.*

She found a rack of bib overalls in the women's section. They would be fun and easy to fit into. She took two and found some T-shirts. There was a table full of generic shorts, so she grabbed a pair of those. At the check-out, Sophie was amazed at the total. She had often spent more on one T-shirt and twice as much or more on a pair of jeans. Andy put the two large rolls of bubble wrap in the back of the car. After a short drive, he pulled into the parking lot of the Econo Lodge.

“Grab a bag – no bellboys here,” Andy said.

The room was small but clean. It boasted free Wi-Fi and had the password taped to the TV stand.

“It’s just for a few days, and you'll only be sleeping here,” he said almost apologetically. “You sure you want to do this?”

Sophie put her bag on the bed by the window. “I’ll be fine. Stop worrying.”

Albert was on the porch drinking coffee when they arrived.

“Hey, looks like she's all ready to go to work,” he said upon seeing Sophie.

“She’s like her mother,” Andy said. “Once she gets going on something, there's no stopping her. We got some bubble wrap to get started with. I’m really hoping Bonnie will pitch in.”

Albert finished his coffee. “Once she settles down, I’m sure she'll help."

Andy sat down next to his father. “I've gotta get going. I haven’t been to work in a week. We got a lot done, but the rest won’t happen overnight. Lilly’ll be here next week, and I’ll be back in a few weeks. Geoff and Don will take care of things and keep me up to date. Call my cell if you need anything or let Sophie know.”

"We got a good start," Albert said, "hopefully it will move along. Have a good trip back."

Sophie went with her father to the car.

"Cookie, I want you to be careful, use Uber or ask Bonnie to get around. I don't want you walking anywhere. You have your credit card and here's some cash. Your mother's worried enough, so don't make things worse. Call her sometime today." He handed her five twenty-dollar bills.

"Thank you. Ya know, I managed in Pittsburgh without a bodyguard or nanny. Stop worrying. Have a safe trip. I love you."

"I love you too, and thanks for helping. I'll see you at home next week. Get those applications finished."

Sophie hugged her father. "I know it's important to you. See you soon."

Andy backed out the driveway and was gone.

Well, I didn't really lie, Sophie thought. *I didn't say I would do the applications, and I'll see him fairly soon.* She knew it wasn't really the truth either.

Her father was right. She had lost some of her innocence.

"Grandpa, do you think we could start in the back and wrap some of those paintings? I don't want to just wrap everything. I mean really, anything you want boxed I'll do, but if we can make some progress and get things sorted, it would help."

Albert looked at the racks of canvases and piles of sketch books and portfolios.

Some of the early stuff is just what I did in school - plus ketches, copies, and things like that. That can be thrown out. I haven't looked at the old stuff in years. I guess we'll just have to go through it and decide. Like I said, none of it will have any value to anyone else."

"Well then," Sophie said, "let's just start and see what happens."

It was three o'clock before Sophie noticed Albert's hands shaking. He had missed his lunch time beer and a shot.

"I can't believe it's three already," he said. "I have to take my nap."

They had made a large pile of drawings and paintings to be discarded, over Sophie's objections. They had also wrapped a series of pastel cityscapes on board and set aside a few oils to be boxed. They left all the portfolios to deal with later.

Albert went down the stairs without saying anything about lunch. Sophie remembered there was a strip mall at the other end of the street and walked to it.

There was a tiny nail salon huddled between a Chinese takeout place and a pizza shop. A lighted sign hanging at one end said:

INS RA CE

H ME

AU O

The store windows at the other end were covered in newspaper. Across the parking lot, beyond the sidewalk, a For Sale sign was listing downwind. Sophie went into the pizza shop. There was an older guy cleaning a big mixer. A baseball game was on the TV. He looked up when the door buzzer went off.

"You surprised me. I didn't see a car drive up."

"I walked. Do you have wraps?"

The man wiped his hands on a towel and pointed up to one of the menus hanging above the counter.

"Where did you walk from?"

"From down the street. My grandfather lives behind you."

The man looked at Sophie. "You're Al's granddaughter? I've known him for years. He used to stop at the liquor store next door and come in for a pizza once in a while. Haven't seen him since the liquor store went out of business. How's he doing?"

"He's fine. I'm just helping him for a few days. Could I have a chicken salad wrap please?"

He could tell she wasn't going to give him any more information and didn't want to chat.

Sophie paid with cash. The man bagged up the sandwich.

"Please tell your grandfather Louie said hi. Tell him to stop in for a pizza on the house. I won't be here much longer – business is dead at this end of town."

"I'll tell him. Thank you."

Sophie sat on the porch and ate her wrap and drank a bottle of tonic water.

She didn't want to think, so she went back to the studio and kept sorting and wrapping pictures. She was partway along the bottom of the first rack that reached to the ceiling when the enormity of the undertaking was becoming obvious. At 4:30 Albert came in, a cup of coffee in hand. His tremor was gone.

"You kept going. Find anything interesting?"

"Mostly portfolios. There's a series of acrylics on board that I started on, kind of abstract impressionist. I got a wrap down at the plaza. Louie said to stop in for a pizza. Sounds like he has to close his shop soon."

"That poor bastard raised three kids with that store and should have retired flush. Then the big chain restaurants moved in and destroyed all the family-owned places. Now he can hardly get by. The little guys don't stand a chance in this crooked system."

"Then you should go over and get a pizza for supper tonight," Sophie said.

"Nah, his pizza gives me heartburn. How late you going to work? I didn't get lunch, and now it's almost dinner time."

"I just ate, what do you usually do for supper?"

"I've got some crackers and a can of sardines. I doubt you want that."

"You know, Grandpa, I'm really tired. Would you mind terribly if I just went back to the hotel? We can start again tomorrow."

"Yeah, that's fine with me. Go ahead; I'll lock up. How you getting back?"

"I'll call for a ride. What time do you want me to come back in the morning?"

"I paint Sunday mornings until noon or so."

"Do you really want to keep painting while we're trying to pack up what you have?"

"I always paint on Sundays. You can still come over -- in the afternoon."

"OK, I guess. Bye, Grandpa."

"See you tomorrow Sophie."

When Sophie got to the hotel, she knew she needed to pray. She asked God to convince her she was doing the right thing. She prayed for guidance to deal with her grandfather. She asked for forgiveness for lying to her father. She asked God to show her how she could live here without any help. There she was, alone in a motel room. It had all sounded so romantic -- she would be helping her grandfather, the artist. She would learn so much and start her life as an artist herself. She was starting to understand what her father meant about her grandfather. She had met rude people before, but he wasn't exactly rude. It was more like he didn't expect anything from other people, so they shouldn't expect anything from him.

He must be so lonely, and then to have the memory of his wife dying like that, Sophie thought. Who am I, a twenty-one-year-old girl, to help him? Maybe this whole thing is a mistake.

Sophie got her laptop and opened up one of the grad school applications. It was long and required an essay. Even if she wanted to, she couldn't get it done by the deadline. The prospect of two more years of college deflated her, especially for something she wasn't interested in. It was her father's plan not hers. After being with him on this trip she could see where he was coming from. He had to work hard and stay with a plan to get where he was today. It's the only thing he knew: set a goal and don't let anything stop you until you reach that goal. Then set another goal. Take it one possession at a time. Put yourself in a position to win. Never give up.

He's such a jock, she thought, *and I'm just not like that. I have to be open and free to accept what God puts in my way.*

Andy crossed the Bear Mountain Bridge. The Hudson widened to the south and flowed around Stoney Point on its final run to New York Harbor. He would be home in half an hour or so. The five hours alone had been good to get his head straight.

He went over everything again. *He had completed the unlikely goal of getting his father's place listed, so really, he was ahead of schedule. Bonnie and his father had reacted in their predictable ways – nothing new there. They were just rocks in the road he had to work around. The whole Vermont thing was ridiculous. He wasn't going to waste any time worrying about that. All-in-all, it had been a successful trip, and it had been nice to have Sophie to himself.*

She's young, and that's OK, he thought. She has a plan. As long as she sticks with it, she'll be fine.

≈

Lillian's legs were burning as she turned the corner to the driveway. Pushing through the pain, she finished her twelve miles with a sprint up the driveway. She shouldn't have gone so far; now she would have to hurry before Andy got home. She went around to the yard and walked off the cramping then punched in the code at the back door. She chugged her recovery brew on the way to the shower. She could feel the cool water bring her temperature down and her muscles loosen.

As she dried off, she thought *This hair! I don't have time to dry and curl it.*

She put on the Lascana mini-dress Andy had bought her. It was too young for her, strapless with a built-in push up, but he liked to see her in it. Not that she would wear it in public. She had to admit the dark pink set off her complexion. All she could do was put her hair back in a ponytail.

She was arranging a cheese and charcuterie plate when Andy came in.

"I missed you," she said. "It seems like you were gone forever."

Andy bent down to kiss her.

"I'm so glad to be back. I sure have good taste in dresses. You make it look gorgeous."

"Fiddle dee dee, you say that to all the girls, but I love hearing it. Come on, let's have some wine and cheese then you can get cleaned up while I make dinner."

"Sounds great. Where's Jack?"

"The Billingsbies took him to their beach house for the weekend. He was nervous to go, but I encouraged him. He and Boyd are good friends."

"I'm surprised he would take the time off work. I'm glad though. That should be fun for him. I bought some wine I think you'll like."

"Not real dry I hope."

Andy brought in a case of wine and put a Herman Weimer semi-dry Riesling in an ice bucket.

"Try this. It's a little sweet for me, but really balanced. It's better chilled."

Lillian took a cautious sip. "It's not bad. So, how'd things go with Sophie?"

"We had fun, mostly. Dad and Bonnie put on one of their productions, so unfortunately, she had to see that. Dad got going on Mother, then I had to explain some of that. Of course, she bought into Dad's suffering-artist routine. She thinks he's an undiscovered Picasso or something. That shine'll wear off after she's around him a while."

"This wine is different," Lillian said. "It has a nice aftertaste. The kids have to hear about your family sometime. It's not a bad thing that Sophie gets to know her grandfather. Did she like being at the hotel and traveling with you?"

Andy added some chilled wine to their glasses.

"She likes being waited on and dressing up. I think you need to talk about how she dresses sometimes. I don't think she does it on purpose. I couldn't say anything."

Lillian leaned back. "Her problem is she can make a potato sack look sexy. She has a body any woman would kill for. I'll remind her, but she'll be embarrassed you brought it up."

"I just can't deal with it. How did your week go?"

"The buyers put in an offer, and I think the sellers are going to accept. It'll be a big commission. I really like this wine. I'll take some more."

Andy leaned back and pulled Lillian to him for a kiss. His hands drifted a bit.

"Not so fast Gunner," Lillian laughed. "You have to wait."

Andy gave her a squeeze anyway.

"You always were a tease," he said. "I'll go take a shower."

Lillian filled her glass. As she was headed to the kitchen Sophie's ringtone sounded.

"Hi Mom! Is Dad home yet?"

"Hi, honey. He's home -- said it was an interesting trip. Are you at the hotel?"

"Yeah, I'm kinda stuck here. I worked at Grandpa's most of the day but came back before dinner. Now I don't have anything to do."

"You know, Cookie, it wouldn't take long to finish up those applications. Just get them done and behind you."

"Yeah, I looked at them earlier. I have a lot to do at Grandpa's. It'll take a long time to finish that – way more than a week."

"Yesterday your Dad said Bonnie might do most of it. They'll have to figure something out. I'm not sure yet, but I think I might stay there with you on Friday. Then we can drive back home Saturday. Are there two beds in your room?"

"Yeah, two small ones. Well, I'll see you then. I'll call again soon."

"You sound like you're not sure about this. Is the hotel safe? Are you afraid?"

"No, I'm fine. Just tired."

"I wish you'd come home with your Dad. I miss you. Once you're home, we'll have some fun. I'll take some time off and we'll do something – just the two of us. Do what you can there, your Dad will figure something out. You know that."

"Bye, I miss you too."

"All right, hon. Call me again soon.

Sophie put her phone down. *Now I've been untruthful with my mother too, she thought. This is getting serious. They have no clue I'm not coming home. Not only that, packing Grandpa's paintings is going to take even longer than I thought. Actually, there's no way I can do it by myself. Aunt Bonnie was really upset yesterday, but I wonder if she'd be willing to help. I guess I should just call her.*

Bonnie heard her phone go off. She turned down the stereo and pawed through her bag and flipped it open. She didn't recognize the number.

"Hello?" she said half expecting a robocall.

"Hi, Aunt Bonnie! It's Sophie."

"Sophie? Where are you? Is everything OK?"

"Oh, sure. I'm at the hotel. I wondered if you had time to talk?"

"Yeah, sure. Ya know, I'm sorry about yesterday. It was kind of a shock to me. I lost it. I'm usually laid back and chill."

"It's so much change," Sophie said. "Everyone's stressed out. I hope you aren't mad at me for getting involved."

"I'm not mad at you. In fact, I'd hoped to get to know you a little, then all that came down. You know what? I'm having some friends over later, but I'm here now. Why don't you come over? We can rap and then you can meet my friends."

"That'd be great. Let me write down your address."

Sophie didn't take time to change. She ordered an Uber and waited outside the hotel. On the way, she persuaded the driver to stop at a liquor store. The store was huge. She was looking for the white zinfandel, when a middle-aged man in a baggy sport coat asked her if she could use some help. She said, "I usually get a white zin, but maybe I'll try a sweeter red wine."

"Would you like to try something more local?"

"Sure, I guess. Like what?"

The man led her to the New York section.

"Have you ever heard of Red Cat?"

"No, is it good?"

"It's made in Naples, down in the Finger Lakes, it's the most popular wine around here. Nice flavor but not too sweet. Are you going to a party or for dinner?"

"Just meeting some people. I'll try it, thank you."

The driver dropped her off in front of a green house with steps up to a covered entrance. The windows had metal awnings over them. Some bedraggled shrubs separated the house from a small lawn. Sophie rang the bell, and Bonnie opened the door.

Bonnie's apartment featured a motif from the post-macramé/mid-dream-catcher period. The visual center was an oriental carpet and a low table surrounded by batik-covered cushions. Soft lighting was provided by a pole light with multicolored globes along with large sand-cast candles arranged on mission-style stands. The complementary wall art consisted of rock concert posters and psychedelia. Window treatments were tasteful but colorful tie-dyed drapes. Alone on one wall was a large portrait of Jerry Garcia. Below it was a three-tiered table holding incense burners and votive candles. Opposite that was a turntable, a black multi-knobbed amplifier, and a cassette deck surrounded by crates of LPs which were flanked by two very large speakers.

The first impression Sophie got was from the fragrance. It flashed her back to the off-campus apartments of her art-student friends. It was like patchouli perfume mixed with the sharper animal smell of fresh pot smoke that prickled her nose. There was music playing. It was a jangle of guitar, organ, and a seemingly impossible number of drums. The singer had a really bad voice.

Bonnie had on a long white kurti that came almost to her knees and black tights. Sophie wished she had changed out of her Walmart T-shirt.

"This is so great," Bonnie said.

"It's so nice of you to invite me. I brought some wine."

"Oh cool, Red Cat. I love it. Come on in. Hope you don't mind sitting on the floor. I haven't had chairs in years."

Bonnie went into the kitchen to get glasses. Sophie looked around. *How could my Dad have come from the same family as Aunt Bonnie? It's no wonder they don't get along. They're, like, from different planets.*

Bonnie brought the glasses and Sophie poured them half full.

"I feel like I know you but then again, I really don't." Bonnie said. "You used to come down here when you were little, and Andy has kept me up to date some. You're all done with college, right?"

"Yeah, I graduated this spring, I studied art and sort of the business of art -- how galleries work, some marketing classes, stuff like that."

Bonnie eased into half-lotus position.

"I mostly taught myself art," she said. "I do jewelry design, sculptured candles -- you know, usable stuff. I sell it at music festivals and art shows. Plus, I have an Etsy account, so I do pretty good."

"I love your necklace," Sophie said. "The crystal is so perfect."

Bonnie cradled the double pointed crystal.

"I get a lot of energy through this. It keeps me in tune with the cosmos. You know there are low frequency sound waves that travel through space from somewhere. Some crystals have the same frequency. It's really complicated. Anyway, what's the trip with your grandfather going to be?"

Sophie drank some wine while she pondered that. “I'm not going anywhere with him. I'm just trying to help get his paintings packed up.”

Bonnie laughed. “I forgot how young you are. I mean, what're your plans?”

"Oh. Right now, I'm just here for a week. I won't even make a little dent in it. It'll actually take months to do it right.”

“I'm so bummed about the whole thing,” Bonnie said. “I guess I can't get my head around my Dad getting old. I can see his wheels slowing down. Maybe that's why I got so upset. I haven't been in his studio in years. Is there a lotta stuff in it?”

Sophie couldn't hide her confusion. “That's what Dad said! Why didn't you guys ever look at his paintings?”

Bonnie switched one leg over the other. “I regret it now. His painting has always been his own gig. He never lets anyone in on it. He never once invited us to look at them. But, in fairness, he never showed them to anybody... until you.”

Sophie saw an opening. “Well maybe now things are changing. By letting me in, he's ready to let you and Dad in too. He wants you to help me pack them up.”

Bonnie got up and put both hands against the racks of record albums. Sophie could see she was breathing deep and slow. She wiped her eyes then fiddled through albums and pulled one out and put it on the turntable. This singer had a sad-sweet voice.

“Do you like Jackson Browne?”

“Never heard of him. He has a nice voice.”

Bonnie sat back down. "He sings a lot about being late, missing out on love by just a little. Sort of not recognizing it until it's gone. I hope I haven't done that with my father."

They were quiet. Sophie listened to the music. It was so clear and deep. She could hear every instrument spread across the room. It sounded like she was sitting at the piano with the singer.

“Sophie, can I be honest with you?”

“Of course.”

“I didn’t know what to expect from you. I admit I had a picture in my mind."

“I know--a spoiled brat.”

“I have to start looking at things differently. It’s some kind of karma that this is all happening."

“I don’t know much about karma, but I know God’s hand when I feel it. I know I'm in the right place. I have to be honest with you too.”

“Oh, I know. I’m just the old hippie aunt.”

Sophie chuckled. “Well, there’s that. But, I haven’t told anyone the truth about what I'm going to do. I'm not going back home. I'm staying here in Rochester to get Grandpa’s paintings packed and safe. He's going to pay me. I have a week to figure everything out and tell my parents. They think I'm going to grad school in the fall. Grandpa is the only one who knows, and he doesn’t believe me.”

There was a knock at the door.

“There’s my friends. Sorry, we'll talk again later.”

Sophie saw there were two girls and a guy. The guy was older -- Bonnie's age. He was bald on top but had a long gray ponytail and a full salt-and-pepper beard. He was wearing a well-loved Hawaiian shirt, khaki shorts, and flip-flops. The girls were younger – probably in their thirties. One was tall, her dyed–black hair was cropped short. She had on a black T-shirt and army–green cargo pants. The other was almost petite, with red hair -- maybe natural -- in ringlets. She had on an emerald green peasant blouse over brown capris.

"This is Sophie, my niece. This is Derek -- we call him Bo -- Janice, and Maggie." Janice, the tall one, reached out her hand and gave Sophie a firm handshake.

"Bonnie has talked about you," she said.

Maggie air-kissed her on both cheeks and said, "Oh, so fun to meet someone new."

Derek came close. Sophie was a little startled. He made an exaggerated bow.

"At your service mademoiselle."

Bonnie pushed him away. "Knock it off you old goat! You'll scare her."

They all laughed. Sophie felt at ease from the wine and their easy familiarity with each other.

"Jackson Browne?" Derek questioned. "He always gives you the blues, Bon. Let's get the party started. Here's some wine, but I see you're ahead of me."

"Doubt that," Bonnie said. "Go pick something out."

"I brought some munchies," Maggie said, "but I need a plate."

Bonnie and Maggie went into the kitchen. Janice sat down awkwardly with her feet out in front of her.

"What kind of music do you like, Sophie?" Derek asked.

"Ed Sheeran's my favorite right now."

"I've heard of him, but I don't think Bonnie has any of his stuff. How about the Allman Brothers?"

"Never heard of them."

Derek pulled out a peach colored album. "How bout we do some Bro's? Then you can turn me on to Sheeran. You got any downloaded?"

"Yeah, I've got some," Sophie said.

Maggie brought in a tray of pita bread, hummus, and spinach-artichoke dip, then kneeled and sat on her heels next to Janice.

There was an amplified pop as Derek placed the needle down on the spinning record, followed by a piano which was augmented with what Sophie guessed were guitars. The singer was gravel-throated. Her father would probably like it -- kind of country, like the Eagles. Again, the sound was almost overwhelming. She kept hearing more instruments all over the room. She and Bonnie had finished most of the Red Cat. She poured the rest into Bonnie's glass.

"One moment m'lady," Derek said. "I'll bring you more wine."

Bonnie sat down next to Sophie.

"Don't mind him. He's a clown."

A sad song about a girl named Melissa came on. The guitars seemed to be crying. Maybe it was the wine, but Sophie had never been so into music before.

They all chatted, though Janice was mostly quiet. She said she was a nurse, and just came off a string of night shifts in the cardiac ICU at Strong Memorial Hospital. Maggie was bubbly with a sweet Southern accent. She was a social worker at the hospital where she met Janice. She grew up in Savannah but said she didn't fit in there and moved north for college and stayed. Derek came off as a goof, but it turned out he was an electrical engineer and had worked at a big communications company since graduating from RIT. He said his projects were "top secret," and he could not talk about his job. Eventually it got quiet.

Bonnie turned to Sophie. "We were planning on smoking a little pot. Do you mind? Or do you want some?"

Sophie wasn't surprised.

"No, I don't mind. Some of my friends vape weed, but I don't care for any. Go ahead though."

Sophie was fascinated by the ritual-like way Bonnie brought a wooden box to the table. She deftly hand-rolled a joint and lit it from a candle. She took a puff then passed it to Maggie and around it went until it got to Derek.

"Dude, don't bogart that joint," Bonnie warned him. "I'll roll another one if you need it, but this is good shit. I just got it."

Derek inhaled and the joint glowed until some ash fell onto the rug. Through held breath he said, "Hey Bon, don't you have that Pacific Northwest album?" He exhaled a mighty cloud of smoke.

"Yeah, it's there. You know, that was the '73 tour. I saw them here at the War Memorial. They did China Cat and Box of Rain here too."

"What are you talking about?" Sophie asked.

"They're back in their glory days with the Grateful Dead," Janice said. "Don't get 'em started."

"Oh yeah," Sophie said. "We talked about them in a Pop History class I took. It was pretty funny."

Derek got serious. "You mean they teach the Dead in college now?"

"Yeah, a little. We learned about the '60's and '70's, you know, ancient history."

Janice and Maggie laughed. Bonnie and Derek didn't. The joint went around a couple of times until Derek pinched what was left with his fingernails and sucked it down to nothing.

Sophie thought how different they were from her friends. When her friends did weed, they each took out their own e-cigs. These guys shared a single joint. She guessed that's the way it was in the old days.

Soon the same jangle of music she heard when she came in started up. The singers were terrible, but everybody else seemed to be enjoying it. After a while, the pita and dip started to disappear. Janice laid back on the floor. Derek and Bonnie were far off. Maggie's red ringlets were bouncing to whatever beat there was.

"Well Sophie, what do you think of the Dead?" Bonnie asked.

"They're OK. It would be better if they were all playing the same song at once though."

Maggie fell over laughing. Janice sat up laughing and said, "I like this chick, that's the funniest Dead joke I've heard in a while."

"Yeah," Derek said. "It was so funny I forgot to laugh."

After then it was quiet again for a while.

"Hey, Bon," Derek suddenly asked. "Are my Twinkies still in the freezer?"

"Dude, I don't know, but they were cold the last time you came over. It bummed me out."

Janice snorted from the floor.

"Oh, gross," Maggie said.

Derek stood up directly from half lotus and went into the kitchen. Sophie was impressed.

"I'm going to toast some Twinkies, anybody else want some?" he yelled.

Sophie could tell she had just a little too much wine but was having fun doing something different. Of course, her mother would be mortified she was with people "like these" being "exposed to drugs." Soon Derek came back with a plate of brown cake–like things.

"Here Sophie. Try one of these."

Not one to turn down cake, Sophie bit into one. It was toasted crunchy, warm on the outside with frozen synthetic-tasting cream inside.

"They're like a tiny Baked Alaska," she said. "Yummy."

"They're full of chemicals and preservatives," Bonnie protested. "Not one real thing in 'em. I don't know why I allow them in my house."

"'Cause, my little Bon Bon, you loves me," Derek cooed.

Janice stood up. "That does it. You two need to get a room. I'm heading out. Let's go Maggie."

Maggie slowly rose from the floor. "Sophie, it was so nice to meet you. Hope I see ya'll again real soon."

Janice opened the door. "Thanks Bonnie. See you again soon, Sophie. Later, Bo."

There was an awkward moment after the women left and Derek didn't. Then Sophie suddenly understood -- it was her making things awkward.

Derek took her hand and kissed it.

"I would I were thy bird," he said.

"Good night, good night, parting is such sweet sorrow," Sophie replied.

"I just love a shiny college girl."

"Maybe I should be the one leaving." Bonnie laughed.

"No, please. I'll get a ride. Bonnie, do you want to meet at Grandpa's tomorrow and talk some more?"

"Sure, how about I pick you up at the hotel and we go over together, maybe, like, one o'clock?

Eleven

This was anything but a normal Sunday morning for Sophie. She awoke late but still felt drowsy and had a dull headache. Instead of going to church, as she normally would, she walked to a diner down the street. She felt better after some eggs and toast and a couple cups of coffee. Then she went back to the hotel, hoping Bonnie might come a little early.

By 2:00 Bonnie still hadn't showed, so she called her. At 2:45 Bonnie finally pulled up in front of Sophie's room.

Sophie got in the car.

"We have to hurry," Sophie urged. "Grandpa will be taking his nap soon."

"We'll be fine. Did you've fun last night?"

"Yeah, your friends are nice. They're funny. It's cool the younger girls came over."

"They think Bo is some kind of guru, and I'm the funny old hippie. I think you'll get to like Maggie; she's a hoot."

Albert was on the porch finishing a drink when they pulled in.

"I wondered what happened to you two. I'm heading for my nap. I left the studio open."

Sophie led the way up the stairs and into the upper room. Bonnie took a few steps in and stopped. She felt like a burglar -- entering a place she had no right to.

"This isn't what I expected. It's beautiful," she said.

"I felt the same way," Sophie said. "I expected a mess. Why do you think he let the house get so bad?"

"Did your dad tell you anything about our mother?"

"A little. I'm sorry about what happened. I don't know if I could have gone on like you did."

"You mean about finding her? I'm glad it was me and not your father. I made sure he didn't have to see anything."

Sophie walked over and looked at the new painting Albert had started.

"What did happen?" she asked.

"After Mom had me, she wanted to stay home and take care of me. She was an artist too. She wrote poetry, drew, and liked photography. She was an intellectual and spent a lot of time thinking. She was very delicate and too sensitive for the outside world. That night, she went to bed and just stayed in the dream world. I think the real world finally ate her up."

Sophie studied Bonnie.

"So, you think she died by accident?"

"Oh definitely...of course. She would never have wanted to leave me... or Andy and Dad. I think her meds were too strong. The doctors were always trying to keep her zoned out. They didn't want her to talk about the things she saw and dreamed."

"Dad said that Grandpa slept up here that night. Do you know why?"

Bonnie looked up at the skylight.

"No, I don't know why. Just bad karma, I guess. Anyway, after that I took care of Andy and Dad. I didn't have much of a school life from then on or much of any kind of life. After I left, Dad just completely stopped taking care of the house, and that's why it's such a mess."

"Are you alright being up here?" Sophie asked. "Is it hard?"

"Yeah, a little. I shouldn't be all that surprised. I've always known he's two different people: the painter, who lived up here by himself, and the plumber supporting a family he probably never wanted. Thinking about it, I can see it makes sense that this place would be perfect. No need to get heavy; I can't keep worrying about the past."

"Could I see some of the paintings?" Bonnie asked.

"I'll show you one of his newest ones."

Sophie pulled out the one Albert had just finished and put it on an easel.

"Look at it from back here."

Bonnie was quiet for several minutes.

"This is really good isn't it?" she finally said. "It would be hard to do, right?"

Sophie put her arm around Bonnie.

"I'm just a girl with a BFA, but I've never seen anything like it. I know enough to know it's special and that your father is an incredibly skilled painter."

"Andy and I have been fools all these years, haven't we? We chose to ignore this side of him out of spite or resentment... or just plain ignorance. Now I find out. Now that he'll soon be gone. It didn't have to be this way."

Sophie held her aunt closer. "I don't know you and Grandpa that well, but it seems to me, Grandpa has been really difficult to deal with. It just became easier to leave him alone. You can't blame yourself for everything that's happened over all these years."

"Thanks Sophie. I guess that's it."

They looked at several more paintings. Bonnie didn't venture far into the room but glimpsed around, like a first-time visitor to a new friend's house. Sophie led her to the back, where she looked at the worn furniture and the stacks of books. She couldn't bring herself to approach any closer.

Sophie wasn't sure this was a good time to discuss packing the paintings with Bonnie.

Suddenly the door opened. Albert came in and walked over to the racks.

"Well, Bonnie, do you want to help pack up this junk or not? I wouldn't be able to pay you until the place gets sold."

The light in the studio undulated softly as pregnant clouds sailed over the north facing skylight. Bonnie studied her father. He was an apparition to her, floating in the light. Here was the father she had missed.

"Dad, I need to talk to you first. I'm not sure what to say. I'm just so sorry how our lives have been. I wish with all my heart I had come up here years ago."

"I never thought it was anything anyone would care about," Albert admitted. "I didn't think anyone should be exposed to it.

Some of it's not good -- not bad painting, but not good to look at. I don't have an excuse. It was just something I had to do. It's not good to have to do something. Anyway, that's neither here nor there. We need to get rid of it."

Bonnie tried to hold her father.

"Oh, come on, let's not get sappy," Albert said as he pulled away.

Bonnie got a hold of him anyway -- for just a moment -- then let him go.

"I guess it would be good if I helped get things packed up," she said. "I'll give it a try."

After about an hour, Albert had enough and went back to the house. The women were noisy, asking questions, discussing his old paintings and wrapping them in plastic, probably never to be seen again. The thought of moving had been grinding in his brain for a year or more. Now, it was happening, and everything he dreaded was coming true. People were all over his property -- poking around, asking questions, making decisions for him. Now he was trapped with these interlopers and worse, dependent on them. The absurdity of living beyond his usefulness was a cruel fate.

He heard Bagger drive in for his Sunday checkup. His old friend came into the house without knocking.

"Hey, ol' man, you alive?"

Albert waited a few seconds then called from the living room.

"Let me check."

“I brought some ham and greens my daughter made. You can have it for supper.”

Albert walked into the kitchen. Bagger was standing by the table holding a paper plate wrapped in foil. He looked old – gray and old and bent.

"Damn, Bagger, it’s a terrible thing. How’d we get like this? Why the hell aren’t we gone yet?”

“Al, you know what I think. The Lord will call us when he's ready – when he’s done with us down here. It just ain’t our time yet. Wish you could understand that.”

“Yeah, you got all filled with the spirit today. All I know is I woke up again to face this mess. Nothing I asked for.”

“You just feelin’ down ‘cause all the changes. It'll pass. You be lucky to have kin to help you. Anything you need me to get? I suppose you gettin’ low on booze?”

“No, I got enough. I've got one leg on the wagon – hopping along on the other.”

Bagger kept a hand on the table and raised the other.

“Well, hallelujah! He’s seen the light! How you feelin’?”

“Way too much. That’s the problem. But I got to get my head straight. I might even try to get my license back.”

“Well, wouldn’t that be somethin'. It’s been awhile. I'll be seein' you. I've gotta get to evenin' service. Hope you like the ham and greens.”

“Thanks, Bagger. Thank Eugenia for me.”

≈

After church Andy and Lillian took the 'Vette out for a drive. They stopped for ice cream, so they were not very hungry for dinner. As the sun was going down Andy whipped up some omelets.

They carried them over to the nook. Andy asked.

"I put in some lox, are they good?"

Lillian smiled. "You make the best omelets, honey, everybody knows that. For some reason we didn't get to talk much last night. I have to tell you about Mrs. Kowalski and a couple other things."

"I wanted to talk, but you wouldn't leave me alone," Andy said. "I felt used."

"Stop that; it's Sunday. I'm serious about Mrs. Kowalski. I really feel God sent her to teach me a lesson. You were sort of right, and I was mostly right, but anyway, we should work as a team. That's what being married means. It's not about what we do separately; it's who we are together. The more we put the other first, the stronger each of us is. It's the whole servant thing. It sounds impossible, but it works."

"All I know is she sure can clean a floor. It looks great."

"Andy, I'm being serious."

"I know, Lil. I think we just -- or at least I -- forget once in a while what's important. We have all this stuff and all this money, but my happiness comes from you and the kids. We were just as happy when we had a lot less money."

"The money is only the result of us working together, using the gifts God blessed us with. It's a by-product not the goal. That's why I want to make some changes."

"What kind of changes?" Andy asked seriously.

"Since I decided not to give your money back – our money back – I want to go ahead with bidding on Frank's plaza. One of my tenants wants to buy the duplex. With that plus the commissions I've saved, I can make a cash offer. If I do have to borrow, I can pay it off in no time with more commissions. How does that sound?"

Andy considered worst case scenarios, and there wasn't anything they couldn't handle.

"Other than having to deal with Frank, it's a good plan," he said. "The plaza will eventually have a better return than the duplex. You did a great job with the other plaza, so you know what you're getting into. You should go for it."

"Do you really think so? That means a lot to me. Thank you. I was worried we were getting to a bad place."

"Things are changing fast, Lil. I'm trying to deal with it. I know it isn't easy for you, and my issues make it tough."

"We're good," Lillian said. "Thanks for the omelet."

TWELVE

On Wednesday, Sophie had run out of bubble wrap. She thought that would happen sooner. It was becoming obvious Bonnie wasn't going to be much help. She showed up midmorning, left for lunch, and then worked a couple of hours in the afternoon. Albert came and went -- sometimes working on his new painting, sometimes giving tidbits of information about a previous painting, or simply reminiscing. Sophie pumped him for information so she could date and label the wrapped paintings. She was determined not to rush through. The ones to be boxed were set aside. She wanted to photograph each one and label them accurately.

She was praying more than ever, especially after talking with her mother. She was lying to her every day. She asked God for forgiveness but also to show her how she was going to stay there. She had no place to live after Friday. There wasn’t time, and she didn't have the money to get a place of her own. She saw only two options. She had to ask Bonnie if she could stay with her or ask her grandfather. She decided to ask Bonnie first.

≈

Albert took a shower and shaved. He was feeling much better since cutting back on the bourbon. He had finally slept through the night and had no nausea in the morning. He made scrambled eggs and ate a little bacon. Sophie was already up in the studio.

"Look at you," Sophie said when he entered. "Shaved and everything. Are you feeling better?"

"I am...finally. I must have had a bug or something. How is it going?"

"I'm out of wrap. When Bonnie gets here, we'll go get some more. I'll need some money to get it. Sometime, we have to get cardboard and Styrofoam too."

"You've been working hard, Sophie. You must be getting tired of this."

"Not bad for a spoiled college girl, huh?"

"I'll admit it, I'm a little surprised, but your dad and mom have always worked hard. Just too bad they're cogs in the machine, but that's neither here nor there. Sounds like Bonnie is here, earlier than usual."

The studio door opened, and Bonnie stepped inside.

"Hey you two, what's happenin'?"

"I'm just cleaning up a little," Sophie said. "We need to get some more bubble wrap. I googled a place on Mt. Read Boulevard that sells packing supplies. It's cheaper than Walmart. Do you mind going there?"

"No. Bonnie said. Let's boogie."

On the way Sophie turned to her Aunt. "I need to ask you a question, and I want you to be honest. I mean, don't feel bad about anything."

"What's the matter, Sophie, is something wrong?"

"Well, sort of. I told you I want to stay here in Rochester and not go back with Mom this weekend. Problem is, I don't have any place to stay. I was wondering if you had room at your house for me to stay a while?"

"Oh, wow, I hadn't thought about that, I was so hung up on the paintings and everything. My second bedroom is where I make my jewelry and candles. It's full of worktables and supplies. I don't even have a couch."

"No, that's OK, I just wanted to check with you first. I'm sure something will work out. Don't worry about it."

"I could, like, make room for a mattress to crash on if nothing else'll work. I'd love to have you. It'd be fun."

Twenty minutes later they arrived at the mover's supply store. Sophie was able to get bigger rolls of bubble wrap and tape in bulk supply. They loaded everything into the Volvo and headed back.

Sophie was surprised. Bonnie dug right in, and they worked steadily until lunch time. She had brought a couple apples and a bag of nuts. They shared those and went right back to work. By three o'clock, she was slowing down, and Bonnie was resting at the worktable.

"I'm going home. I'm meeting Bo and Maggie when they're done with work, plus I have some jewelry orders to do. Hey, why don't you come with? We're just getting together at Red

Fern. It's a vegan place that has wine and beer. It's not far from my house. They'll be there by 5:30-6.

Sophie googled it.

"It's on Oxford Street?"

"Yeah, that's it. Can you come?"

"Sure, I like Maggie. "What's up with Derek?"

"Don't let him freak you out. He's harmless. He's actually a genius. He remembers everything – likes to write, plays guitar a little, reads a lot. And, hey little girl, don't tell me he's the first guy to go gaga over you. He wasn't hitting on you. He's just really friendly and likes talking to smart girls. He doesn't mind if they're gorgeous too."

"I wasn't afraid. He's just different. I didn't even change that night. I looked gross. It'll be interesting to see him again, I guess. We got a lot done today, thanks. Can you drop me off at the motel?"

After she got to the motel Sophie had second thoughts. She was quickly depleting the cash her father gave her, but she had to eat somewhere. She took a shower and did her hair. She thought for sure Maggie would have something nice on. She tried several combinations and settled for the Frame jeans and the sailor top with the denim jacket. Nobody there had seen the outfit, and it looked the most mature. She didn't want to be early, so she waited until 5:45 to get an Uber.

Sophie found the three friends at a table near the front. They all seemed glad to see her. Maggie jumped up to hug her. Derek seemed subdued but friendly. He had his work clothes on -- a white short-sleeve button-down shirt and black slacks.

She ordered a beer. It was cheaper than the “sustainable” wine. The beer was harsh, so she just sipped on it. Bonnie started telling them about her father’s paintings and all the work Sophie had been doing. Derek was really interested and started asking questions.

“He was painting in New York in the 50’s?”

“Yeah, but he won’t tell me much," Sophie replied. "Do you know who Willem de Kooning was?”

“Of course. He was the most important painter -- other than Pollock -- at the time. After Pollock died, he was the most well-known.”

“He told me he knew him and his wife Elaine, but really, I haven't been able to get any details out of him. Some of his paintings are obviously studies of de Kooning, and I think Elaine also. Most are figurative in some way, not like totally abstract.”

Derek delivered a monologue about the evolution of Abstract Expressionism and how it brought the center of the art world from Paris to New York after the war. Sophie was particularly interested in the connection between Existentialism and the New York artists. She would have to learn more about Sartre.

“Wow,” She said when Derek finally slowed down. “Where’d you study art and philosophy?”

“I've done a little reading."

He seemed to be finished with that subject and ordered another beer.

"He's like having a private professor," Maggie said. "You never know what he's going to go off on."

"How do you two know each other?" Sophie asked.

"Janice and I rent an apartment from him."

Bonnie jumped out of her seat. "Oh my God! How could I be so stupid? Bo, do you still have that apartment open?"

"I just have the studio. It's hard to rent because it's so small and doesn't have a kitchen. Why are you so jacked up?"

Bonnie sat back down. "She wants to move here and needs an apartment. Tell him Sophie."

"Well, I'm working for my Grandfather, like I said, packing his paintings. It's going to take all summer at least. If I can't find a place to stay this week, I'll have to move back home with my parents."

"If you're not afraid of living in the big bad wolf's house, we could talk about it."

"What do you mean?"

"Bonnie said I scared you the other night."

"Oh, kind sir, I'm but a silly country girl, not accustomed to gentlemen of the world. I was innocently taken aback by your boldness. Be assured I wasn't offended. Indeed, I was charmed."

"Where did you get that? I take it there's a repressed theater major in your past."

"Too true. Drama is in my blood."

Derek boldly studied the young girl. She had a face by Botticelli and a body by Vargas – whip smart, but innocent – a rarity to him.

“Here’s the deal, I have to get $400 a month. I usually get $200 security deposit and two months’ rent, nonrefundable. But for Bonnie here, you give me $400, and you can move in. You should look at it before you agree; it’s small. Has a bathroom and a bed and a small closet. It’s on the third floor. Maggie and Janice have half the second floor. There’s a married couple in the other half, no kids. I have the first floor.”

“It'll be just perfect," Bonnie said. "It's real safe. Bo keeps an eye on everything. Maggie don’t you think so?”

“Janice and I love it there. It’s a beautiful house and a cool neighborhood. Our landlord or, as he says, 'owner of the estate' is great. Never had a problem.”

After they finished dinner, they repaired to Derek’s house. Sophie recognized the street where she had dinner with her father and grandfather. After another turn onto a bigger street, they pulled in front of a large house. They all went into Derek’s apartment. It had dark woodwork with scrolling in every corner. Some of the windows had stained glass. Sophie could see a library through French doors on the right. On the left was the living room and beyond that a dining room.

“I found the key,” Derek announced. “Let’s see what you think.”

They went back outside to a metal door with a bright light overhanging. He punched a code into a pad and opened it. It was a long steep climb to the third-floor landing. He unlocked the knob and deadbolt and let Sophie in first.

Sophie was enthralled. Her artist’s garret-fantasy had come to life. The apartment occupied a dormer; the small paned window stopped at a storage bench. There was a straight-back chair and small table to the right. A child-size bed filled the space opposite the window leaving just enough room to walk around the end. Beyond the bed were two narrow doors covered by curtains. Behind the one on the left was a toilet, a powder room sink, and a slender tiled shower. Behind the other was a clothes rod, a stack of plastic totes, and a pile of bed linens and towels. The entire space was smaller than her walk-in closet at home, but to her it was the coziest, cutest thing she had ever seen.

Maggie and Bonnie crowded in and stood in front of the door.

"Ya'll could fix this up real cute," Maggie said. "It wouldn't take much; that's for sure."

"It's fine the way it is," Sophie said. "I love it."

They all went back out on the landing.

"Are you sure you want to do this?" Derek asked. "We won't do a lease or anything, so if it doesn't work out, it's no problem to me."

"I have to see if Grandpa will pay me a little ahead. I'll ask him tomorrow. I just have two suitcases, so It won't be anything to move. Bonnie, will you help me bring my stuff?"

"Sure. Dad will give you the money. Don't worry about that. You know what? He'll still be awake; let's do it now and be done."

"Don't bother with that," Derek protested. "Just get your stuff. I'll catch up with you tomorrow, here's the key. I'll write down the code for the outside door."

Sophie made sure she could work the locks, then she and Bonnie went back to the hotel. Sophie packed her bags and checked out. She was determined to make this the last time she used her father's card.

Derek heard them pull up, and he carried Sophie's suitcases up to the room. Sophie thanked Derek and Bonnie. Then they left, and she closed the door.

She sat on the chair in a daze. What had just happened? The only feeling close to this was when her parents left her at college her freshman year. She remembered their footsteps echoing down the hallway. At that time, she felt she had crossed an open boundary. Now, she felt exiled from the secure land of her home, but most of all she felt excited. She had done it. She had her "own place."

The stale, warm air triggered her memory of the little hotel room in Paris during her senior trip. That was the last time she had slept without air conditioning. She opened the window. It wasn't Paris, but the city noise made her feel she was in the middle of a new adventure. Her reverie ended with the sound of her mother's ringtone.

"Hi, Mom."

"Hi, sweetie, are you at the hotel?"

"Yeah."

"Is everything all right?"

"I worked all day at Grandpa's. Just a little tired. How are you?"

"I'm fine."

"That's good. What time will you be here Friday?"

"I'm not sure yet. I'll let you know."

"I'll wait for you at Grandpa's. See you then."

"Sophie, is something wrong? You don't sound right."

"Mom, I told you I'm fine – just tired. I'm getting ready for bed."

"I'm sorry. I just feel like something's wrong. You'd tell me, wouldn't you?"

"There's nothing to tell. I'll see you Friday. Goodnight."

"OK. Call me tomorrow. I love you."

"Love you too."

Sophie knew this was just the beginning of the guilt she would be feeling to do this. Like her grandfather said: Every choice comes with consequences.

Even that couldn't shake the joy she felt crossing this new threshold. She still wasn't tired after organizing her clothes and getting settled in. She tried sketching for a while. She finally fell asleep but awoke with the city as light cut through her window. After a shower -- in her own shower -- she walked back to the street where she remembered there were restaurants. As she was walking a city bus went by. She found a cute coffee shop. While she ate her breakfast sandwich, she Googled the bus lines. It would take at least an hour, and she would have to walk some to her Grandfather's house, but it was only two dollars, compared to almost fifteen by Uber. She had ridden busses in New York City; she was sure she could navigate Rochester. Another problem solved.

THIRTEEN

Albert awoke feeling more rested than he'd felt in years. After a big breakfast, he was on the porch with a cigarette and half ration of bourbon when Sophie came walking up the driveway.

"Morning, Grandpa. I have some news."

Albert was wide-eyed as he listened to his Granddaughter relate she was not going home. He never really thought she would stay in Rochester and defy her father.

This girl has more backbone than I gave her credit for, he thought. *There's going to be trouble when Lillian shows up. Andrew will be furious!*

"Sophie, I'm afraid of what your mother and father are going to say. Haven't you told them anything?"

"No. I have to tell Mom in person. I don't know how I'm going to do it, but I'll tell them you told me I shouldn't, so they won't be mad at you."

"I doubt that."

"We just have to stick with the plan," Sophie said. "You'll find a better place to live and keep painting. We'll get your paintings stored so they're safe. Then after that, who knows. I hope you can teach me to really paint once things are more settled."

Albert watched her as she went to the studio. He could not remember the last time he had a young person in his life. *She lived in assured hope and held to the belief that love conquers all. He had confronted optimism years ago. He executed it then threw its cremains to the winds. He had made a truce with resentment; now they stared at each other across no-man's-land. This youthful new force, this young girl, was disturbing the balance of power. She stirred his memory: Faded tableaus of sunny days, easels standing by a river, dancing, and lullabies sung in French passed dimly across his mind. Sophie, sanguine and radiant, was like a distant flare lighting up the trench he had dug – deep and dark. Alcohol and painting had long protected him like barbed wire strung on bent posts. Should he dare to poke his head out, extend a hand and climb out into the world, or was this just another apparition that would vanish into the fog?*

He stubbed his cigarette in the film of bourbon shining in the glass and went into his basement.

He was inspecting the piles of scrap pipe, boxes of brass fittings, old lumber, and moldering piles of summer furniture when he heard the lawn service truck pull in. By the time he got back up the stairs, the lawn guy had started the mower. Albert went out to watch. He was pleasantly surprised to find the young man had actually listened to him and was leaving delineated rows cross-lit by the late morning sun. He went into the kitchen and brought two glasses of iced tea to the porch.

After he was done mowing, the young man blew the clippings from under the hedge and came to the porch.

"Good morning, Mr. Martel."

"Come on up; have some iced tea. It's getting hot. What's your name, anyway?

"Thanks. It's Randall Johnson. I have to tell you something."

"What's wrong?" Albert handed him the glass.

"This is the last time I'll be mowing your lawn. My boss let me go."

"Did you do something wrong?"

"I don't think I did. I was doing some moonlighting – mowing and hardscaping. It was all down near where I live, not here in the city at all. I hadn't missed any work for him. I did it weekends and nights -- even did hardscape under lights. He still didn't like it, so he fired me. Someone else will be coming here next week."

"I just got you trained. I want you to do it."

"I can't. It's his contract."

"Well piss on him. I'm not going to deal with his company anymore. Besides, I have a mower here. You could use that."

"I'm not sure that would be right," Randall said. "I'm not into stealing jobs."

"You're not stealing from him, 'cause I won't have him back anyway. You don't have to put up with some fat cat in a Cadillac. You're not a slave. If I want to hire you, then you can work for me. Come on out and look at my mower."

Randall followed the old man to the garage and helped open the door. Albert pulled a tarp off a shiny red zero turn.

"That's a really good mower. It's like new. When did ya get it?"

"I've had it seven or eight years. Probably overkill for what I need, but it does a good job."

"I bet. You must really like your lawn."

"I used to. Now it's mostly a pain in the ass. I'm too old to mow it."

Randall looked around the garage.

"Wow, that's an old truck. Like a '90?"

"It's an '88. It was my work truck. It's not all that old."

"That was eight years before I was born. It's old to me. Looks like it got banged up a little. Do you drive it?"

"No. I haven't in a couple years. I'm planning on getting it back on the road though. I have to get it started and take it to a shop so it'll pass inspection."

"It wouldn't be hard to fix. They'd just put on a new fender, headlight assembly, and a grill."

"Do you fix cars?"

"A little -- for friends and family. I took auto-body and mechanics in high school. It was better than sitting in class. Plus, I grew up on a farm, so we were always fixing stuff. No big deal."

Sophie saw her grandfather and the lawn guy on the porch. Now she heard them in the garage and wondered what was going on. When she came down the stairs, the lawn guy was bent under the truck hood fiddling with something. She walked around the back of the mower and tried not to startle them.

“Hi. I was coming down for some iced tea. What’s going on?”

“Randall here is looking at my truck,” Albert replied.

Randall turned around.

“Hi! You’re still here,” he said.

Sophie came closer. “Yeah, I still am. I’m living here in Rochester now.”

Randall looked at Albert then back to Sophie. “I’m just checking out his truck. I have to get going.”

“Hold on a minute," Albert said. "I need to talk to you. Come on back to the porch and finish your ice tea. This is Sophie, my granddaughter. She can join us.”

Sophie went into the kitchen and brought out the pitcher and refilled their glasses.

“So, it sounds like you'll be looking for some work, Randall.” Albert said.

“I’ll find something. I have some other patio jobs lined up. I can always work for my father on the farm when he needs me. I’ll be fine.”

“I could use some help around here for a few weeks. I’d hire you to fix my truck. Also, I’m selling this place and need help getting it cleaned out. Especially the basement.”

Sophie sipped her tea and studied Randall. He was tall with nice dark eyes. He had thick black hair – not shaved on the sides like most guys. His nose was a little flattened to one side but not in an ugly way. He had on a green T-shirt. It was stretched tight across his chest and upper arms. He was staring directly at her grandfather and not even sneaking a look toward her.

Her grandfather continued. "I'll pay you twelve dollars an hour. What d'ya say?"

Sophie got up from sitting on the steps and sat in the chair between Randall and Albert.

"I'd have a day here and there," Randall said. "I could order the truck parts for you and just give you the bill. I have a friend that could paint the fender, then I could put it on here. Looks like you've got enough tools to do it. I could get it started too. I can come up with a price for all that. What's in the basement?"

"Quite a bit of iron pipe and brass plumbing fittings, some copper. Plus, piles of other junk."

"My cousin is a scrapper. He'd probably be willing to clean the whole thing out if he could have the metal."

"Well Sophie, do you think Randall here is a coincidence or did your god send him? Randall, Sophie thinks god plans everything out for the good of us all."

"I believe He opens a new door when one closes," Randall replied. "It happens to me all the time."

"It sounds like Randall could be a big help, and you need it." Sophie said to her grandfather. "You can believe what you want."

She studied Randall again. He was definitely cute and maybe a Christian. *Too bad I don't have time for a boy right now,* she thought.

He finally looked at her. "How come you moved to Rochester?"

“I'm on the payroll here too. I'll probably work most of the summer – getting things ready for his move. I just found my own place to live.”

Randall had to wet his mouth with the tea. “That's nice.”

"When can you get started?” Albert asked.

"I have jobs lined up the rest of the week. I could come back Monday with a price for the truck. I'll see if my cousin will come with me to look at the basement. I can text you Sunday to set a time.”

“My grandfather doesn't have a phone, so you'll have to call his landline, but he probably won't answer it,” Sophie said.

“Sophie is tapping on her phone most of the day, you can text her,” Albert said.

“I'd have to get her number. I doubt she'd want to do that. Let's just say I'll be here at nine o'clock.”

“I'll give you my number," Sophie said.

“Well, if you want. My phone's in the truck. Goodbye, Mr. Martel, thanks for the tea and for the work. I'll see you on Monday. We'll get that truck started and the fender off. No big deal.”

Sophie and Randall walked over to the Lawn Order truck. Sophie stared at him as he put her number in his phone. She saw that he turned red again. He got into the truck and before he closed the door he said, “Maybe I'll see you Monday.”

“I'll be around. Bye.”

Randall looked in his side mirror as she walked away. *I've never seen a girl like that,* he thought. *She's so far out of my league, it isn't even funny.*

Sophie went back to the porch. “Grandpa, why do you want to fix up that old truck?”

“I thought with everything we need to do, it would be good to have a truck. I'm going to get my license back. Plus, you could use it when you need to go somewhere.”

“Yeah, like I'm going to drive that thing. I'm going back to work. I hope Bonnie comes soon.”

Albert followed Sophie back to the studio, and they worked together sorting and wrapping paintings. He talked about going to New York City. He had enlisted in the Army in 1958 to get out of Rochester. He signed up to do graphic arts or communications, so naturally, the Army trained him to be a plumber. He got stationed at Fort Hamilton in Brooklyn.

“It's still there today," he said. "It's the last active fort in New York City. I did maintenance and plumbing all over the base. I took art classes and painted when I was off duty. I spent my entire four-year tour there. I liked it, so I just kept my head down and the Army forgot about me.”

They quit at lunch time when Bonnie came with some groceries. By four o'clock they had made it to the end of the first rack. Sophie made notes and pried as much information from her grandfather as she could in an effort to make a rudimentary catalogue.

“Do you mind leaving soon?” Sophie asked Bonnie. “I want to meet Derek when he's done with work so I can pay him.”

"That would be good," Bonnie said. "I still have some orders to get out. Seems like as soon as I started this, I got busier with my jewelry. When it rains, it pours.”

“Grandpa, could I get that money?”

They all went back to the house. Albert went upstairs and brought down four one-hundred-dollar bills, then went back to the studio.

"I'll make up the extra next month," Sophie promised.

"Let's call it a starting bonus," Albert said.

In the car, Bonnie asked Sophie, “What time’s your mom coming tomorrow?”

“I don’t know yet. I have to call her. I'm dreading it so much.”

“Do you think she’ll be upset?”

“Upset? She's going to be totally pissed off. I've never done anything like this. She has no idea what's happening.”

“I can see your Dad freaking out," Bonnie said, “but I thought your Mom might be cool with it.”

“No way. They're both the same -- absolutely goal-driven. This isn't part of ‘the plan.’ It’ll be a nightmare to them. I just don’t know what I’m going to say.”

Bonnie pulled into Derek’s driveway.

“Will I see you tomorrow?” “Can you pick me up?”

“Yeah, I want to get an early start. I’m just gonna work in the morning, I’m visiting a friend out in the country for the weekend. Say hi to Bo for me.”

Sophie got out of her work clothes and put on her one pair of shorts and the baggy white shirt she had brought. She waited twenty minutes after Derek got home then went down and knocked on his door.

“Hi, Sophie. Did you sleep last night?”

“Hi, Derek. I was pretty excited, and the noises were different. I didn’t sleep much, but I still love it here. I have the rent money.”

“Come in a minute. I’ll give you a receipt. Did Bonnie bring you back?”

“Yeah. She said hi. I guess she’s going away for the weekend.”

“She has a friend out in the sticks somewhere. Would you like some wine or a beer?”

“Some wine would be nice. Your house is beautiful.”

“I was lucky. It came on the market during the last real estate bust. I got it cheap and have gradually redone it. I’ll get the wine and the receipt and meet you back on the porch. It’s nice out today.”

Sophie was glad to have a diversion before she called her mother. Derek was funny and they talked about art again. He told her he had a friend who worked at an art gallery just down the street. He said she would be happy to show her around the gallery. They sipped their wine, and Derek brought out some cheese and crackers.

"I googled a little on Sartre,” Sophie said. “He was so pessimistic and dark."

"Don't forget, he was writing after the Holocaust and Hiroshima. He wasn't the only one who wondered where God had been."

"Did he say God is dead?"

"No, that was Nietzsche. Not so much dead as irrelevant. If man can cause the apocalypse there isn't any need for a god to do it."

"Wars aren't started by God," Sophie said. "People do that. It's our evil nature."

"That's kind of what some of the Existentialists said. 'We can't blame God, or thank him.' They believed everything is up to the individual. Even to the point of choosing to live or die in a hopeless world."

That's also what the Abstract Expressionists were doing. Their art was an expression of their true selves, not a comment on anything else. They were rebelling against the old European stuff – making something new. They were rebelling against government -- capitalism, and religion too."

"Are you a rebel like that?" Sophie asked.

"Not really. My parents were Unitarians, so I didn't have anything to rebel against. I believe there is a God, but I'm not sure she's all that interested in me. I admire Jesus, but he wasn't divine."

"So," Sophie asked, "do you think he was a liar or insane?"

"Interesting point. Did you come up with that?"

"No. It's something C. S. Lewis said."

"I'll check that out." Derek studied her and thought, *This is not a typical twenty-one-year-old.*

"You should do that," she said. "Thanks so much; this was nice. I have to call home."

"Thanks for talking. Let me know if anything isn't right with the room."

Sophie went back up to her room and sat on her bed. This was the last time she would have to lie to her mother. She would need all her drama skills to get through it.

“Hi, Mom. How’s Daddy and Jack? Sorry about last night. I was tired and had a bad headache.”

“I knew something was wrong. You just didn’t sound like my Cookie. Dad is good. He’s been home early every day this week. He seems more relaxed. Jack is nervous about golf camp. We have to keep encouraging him to go.”

“He's so shy. It’ll be good for him. I miss him.”

“Well, you’ll be home soon. Jack is staying with the Andrews on Friday, then he'll move into the dorms for camp on Saturday. I’ll be in Rochester by two o’clock. We can go shopping and have dinner then come home Saturday morning. How does that sound?”

“I can’t wait to see you. Bring my camera with you. I want to take a couple of pictures of Grandpa’s paintings before I leave. It's on my desk.”

"I can do that. How’s Grandpa?”

“He’s good. I’ll see you tomorrow. Love you, Mommy.”

“Love you too, sweetie. Bye-bye.”

Lillian put her phone down. She still had a feeling deep in her maternal core that something was amiss. Her daughter had always been a changeling, but this overnight sour-to-saccharine was forced somehow. She had been looking forward to this week-end. It would be one totally dedicated to helping her two children. Things were better with Andy; now this would be a chance to reconnect with her kids. Jack needed support, and Sophie was obviously having trouble transitioning from college life. Getting them trapped in the car would give her a chance to talk to them.

FOURTEEN

Friday morning finally came. Andy found Jack sitting on his bed staring at his half-packed suitcase. "You about ready to go, Bud?"

Jack picked up a shirt. "Almost. I'm not sure what to take. I don't know what I'll need."

"Come on, Jack," Andy implored. "You're getting yourself worked up over this. I know you're going to do great and enjoy it. Nobody's judging you. Just go and enjoy yourself. It's just golf. It should be fun."

"I don't like people looking at me when I play. I get nervous."

Andy sat on the bed. "Well that's a big part of the game. You have to learn to focus and put everything else out of your mind. The more you can do that, the better you'll play. You have to work on that part of the game as much as your swing -- probably more. It'll come. And guys joke around and trash talk. That's part of the game too. Don't take it so seriously."

Jack smiled. "Is that a 'do as I say, not as I do' thing?"

Andy laughed. "You got me there. I'm hoping you'll be better at that part than I am, for sure. I have to get to work. I'll see you next weekend."

Jack stood up when Andy did. Andy hugged him.

"Have a good time. Call me tonight or anytime."

Andy met Lillian at the bottom of the stairs. "He's stalling up there. Poor kid is so nervous."

"I guess I'll have to help him. I was trying to get him to be responsible, but he's too stressed out."

"I've got to get going," Andy said. "Have a good time. I haven't heard from Geoff or the realtor. I'll text you their numbers. Maybe you can touch base with them. It'd be good for you to get up to speed on the deal."

"I'll miss you too, Mr. Martel."

"I was getting to that. Come here and give me a kiss."

It was a pretty drive upstate. Jack was quiet at first. Lillian peppered him with questions about golf, possible colleges, his friends -- but she was getting nowhere. Finally, she stopped talking until Jack asked, "So, Coach Andrews was in Dad's fraternity?"

"Yeah. Their fraternity was mostly athletes and guys from fairly-rich families -- but not the really rich. It was kind of an odd mix, but that's who they allowed in. Mr. Andrews played golf; of course, your father played basketball."

I've seen Dad's scrap books from college. He won some big awards and Princeton won the Ivy League his senior year. I've always wondered: If he was so good in college why he didn't try for the NBA when he had the chance? He got drafted, right?"

"Finally, in the late rounds by Dallas but didn't go to camp."

Jack looked at his mother. "Dad always told me he didn't want to move to Dallas. Is that really why he didn't go?

"He wanted to stay near me and go to law school. He made the choice to give up basketball."

"Is that when you got married?"

"No. That was when I left to train for the Olympics after I graduated, so we weren't together anyway."

Jack was quiet for several miles.

"That kinda sucks."

"It all worked out," Lillian said.

It had been over two hours since Jack had eaten and he was getting hungry. They pulled off the highway and into a McDonalds. Lillian got a coffee. Jack stayed busy with his Big Mac as they drove through rolling hills and farmland and on into Ithaca. The dispassionate female voice tracking their progress took them through the hilly town until their "destination was on the left." The driveway led off the road to a house overlooking Cayuga Lake.

Lillian had seen Sandy Andrews at their weddings and at a couple of reunions since college. Her cheerleader body had rounded out only a little, and the bubbly personality was unchanged. Her thick brown hair was cut in her trademark bob – designed to frame her dancing dark eyes. Insufferably cute and perky was her college tag. She was born to be a kindergarten teacher from which she was on summer break.

"Lillian, I'm so glad to see you! Hi, Jack; we haven't met. I'm Sandy. What fun to have you here! My husband talks about your Dad all the time. You're tall just like him. Come on in; we'll get your bags later. I have lunch almost ready."

Jack concentrated on his BLT as the two women caught up on their interim histories. They got to laughing about their husbands and golf.

"You would think their lives depended on how they hit a little white ball." Sandy said.

"I know, it's like torture to them, but they can't stop. Of course Andy tells Jack 'it's just a game', like he really believes that."

"It's a good game, just really frustrating. It drives you crazy," Jack interjected.

"They could do worse things, I guess," Sandy said.

"Yeah, like running every day," Jack said.

"Touché." Lillian said.

They finished up lunch and Lillian helped clear the table while Jack brought his bags in.

"Thanks so much for lunch, Sandy. I want to get going so it won't be too late when I get to Rochester."

Lillian captured Jack for a hug. He made a show of resistance but bent down and buried his head in her shoulder for a brief moment.

"We'll take good care of him. Don't worry," Sandy said.

"Jack, you can call anytime," Lillian said. "Just have a good time. I love you."

"Bye, Mom. I'll be fine. Stop worrying."

It was a gorgeous drive up through the Finger Lakes region and on into Rochester. Lillian had always loved this area. She and Andy had talked about a vacation home, and she figured they could probably get three times the place up here compared to downstate. It was worth considering.

After she got off the expressway, she almost didn't need the GPS to find Andy's boyhood home.

Sophie heard her mother drive up.

"Grandpa, I still haven't told Mom about the apartment and everything. I'm going to today."

"I won't say anything. It's almost time for my nap anyway."

Sophie went down the stairs and out through the garage to her mother's car.

"Hi, Mom!"

"Hi, Cookie! Give me a hug. I've missed you so much."

"Me too. Did you get Jack to Cornell?"

"Oh yeah; he'll be fine."

"Come up to Grandpa's studio and see what we're doing."

Lillian stepped around the lawn mower and went up the stairs.

"I've never been up here. This is beautiful. Are those all paintings?"

She spotted Albert across the room. "Hello, Dad. Andy was right, you look great. How're you feeling?"

"I feel good. I get a little tired this time of day. Did you have a good trip? What route did you take?"

"I came from Ithaca -- not sure of the route number, but it was a beautiful drive. How are you feeling about selling the place?"

"I haven't heard anything yet, but I'm glad we're getting started."

"It's still early in the process. I thought you could show me around, just so I know what we have here. Do you mind?"

"No, go ahead yourself. I'm going in for my nap. Use the bathroom or get something to eat if you want."

"I was hoping to visit a while," Lillian said. "Don't you want to walk around the property with me?"

"No. It's my nap time. Maybe I'll see you later."

"I didn't have any idea you had so many paintings up here."

Albert stopped at the door and turned around.

"Sophie is doing a great job getting them packed. But it'll take a long time to do them all. She's a hard worker. I'll see you if you're around later."

Albert closed the door.

"He's the most difficult man I have ever known," Lillian said, shaking her head. "I drove all the way up here, and he can't give me five minutes? Typical of him though. Let me see some of these famous paintings."

Sophie opened up three easels and set Albert's last three paintings on them.

Lillian studied them carefully, tilting her head back and forth.

"They wouldn't match anything in our house. I suppose they might work for someone though. They would clash with most of the colors people are using this year. Does he have any landscapes or things people might recognize?"

Sophie put the paintings back in the rack.

"I doubt there's anything you'd like here," Sophie said sharply. "Didn't you want to walk around?"

"You don't have to get mad," Lillian replied. "I guess I don't understand art. But really, if he'd made things people liked, he wouldn't have a barn full of paintings to get rid of. Just sayin'."

"Real artists paint for themselves – not to sell for decoration. Come on. Let's get outta here."

They walked the perimeter of the yard, then Lillian wanted to see more of the neighborhood. Sophie led her up the street to where the pizza place was.

"This looks familiar," Lillian said. "These old strips of stores are failing everywhere. They're wearing out, and the business centers have moved. Most of them are on the outskirts and getting killed by the big-box stores."

Lillian could see it was a neighborhood in decline. It was too far from the city center to attract young couples and probably too expensive for people displaced by gentrification in the city. *The realtor was right, she thought. It might be harder to sell Dad's house than Andy thought.*

"Let's go to the hotel," Lillian said when they got back to the house. "You can get changed, and we can go shopping. There's the Park Avenue area. That has cute shops."

Sophie knew the time had come to be honest with her mother but couldn't make herself do it. She got in the car. Lillian pushed the ignition button.

"Mom, wait a minute. I need to tell you something."

"What is it honey? I knew something was wrong."

"I'm not going home with you."

"Well, how will you be getting there?"

"I'm not going back. I'm staying here. I have an apartment. I'm going to live here and help Grandpa."

"What do you mean you 'have an apartment?'"

"I moved from the hotel on Wednesday to an apartment. I paid for it with money Grandpa paid me."

"You did this without discussing it with your father and me? Why would you do something like that? I don't understand. It doesn't make any sense to get an apartment for just a couple months. It won't be that long until you go to school."

"I'm not going to school. Mom, listen a minute. I've never wanted to go to grad school. I'm sick of school, and I want to help Grandpa. Mom... I never did the applications. I'm not going."

Lillian turned off the car and leaned her head against the seat.

"Have you been talking to Bonnie? Did she put this in your head?"

"No, Mom. It was totally my idea. Grandpa said I shouldn't do it. Bonnie didn't say anything about it."

"How did you find the apartment?"

"It belongs to a friend of Bonnie's."

Lillian leaned forward and gripped the wheel. "I knew it! She's a conniving bitch, just trying to aggravate your father. This isn't going to happen. You're going to get your clothes. I'll get the money back from her druggie friend, and we'll head home tonight. You show me how to get there right now."

Sophie got out of the car and closed the door. Lillian came around and faced her.

"Mom, it doesn't have to be like this. I've thought it through, and I know it's right. I'm sorry I've been lying; I really am. Please forgive me. I just know this is what I need to do."

"What you need to do is get in that car. You're going home with me right now. I don't want to hear anymore. This isn't fair to your father or to me. You're acting like a child, not a responsible adult. I'm disappointed in you. Now get in the car."

"Mom, please. You know you can't make me go. Please listen to me."

For a moment Lillian was going to grab her daughter and sit her in the car like a runaway toddler. It was past that – way past that. She told herself she wasn't going to cry. She truly didn't know what to do. Now she was in a corner. Sophie wouldn't get back in the car.

"Can I at least see the apartment?" Lillian asked in the calmest voice she could muster.

"I'm not getting in your car again," Sophie said. "You can see it the next time you come up."

"Sophie, please. Listen to me. You're making a big mistake; believe me. Come home. If you don't want to go to school this year, that's OK. We can figure something else out. You can't stay here. Just get in the car, and we'll talk some more."

"Mom, can I have a hug before you go? I love you and Daddy so much. Please try to understand; this is where I have to be. I'll be fine. If anything happens, I'll let you know. Please. I love you."

Lillian got back in the car. The mix of anger and love finally welled out of her eyes. Her hands were shaking as she reached for the ignition. She got back out.

"I'm going to get a room for the night and talk to your father. I won't leave until I see where you're staying. I expect that much respect from you. I'm also going to have a talk with Bonnie. I know where she lives."

"She isn't home this weekend. She didn't do anything. Do you promise not to kidnap me? I'd like you to see my place."

Sophie broke the silence as they drove.

"How was Jack?"

"He's fine. Worried about meeting new people and being away from home. He doesn't want to leave, and you don't want to be there."

Lillian wound her way from the suburbs back into the old residential area of Sophie's neighborhood.

Sophie pulled open the heavy door and led her mother up the stairs. She was deliberate as she unlocked the deadbolt.

"It's nothing but part of an attic! There isn't even a kitchen," Lillian said as she looked around.

"It's all I need. I'm at Grandpa's most of the time. I eat my meals with him. It's really safe, and the owner is great."

"Sophie, I just wish you'd been honest and discussed this with me. Why didn't you feel like you could?"

"It happened really fast. I should have told you I didn't want to go to grad school. I just couldn't bring myself to say it. I'm really sorry about that. Grandpa needs help. I'm learning so much from him, and soon he'll teach me painting. I want to get to know him."

"Your father is going to be furious at him, at Bonnie, at you, and probably at me. He isn't going to take this well, and I don't blame him. Sophie, honey, let's pack your things. We'll go home and all of us can discuss it and come up with a plan. I think you owe us that."

"Mom, I have a job with Grandpa. He's paying me, and I want to do it. Maybe this won't be for all that long, but right now I'm staying."

Lillian had to sit down. She sat on the straight chair and put her head in her hands. Her mind was jumbled. Her daughter had never treated her like this; it was totally unexpected. She tried to calm herself and go through the options and come up with a plan.

"There's no use of me staying here. Your Dad will work late tonight because I wasn't going to be home. I'll probably still be back before him. I'd rather tell him this in person. I don't know what he'll do. I wouldn't be surprised if he drives up here tomorrow."

Sophie sat on the bed.

"Please don't let him do that."

"Do you think I can stop him?"

"Yes, I do. He listens to you. You shouldn't let him get upset. Tell him I don't know what I'm doing. You should tell him to leave me alone for a little while. Tell him to think about it and come up with a plan. Just tell him that – you know how to handle him."

"I don't 'handle' him. Just because you can melt him with your tears and get what you want with those eyes doesn't mean I work that way. That isn't me. Besides, I doubt even you can change him on this. If you want to do it, you're going to have to face him alone. I'm not protecting you. Good luck. I'll call when I get home... if you want me to."

Sophie didn't bother letting her tears go; she knew they wouldn't affect her mother. She had to stick with reason.

"Mom, this had to happen sometime. I'm twenty-one. It's time I make my own decisions."

"You lied to us. You've gone behind our backs. I didn't think you had that in you. I'll give you one more chance to pack up and come home with me."

Sophie closed her eyes and prayed. *Please God, give me strength.*

"I love you Mom. Please let me know you got home safely."

About an hour from home, Andy's ringtone lit up Lillian's phone. She was tempted to not answer but knew that would make things worse. She pushed the phone button on the steering wheel.

"Hi."

"You left a message to call. Is everything OK with Jack?"

"Jack's fine; it's Sophie. She doesn't want to come home. She wants to stay at your father's and work on the paintings."

"Well, just tell her she can't. Put her on the phone; I'll tell her."

"I want to discuss this in person. I'm almost home. Sophie stayed back in Rochester. I'll explain everything when I see you."

"You mean you left her there? Why didn't you just bring her back? Why'd you let her stay?"

"She refused to leave. There wasn't anything I could do. It's better if we talk at home. When will you be there?"

"I don't believe this. *She's your daughter*. What do you mean she refused? You should have made her!"

"Andy, be real. I'll talk to you at home."

Andy looked at his list of emails to answer and the piles of reports on his desk. He wished he could bury himself under the concrete world of work. He hit the intercom button.

"Miss Ryan?"

"Yes, Mr. Martel."

"I'm not staying late after all. Call for the limo."

Andy called Sophie's number on the way home. She didn't pick up. He was sure his father and Bonnie were behind this. He expected as much of them, but he couldn't understand how Lillian could just leave her there. He would take care of it tomorrow, maybe even tonight.

Damn them all! Dad can rot in that dump until it falls down around him. Him and his damn paintings.

Andy got out before the driver did and almost threw the hundred-dollar bill at him.

The Audi was in the drive way, and the trunk was open. Andy closed it as Lillian was coming back out.

“I’m going to change and drive up there tonight," Andy said. "I’ll have her home by morning. I can’t believe you screwed this up.”

“Andy, let’s talk first. Come on in and rest a minute before you do anything. Do you want a soda or a drink? Sit on the couch. I’ll bring it to you.”

Lillian poured just a little whiskey into a glass of ice, just in case he did take off driving. She sat close to him on the couch.

“Let me take your tie off.”

Lillian repeated everything Sophie had said about grad school and the applications. She told him about the apartment. She could see him tensing up even more as he sipped on the watered-down drink.

Andy was seething. *Getting at me by exploiting my daughter is a new low for them. Sure, Sophie’s at fault too, but she wouldn’t have done it on her own. She’s too innocent for anything like this.*

Lillian pressed against her husband and massaged his temples and neck.

“I’m sorry I couldn’t get her to come home. I don’t think she really knows what she's doing. You shouldn't get so upset. Wouldn’t it be a good idea to take a day or two to cool off and give her some time to think about it? I’m sure if you give it a couple of days, you'll come up with a good plan. You always know what to do. You're such a wonderful father.”

She turned his head so he could look at her.

“Why are you blinking," he asked. "Are your contacts dry?”

Lillian gave that up and got Andy another drink and herself a glass of wine.

"It's not your fault, Lil. I'm sorry I said that. I think I'll wait and come up with a plan. It would be good for her to think about it and see what living on her own is like."

≈

Her mother hadn't closed the door behind her. Sophie got off the bed and shut it. That went worse than she expected, she thought. She had hoped her mother might understand more and not be so angry. *She probably isn't going to be any help with Dad.* She felt trapped in her room and decided to go for a walk.

She knew East Avenue was a main route and turned left on it. She passed some beautiful mansions, and after three blocks, she saw a big church on the other side of the street. She was drawn to it. The door was open, and she sat down in a back pew. It was a Methodist Church with a large, ornate sanctuary. She took a moment to collect herself and prayed. She prayed for forgiveness, for her parents, and for guidance. She was again filled with a sense of purpose. She thanked God for giving her that feeling.

She continued on East Avenue until she recognized a street that went to Park Avenue. The sidewalk cafes were filling up as people met after work. *This is as close to Paris as I'm going to get for a while,* she thought.

She took a seat at small wrought-iron table beneath a green awning and ordered a mocha latte. She checked her purse. She had some cash left from her father. It felt lame to use cash, but what else could she do? She sipped her latte and people-watched. Finally, she daydreamed of the Left Bank and lost herself in the street scenes. She was suddenly jolted back to reality.

"Tiens! Bonsoir, mademoiselle."

"Derek! Bonsoir! Bonsoir! Joignez-vous à moi, s'il vous plait."

"Avec plaisir, ma chère. Merci."

"Tout le plaisir est pour moi. Puis-je vous offrir un café?"

"Oui... avec joie". And that's as far as my French will take me. How are you?"

"Actually, I had a stressful day. My mother came to take me home. I didn't go. Are you meeting friends?"

"Yeah, just one. She should be here soon.

Sophie filled him in on the grad school thing. She told him what her mother had said and how angry and disappointed her father was going to be.

Derek sipped his espresso. "I still remember when my daughter left home. I didn't believe she was ready. But I also remember feeling jealous. Jealous that she would have people in her life more important to her than me. It's a real comedown but one every father has to go through."

"That doesn't make me feel much better," Sophie said quietly.

"You might not feel very good for a while. It's just a road you gotta travel. You're a young woman now; you have your own decisions to make... and the consequences to live with."

Sophie laughed. “Are you an existentialist now? My Grandfather says he is.”

“I've been a lot of things. I’m just me now. Oh, there's Monique. I told you about her. She runs an art gallery.”

Sophie saw an attractive older woman, about Derek's age, approach. She was tall, her graying hair was up in a bun. She was wearing some worn mom jeans and a paint splattered t-shirt.

"Hi, Derek. I didn't know you were meeting someone."

"Monique, this is Sophie, she rents a room from me. She just moved here."

"Nice to meet you," Monique said. "I'm embarrassed I look so grubby. Today was a clean-up day at work."

"Nice to meet you too," Sophie said. "Derek told me you work at a gallery."

"At the Memorial, just up East a little way. We had to tear down an exhibit today."

"You two will have a lot to talk about," Derek said. "Sophie is an artist and is interested in gallery work."

"Really?" Monique said. "Tell me more."

They ordered more coffee then the three of them fell into a conversation about art and the Memorial Art Gallery. Monique asked about Sophie's education and her art. Sophie told her about what she did with her Grandfather.

"Monique," Derek said, "Sophie est très à l'aise dans Français"

"Belle, intelligente, et parle Français? Le monde est à toi," Monique said

"Je ne suis qu'une fille. J'ai beaucoup à apprendre," Sophie replied.

" N'est-ce pas? I would like you to see the gallery. Here's my card. Call some time and I'll give you a tour."

"I would love that," Sophie said, I certainly will. I must be going. Bonne soirée!"

Monique and Derek replied in unison,"A bientôt."

"An interesting young lady. No?" Monique said.

"Yeah, the operative word is young. Another time, another place," Derek sighed.

"No, Derek, you need a woman whose been around more than her," Monique said.

On the way back to her apartment, Sophie noticed a laundromat not far from her street. *What could be more apropos than spending my first night of emancipation doing my laundry?* she wondered. She collected her laundry, bought a sub, and went to the laundromat. There was a take-one/leave-one bookshelf near the door. She found a well-traveled Nicholas Sparks novel and escaped onto an emotional rollercoaster. She continued reading when she got back to her room. She started nodding before the first heartbreak, turned her light off, and fell asleep.

FIFTEEN

Albert awoke Saturday morning assuming Lillian took Sophie home, so he was surprised when she walked up the driveway.

"Hey, Grandpa. I'm still here."

"I wasn't sure you would be. How'd it go with your mother?"

"She's really upset. I expected it. It's just a road I have to travel, but I'm more sure than ever that God wants me to be here."

"Don't put that god thing on me. It's you that's doing it, no one else."

"Sorry Grandpa, but God helps people who don't even believe in him. That's the way He is."

"Tell your god to leave me alone. I can screw up my life without his help. You going to work weekends too?"

"What else do I have to do? I know all of five people here. Besides, we haven't even really cataloged and packed any of the important paintings. We have to keep moving."

"I want to mess around with my truck this morning. I'll be up in a while."

Albert lifted the hood of the truck. It hadn't been started in two years. He gave it a try, and it didn't even grunt. He got his multi-tester and a hydrometer out of a drawer. The battery was totally discharged and had two dead cells. He would need a new one.

He called Bagger for help and soon he arrived with one of his grandsons. The grandson drove them to an auto-parts store where Albert bought a battery, filter, oil, starter fluid, and dry gas. Bagger's grandson got the old battery out and lifted the new one in. He also put five gallons of fresh gas in the tank. Albert slipped the kid a ten and walked Bagger back to his car.

"Thanks for the help. I can get it from here."

"I hope I don't come back and find you dead under that piece a junk." Bagger said.

"If you do, throw me in the back, and send it all to the scrap yard," Albert replied.

Albert knew he would need a little extra tremor medicine that day. He sat on the porch to rest and had a short one. Then he went back to the garage and got to work. He had to put a cheater on the oil filter wrench, but other than that he had no trouble.

Sophie was quitting for lunch when she heard the truck making a terrible noise. She went down to check on her grandfather.

"Hey, Sophie, you want to help?"

"I don't know anything about trucks."

"Just get in and turn the key when I tell you and push the gas pedal down."

Sophie climbed in the truck. The burning smell of the starter fluid filled the garage.

"Crank it!" Albert yelled.

Sophie turned the key and pushed down on the pedal. The engine roared to life then quit.

"Now pump the pedal and turn the key again!"

The spray burned Sophie's nose. The engine fired, jumped and bucked for a few seconds, then quit again."

"Get out. Let me try it."

Albert gave it another blast of starter fluid and pulled himself behind the wheel. It fired again. This time Albert gently played the pedal and the engine kept running, missing a beat here and there.

"Put the hood down and get outta the way!" he shouted.

Sophie closed the hood. Albert put the truck in drive, it hesitated at the doorway then lurched out of the garage, protesting with backfires. It wasn't long before the fresh gas mixed in and it fell into a syncopated rhythm.

Albert yelled at Sophie though the open window.

"I guess I won't need that kid to start my truck! Let's go for a ride and clean out the pipes."

"Grandpa, you don't have a license and neither does the truck."

"Oh, hell, nobody'll see us. We'll just go down the block and back. C'mon." He leaned over and opened the passenger door.

Better to be with him than not, Sophie thought.

Albert eased the still-complaining truck down the driveway and onto the street. As he gently accelerated, white smoke billowed from the tail pipe. When he got to thirty, the engine suddenly smoothed out, so he slowed back down. Albert was sitting straight backed, staring intently at the parked cars as he went by. He turned around in the church parking lot and slowly retraced his route back to his driveway. He shut the engine down then retried it. It started again easily. He beamed at Sophie.

"Not bad for a half-dead man. Couldn't have done it a week ago."

He removed the key and put it in his pocket.

"Let's get some lunch."

Sophie made them sandwiches, and Albert grabbed a couple of beers from the fridge. They retreated to the porch and sat quietly eating. After a while, Sophie broke the silence.

"Grandpa, it's amazing you got that thing running. How long's it been?"

"Almost exactly two years. I parked it when they took my license away. I haven't touched it since."

"Did you have an accident?"

"I ran into a light pole. They said I was drunk. I'd hardly had a drink yet that day. The town just wanted to collect a fine. I told 'em I wouldn't pay it, so they took my license. I'm going to get it back though."

"It would be good if you could drive to the store yourself."

Albert finished his beer and stood up. The conversation was over.

"I gotta get the air cleaner back together."

Albert felt his joints stiffening as he bent over the engine, but he actually welcomed the pain of accomplishment.

I doubted I could do it, but damn if I didn't, he thought. *That's it for the day though.*

He pulled himself up with the handrail to the studio to tell Sophie. She started in with questions about a painting. He wished he could give her the insight she was looking for, but he just didn't remember, so he made up something close, and she seemed satisfied.

"I guess I overdid it. I have to go lie down. I might take a Tylenol."

Sophie came to him and gave him a gentle hug and a kiss on his cheek.

"You worked hard today. You're quite a man."

"I was a long time ago. Are you coming back tomorrow?"

"No, I'm going to take a day off. Could I borrow your pastels and some paper? I have a few sketches I want to work on."

"Sure, take whatever you need or work here if you want."

"Thanks, Grandpa, but I'll work at my place for now. Call me if you need anything."

After he had made his way back to the house, Albert eased onto the couch.

I fixed a truck and a young woman called me a man. I don't know where all this is coming from, but since my granddaughter has been here, something is changing.

For the rest of the weekend Sophie felt like she was living out a fantasy. The feeling of freedom and accomplishment dampened her guilt for what she had done to her parents. She was living on her own and drawing in her little attic room -- like a real artist. She lost herself in her art. She wandered the neighborhood streets having lunch and coffee at the cafes. She ran into Derek and Maggie, but they were busy also, so she kept to herself and worked. By Sunday night she had completed two pastels. She was happy with them. They were more free -- different from her school assignments. She was torn about calling her father. The plan was to give it a few days. She would stick with the plan.

Monday morning broke warm and fair. Sophie caught an early bus and was in the studio before Albert was up. She had worked almost two hours when she heard the bumbum bumbum of a motorcycle slowing down, then podatopadatopadato as it idled into the driveway. She looked out the window and saw Randall getting off a big black and chrome bike. Then a pickup truck pulled in behind him. A large man got out of the truck. He had on a straw cowboy hat and bib overalls. He looked to be at least fifty. As they were talking, her grandfather came out and joined them. Randall went to the garage and opened the door. All three went inside. She heard the truck start up and drive out of the garage. She kept working, trying to ignore the activity outside. She was getting hungry when her grandfather came into the studio.

"I thought maybe we could have pizza for lunch," he said.

I know where this is going, Sophie thought.

"Sounds good. Let me know when it's here," she replied.

Albert looked at his shoes. “I thought we could get it up at Louie’s.”

“And who is 'we,’ Grandpa?”

“Well, I guess I could walk all the way up there.”

Sophie tried to sound angry.

“No, no, I’m the girl here. I’ll go get you big strong men lunch. It’s my place.”

“True, hadn’t thought about that," Albert joked back. "I bet Randall would help you. Pick up a couple large. The cousin looks like he could eat one himself.”

Sophie followed Albert down to the driveway. Randall was coming out of the basement with a box to put into the truck. Then his cousin came out with an armload of pipe and threw it in. Randall came over to Sophie.

“Hi. Sophie, this is my cousin, Daryl.”

“Hello,” Darryl said, “look at that, we’re twins -- got the same bibs on. You get yours at Walmart?”

“As a matter of fact, I did." Sophie replied. "Nice to meet you. I've been ordered to go get pizza. What kind do you want?”

“We tried to tell Mr. Martel we don’t need lunch, but he insisted," Randall replied. "I can help you.”

“I’m sure I can manage," Sophie said, "but you’re welcome to come if you want.”

“Told you he’d like to walk with you,” Albert said.

“Grandpa, mind your own business.”

Randall and Sophie headed up the sidewalk.

“I can see why RJ can't stop talking about coming back here,” Darryl said, smiling. “She's one fine lookin' gal.”

"That she is, but there's a lot more to her than looks," Albert replied.

Randall was quiet. *I'll let her talk first. Less chance of me saying something lame.*

They were halfway to the pizza shop, and still Sophie hadn't said anything.

This is dumb, Randall thought. *I have to say something.*

"Your grandfather is quite a guy. I can't believe he got that truck started and changed the oil. That was a lot of work. I figured it'd take me most of today."

"Pretty much if he decides to do something, he does it." Sophie said.

"I'll get the fender off this afternoon while Daryl takes away the scrap."

"What does he do with that junk?"

"He takes it to a scrap yard. They pay by the pound. It's one of the things he does for a living."

"Is he off from his usual job?"

"He doesn't work for anyone regular." Randall replied. "He does welding, sells firewood, raises some beef, and does the scrapping. He's got a backhoe. He'll do most anything someone wants to pay him for. He hunts and puts meat in the freezer that way."

"Is he married?"

"Oh, sure. His wife home-schools their three kids."

There were no other customers in the pizza shop when they arrived.

“Hi, Louie,” Sophie said. "Remember me, Albert’s granddaughter?”

“Of course. How’s Al today?”

“He’s doing fine. He sent us to get a couple pizzas.”

“Great, what'll it be.”

Sophie looked at Randall.

“What do you think? Two large pepperoni?”

“That’ll be plenty.”

“Good,” Louie said, “Gimme 20-25 minutes.”

As they sat down at a table to wait, Sophie thought, *This is going to be awkward. He’s obviously uncomfortable too.*

Finally, Randall spoke. “Your grandfather told me what you’re doing back there. It sounds like a big job you're getting into. Is anyone helping you?”

“My aunt helps once in a while. She might be here later. Grandpa helps a little. But mostly I’m doing it. I learned how in college.”

Randall was quiet again. The silence got to be too long for Sophie.

“So, you hope to get Grandpa’s truck fixed?”

“Yeah, it’s no big deal. Probably come back next weekend and put it together.”

“That’ll be nice," Sophie said. "He’ll feel better if he can drive again.”

Mercifully, Louie slid the two warm boxes across the counter. Sophie paid, and they each picked one up.

"You know," Randall said, "I was serious the other day about God opening doors. I need some new things in my life. Maybe some changes are coming."

"Changes are good sometimes. Hard to do though."

Albert and Daryl were waiting at the picnic table taking apart a six-pack.

Sophie ate her pizza while the men discussed the finer points of pickup trucks. She left them at the table and went back to the studio. She thought about Randall and Daryl. She had heard redneck jokes but never expected to actually meet people like that, certainly not back in Chappaqua.

Around two o'clock Bonnie showed up. Sophie filled her in on what happened with Lillian.

"You've got a lot going on," Bonnie said. "Are you still cool with staying here?"

"I know it's the right thing to do," Sophie replied. "I just have to get through to my parents. I mean, like, I feel bad for the way I did it but not for doing it. Does that make any sense?"

"Totally. You just gotta do what feels good. They'll have to get into what you're doing and stop being so uptight. Your dad will be blaming me anyway."

"I told Mom you and Grandpa had nothing to do with any of this. They can't blame anyone but me."

"They will though, for sure."

By five o'clock, Bonnie was ready to go home. Randall and Albert were working on the truck. The fender was gone; now they were taking the toolboxes off the back.

"Five o'clock – quittin' time," Albert announced. "Randall, you going to mow my lawn this week?"

"I'll do it when I bring the fender back, probably Friday or Saturday. Will that work?"

"Either one, just let Sophie know when you're coming. See you then."

Randall went back to the garage for a few minutes then closed the door and walked to his motorcycle. As he was putting on his jacket Sophie approached him.

"Randall, thanks for letting Grandpa help. That was nice of you."

"He's a tough old guy for sure. Um, Sophie?"

"Yes, Randall?"

"My friends call *me* RJ."

Sophie couldn't resist torturing him just a little. She caught him with her eyes and smiled.

"Would you like *me* to call you RJ?"

Randall zipped up his jacket.

"I would much very...like that... very much."

Sophie laughed.

"Well then, RJ it is."

What a loser, RJ thought on the way home. *I can't even talk around her. Why am I even thinking about her? I made a great impression today. She'll be on Instagram laughing about the biker and his redneck cousin, the scrapper. I just have to forget about her.*

≈

Tuesday, Sophie and Bonnie were at the studio by nine. Bonnie hung in there until four, then Sophie rode back with her to avoid taking the bus.

Sophie had decided this was the day she would call her mother. It was only fair.

Lillian was driving home when Sophie's ringtone sounded.

"Thank you, God. Now give me strength," Lillian whispered. "Hello?"

'Hi Mom, can you talk?"

"I'm in the car. How have you been?"

"I'm good. I got a lot done the last two days. Bonnie's been helping. How's Daddy?"

"He's still very upset. He almost drove up there to drag you home."

"But you did what I said, right? Did he calm down?"

"We discussed it rationally, and he decided to give you some time to reconsider. After that I don't know what he's going to do. Hopefully we'll talk about it again tonight. It would be nice if you called him."

"I will if you think he won't just get mad and yell."

"I'm not guaranteeing anything. Do you have enough money? Are you eating good?"

"I'm fine. Would you call me after you talk tonight and let me know how he is?"

"I told you. I'm not going to be a buffer for you. You have to deal with him, not me. The longer you wait the harder it'll be."

"I hoped you would feel better about this by now. I guess not."

"What's to feel better about? You've disappointed us terribly; that hasn't changed. Are you sure you're safe?"

"I said I was sorry. I guess I'll talk to you later. Is Jack OK?"

"He texted me today. He seems to be doing well."

"I'll text him. I have to go," Sophie said. "We'll talk again soon."

Lillian was determined not to cave.

"You can call anytime. Goodbye."

"Bye, Mom, I love you."

Lillian choked, but pushed the end-call button.

That evening after Andy had changed his clothes and come down to help with dinner, Lillian said, "Sophie called me this afternoon."

"Is she going to call me?"

"She's afraid you'll yell at her."

Andy formed some ground chuck into patties.

"I've given the whole thing some thought. I have no doubt she'll get tired of living on her own. But more than anything, she'll soon find out what her beloved grandfather is really like. I think we just have to let this run its course. The more we push it, that more stubborn she'll get. I'm going to concentrate on moving her back on track to grad school. She's just getting back at me for not sending her to Europe last year. So, I'll back off and let her go to France. Then maybe she can start school in January, or we may just have to wait a year. That'll get her away from Dad and Bonnie. She won't be able to resist it. Sometimes you have to reset and call a new play. What do you think?"

"I hate to indulge her after she acted this way, but you're right; she wants to go to Paris more than anything. This is what we get - you get - for spoiling her. She always gets her way with you in the end. What's to guarantee she goes to school after you give her Paris?"

Andy sliced some onions.

"I trust her. She'll promise."

"You're hopeless. But I love you. You going to call her?"

"No, I'll wait. Maybe I'll yell a little for effect when I finally do. I bet we'll have her home on the weekend."

Andy grabbed a beer and went out to grill the burgers.

Lillian texted Sophie.

Call your dad, he's better now.

After dinner, Andy was in his study reviewing a contract when Sophie called.

"Hi Daddy, I miss you. Do you still love me?"

"I'm not happy with what you did. I just don't know what you were thinking. You had all that time when we were together to discuss school. If you had decided not to go, you could've told me. Of course, I love you."

Sophie started to cry. "I know I was wrong, Daddy. I should have told you. I just didn't want to disappoint you. I want to make you happy, not upset."

"Cookie, it's not about making me happy, it's about what's best for you. I still think going to grad school is best. Maybe it's just too soon. Maybe you need some time before you go."

Sophie brightened.

"So, it's all right if I stay here and work with Grandpa?"

"Not really. You're just wasting time. I think we could come up with something better."

"Like what?"

"If you're not going to school this year, I think studying in France would be something to consider."

"You would send me to Paris? After all this?"

"It would look good on the applications and give you some experience. Hopefully we can find an internship or something."

"But I've hardly gotten started on Grandpa's paintings..."

"You just think about it. Make a pro-con list. You can live in an attic in Rochester and waste your education or go to Paris and study art. It's a no-brainer."

Sophie stared at her phone for a long moment.

"I'm so confused. I need to process all this."

I've got to stick with the plan, Andy thought. *Let the game come to me.*

"I'm not going to pressure you, but this is a once-in-a-lifetime chance to do something you've wanted to do. Just let me know before Friday if you want us to pick you up."

"I'll call again soon so we can talk some more. I love you, Daddy."

"I love you too, Cookie. Please be careful, bye-bye."

SIXTEEN

For once, Sophie was glad Bonnie was late. She hadn't slept much and was slow getting going. She had spent most of the night making pro-and-con lists in her head, thinking about what-ifs. She tried praying for guidance, but no answers came. Even after weighing it over and over, there was something short-circuiting the process. Finally, Bonnie showed up.

"Sorry I was late. I stopped for groceries on the way here. How's it going?"

"I talked to Dad last night. He wants to send me to Paris."

"He wasn't mad at you?"

"Yeah, he is, but he wants me to get me away from here, so he offered to send me. I don't know what to do."

Bonnie was quiet for several blocks.

"Would you pass up a chance to go to Paris?"

"I just don't know. I really don't. It's like I can't even think straight. I committed to helping Grandpa, so I feel guilty even thinking about leaving. But I feel guilty for what I did to my parents too. And I really want to go to Paris."

"Your grandpa and I appreciate all that you're doing, but you gotta think about your future, like, you're so young. Not that I ever had a chance to go to Europe, but if I had, I would've gone for sure."

Sophie sighed. "I know it's a great opportunity. Let's not say anything to Grandpa for now."

By four o'clock Bonnie wanted to leave. Sophie didn't want to go home yet. She told Bonnie she would take the bus.

"OK, cool. I'll be at Derek's. Stop in when you get home."

Sophie tried working some more but hadn't been able to concentrate all day. She walked around the yard then came back and sat in Albert's library in the back of the studio. She tried praying again but could not get into it. She was sleepy, so she laid on the couch and fell asleep.

A beautiful woman walked out of her grandfather's painting, then became an owl and flew away. It landed on a cross and turned into a woman again and slid down the cross to the ground. Sophie followed the woman, now bent over then floating, up a mountain path past dark trees. The woman motioned to Sophie to sit with her by a spring. A cool mist enveloped them both. Then Sophie, alone, continued up the path. An old bear lay among the rocks. He sniffed the air and turned his grizzled head toward her. His eyes were white, unseeing. Sophie whispered in his ear and the bear followed, struggling up the narrow path. The bear growled and huffed, but Sophie wasn't afraid. They came to a clearing. The bear turned into a hawk and circled high above the mountain.

Sophie awoke with a start. She prayed. This time she got lost in her prayers and felt a calmness fall on her. She opened her eyes. She knew.

She would stay.

≈

Bonnie had let herself into Derek's apartment with the key he had given her a year earlier. She was sautéing eggplant for ratatouille when she heard him open the door.

"Hello," he shouted. "Is that you, Sally?"

"No, it's Audrey."

"That's right; it's Wednesday. I can't keep all you women straight."

Bonnie looked over her shoulder. "In your dreams, old man. Go get changed. I just have to put this together and let it simmer. You can make me a drink."

Derek made two Dark and Stormys and Bonnie followed him out to the porch.

"It looks like you won't have a princess in your attic much longer," Bonnie said, waiting for his reaction.

"Really? Why's that?"

"Her daddy wants to pack her off to Paris."

"She told me she'd decided against grad school and wanted to stay here. Must be she really wants to go to Paris."

"Andy will get his way no matter what it costs. It's just as well. We really don't need her here complicating things."

"That's a little harsh," Derek said. "I thought you liked her."

"It's hard not to -- she's a sweet girl. But Dad is, like, infatuated or something. He's almost stopped drinking and smoking. He shaves every day. Sometimes he acts almost happy. I still hope I can convince him to save the house from Andy. Pretty soon, he'll do whatever she says. She has a way with men. Wouldn't you agree?"

"Is it a bad thing your father is happy? And she's younger than my daughter."

"I just don't want Dad taken advantage of. He and I have gotten along fine without Andy and his big plans. I thought someday I would move back in there and take care of him. Now I'll end up with nothing after all these years. And, yes, she's young, but you're still a man."

Sophie halted at the corner of the house when she heard Bonnie say "princess." She was out of sight but within earshot of her aunt and Derek. When they were done talking about her, she turned and went around the house and up to her room. Now she understood her feeling that Bonnie was almost sabotaging the work on the paintings.

I'm the only one who cares about Grandpa and his art. I'll show her a princess. Wait til she finds out I'm staying.

She put on her white cami and a pair of tight capris. She went back down to the porch and bounded up the steps.

"Hi, Derek! Bonnie invited me. I hope you don't mind."

Derek jumped out of his chair as she came up the steps.

"No, I'm glad she did. You're having dinner with us, right? Bonnie made ratatouille. Can I get you a drink or anything you want?"

"Sure, I'll try whatever you're having."

"I'll be right back. Don't go anywhere."

Sophie half-sat on the railing.

"Did you get much done after I left?" Bonnie asked.

"Not really. I couldn't concentrate today."

"I was telling Bo you're going to Paris."

"Well, I did get that much done. I've thought and thought. I'm not going. I'm staying here as long as it takes to help Grandpa get moved. It might take months; who knows. Plus, I love living here with Derek."

Sophie was a little ashamed and thought, *You cat you, stop that.*

Derek mixed the drink then stirred the ratatouille. *Get a grip,* he thought. *Think of her as your daughter and don't stare.*

Bonnie took a sip of her drink. "I hope you aren't passing up something you'll regret later."

"You know what Grandpa says, 'You'll always regret what you don't do as much as what you do.'"

"I've never heard Dad say anything like that."

"We talk about stuff all the time. I think he's wrong because I believe this is what God wants me to do, so I'll never regret it."

Derek brought Sophie's drink to her. He could sense some tension between the women. He gave a short discourse on the history of the Dark and Stormy cocktail after which they went in for dinner.

Over dinner Sophie and Derek discussed books Bonnie hadn't read and plays she hadn't seen. Sophie could recite lines from every high school and college play she had performed, to Derek's great delight. Bonnie watched the refracted light from the stained-glass windows shine in Sophie's black hair. She saw how the wine had caused the young girl's flawless complexion to glow. Derek insisted on clearing the table and washing the dishes by himself. He left the two women lingering over more wine.

"I'm going to call Dad tonight and tell him I'm staying here," Sophie said. "I have a feeling he's trying to wait me out. He doesn't think I can make it on my own."

Bonnie poured herself another glass of wine. Her speech was a little slurred. "You think this is living on your own? Your grandfather or me are feeding you most of the time, and he's giving you money. Derek is letting you live here for almost nothing. And besides, any time you want you can run back home to Daddy. This ain't real, honey."

Sophie was a little shocked but glad this was coming out.

"I'm working hard for Grandpa, and he's going to pay you too. Derek isn't charging me less than anyone else. I appreciate what you've done for me, thank you. I hope someday I can repay the favor."

Bonnie looked away. "I just want what's best for my dad."

"That's what I want too. If we both keep that in mind, we'll get along great. Thank you for dinner."

Sophie went into the kitchen.

"Thanks Derek, I have to get going and call my father."

"Nice to see you again. Is everything cool with you and Bonnie?"

"We had a little chat. We're fine."

Bonnie was finishing her wine when Derek came back in.

"I'm going home," she said.

“You’re not staying tonight?” Derek asked, sitting down.

“No, I don’ feel like it. See you later.”

“I don’t think you should drive. You had quite a bit to drink.”

Bonnie pushed up from the table. “Sorry to waste your wine. I’m drunk, but you ain’t gettin’ laid tonight.”

"I'll take you home if that's what you want."

On her way up to her apartment Sophie thought, *It was weird with Bonnie tonight, but now I know where she stands with me.* She wanted to put off calling her father, but she was certain of her decision and wanted to get it over.

Andy muted the Yankees game when his phone vibrated. He saw it was Sophie.

Good, this mess will be over with soon, he thought.

"Hi, Cookie. I'm glad you called."

"I said I would. How was your day?"

"I got home fairly early. Work has been hectic though. Have you given some thought to going to Paris?"

"That's all I've been thinking about," Sophie said. "I still can't believe you would do that."

"I can admit when I'm wrong. We should've done it sooner. I see now you need some more time to grow up a little."

"Dad, I'm twenty-one. I know what I'm doing."

"I know, Cookie. To you that seems grown up, but you're really just getting started. We'll get you to France then plans will fall in place. When you coming home?"

"Daddy, you don't know what it means to me that you offered it to me. But, I just can't go. I have to stay here with Grandpa for now."

Andy put the phone down and took a deep breath and thought, *Got to let the play develop, don't rush it. Wait for an opening.* It took all his self-control to even out his voice.

"I'm disappointed, Sophie. I thought you would make a better decision. You won't be twenty-one again; now is the time to learn and grow. Later on it won't be right for me to support you like this. You have a lifetime of responsibility ahead of you, take advantage of who and where you are right now. Just tell me you'll think about it some more."

"That's what I mean. I want you to know I appreciate everything you do for me and have. I just know I need to stay here and help Grandpa."

Andy knew the worst thing he could do was make this about his father. That would back Sophie into a corner. He would deal with that later.

"Let's just leave it there for now. You're welcome to come home anytime you want."

"I love you, Daddy. I'll call again soon."

"Please do that. I love you too Cookie."

Andy turned off the big screen, went to his bar and poured a Scotch. He walked out on the patio. The pool was blue against the expanse of the green yard. Despite the glow of the metropolis to the south he could see a pale moon rising in the east. *I thought I had my father in the past where he belongs. Now, he's using my daughter to get back in my life. It's not going to happen. I won't let it. I just won't.* He sipped on his drink and watched the bats frantically harvesting mosquitoes over the garden. When he was done, he rattled the ice, threw it onto the patio and went back inside.

SEVENTEEN

The next morning, Bonnie called Sophie to let her know she wasn't going to the studio until later. She had spent much of the night and the morning cutting down her dread-locks and combing them out. She then went to her friend's beauty shop. She had her hair styled in a wedge cut, colored brown with highlights. She gave her friend a half bag of buds and headed for her father's house.

Sophie was taking a three o'clock break when Bonnie came into the studio.

Sophie stared for a moment. "Oh my goodness! Look at you! What a cute cut! Your dreads were nice, but this is awesome on you. Why'd you do it?"

Bonnie flipped her hair. "Oh, just thought it was time for a change. Do you like the color? I wasn't sure."

Sophie came closer. "It's perfect for you! They did a great job. Wait 'til Derek sees it."

"He's never seen me without dreads. I hope he likes it."

Sophie lightly touched Bonnie's shoulder. "He's going to love it. I know he will."

"Sophie, about last night. I'm not going to lie. I wish my father could stay here, but my hassle is with your dad, not you.

These paintings need to be dealt with no matter what. It blows my mind you would stay here and not go to Paris. That tells me a lot about you. I'm sorry for the way I acted."

"I was bitchy too," Sophie said. "There's a lot of stress on everybody -- my dad included. I don't know what you think, but I know he cares about you. I care about you and Grandpa. I'm so glad I have this chance to know my family."

Just then Sophie's phone buzzed with a text. It was from Randall.

Fender won't be done til sat. Staying with a guy I worked with in Roch so will be around sat night. Will come on sun.

Sophie didn't text right back.

He's hinting that he wants to go out, she thought, but he's too shy to ask. Maybe if we went with some other people it wouldn't be so awkward. It would better than doing nothing again this weekend.

After leaving him on read for a while, she texted him back.

Are u going out with your friend on sat?

Yeah, he's married. I'm going out with them.

Like some company?

Sure. Would you like to go?

Where you going?

Prob for dinner and music club. We can pick you up.

Sophie considered this. He seemed like a nice guy. She could always Uber back if it didn't feel right.

Is it close to Culver and East?

Prob 10 min.

Send link for club. I'll let you know.

K

Sophie checked the site. It was near other clubs, not in the middle of nowhere. It should be safe.

Looks cool. Text me with time.

Randall put down his phone. His cousin was sitting next to him.

"Holy shit! You were right, dude! She said she'd go out with me."

"I told you, she puts her pants on one leg at a time, like everybody else. She's got nothin' on you."

"Yeah right. She's just bored and wants to get out. I don't care though. I still can't believe it."

"What was that all about?" Bonnie asked.

"I'm going out with that lawn guy and some of his friends on Saturday. I thought it would be fun to see what the clubs are like here. I think it'll be safe, and I won't be alone with him. I wouldn't do that. He seems OK."

Bonnie laughed. "OK? He's a hunk."

"He's kinda a redneck. I don't know what we'll talk about. He's cute, but so shy."

"You might be surprised. Just 'cause he lives in the country doesn't mean he's dumb. I've got friends down there. They're way cool."

For the rest of the afternoon they chatted and plugged away at wrapping paintings. At five, Albert came up and gave Sophie her two one-hundred-dollar bills. He looked at Bonnie and smiled.

"You combed your hair. It looks like it used to... You look nice."

Bonnie engulfed her father and sobbed. He brought his hands up and fluttered his fingers on her shoulders. She had no memory of the last time he complimented her.

"OK, OK, that's enough. You don't need to get all upset. Let's go down and have a drink."

They sat on the porch and chatted. Bonnie let it out about Sophie's date.

"So, he called you," Albert said. "I told him to, but he said he would never dare. Glad he changed his mind."

"Grandpa, why would you do that? You probably embarrassed him."

"It'll be good for you to meet some new people. He's a hard-working boy -- seems real responsible."

"I just want to go out, that's all. He said he can't come until Sunday to work on your truck."

"That's fine, maybe I can get it registered and inspected next week."

"Can I just drop you off?" Bonnie asked on the drive to Sophie's apartment. "I want to go home and change. I'm going to see if Derek will go out tonight. Do you have any plans?"

"No, not yet. Do you think Maggie will be around?"

"Probably," Bonnie said, "depends if Janice is working or not."

"I'll be fine. I'm tired anyway. I'll check with you tomorrow.

Maggie's car was in the driveway, so Sophie sent her a text.

Hi, can I come down to see you?

Sure come on down. Janice just left for work.

Maggie's apartment had the nice woodwork and windows like Derek's. It was spare and clean. It had a small enclosed porch off the back, under Sophie's room. They sat out there. The evening was warm with a nice breeze.

Maggie brought out two glasses of pink wine.

"I'm so glad you called. I was just going to do housework. This is much better. How're you doing?"

Sophie explained what happened with her mother and father. About her guilt, her excitement, and fear. She felt she could open up to Maggie for some reason. Maggie talked about how she left home and how disappointed her family was.

"Well, enough of that," Sophie said. "I wanted to tell you. Bonnie had her hair done."

Maggie sat up.

"No way! The dreads are gone? I've never seen her without them."

"I'm not judging, but she looks at least ten years younger. She dropped me off because she wanted to change clothes before Derek saw her. She was cute -- like she's nervous about him liking her this way."

"That's too funny. They're an odd match -- kind of on-again, off-again. Must be Bonnie wants to move the relationship along for some reason."

"I have some other news too," Sophie said. "I have a date Saturday night."

"That didn't take long. Who is it?"

"Just a guy that does lawn work and stuff for my grandfather. I don't know him very well, but he seems like a nice guy."

"Where you going?"

"A place called Abilene. I guess it's a dance club or something."

"Uh, it's an older crowd than ya'll but has good music -- different stuff. What're you going to wear?"

"I thought I might look tomorrow. You always have cute clothes. Where do you shop?"

"To tell the truth, I get almost all my clothes at a consignment shop. I can't afford the same stuff new."

"You mean used clothes?"

"Yes ma'am, but they're hardly used. Girls from out in Pittsford buy designer stuff, wear it one time, and then put it in consignment shops to make room in their closets. Of course, they wouldn't be caught dead wearing the same thing twice. Maybe you know the type?"

"Ha, ha, you got me pegged. But that's not me now. Where is it?"

"Let's go together. We'll have a girls' day out. Janice will be sleeping anyway."

"That sounds like fun. I have to go to a bank in the morning. There's one just down the street. But after that, I'm good."

"Let's try for eleven." Maggie said.

"Great, it'll be fun."

EIGHTEEN

Years earlier, her father had taken her to the bank to open an account. Now, Sophie was getting one on her own. After she deposited the two hundred dollars her grandfather had given her, the bank representative activated her debit card. On her way back home, she got a bagel and coffee and didn't have to pay with cash.

Upon reaching the yard, she saw Derek working in a flower bed.

"Hi, Derek! Anything new?"

He looked up.

"Just weedin' this mess."

"No, I mean anything new last night?"

"Oh, Bonnie and I went to a jazz show. It was really good."

Sophie stamped her foot.

"No, you doof. How was Bonnie? Do you like her new haircut?"

"Oh, that. Yeah, I like it a lot -- big change for her. She seems happy with it."

"She did it for you, you know."

"I told her it looks real nice. She ran home – be back this afternoon."

"Fine, Derek... *Have a nice day*."

As she walked away, he thought, *What the hell's up with her*?

Sophie picked up her loft until Maggie texted, and they met at her car. She said they were going over to Monroe Avenue -- another cool neighborhood. When they got there, she parked, and they walked to a store called:

Your Pretty Sister's Closet

"So, Maggie, what do people wear around here, like, to the place where I'm going? I'll probably just wear jeans and look for a top."

"It's such a mix of people here. You'll see everything. Some people dress up, but a lot are casual. Let's just look around."

Sophie looked through the racks of tops. There were some good designer labels, and not all of them were last year's style. She tried on a couple but kept looking. As she was coming back from the changing room, she saw a dress on a mannequin. It was obviously an Alice and Olivia tunic with tiers on the bottom. It had a tile pattern of red, green, and black and just a small slit down the front tied with ribbon -- short, but not mini. It was only ninety dollars. She knew it would be three to four hundred new.

She tried it on. It was a little snug on top.

"Maggie, what do you think of this? Is it too much?"

"Honey, that's you all over. Ya'll might want to loosen the ribbon and give those girls some room to move."

"Maggie, stop. Is it too dressy for tonight?"

"Darlin', you just wear what you like. Don't worry 'bout it."

"I don't know. I don't have any idea what this guy will be wearing or his friends."

"Sophie, you're a city girl and gorgeous. Be who you are; they can be who they are. Buy it if you like it."

They had lunch, and Sophie paid. They got their nails done and stopped for a mocha then went back home.

Sophie tried on her jeans and all her tops then the dress again. She couldn't really see in the bathroom mirror. The dress felt so good and fit her perfectly. She retied the ribbon. The slit became a gap and some cleavage showed but not too much.

It was too early to shower and do her hair and makeup. She tried to sketch. She went for a walk and sketched outside for a little while as the sun was getting lower then went back to get dressed. Finally, her phone buzzed. It was Randall.

In driveway which door are you?

Meet at metal door under the light.

K

As Sophie pushed the door, Randall pulled it open and held it.

"Hi!" he said.

"Hi, Rand... I mean RJ."

Randall turned around. "We'll be riding with my friends tonight."

He was wearing boot-cut jeans with boots, a black and green plaid shirt, and a denim jacket.

Kinda cowboy, but not, Sophie thought.

He opened the driver's side door for her. She swung her legs in and smoothed the dress underneath her. After he closed the door, he took a second to collect himself then went around to the other side.

"Sophie, this is Sue and Tom."

Sue looked back over the seat. "Hi, Sophie. Glad you could join us."

"Nice to meet you," Tom said, eyeing her from the rearview mirror. "Have you been to Abilene before?"

"No, I've only been here a few weeks. This is my first time out."

"I think you'll like it. We'll get dinner then go there."

"I'm sure I will. Thanks for having me."

Randall explained that Tom was a salesman and bid jobs for Lawn Order. They became fishing buddies, so Tom and Sue kept their boat at Randall's family cottage. Sue said she taught Earth Science at a suburban school.

They were shown to a table. After they ordered Tom carried most of the conversation. Eventually Sophie learned that Randall had finished community college with a degree in vineyard management. His father owned a grape farm that had been in his family for three generations. Sophie told them her father was a lawyer and her mother sold real estate, but she tried to avoid the whole Wall Street thing. Randall started to relax and talk about wine. He seemed to be an expert on the wineries around the Finger Lakes. Sue explained how the lakes had been formed by glaciers and how beautiful that area was.

After dinner, they headed to the club where Sue and Sophie went to the ladies' room while Tom and Randall found a table.

Sophie freshened her lipstick.

"That's a beautiful dress," Sue said. "It looks so nice on you. Not many girls could wear it."

"Oh, thanks. I like yours too – so summery. This is fun. Thanks again for having me."

"I should tell you, RJ asked us to come. He was afraid you wouldn't go with him alone."

"I probably wouldn't have."

Sue brushed her hair. "He's a sweet guy. Once he relaxes, he's fun. You'll see."

"He's been nice to my grandpa, so I can tell he's a good guy."

Randall looked across the table at Tom. "What d'ya think of Sophie?"

"She's a nice girl. *Reeeal* nice."

"I know -- out of my league."

"I don't know about that – maybe – probably. Are you ready to get involved again so soon?"

"She won't get involved with me. I'm not worried about that. She didn't say, but her father is a millionaire lawyer in New York City. I met him once. He looked at me like I was a bug. She'll go back home soon, and I'll never see her again."

The ladies returned. RJ stood up and pulled out Sophie's chair. Tom half stood up. Sue pulled out her own chair.

When the server came and asked for their drink order. Sophie smiled at Randall and said, “I’ll have a white wine, would you pick one for me, RJ?”

The band came on. It was twangy, but the female singer was good. It was like country but not really. The songs had nice lyrics. They played a slow song, and Tom and Sue got up to dance.

Sophie could see Randall was getting nervous.

“I've never heard music like this,” She said. “I wouldn’t know how to dance to it.”

“Do you like it?”

“I do, actually. I wonder if they’re on iTunes.”

Sue leaned back as she and Tom danced. “So, what d’ya think of Sophie?”

“There’s nothing I can say that won’t get me in trouble.”

Sue poked his shoulder.

“I don’t mean that dress. What about her?”

“Really smart, well-educated, confident, kinda pretty. Not my type though.”

“Bullshit.”

“See? I got in trouble anyway.”

“I think she's real sweet." Sue said. "Poor RJ. I hope he relaxes. Don’t pick on him.”

They stayed until the band took their second break, sometime after 10:00. When they got back to Derek’s driveway, Randall and Sophie had the awkward first date goodbye. She offered her hand, and he shook it gently.

“Thank you so much. This was nice," Sophie said. "I like Tom and Sue.”

Randall released her hand.

"I wasn’t sure you’d like the place -- or the music. I had fun... It was fun to be with you. Will you be at your grandfather’s tomorrow?”

“I’ll be there. I have to take the bus, so it’ll be later.”

“I have my truck at Tom's. I can pick you up.”

“That would be nice, thanks.

“Is nine too early?”

“Not at all. See you then.”

NINETEEN

Sophie was waiting outside enjoying the morning sun when Randall pulled in.

"This is a big truck," she said as she climbed in.

"It's my work truck. I usually take my bike. I have a car, but it's not on the road right now."

"Do you like doing lawns and stuff like that?"

"It's all right. I like being outside. I like building patios and walls. It looks nice when they're finished, like you did something. What I really want to do is to get a job at a winery doing vineyard management. I've been talking to some people, but I'm kinda young to get a job like that. I'm doing OK right now."

When they got to Albert's house, Randall unloaded the truck parts and opened the garage door.

"I want to show your grandfather the fender and make sure the paint job is right."

"You can't talk to him until after noon," Sophie informed him. "He's painting now."

"It'll just take a minute."

"He won't talk to you until he's done for the day at noon. I can't even go up there now. I just have to hang out."

"Well," Randall said, "I guess I can get started. Hopefully he'll like the color."

"Is there anything I can do to help?" Sophie asked.

"Really? It's easier if someone holds the parts while I bolt 'em on."

To Sophie' surprise, she was actually helpful, and they worked together for a couple hours without stopping. Randall hooked up some wires and made some final adjustments to the grill and inner fender, getting everything ready to put the fender on.

"I guess I'll mow until he comes down, then he can see the fender before I get it fastened on. It feels funny to be working on a Sunday morning. I'm usually in church."

Sophie handed him some iced tea.

"I haven't been in a couple of weeks," she said. "Where do you go?"

"It's a church down in Canandaigua. I've gone there since I was a kid. Most of my friends are from there. It has a great youth program and good music."

"Sounds like my church."

Sophie sipped on her iced tea and looked at Randall. She could see the redness starting on his ears.

"This is where you say, 'Gosh, Sophie, if you wanted to I could take you there next weekend.' Then I say, 'Oh, but that's so far for you to come and get me.' Then you say, 'I don't mind, really. I'd love to have you come with me.'"

Now, the redness had infused his face and neck.

"Or don't you want to take me? Maybe you don't want me to meet your friends. That's all right if you don't."

Now Randall felt the sweat starting. *What is my problem? I'm not like this.*

Sophie could see she had embarrassed him. "I'm sorry, RJ. I shouldn't be so forward. We hardly know each other. I didn't mean to make you uncomfortable."

"I don't know what's wrong with me," he stammered. "Of course, I'd like to take you to church."

Before Sophie could say more, Albert came over and inspected the work on his truck.

"Looks like you're almost done."

Randall unwrapped the fender.

"I wanted you to see the paint before I put it on - make sure it looks right to you."

"It looks fine. I just want it to pass inspection. Here, I'll hold it up for you."

Albert's tremor made it difficult, but eventually Randall got all the bolts in. After a few minor adjustments he tightened everything down. He checked all the lights and turn signals.

Sophie made grilled cheese sandwiches for everyone, and after lunch she went up to the studio and started working. Albert and Randall finished their beers.

"Mr. Martel, I was thinking. You said you wanted to get the truck registered. You can't register it without insurance, and you can't get insurance on a vehicle without a driver's license. I just happened to think of that."

"You can't insure a truck without a driver's license?"

"It's no big deal. You just gotta get your license before you insure it. I guess I'll start mowing."

"I'll get your money," Albert said. "I'll be sleeping when you're done. How was your date with Sophie?"

"It was fun, but I'm just so lame around her. She makes me nervous."

"She's pushy. Don't take her crap; give it back to her. You'll get along better if you do."

When Sophie heard the mower stop, she went down to the garage. Randall was in the driveway hosing off the mower deck.

"That's a nice backboard," he said. "Who's was it?"

"My Dad's when he was a kid. Do you play basketball?"

"Just two or three times a week now. I used to play a lot. I've got a ball in the truck. C'mon, we'll play some one-on-one."

"I haven't played in a long time," Sophie warned.

"You afraid to break a nail, girly-girl?"

"Hey, I put the truck together for you. You couldn't've done it without me."

"Well then, let's see what you got. I'll get the ball."

They played. She hoisted up shots from her waist; he shot over her. She slapped at the ball as he dribbled; he left her falling down with a crossover. There was some incidental contact and some intentional fouls on her part. She got up close and pushed her hand against his chest. His shirt was moist. He smelled of gasoline and man sweat. He faked right, spun left, took one dribble, and dunked the ball.

"OK, OK, show-off, I'm done. You can get me some iced tea now."

They sat on the picnic table and laughed. Sophie noticed his face wasn't pinched together. His smile was real; his eyes were soft.

"Would you mind driving me back to my apartment? It'll take forever by bus now."

"Sure, I have to get going anyway. My mom will be expecting me for dinner."

When they got to the apartment Randall told her, "I won't need to mow again til next week. Do you still want to go on Sunday? I go to the eleven o'clock service."

"I'd like that. Text me this week sometime; we'll figure it out. Thanks for the ride."

She impulsively kissed him on the cheek.

"Thanks again…for everything," he said. "See you next Sunday."

On the drive home, Randall tried to concentrate on his week ahead. *I'm just not going to think about her. There's no point. She's just messin' with my head.*

Sophie took a shower and did some sketching outside but couldn't get into it. *What was that all about? I shouldn't give him the wrong impression. I need to keep focused on me.*

Andy and Lillian tried to have a good time with the Andrews. They went out on their boat and went to some wineries. Lillian hoped they didn't hear her and Andy arguing Saturday night. Andy refused to drive up to Rochester and see Sophie on Sunday. He said they had to stick to their plan and let her get lonely and tired of struggling on her own. She had to come to them. He would wait a week; by then he would need to meet with the realtor anyway. Jack had done great at camp, and Andy didn't feel it was fair to let Sophie's selfishness detract from him.

When they got home Sunday night, Lillian called Sophie.

"Hi, Hon. Sorry we didn't get up to see you. We didn't leave Ithaca until later."

"That's OK. I worked at Grandpa's most of the day. How's Jack?"

"He had a great week. The coach said he was one of the top five golfers there. He got a chance to walk around Cornell, and he really liked it. He seems happy with how he did. How are you doing?"

"Really well. I've made friends with the girl that lives downstairs. The guy that owns the house is really nice too. How's Daddy doing?"

"He wants you to come home. He's worried about you. I can't believe you're throwing away the chance to go to Paris."

"I know he is. I just hope he can understand. He needs to listen to me. This is important -- more important than Paris."

"I don't know about that," Lillian said. "Do you need anything?"

"No, I got my own bank account and card. I'm doing fine."

"Sophie, you're getting too settled up there. I want you to pray on this and get yourself together. I've had just about enough of it. You need to get back home."

"We've been through all this. I'm glad Jack did well. I'll text him. I'll call you later this week. Goodbye. Tell Daddy I love him."

"Sophie, please think about it."

"Bye, Mom. I love you."

TWENTY

Monday morning, Bonnie and Sophie got more supplies and groceries before going to Albert's. He had pulled the mower out and was wiping it down and cleaning out the tires. Randall had done a pretty good job, but Albert couldn't help checking it over.

"Hey, Bonnie," he called to his daughter, "can I talk to you a minute?"

They went out to the picnic table while Sophie carried in the groceries.

"The truck is ready to get registered, but I was thinking it would be better if we registered it in your name. Then when I kick off, it'll already be done and save you a lotta work. If you don't keep it then it'd be easier to sell. I'll still get my license, but this part would be done. We need the truck to get the house cleaned up."

"Dad, nothing's going to happen to you. We can wait on stuff like that."

"I could keel over sitting here. Face it, Bonnie, we have to take care of some of these things. I'm just looking ahead for you. You'll be the one to have to mess with it."

"I'm sure Andy will take over. He always does."

"Well, whatever, it would be a load off my mind if you'd do it. We can walk up to the corner and get the insurance then go to the DMV."

Sophie came down for another load of bubble wrap.

"I'm taking Dad to get his truck registered," Bonnie informed her. "Going to the DMV, so who knows how long it'll take. Do you need anything?"

"No. That'll be good. He wants to get that thing on the road. See you later."

Albert had all his papers in order, so the process went as well as could be expected. He also picked up the forms for getting his license reinstated.

Bonnie worked full days the next three. Each evening she made dinner for Derek. Sophie enjoyed walking around "her neighborhood." She was getting to know some of the people at the coffee shops. Maggie and Janice joined her one evening, other times she worked on her sketches. Randall texted her every day. She couldn't help hinting she was available in the evenings, but he didn't bite.

Wednesday evening, Sophie went for dinner with Bonnie, Janice, and Maggie. They had just been served dessert when Randall called. Sophie stepped away and took the call then came back and started on her cake.

"Well? Was that farm-boy?" Maggie asked.

"Yep," Sophie said and sipped her coffee.

"And… is he coming to see you?"

"Not until Sunday. He's 'putting up hay' all weekend."

"What does that mean?" Janice asked.

"I have no idea, but it sounded important."

≈

Andy came home early Thursday and got in nine holes with Jack before dark. He was back in form and beat his son by three strokes. Lillian was home cleaning when they got there. She turned off the vacuum when they came in.

"Hi, Lil, did you've a good run?"

"I didn't go - didn't feel like it. I haven't started dinner. There's some leftover potato salad. Cook some burgers or something. I'm not hungry."

"Come on Lil, let's go for a walk. Jack, could you grill some burgers, please?"

Lillian let Andy take her out to the gardens.

"I know this is hard on you."

"I can't stand it anymore. You've got to do something."

"I talked to the realtor today. He has a meeting with a developer on Monday. I'm going to take the limo to Rochester on Wednesday to talk it over. You can come. We can talk with Sophie again. We'll get her back home. I promise."

It had been a couple of Thursdays since Bagger and Albert had been to the Back Door.

"I thought you two had run off somewhere," Mrs. Beasley said when she saw them come in. "What's been going on?"

"It took this long to recover from the last time we ate here," Albert said. "We're back for more punishment."

"I'll get your drinks."

Mrs. Beasley set a Genesee Cream Ale and a shot of whiskey in front of each man.

"I didn't order any whiskey," Albert protested. "Why'd you bring that?"

Mrs. Beasley put the shot to her lips and knocked it back.

"Thanks for the drink, Al. Anything else I can get you?"

Albert had the meatloaf. Bagger had lasagna. Neither could face a steak while remembering the last ones they had with Andy.

"So, Pablo, did you get that Chevy running?" Bagger asked.

"I did. I'm still sore, but I did it. The kid got the new fender and grill on. It's all registered and inspected."

"Now all that's done, who's going to drive it?"

"I'll have my license soon. I got the papers all filled out. I'll mail them tomorrow, and soon they'll send it to me."

"I thought you had to take classes."

"Yeah, just a couple of hours. I'll get that done. Don't you worry. I'll have it in a week or less."

"That's mighty quick for the DMV."

"It's all computerized now -- lots faster. How's Eugenia doing?"

Bagger couldn't help but notice Albert's improved mood. He had cleaned himself up and was looking forward again.

The Spirit of the Lord must be movin' through him, he thought. Nothin' else could get him to change.

TWENTY ONE

Lillian finally found a time on Friday when she could get together with Mrs. Kowalski. They met at a coffee shop in town and settled into a booth.

"Is floor good still?" Mrs. Kowalski asked.

"Yes, it still looks like new. My husband loved it," Lillian said.

"And how is Mr. Martel? Very busy I s'pose."

"He is, but he's been trying to spend more time at home with our son."

"Your son, how old?"

"He's seventeen, starting his senior year of high school. Do you have children, Mrs. Kowalski?"

"Please, I am called Dottie. I have two sons and daughter. My sons, very happy. One graduate community college. He does something with the computers, has seven people to work for him. The other, he is in construction like his father, but as crew chief -- builds big houses like yours. They give me three grandchildren. My daughter, she is twenty-six years, not yet married. You have daughter, no?"

"I do. She just graduated from college -- doesn't know what she wants to do yet. She's living in Rochester at the moment, helping her grandfather."

"Is good she help grandfather. She sound like fine daughter. Many old people have strangers only to help. He sick, the grandfather?"

"Not really. He's selling his house and needs help getting things organized. It isn't really where I want her to be."

"She is how old, your daughter?"

"Twenty-one. I know, she's an adult, but I just don't think she's ready to be on her own."

"She is not ready... or you not ready?"

"I miss her more than I did when she was at college. We were just starting to understand each other. We were opening up. Now I'm afraid I'll never have that again. She's my first, my girl."

"My daughter, she get money go free to college. She go four years – did not find husband. Now she live in Boston, working in office full with men – still no husband. I too miss her. We were close.

"It sounds like she's very successful."

"Yes, she is successful," Mrs. Kowalski said, " but happy? I am not sure.

I really did never understood her, but she loved me and was good daughter. I cry when she move away. Mister Kowalski, he too cry."

"I guess it's part of growing older," Lillian said. "You expect it but aren't really prepared when it happens.

Mrs. Kowalski reached across the table and pulled Lillian's slim, manicured fingers into her thick, chapped hands.

"I tell you what my mother say to me when I leave home. She say, 'There is pain to bring child into world, but pain to let go is worse.' It must be done. If stay too long, they do not grow."

"It's just not happening the way I had it planned. I'm worried."

"We are not to worry, my dear. God's will be done -- in His time, not ours. Trust Him."

≈

Sophie worked all day Saturday and rode the bus home. She was walking back from dinner as light rain and darkness fell together. She just made it home before the rain could soak her. As she was toweling her hair, her phone buzzed. She recognized Randall's number.

"Hi, RJ."

"Hi, sorry to call so late. We just got done with the hay – missed the rain by half an hour."

"That's fine, I just got back from dinner. I worked all day too."

"I was thinking... you seemed interested in wine. Would you like to go to some wineries after church?"

"Just the two of us?"

"Is that OK?"

"Sounds like fun. Will we be taking your motorcycle?"

"I got my car back on the road. We could ride the bike, but we wouldn't be able to buy any wine."

"The car would be good. Sorry to ask so many questions."

"I understand. You're just being smart. I'm sorry, but I gotta put away the tractors. I'll see you in the morning."

"Bye, RJ, thanks for calling."

Sophie clicked off. *Whoever thought I'd know a guy who has to put away his tractors?*

Randall backed the tractors into their shed and went into the barn. The hay was neatly stacked in the mow. On this day, the roulette wheel that is farming had paid off. The gathering rainstorm beat on the roof and the earthy fragrance of the fresh breeze melded with that of the new hay.

Daryl got a cooler out of his truck, brought it into the barn, and handed Randall a beer.

"Well, your dad should be happy. We got both fields done before it got wet. Nice hay too. I guess he was too tired to wait for a beer."

"He's slowin' down for sure. I wonder how much longer he can do it. But anyway, thanks for your help, dude. We got 'er done, didn't we?"

"That we did, my man. My ass is draggin' though. Hey, did ya call that girl?"

"Yeah... Have you ever done something you know you're going to regret?"

"Not today yet. Night is young though."

Randall took a long pull on the cold beer. "I've made a list of why this relationship is doomed. Her father's a millionaire;

I've got nothing. She's city; I'm country. She's smart – been to real college. I got a degree in killing weeds and bugs. I just got dumped. I should be playin' ball, fishin', and workin' – not chasin' another girl around fixin' to get busted-up again."

"But?" Daryl asked.

Randall picked at the beer label. "I can't stop thinking about her. And not just her looks; that's not it. I've never felt this way. Not even with Angela."

"You got it bad, boy. You gotta stop sellin' yourself short. You're a winner – always have been."

"This isn't basketball, but thanks, man. I'll take another beer."

TWENTY TWO

It was still raining Sunday morning. Sophie waited in her room until Randall texted from the driveway. He was driving a medium-sized, four-door car. When she got in, the smell reminded her of her father's car after she cleaned it. There were new brown seat covers and shiny rubber floor mats. He was wearing a generic polo shirt, cargo shorts, and a green windbreaker with a big white N on the front.

"Still raining," Randall said. "Thank God this wasn't yesterday. We would've lost a lotta hay."

"Where would it have gone?"

"No, it would've been ruined -- got wet -- couldn't have baled it even if we raked it again."

"Oh," said Sophie, "I guess that'd be bad."

"You don't have a clue what I'm talking about, do you?"

"I know what hay is. Horses eat it. Do you have horses?"

"No, but we take it to a racetrack in New York City. They pay top dollar, but it has to be perfect."

"Sounds complicated."

"Ever heard 'make hay while the sun shines?'"

"Yeah, I guess."

“Well, that’s what we did. It's a good feeling to have dry hay in the barn."

"I don't know much about farming," Sophie said.

"It's all I know about," Randall said with resignation.

The route took them on expressways and down a commercial street of car dealers and fast food places. Sophie was surprised when they came into Canandaigua. There was a wide Main Street with beautiful homes and cute shops. After about a half hour, they pulled into a large parking lot and joined many others walking into the church.

Everything about the church was familiar to Sophie. The greeters at the door were friendly. It had a coffee bar and tables in the foyer. She noticed a group of girls and guys staring at her and Randall as they went by.

The service was in a gym with basketball nets folded up to the ceiling. There was an elevated stage with video screens above and a smaller platform for the pastor, below the stage. There was a countdown clock on the screen. When it hit 00:00 the band struck their opening chord. Sophie knew the song. She looked to see if Randall was singing. He was, so she did too. They sang two upbeat songs, had announcements, and welcomed the first-time guests. When the baskets came around for the offering, Randall put some cash in. Sophie put in a five. After that, there were three quieter songs and the message. It was based on Psalm 118:24: *This is the day the Lord has made. Be glad and rejoice in it.*

As they sang the closing song, Sophie thought, *Wouldn't that be a blessed way to live? Just trust and enjoy every day, no matter what happens. Something to strive for.*

On the way out, two girls approached. One was tall and pretty. Her blonde hair was up in a chignon. The other was shorter and plain.

"Hey, RJ, what've you been doin'?" the taller one asked. "I haven't seen you lately."

"I've been busy, mostly working. This is Sophie… She wanted to check out the church."

"Nice to meet you," the short one said. "Where are you from?"

"I live in Rochester. Sorry, I'd love to chat, but Randall and I have plans."

"Your friends will have something to gossip about over coffee, won't they?" Sophie said when they got outside.

"I've known them a long time. Yeah, they'll gossip. That's what they do."

"Did I embarrass you? I didn't mean to."

"Just a little awkward – not your fault. No big deal."

"So, where are we going?"

"I thought we'd cut over to Keuka Lake and have lunch at Heron Hill. Then check out Dr. Frank and come around the other side of the lake and hit a couple more wineries on the way to Penn Yan and back to Rochester."

"I've never heard of any of those places," Sophie said.

"They're some of the best wineries in the area. And it's a really pretty drive."

At the first winery Randall knew the taster. He gleaned information from her about who was leaving, who was getting hired, and what was happening behind the scenes. Sophie bought one bottle of a rosé that reminded her of Provence.

They stopped at Dr. Frank. It was very crowded, so they waited on the patio. Randall stood in line while Sophie admired the view. Mist was rising from the lake below and flowing over the hill beneath thin clouds retreating to the east. Sophie imagined herself as a figure in a Monet. A splash of black hair, dying rose of her skin, and a splotch of purple blouse set against the soft greens and pale blue sky. Out of the corner of her eye she saw Randall staring at her. She held her hair behind her ear to reveal her profile, waited a beat, then turned her tilted face toward him. He blushed but then smiled. She smiled back and locked her eyes on his until he glanced away. She turned and continued to study the landscape.

At each winery, Randall discussed the finer points of the wines and how they were made. Sophie learned more about wine than she thought there was to know.The drive back was sublime. The sun was low--shadows sharp. The rain-washed air was crystalline. Every tree on every distant hill was distinct. They were passing through Mennonite Country. Composed against the green and gold fields were barns, silos, jigsaw-patterned cows, and flower gardens in front of white porches. They passed buggies pulled by shining horses carrying men dressed in black and women in calico dresses. Impossibly cute kids, hanging out the back, stared from under hats and bonnets. It was like being transported to a different time and place. There was a lifetime of paintings to be made just along this one road.

Despite the scenery Sophie's mind kept returning to the girls at church. *Why was he so shy and uncomfortable?*

They pulled into her driveway.

"RJ, this was a wonderful day. I can't thank you enough. I had no idea there were places like that in New York. I had a fabulous time and thanks for taking me to church. I needed that."

"I'm so glad you could come. I... it was... a really great day."

"RJ, can I ask you something personal?"

"I guess."

"Do you have a girlfriend?"

He hesitated.

"Do you?" she asked again.

"I did... a fiancée. She broke it off in February."

"You were going to get *married*?"

"After she was done with college, but she met someone else. I haven't dated anyone since then. Maybe that's why I'm so awkward with you. I don't mean to be."

"I'm sorry. I shouldn't have been so forward. It's none of my business. You must still be hurting."

"It was a shock. I'm fine now. No big deal."

They met in front of the car. It was just an A-frame hug -- brief and reserved -- but full of softness and the smell of her hair.

"Can I call you tomorrow?"

"Yes, RJ, we can talk."

Sophie took her wine to the door and watched him go out the driveway.

Now, She was sure she couldn't even think about getting involved with him. It was too soon for him, and she wasn't going to be a rebound. She would keep it friendly, but that's all. She got out her sketch pad and recorded the day's scenes.

TWENTY THREE

Monday morning greeted Sophie with rain. She wore her raincoat and hat but still got wet waiting for the bus. It was a miserable ride, followed by an equally miserable walk to the studio. Albert joined her at about ten o'clock and started to help.

"Where's Bonnie?" he asked.

"She stayed at her friend's house again last night. She said she wouldn't be back until later today."

"We don't have much for lunch."

"I can look. There must be something."

Albert pulled a painting off the rack. "I remember this one. It was shortly after I met Elaine de Kooning. It's one of the first abstracts I did. She was into cave paintings at the time. I did it at the zoo."

"How'd you meet her?" Sophie asked.

"There was a bar, The Cedar Tavern, where artists hung out -- Elaine and Bill, Rothko, Motherwell, Kline. Pollock had died in '56. I was doing a sketch, and she came over to look. We got to talking. She told me to stop by her studio sometime, so I did. We could take the truck to get groceries."

"Did she give you lessons?"

"We worked a little together in her studio, but then I took classes from her later on. I'm sure you could drive the truck; it's not hard."

"Grandpa, lunch can wait. I'm interested in how you got started."

"I could always draw. It was the de Koonings -- Elaine and Bill -- that taught me about making real art -- my own art. We can talk more over lunch. C'mon."

Sophie remembered trying to drive her father's SUV. She was afraid she would hit something because it was so big and hard to see out of.

"I'm used to little cars. I don't like big trucks. I don't want to crash into some-thing."

"Just try it here on this side street," Albert said.

He got the garage door open and gave Sophie the key.

"Start it up like anything else.".

The truck started easily.

"Where's the shifter thing?" Sophie asked.

"It's the lever behind the steering wheel."

Sophie started slowly out of the garage and onto the street. The steering wheel was harder to turn than in her car. She drove carefully by the parked cars and pulled into the church parking lot.

"Just drive around here and get used to turning it," Albert said. "You'll see; it isn't hard."

She turned some circles then pulled into a parking spot.

“I guess it's not that bad. I’ll try backing up.” She backed out and turned towards the exit. “Do you know how to get to that Wegmans place?”

Sophie was proud of herself for driving and getting her own groceries. During lunch she quizzed her grandfather about New York. He opened up somewhat. He had studied at The Cooper Union where Elaine de Kooning taught. He also took other classes on his off-duty time. He had planned to finish art school after his enlistment.

“That didn’t work out," he said, "so I moved back here.”

By Albert’s nap time the rain had picked up again.

“You did so good with the truck,” he told Sophie, “why don’t you drive it back to your place? It’d be better than the bus.”

“I don’t want to take your truck. It might get hurt. The bus isn’t that bad.”

“Well, think about it. I’ll see you after my nap.”

Sophie had a cozy feeling the rest of the afternoon. The rain drummed on the roof while a soft light filled the studio. She studied the paintings. A progression was starting to show. There were fewer landscapes but more and more impressionistic images leaning to abstract. His palette changed to bolder, more primary colors. Around four o'clock Albert came back in; his yellow slicker was dripping.

“Sure you don’t want to drive home?”

“I guess I could,” Sophie said. “Maybe this one time because it’s raining.”

She pulled the truck out of the garage. She asked her phone for directions and stayed in the right lane as much as possible.

The traffic wasn't bad at all. The drivers were nowhere near as obnoxious as downstate.

When she arrived at her place, she parked next to Maggie's car. She felt liberated from the chains of the bus schedule and glad to be home early.

≈

Lillian had a late-afternoon showing on Monday. Andy ordered out after the limo dropped him off.

"It's all set for Wednesday," he said. "The limo will be here before six. We have a lunch meeting with the realtor, then we'll go see Dad and Sophie. I have to work on the way. Will you have something to do?"

"I can do some bookkeeping," Lillian said, "and I need to set up the closing on the duplex. Will that disturb you?"

"No, that'll be good. We can both get some work done."

"What are you going to say to Sophie?"

"I'm sticking with the plan – offer Paris again. The other factor is, if this is going to take a long time, there's no hurry on storing the paintings. I can tell her she can always come back to it. Really, it's Dad who's the problem. He's trying to keep her there. He's the one that needs to change."

"At least we can all sit down together and discuss it. That's a start."

That evening Lillian spent some time praying and thinking about what Mrs. Kowalski had said. It wasn't time to bring it up with Andy, but maybe they had to face some facts. Maybe they were the ones who needed to change.

TWENTY FOUR

The limo was right on time Wednesday morning, and Andy and Lillian were on the road by 6:00.

"Thanks for this, Jeff," Andy told the driver. "It's going to be a long day."

"I enjoy these long trips – get some different scenery, get out of the traffic. What time's your meeting?"

"Noon or so."

"Sounds good. Let me know if you want to stop along the way."

Lillian pulled the fold-out desk into place and started working on her spread-sheets. She had trouble concentrating.

How did it happen I'm married to this wonderful man, riding in a limousine, crunching six figure numbers from my own business? How did it happen? Where has the time gone?

For five hours, Jeff expertly chauffeured them along the Thruway and onto the expressways of Rochester. He followed his navigation system and pulled into a congested area next to the Erie Canal. Don was waiting outside and escorted them into Richardson's Canal House. They settled into a secluded table.

"This is lovely," Lillian said.

"I thought you would like it," Don said.

"Glad it's on your expense account," Andy joked.

Don laughed. "You can make it up to me in Manhattan someday. I think it'll wash. Well anyway, I met with the developer I know. He's the CEO of a non-profit that does senior and low-income housing, among many other things. He has a grant he needs to use for housing. Your father's lot would be a good fit. However, as I said on the phone, zoning is a problem."

"Can't we get a variance?" Andy asked.

"This guy has pull -- a lot of connections at the local, county and even state level. He thinks it can be done, but he won't commit until the zoning is resolved. He's willing to do what he can, but it's definitely going to be a long-term project."

"What about a private developer?" Lillian asked.

"I doubt a private developer would have the juice to get the zoning changed. If they did, they wouldn't be the kind of people I want to work with, if you know what I mean."

"I work in Manhattan. I know what you mean. Any chance someone would want it for a single residence?" Andy asked.

"That would be my suggestion for right now," Don replied. "Get it on the market, set a fairly high price, and see what happens. If we get a reasonable offer, great, if not we keep working with my friend at Corner Stone, the non-profit I was talking about. What'll your dad think?"

"He'll be convinced us capitalists are trying to steal his property. Go ahead and get a sign up. We're on our way to talk to him after this."

On the way to Albert's house, Andy turned to Lillian.

"You take Sophie and talk to her somewhere. I want to talk to Dad alone first."

"Good idea. Maybe we can go up to the studio."

Albert was on the porch having his afternoon fortified coffee and Sophie was cleaning up after lunch when the limo pulled in.

Could he be any more ostentatious? Albert thought. *Who does he think he's impressing?*

Sophie came out of the house and hugged her mother as she got out of the car. Then she ran around to the other side and nearly tackled her father.

"Daddy, I missed you! I'm so glad you're here."

"I missed you too, Cookie. I've been worried. We need to talk."

"We can talk. You'll see I'm doing fine, but I missed you so much."

"C'mon Sophie," Lillian said, "Show me Grandpa's paintings. I want to learn more about them. Dad and Grandpa are going to talk about the house."

Andy slowly walked up the porch steps.

"Do you want a beer?" Albert asked. "Does your chauffeur need anything?"

"He has stuff in the car. I don't want a beer. Let's talk. I met with the realtor."

Andy explained the situation and how they had left it. Don would be coming by to put up a sign and would start advertising.

"I wouldn't put the price too high," Albert said. "I want it sold. I don't need all that much. I would rather sell it low than be stuck here any longer."

"We want to get a fair price. We can't just give it away. Anyway, Don knows where to start. We can always adjust it. It does mean we should get the place cleaned out in case someone wants to look at it."

"I can take care of that. I may need an advance to hire some help, though.

"I'll have Geoff set up an escrow account you can draw on for expenses. He'll give you a sort of checkbook. Anything else about the house?"

"No, I guess not. When are you heading back?" Albert asked.

"Not right away. I want to talk about Sophie. This whole thing has disrupted her plans – really set her back. I want you to make her understand she should come back home."

"I've tried to tell you before. I did try to talk her out of it. I told her she shouldn't get stuck in Rochester. She wants to stay."

"She wants to stay because you manipulated her and turned her against me. I know how you work. She'll listen to you either way, so get her to come back to us. I want her home with me."

"Who the hell do you think you are coming here in your limousine and telling me what to do? I'm not one of your lackeys. She's learning more about life living here than she ever has in the one-percenter world you want to trap her in."

“She belongs in that world," Andy said. "She has too much on the ball to waste her time packing up your worthless paintings. Admit it, you’re doing this to get at me. Find some other way, and leave my daughter out of it.”

“I’m not trying to get at anybody. All I want is to get out of this place and away from all of you. I want this place sold and sold soon. If you can’t do it, I’ll hire my own damn realtor.”

“You can’t for ninety days. Just talk to Sophie. You know I’m right.”

Andy turned his back to his father and headed down the porch steps and made his way up to the studio.

“How did it go?” Lillian asked.

Andy glared at her. “Not good – about as I expected. Sophie, I want you to listen to me. Don’t jump to conclusions; just listen first. I know you think you're helping your Grandfather. I know you think he's just a harmless old man who needs help.”

“He does need help, and I’m learning from him.”

“That’s what he wants you to believe. These paintings don’t need to be cared for like this. He’s just paying to keep you here. He and I have a complicated relationship. Anyway, he's using you to aggravate me. It’s just the way he is.”

“Dad, you're so wrong.”

“I've given you everything you have. I have loved you your whole life, not him. I want what's best for you. He wants to use you. He doesn’t care about you -- he doesn’t care about anyone. I know it's harsh, but that's the truth.”

“Dad, you're missing something really important here. Say you're right, that he's like what you say. That means I need to be here even more. I need to teach him that people care about him so he can learn to care about others. You believe that, don't you?"

"It's not your responsibility to save him."

"I believe it is."

"You're throwing away your opportunity to study in Paris. You've always wanted to do that. I should have sent you. I was wrong. I want to make it up to you. Come home; you'll go to Paris. This place won't sell for months and months. After that, if you still want to come back, I'll get you an apartment here."

"Dad, sometimes plans have to change. I'm staying here. As much as I want to do what you want and be with you, I know this is the right thing. I'm sorry. I really am."

Andy sat down and turned away. Lillian went to him. He let her hold him briefly .

"I want to be alone a minute, " he said.

Lillian and Sophie went outside. Sophie sat on the bench by the lawn, Lillian went to sit with Albert.

"Andy is really upset," Lillian said. "He's worried about Sophie."

"I know he is," Albert said. "I can understand that. What I can't understand is why he blames me. I've told her to go home; she won't. She thinks her god is telling her to stay."

"What do you mean?"

"She says she prayed, and her god told her this is where she should be -- here with me.

"She never said that to me."

Lillian went over to Sophie.

"Do you feel you're being called to be here?" she asked her daughter.

"Who told you that?"

"Your grandfather."

"He doesn't believe it. Why would he tell you?"

"Is it true? Is that what you believe?"

"I didn't want to say. Dad -- and probably you -- would think I was just using God as an excuse. I'm not. I know I need to be here. I'll do whatever it takes and accept the consequences."

"Wait here. I'm going to talk to your father."

Lillian could see Andy had been crying.

"I want her back, Lil. I don't want to lose her, especially to him."

"We just have to give it more time. I miss her too. You're not losing her. You're her father, nobody is more important to her – even now. It's just something she has to do."

"She doesn't have to. She's got herself trapped by my father."

"Andy, we did our best to raise her as a Christian, right?"

"Of course. We took her to church. We sent on the mission trips and all that."

"We did more than that. She has a real faith, Andy. She feels in her heart God wants her here. I believe she's sincere."

"Now she brings God into it? Are you both blind? Can't you see what he's doing?"

"What your dad is doing?" Lillian asked.

"Who else?"

“So, this isn’t really about Sophie, is it? It’s all about you and your father.”

"If you’re not on my team I should just forget it," Andy snapped. "Let’s go home.”

He went back to the porch.

“Don will be bringing a sign. Tell him what price you want. Give it away for all I care. I don’t give a damn anymore. Geoff will call you later this week.”

He then went over and sat on the bench with Sophie.

"Cookie, I know you're growing up, but all of us, no matter how old we are, sometimes have to admit someone else knows more about a situation than we do. This is one of those times. I'm telling you I'm right, and you don't have enough information to make this decision. I want you to come home with us today."

"Daddy, you have no idea how this is breaking my heart. I want to be with you, but this is bigger than any one of us. Please trust me. I know this is the right thing to do. I'm not coming home."

Andy felt the breath go out of him and a weight rounded his shoulders. He took another look at his daughter and walked back to the car.

Sophie followed behind and went to her mother.

“We'll be back soon,” Lillian promised. “If your dad can’t get away, I’ll come. Call me more often. Let me know what’s going on, please.”

“I will Mom. Try to get Dad to understand. It’s awful having him mad at me.”

“I'll help him get through it. Bye baby; we’ll talk soon.”

Lillian went back to Albert. "I had hoped she'd come home," she said," but she's made up her mind."

"This is exactly what I didn't want to happen. I just want to get out of everybody's way and be alone. I'm sorry I'm disrupting your life."

"We should have known it wouldn't be easy. It'll work out. Goodbye."

When they got on the Thruway, Andy opened the bar and took out a bottle of scotch. He poured himself three fingers and stared out the window as he sipped it. After his second glass, he reclined the seat and went to sleep. Lillian knew this mood. Talking would not help right now.

“That went even worse than I expected,” Sophie told her grandfather.

“He’s right," Albert said. "You should have gone home with them.”

“That would have been the easy way. I hate disappointing my father. I would love to go to Paris."

“You’re willing to give that all up to stay with me? Why would you do that? It makes no sense.”

“I’m not going to be a hypocrite. I believe God wants me here. He wants me to be with you.”

Albert shook his head. “I’m late for my nap. Will I see you later?”

"I'll stay for dinner."

Sophie worked until the light in the studio warmed then dimmed. She made dinner and cleaned up. Albert was quiet all evening. She left him on the porch smoking a cigarette.

Back at her apartment there was nothing she could do but turn out the light and try to sleep away what she saw in the eyes of her father.

TWENTY FIVE

Another Thursday night came, and Bagger drove into the driveway. Albert came out to the porch to see him setting a cardboard box on the picnic table.

"Eugenia made us dinner. I thought we could eat here. She did up a mess a short ribs."

"I'll get some beers," Albert said.

Bagger set out paper plates, plastic forks, and foil-wrapped pans of ribs, corn-bread, coleslaw, and beans.

"Who else is coming?" Albert asked upon seeing all the food.

"She can't stand see no one go hungry. You know that."

They slowly worked on the ribs and sipped at their beers. Bagger mostly picked at his.

"Don't got much of an appetite, Pablo," he said.

They got to laughing about old times, the characters they had known, and the pranks they had played. They marveled at the physical feats they once performed and laughed at themselves as they were today.

"We sure have been through some times," Albert said. "We sure have. I take it you got something you want to say since you got me here alone."

"That's true. You guessed it."

"Well, get on with it."

"You've been a good friend, and I hope I've been a friend to you."

"You're the only one left that'll put up with me."

"I'm doing poorly, Al. They want me to go on a kidney machine. I ain't gonna do it, so I won't last long. There's some things I have to get off my chest before it's too late. Will you listen to me?"

"Is it about Vermont?"

"Well, yes, and some other things."

"Bagger, I won't be around much longer either. That's why I have to move -- to keep some independence, not be dependent on my family."

"Al, we is old. We ain't never gonna be on our own again. Who would you rather be dependent on -- some strangers in Vermont or your own family here at home? Albert, these people love you. You ain't perfect, for sure, but they still love you."

"My son, Andy, he wishes I was dead. He thinks I'm stealing his daughter. My own daughter circles me like a buzzard waiting to move into my house. The rest of 'em don't know me well enough to hate me."

"That ain't true, Albert. They may not always like you, but they love you because you're their father. That's the kind of love they have. You just need to believe that."

“If I believe in love, then I might have to believe in God. If I believe in God, then I've given up. It would mean I've become afraid to live life as it is. I’m too old to change what I believe.”

“You ain’t never too old to change. People change on their death beds. The Good Lord is just waiting for you to say 'yes' to Him. You gotta give up your pride. Stop being afraid. Have some joy before it’s too late.”

“Bagger, all that's a comfort to you. I don’t believe in it. I would be a hypocrite to change. I've lived my whole life without it. I’m not going to give in now. Life is only what you see; no amount of wishful thinking can change it.”

“It tears me up to hear you say that. I feel like I've failed, after all these years, to bring you to Jesus.”

“I know you mean well. Your conscience can rest easy; you tried. I’m not your responsibility anymore.”

“I pray for you every day. The Lord will answer in His time, not mine.”

After Bagger left, Albert went up to the studio and sat in his library. He looked at the shelves full of books -- old books, worn books, books by self-assured geniuses who had all the answers -- even if the answer was: There are no answers. He sat for a while in deep contemplation.

A man’s life is an act shaped by the books he reads and the books he doesn’t. There are so many scripts to follow in this theater of life. Why one and not the other? In the end we're alone on this stage; we play our role without direction. We have to hit the marks we set. We have to deliver the lines we write. We can’t pass that responsibility off. If Sophie and Bagger want to play martyrs, so be it. I can't stop them. But why do they do it, and why do I feel better when they're with me?

TWENTY SIX

After Randall was done mowing on Friday, he and Sophie walked down to Park Avenue for lunch. Sophie tried to keep it light but couldn't help talking about what happened with her parents. Randall seemed sincerely concerned and listened to her think through what had happened.

He really is a nice guy, Sophie thought, *but I can't let this go any further. Oh but his eyes are so inviting. He doesn't look at me like other men do.*

"RJ," Sophie said, "this has been nice. You're being a good friend."

"But... that's all you want... right?"

"I just don't think this is a good time for either of us. I'm, like, in over my head here. You just broke up. We both need a friend but not a boyfriend or girlfriend."

"I'm over that. She wasn't the person I thought she was. She changed in college, but I'm glad it happened. Getting married would have been a disaster."

"That's the other thing. She became different than you, just like we're so different from each other now. We don't have much in common."

"Will you come to church with me again?" he asked.

"I'll meet you there. I'm driving Grandpa's truck now. Can you believe it?"

"Not really. You don't seem like the truck type."

Sophie was going to answer with a flirty "What type do you think I am?" but didn't.

"It's better than the bus. I'm getting used to it," she said.

They slowly walked up the crowded avenue back to Albert's. They stood next to Randall's motorcycle.

"I guess I won't see you until Sunday," Randall said.

"Maybe we can have coffee after the service."

"Yeah, see you then." He pushed on his helmet then kicked the motor until it growled. Sophie listened as the sound of the big bike faded to grumbling thunder in the distance.

As she headed to the studio, a white van pulled into the driveway. A skinny woman with a kerchief covering short black hair got out and headed for the porch.

Albert came out to greet her. "Hello, Vivian, did you meet my granddaughter?"

"Hi, it's Sophie, right? Sorry I haven't been back. I've been up to my elbows in alligators since I was here last. Most of my customers came back, plus I got more. Bonnie says you want some more work done. She was supposed to meet me here."

"She'll be late. My son has decided we should get the place cleaned up to sell. Take a look, and see what you think."

Vivian went to her van and came back with a pad of paper and a measuring tape. While she was gone Bonnie pulled up.

Vivian came back out. “I’ll put together a bid for getting it ready to sell. You can pick and choose how much of it you want me to do.

“I can get a couple trucks to haul stuff away and some kids to help carry junk,” Albert said. "So, figure on that.”

“Right, I’ll drop off the quote tomorrow. See ya.”

She and Bonnie talked by the van for a few minutes, then Bonnie came up on the porch.

“Well, it’s all set,” she announced. “I start with her on Monday. I'll work at least three days a week. I’ll still have some time to work here on the paintings. It’ll give me a good steady income.”

“That's great, Bonnie. I’m going out to get the mail,” Albert said. “Then I’ll make some coffee."

A short time later he returned with a tray of coffee and cookies. He unfolded an official looking letter.

“Well, it finally came. I sent in my fine, and they sent back the receipt. Now I can sign up for the class to rehabilitate me. After that's done, I can get my license back. I’ll call today to sign up.”

“That’s great, Dad! You don’t plan on driving much do you?”

“I’ll take it easy at first, but I’m fine to drive; I’m sure.”

Andy made it to Friday without many problems. He had passed much of his work off to the associates. But today, he had too much to drink at a lunch meeting and just wanted to go home.

"Miss Ryan, call the limo. I'm leaving early."

"Sir, you have a three o'clock with the Dunning account."

"Cancel it. Call the limo."

"Sir, Mr. Dunning himself is going to be here. Mr. Martel, do you feel alright? Can I get you something?"

"Miss Ryan, you can do your job. Call for the limo now."

Luckily, Lillian and Jack were still at work when he got home. He went to bed. When Lillian got home, he feigned a stomach bug, and she left him alone until dinner. He ate some of the salad. He deflected Lillian's questions and pretended to be interested in Jack's stories about who he caddied for. He left the table, and after watching TV for an hour went back to bed.

In the morning he heard Lillian get up, but he stayed quiet and she left him alone until ten.

"Andy, don't you have a golf game this morning?"

"I'll call and cancel it."

"OK I'm going for groceries. I'll check on you later."

When he was sure Lillian was gone, he got up and ate some leftover pizza cold and a glass of tap water. He was sitting on the couch watching baseball with the sound off when Lillian came back. After she carried in the groceries, she came to him.

"Are you alright? Is your stomach still off?"

"Yeah," he said. "I just don't feel good."

"What's going on Andy? This isn't like you."

"It is sometimes. Just leave me alone for a while."

"You didn't stop taking your pills, did you?"

"I can't remember. Just let me rest. I'll be fine."

"Andy, should I call Doctor Grant?"

"God dammit, Lil! Get off me, will you?"

Lillian went outside to the patio. The last time she waited too long. She looked up the number for Andy's psychiatrist. She was relieved that he was the one on call this weekend.

"Let me talk to him," the doctor said. She took the phone to Andy.

"Sorry she bothered you, Cyril. I'm fine."

"Andy, do you trust me?"

"You've always helped me," Andy said.

"Then I want you to do what I tell you now. Double up on the bupropion, and stay on a double dose until I see you. I want you to get up and go for a run right now. I want you to do whatever Lillian tells you to do. Do you understand? Listen to your wife. Now give me back to Lillian."

"I'm glad you called. Take him out for a run. Don't let him get drinking, and keep him busy but don't push too much. I'm on call all weekend. Contact the office on Monday and get him an appointment for next week."

Andy and Lillian had a leisurely run, then they spread some mulch the gardener had left. Andy swept out the garage. Eventually he was back on the couch and fell asleep watching golf. Lillian got him to grill steaks after Jack got home from the club. They all had a soak in the hot tub after dinner. Lillian shaved her legs before bed, but Andy was already asleep when she slid under the covers. In the middle of the night, she felt him stir and go downstairs.

≈

Sophie thought she could find the church without Google but got lost and was a little late. She saw Randall in the crowd. He was sitting in the middle of a row, so Sophie slipped into the back. After the service she waited near the coffee shop. Randall and the tall girl she had met last week came up to her. She had her blonde hair down, and it flowed in waves past her shoulders.

"Sorry. I got lost and was late," Sophie said. "Do you guys want to get coffee?"

Before Randall could say anything, the girl said, "Sorry, but RJ and I have plans."

Randall started to say something but then hardened his mouth and let himself be led away.

I'm done with high school drama, Sophie thought. *She can have him if he wants it that way.*

Andy let Lillian drive him to church. The music was loud, and the sermon was long with multiple pointless conclusions. Then, off to the club brunch to be water-boarded with small talk. On the way home, Jack asked to go hiking – undoubtably put up to it by his mother. So, hiking they went at Butler

Sanctuary. Finally, in the late afternoon, they left him alone to watch the end of the golf tournament. He fell asleep until dinner.

He was up at three AM watching a sad old movie. He had to retreat to bed to escape a bottle of Scotch calling from the bar. He fell asleep shortly before his alarm went off. Before long, he was back in the limo and then back at his desk. He apologized to Miss Ryan and then to Mr. Dunning.

He pushed himself through the succession of beige days and gray nights. On Thursday he said all the right things to his psychiatrist. He left with a new pill and a promise to keep a counseling appointment. Sophie called, and he managed to put on a happy voice but broke down in tears when they hung up.

On Friday he worked from home and got in a round of golf with Jack. He hit some good shots, but Jack beat him again. That evening they had dinner on the patio. They gathered around the fire and the bouquet of the rose garden mixed with the wine. That night he lost himself in the arms of his wife. After, as she melted off to sleep against him, he wondered why he deserved such a faithful, beautiful woman.

TWENTY SEVEN

Sophie couldn't believe almost a week had gone by already and another Thursday had come. She had fallen into a routine of working, and the days had flown by. She had managed to mostly keep Randall far in the back of her mind, until she had to call and ask him to come and help that day. She made sure that conversation was all business.

Now she couldn't stop thinking: *It's been almost two weeks since I saw him. Today he'll be here. Did that girl at church reeled him in? She sure had her hooks out.*

By afternoon, Vivian, Bonnie, Bagger's grandsons, and Randall were there. Sophie couldn't stop herself from playing the role of a scorned woman and coldly said hello to Randall. He avoided her stormy eyes the rest of the day. The assembled crew filled both trucks with newspapers, magazines, and romance novels. Then Randall and Bagger's grandsons drove the trucks to the recycling center.

While they were gone, Vivian, Sophie, and Bonnie surveyed the living room. Dust sparkled in the sun beams that exposed corners not seen in decades. Summer smells from the open windows had replaced the miasma of stagnate air. Remarkably, not one of the hundreds of figurines that seemed to cover every horizontal surface had fallen during the dozens of arm-laden trips amongst them. They were curated in tableaus of ballet dancers, angels, unicorns, and birds in flight covering end tables, sofa tables, open cabinets, and wall shelves. Most were cheap porcelain; some were plastic.

Bonnie knew they had to be dealt with before the furniture could be removed. “Well, we can’t ignore this any longer".

“Yeah, they're the unicorn in the room, for sure,” Vivian said and giggled.

“Where’d they all come from?” Sophie asked.

“This was before QVC or eBay," Bonnie said. “Mom ordered them all through magazines -- cut out the ads and mailed them in. I guess she might have been a little compulsive.”

“Ya think?” asked Vivian.

“It’s years of work. She spent a lot of her time with them. What do we do?” Bonnie asked.

“If it don’t bring you joy, you gotta let it go,” Vivian said. “Plus, we ain’t talkin’ Hummels here. This stuff's a buck a box at yard sales. Sorry, I suppose it gave her something to give her left over love to. For my mom, it was parakeets. She'd mourn for weeks when one died."

“Kinda sad, really. This was her life,” Bonnie said.

“Vivian, let’s give Bonnie a minute," Sophie said. "I could use a break, and you haven't eaten.”

Albert was up from his nap. Sophie found him out looking at the lawn.

“Grandpa, Bonnie is looking through her mother’s collection. Could you go help her?”

In one of the rare times, Albert made eye contact with his granddaughter. She saw a glimmer of compassion, some understanding. He went into the house.

As the guys came back with the trucks, Bonnie and Albert came out of the house. Each had a cardboard box.

"We told Vivian to take everything else away. I'm going home," Bonnie said.

"Before you go," Albert said, "I have my driving class tomorrow at nine o'clock down at the DMV. Can one of you take me? I'll be done by noon."

"I can take you," Sophie said. "I'll be here by eight."

In the afternoon Albert got a call from Bagger's daughter. Her father wasn't feeling well enough to go for dinner. It would be one of only a handful of times they had not been together on a Thursday evening.

The next morning, Albert put his DMV papers in a manilla envelope along with his well-worn book of short stories by Dostoevsky. Sophie dropped him off in front of the DMV at quarter to nine. He went in and watched as she drove away then made his way to the Tim Horton's next door. He stood in line for a coffee and two donuts then found an empty booth in the corner. He sipped his coffee and read his book. He bought another cup and found an abandoned morning paper. He studied the real estate listings and read the local news. At eleven thirty he walked back to the DMV and waited there on a bench until Sophie collected him.

"How'd it go?" she asked.

"It was boring -- nothing I didn't already know. They gave me my license back though, so I'm done with them. I'd drive home, but you're already there. I'll go out later, maybe."

Well I've done it, he thought. *I lied and pulled off this ruse. It's wrong on some levels but really a victimless crime and the only way I can get out of here. Everything will be set. When they sell the place, I'll be free and can get back to work. I'll miss Sophie when it happens, but that can't be helped.*

In the afternoon the cleaning crew gathered in the living room. They put the chairs in Albert's truck. He watched as they lined up three to a side and slid the couch into the back of Randall's truck. Then they left in a procession for the land fill.

Albert stood in the empty room. He remembered it empty and full of promise once. In those days the trees outside were small, and sunlight streamed through the windows. As the trees grew over the years, their leaves shaded the windows. Even in winter, the dark branches veiled the low, cold light. Eventually, pulled-shades, yellow and stiff, finished what the trees could not.

Sophie broke his brooding. "This could be such a nice room. A little paint and a new carpet-- it'll be beautiful."

"This was a good house once," Albert said. "It could be again for somebody, maybe."

"Well, right now you're here, so we should make it nice for you."

"Sophie, you know I don't want to stay here, don't you?"

"I thought you might have changed your mind and are thinking of it as an option."

“No," Albert said, "it's not an option. I might as well tell you. I’m going to Vermont to sign up for the place up there. Then I'll be able to move as soon as we can get this place sold.”

“Grandpa, how will you get to Vermont?”

“That’s why I got the truck fixed and my license back. I’m going to drive there.”

“You told me it was just so you could go to the store and places around here. Have you been planning this all along without telling anyone?”

“I didn’t want to worry anybody. I’m sure I can do it.”

“I think you should wait until you sell this place, then we can take you to Vermont if you still want to. You can’t drive that far by yourself.”

“Maybe I can, maybe I can’t, but that’s what I’m doing.”

“We need to talk to Bonnie about this when she gets back,” Sophie said.

Albert straightened to his full height. “You can talk about it all you want, but it’s my decision and nobody else. If I don’t do it, I might as well just give it all up. I have to get out of here. Why can’t you understand that? It won’t affect you one way or the other. I’m going up to the studio. Don’t bother me anymore today.”

Her grandfather had never turned on her like that. Sophie remembered how her father had told her this could happen. He was frightening; she didn’t know what to do.

After an hour or so Bonnie and Vivian came back from getting supplies. Sophie took Bonnie aside and filled her in on what her grandfather had said.

“There’s no way he can drive that far," Bonnie said. "I hope he isn't slipping, you know, mentally.”

Bonnie went up to the studio and knocked on the door and called to her father. Eventually she heard him unlocking the door.

“Dad, we need to talk.”

“I suppose Sophie talked to you.”

“Of course she did. You freaked her out. I know you didn’t mean to. Let’s talk about this... please?”

They went back to his study. Bonnie couldn’t remember ever being there.

“Dad, you know you can't safely drive to Vermont. What if you hurt someone?”

“I've been thinking about it. I know you’re right. I may have lost my mind a little. I’ll have to figure something else out, I guess.”

“I'm still hoping you can stay here. It’s possible. We just have to want it. That would be the best.”

“Maybe so. I’m tired. I have to talk to Sophie.”

He wouldn’t look her in the eyes, but Albert apologized to Sophie and told her she could keep the truck like before. He let her hug him before he trudged into the house.

The women worked in the living room until mid-afternoon while the men finished cleaning out the basement. When they quit, they gathered for a late lunch of pizza. Bagger’s grandsons hurried away to be with their grandfather. Vivian packed up and left Randall and Sophie to clean up while Albert and Bonnie sat on the porch.

Working in the kitchen, Sophie and Randall couldn't avoid each other any longer.

“I want to apologize about Sunday,” Randall said.

“There's nothing to apologize for."

“Well, maybe an explanation then. That girl, Leslie -- we've been friends since fourth grade. Now she tells me she always had a crush on me.”

“Oh, I couldn't have guessed,” Sophie said with a smirk.

“Now that I'm not engaged, she thinks we should be together. I'm not interested in her that way. I never have been. It's just really awkward. I'm sorry I didn't say anything that day.”

“Believe me, it's not your fault. Any girl like her would go after you if they thought they had a chance.”

“But not a girl like you, right?”.

Sophie couldn't keep up her act any longer, and finally looked him in the eyes.

“RJ...”

“I know," Randall interrupted.

“I'm not going to lead you on," Sophie said. "I wouldn't do that to you. And like I said, I won't be your rebound. Please, let's try to be friends.”

“I'll take that... for now. Don't let what happened keep you from church. I told Leslie to back off. You can meet some of my other friends.”

“I'll see. Thanks for helping clean up."

"No big deal," Randall said. "Maybe I'll see you on Sunday. I better get going."

TWENTY EIGHT

After Randall left, Sophie said goodbye to Albert and Bonnie on the porch, opened the garage door, and got into the truck. She turned the key, but nothing happened. She tried again with the same result. Albert came to her window.

"What's the problem?" he asked.

"It won't start."

Albert opened the hood and wiggled some wires. "Try it again."

Sophie turned the key and still nothing. Albert went into the garage and came out with a tester.

"This battery is brand new, and now it's dead. I'll have to get it out and take it back."

"Do you need help?" Sophie asked.

"No, I can get it. Maybe Bonnie will take me tomorrow to exchange it. She can take you home. I'll see you in the morning."

On the way home, Sophie told Bonnie, "Maybe the truck's dead. If it is, that might be the best thing."

"He'll never give up on it," Bonnie said. "Nothing stops him from getting his way."

"Like father, like son," Sophie said.

Albert reattached the battery cable and closed the hood. He went back in the house and finished packing his satchel. He put some cash in his wallet and picked up his Rand McNally. He hesitated then left a short note on the kitchen table. He had his route planned: a turn east on Monroe Avenue would become Route 31 which would eventually carry him to a jog down to Route 20 to avoid Syracuse then to Route 7 north. Luckily, the girls left early. There were still a few hours of light left. If he got a head start, he could be there tomorrow easily.

He was enjoying his long-lost freedom, but it was tempered by the need for intense concentration. It wasn't easy to keep the truck straight and cars were lining up behind him. Sometimes one would streak past him then dart back in front. That would cause him to slow down even more. He successfully navigated the worrisome Route 5 and 20 split in Auburn and relaxed a little, thinking he would stop at the next motel he found. The sun was shining into his rearview mirror as he headed down the hill into Skaneateles.

I haven't been here in forty years or more, he thought. *Not since my plein air days.*

It was still beautiful. The street was lined with mansions surrounded by formal gardens. He passed the town park. The lawn, crowned by a bandstand, was dappled by sunlight through the trees. The lake beyond shimmered like a fallen chandelier. The scattered groups of picnickers and running children brought the Impressionistic composition to life. He decided to stop for dinner and inquire about a motel. As he slowed down to survey a parking spot, his mirrors lit up red, white, and blue.

“Sir, do you know why I stopped you?” the officer asked.

“No,” Albert said.

“You went through a stop light. Please show me your license and registration.”

The personnel at the police station were very polite and attentive to Albert. He quickly surmised they thought him to be feebleminded, so he went with that. He had Bonnie’s phone number on a faded slip of paper in his wallet. After he made his phone call, they had a fish fry delivered which he ate by himself in the holding area.

It was just getting dark when Bonnie's phone rang. She was shocked to hear her father's voice. His story was so bizarre she told him to give the phone to an officer. She confirmed that indeed her father had been arrested. His truck was impounded and would need two hundred dollars to get it released in the morning. The officer gave her the name of the motel they would take him to.

Bonnie called Sophie. "Well, you just got scammed by your grandfather. He took off in the truck and got arrested in Skaneateles."

"Skinny-what?"

"Skaneateles. It's a little town almost all the way to Syracuse. The police are going to get him to a motel. We can't get his truck back until morning."

"Are you going to tell my Dad?" Sophie asked.

"He begged me not to. I guess it isn't necessary right now. He's safe and can't get the truck again."

The roadside motels were out of town beyond the Inns, B&Bs, and Spas. The arresting officer dropped Albert off in front of a "vintage motel" and wished him good-night and a safe journey home. The desk clerk reluctantly handed over a key after Albert paid in cash but without a backup credit card.

Albert had spotted a small lounge and grill on the way and carefully walked on the shoulder of the road back to it. It looked to him to be full of the laborers, house-keepers, and public servants who catered to the one-percenters living along the lake. He felt at home.

Morose at first, the second round brought fresh determination. The situation had not changed, he had no choice but to find a different way to Vermont. Going alone was beyond his capabilities. He would have to use his other strengths to get the job done. He had a third beer but no chaser and made his way back to the motel.

Sophie and Bonnie got an early start in the morning and headed east on the Thruway.

"Now, maybe you understand what your father warned you about," Bonnie said.

"I just can't believe he would risk hurting himself or other people, and he lied about having his license," Sophie replied.

"People don't change much. We all have a path to follow. Some will do anything to stay on it."

"Maybe. But people can change paths. They need to follow Jesus and stop trying to make their own path. I believe everyone can if they want to."

"That's a nice way to think, but I don't see it happening much. Funny, Bo has been saying sort of the same thing lately."

Albert was sitting on the bench outside his room when they pulled up in Bonnie's Volvo. There wasn't much to say, so they rode in awkward silence to get the truck. He paid the impound fee in cash and waited for the receipt to print. Albert wanted to ride in the truck, so he got in beside Sophie, and they headed west, back to Rochester.

Suddenly, Albert broke the silence. "You know how you told me you know your god wants you to be here and help me?"

"Yes, that's right. That's what I believe. What you did yesterday makes me wonder though."

"How did you come to believe that?" Albert asked.

"It's just a feeling, and when I prayed about it, I felt it even more. I believe God can speak to me. I've learned a lot about God and faith at church and by studying."

"Do you think people who don't believe in God can get those feelings too?"

"I suppose, but I don't know where the feelings would come from. Maybe God."

"I've done years of reading and thinking, and I have beliefs too," Albert said. "They aren't the same as yours, but they're how I live my life -- just like you."

"I think everybody has different beliefs. All Christians aren't even the same. I can see how your beliefs are as important to you as mine are to me."

"What's important is what works for each one of us," Albert said. "Just like you believe you're supposed to be here with me, I believe I should be in Vermont. I need to be there to fulfill my life. I believe I should be where I can finish my paintings. They're the only thing real to me. If I don't keep painting and if I don't live true to myself, I'm a failure. Dying with regrets is the closest to Hell an existentialist can get."

"But Grandpa, going to Vermont is just one option. There are other ways you can keep painting."

"There's other ways you could help me, or you could be helping someone else. But you're not. You're here because that's where you think you should be. I think I should be in Vermont."

"But won't you be lonely there?"

"I'm lonely because I'm such bad company. That won't change in Vermont."

"I think you're lonely because you won't let people into your life."

"That won't change either," Albert replied.

Sophie tried to think objectively about what her grandfather had said. *In his mind, going to Vermont is as important to him as being a Christian is to me. He's probably delusional, but that's what atheists say about me. Is it right for me to deny him acting on his beliefs any more than for someone to do that to me? Besides, God wants me to stay with him, so that's what I'll do*

TWENTY NINE

Andy thought his week was going better until the partners' meeting on Friday. Sitting around the big table, he was told Mr. Dunning had requested that a different partner take over his account. The senior partners were "concerned" about Andy's health. They "suggested" he take some time off to get settled. They would divide his projects between them and the associates. It was "advised" he needed to work in a more consistent way to eliminate the ups and downs of recent weeks. His salary would remain in place, but the incentives would go to the partners managing his projects. The limo benefit would be put on hold starting the next day.

Andy told them he was sure he would be back on track next week. They said they held a vote and the decision was made. They would review the plan in thirty days. Andy talked with Miss Ryan and told her what was going on. He reassured her she would continue on with another lawyer.

"Please take care of yourself, Mr. Martel."

"I will. Don't worry: I'll be back before you know it. Miss Ryan?"

"Yes?"

"Thank you."

As the driver worked his way out of the city, Andy wondered if he would ever have a limo again. He tried to relax into the deep seat but couldn't close his eyes. Sixty-five minutes after walking out of his office, he was dropped off at his home. He tipped the driver and watched the limousine turn out of the driveway.

Lillian was sitting at her dressing table putting on makeup when Andy came into the bedroom.

"Guess what, Gunner. I'm taking you out for dinner tonight. We're celebrating!"

"Really? What are we celebrating?"

"The renters buying the duplex asked to take both duplexes. I guess they came into some money and want to put it somewhere. I decided to jump at the chance. They wrote me a check for almost my asking price. And... that big commission check came in today. With that and everything else, I'm now officially a millionaire! What do you think of that, Mr. Wall Street?"

"You've done a great job, worked really hard. I'm not surprised. That's something to celebrate, that's for sure."

"I even got us a nice table at Crabtree's. How was your day?"

"Not bad. Glad the week is over though."

"We'll just forget all about work and have a nice evening. I laid out some clothes for you."

Andy and Lillian Hi, how-are-ya?-Find'd their way through the room, stopping at tables filled with friends and acquaintances. Lillian looked spectacular in a clingy, blue-silk creation. Andy's gray dinner jacket provided her a complimentary back drop. Out-of-towners turned to see the power couple led to a window table.

Over after-dinner drinks Andy asked, "What would you say if I took some time off work?"

"I think that would be wonderful. A week like before would really help you."

"I was thinking more like at least a month. I asked the partners for a leave of absence."

"Why did you wait until now to tell me?"

"This is your night. I love seeing you so happy. I really am proud of you."

"I didn't think today could get any better," Lillian said. "We could go on vacation – a real vacation. We can go visit Cookie, maybe make some progress with her."

"I just think with everything going on, I need some time away from work. I'm glad you understand."

"Oh honey, it'll be fabulous. I know it will. Let's get home. I'm not done with you tonight."

THIRTY

On Saturday morning, Sophie found Bonnie and Derek on his porch.

"I was telling Bo about Dad's excellent adventure. Hopefully leaving here is out of his system now. Do you think he's given it up?"

"You know he won't give up," Sophie said. "Now he wants me to take him – drive him to Vermont."

"What a pain in the ass. What'd you say?"

"Do you two want to be alone?" Derek asked.

"No, I could use some advice -- the more the better," Sophie said. "Dad warned me about this. I don't know if Grandpa is trying to trick me. If I don't take him will he just get on a bus or hire a driver?"

"What's wrong with him going to Vermont?" Derek asked.

"It doesn't make sense," said Bonnie. "He can't move that far away; there won't be anyone to take care of him when the time comes."

"Just because it doesn't make sense doesn't mean you should try to stop him."

“It does if he hasn't got it together. I don’t think he's all there mentally".

"So, are you going to force him to be evaluated by a doctor?"

"That's extreme. I don't think we can do that," Sophie said.

“That’s my point," Derek said. "You either have to stop him or help him – tough choice.”

"But I'm stuck in the middle," Sophie said. "I'm the one he wants to take him. I'm the one that has to do it."

“He’s my father,” Bonnie said. “I think I know him best. He can’t move to Vermont; that’s all there is to it. Sophie, you just need to back off. We were fine until you and Andy got into the scene.”

“That’s not fair,” Derek said.

“Oh sure, you would take her side.”

“It’s not one side or the other; it’s just reality. You told me the house is getting sold. He can’t stay there, and he knows it."

Sophie prayed for patience and waited.

“Bon, the most important thing is to keep him safe, even if it's from himself. That’s all Sophie wants too, I’m sure. He believes he has to make a change. You can’t blame him for that. He feels it's his only road.”

“That's a road he wants to travel alone. That's what bothers me. I guess I just have to accept the way he is. He and I had our chances to be close. We both blew it; now this is where we're at."

“So, does that mean I should take him or what?”

“He has to do his trip the way he sees it. I know I can’t change it," Bonnie said. "I just want things to stay the same... they won’t. Sorry I went off on you. If he wants you to take him that's the best of a bad situation.”

“Hey, look at that, it’s after noon, how 'bout some wine?” Derek said.

“I’ll get some of mine,” Sophie said.

She chose a red and grabbed a box of crackers. The porch table was dirty from street grime. She got a towel and washed it. Derek brought out a bowl and glasses. Sophie dumped the wafers in the bowl and filled their glasses with wine.

When they finished the wine, Sophie announced. "I guess I’ll go find out when this road trip starts. Think about me when I’m gone.”

“I’ll always be around if you need anything. Be careful,” Bonnie said.

"Don't worry. I'll come back."

THIRTY ONE

Albert was resting on his porch when Eugenia drove in.

"Mr. Albert, I thought you might want to come and see Dad. I don't expect you'll have a chance to see him again."

Albert stubbed out his cigarette and didn't bother going in for his hat. He quickly got in the car, and they drove away.

"It's sure hard to see my dad like he is. He's so stubborn -- wouldn't go to dialysis like all the doctors said he should. Now it's too late."

"It takes a strong man to make a decision like that," Albert reasoned. "Your father is a strong man."

"Stubborn I say, not strong."

Bagger raised his hand and waved his family out of the room. Albert sat in a chair close to the bed.

"Al, glad you came. I was hoping I could say goodbye to you. You've been a good friend – a brother – to me. I'm ready to move on. I'm not afraid. I'm not."

"I'm glad you're going out on your terms," Albert said. "I'll still miss you though. We've been a pair. An odd pair for sure, but a pair. I won't be the same without you."

"It's been a blessin' to know you. I'm tired."

He closed his dark eyes. There was no pain in his face. Albert went back out to Bagger's family.

"Thanks for coming," Eugenia said. "He's been asking for you. We sure do appreciate all you did for him over the years.

Eugenia drove Albert back to his house. As he opened the car door, she looked at the old man before her.

"We'll stay in touch," she said. "You have a blessed day now."

Albert went to his studio and started a charcoal sketch of his friend. Now there was one less thing to keep him in Rochester. Bagger was the last link to his outside life. Now, that chapter was closed. Only his inside life -- his painting -- remained.

He heard his truck come into the driveway. Sophie quietly entered the studio.

"Is that Mr. Bagwell?" she asked.

"I just saw him. He's dying. I won't ever see him again."

"I'm so sorry, Grandpa."

"He wants to go. He's had enough; can't wish anything else for him. I'll miss him, but that's how it is. Are you going to take me to Vermont?"

"I talked with Bonnie. You know she doesn't like the idea."

"I'm going one way or the other. You can take me, or I'll find someone else."

"I'll take you. Will the truck make it?"

"It'll be fine. We can leave tomorrow. I'll call and get an appointment for Monday morning. We can be back by Monday night."

After much discussion in her head, Sophie decided not to tell her parents she was going. She did call Randall.

“I won’t be in church tomorrow. I’m taking Grandpa to Vermont. I’ll be back Monday night.”

“Are you sure about this?” Randall asked. "That’s a long way in that truck.”

“Grandpa says it'll be fine. Do you think it will be?”

“Probably. I've checked it over -- replaced some belts and things, but you never know.”

“I don’t have much choice. I'll just have to see what happens.”

“Sophie, if anything goes wrong, call me. Promise me. I'll come wherever you are.”

“Thanks, RJ. I appreciate that.”

“I care about you, Sophie. I really do.”

“You're sweet. I’ll call you and let you know how I’m doing. Can we get together next week?”

“Anytime you want.”

Sophie took time to pray before she started out Sunday morning. She felt she was being pulled along -- outside her own volition. There was a sense of adventure though, far outside her white-bread life.

That’s not a bad thing, she thought. Artists have to live that way. You can’t have anything to say about life if you haven't lived it. Oh, I’m so bohemian now -- in my hundred-dollar jeans!

Albert was waiting on the porch when she got there. He was dressed in a white shirt and brown sport coat. White socks peeked out from the cuffs of shiny black pants. He had on a brown trilby hat, pushed back on his head.

“Don’t you look dapper this morning," Sophie said.

“Got my travelin’ suit on. Let’s go.”

He put his leather satchel in the back of the truck and a green thermos of coffee on the passenger seat. He popped the hood and checked the oil and coolant levels before getting in.

He climbed in and buckled up. "Not bad. On the road before eight. Hoping it would be earlier, but here we go."

“What’s the address?" Sophie asked. "I’ll put it in my phone.”

“I have a map, and I already called them. It’s all set. I can figure it out as we go.”

“My phone will tell us. I just need the address.”

“You treat that thing same as your god. Just ask it for help, then you don't have to think".

"Oh Grandpa, you're so deep."

Sophie eased onto the Thruway and settled in the right lane. Cars and trucks were flying by her. After the first half hour she loosened her grip on the wheel and tried to relax her shoulders. She found herself behind a laboring tractor trailer and paced herself with that. Sixty miles-per-hour seemed to be the sweet spot. It was going to be a long trip.

“At this speed,” she said, “We’ll be there in six hours, without stops.”

"No hurry," Albert said. "We got all day; don't push it. You're going kinda fast. Wish we took a back road."

"This is the fastest route," Sophie said. "I'm only going sixty – five miles under the speed limit. Now, Grandpa, I'm not going to sit here in the quiet for six hours. You have to talk to me. When did you first start painting?"

Albert steadily poured coffee into the plastic cup from the top of the thermos and took a sip.

"My mother always said the first time I took up a brush was on one of her paintings. I guess I thought it needed some red, so I smeared cadmium on a still-life she was working on. I would've been about five at the time"

"Your mother was an artist?" Sophie asked, surprised.

Albert didn't often indulge in reminiscence. Reflecting on his life with Bagger had started a cascade carrying him further and further back. Now this benign revenant sitting next to him was asking about her great-grandmother.

"Yes, she was. She had taken lessons before she moved here from France. She painted landscapes and still-life's. She and Dad argued over the money and time she spent on it, but she kept on going. She spent money getting canvas and paint for me also. He didn't like that either. She eventually got a job of her own as a seamstress at Hickey Freeman, then they argued about her working."

"Why wouldn't he have wanted her to work? It would give them more money."

"Back then it was shameful for a man's wife to work. Once she started, she became more independent and had friends of her own -- other artist types. 'Sophisticated people,' she would call them. She would make herself dresses she saw in magazines. She wore them to museums and galleries and sometimes parties with her friends. I suspect now she was having affairs. She was French."

"But what about you? When did you get serious about art?"

"I took all the art classes I could in high school, drafting too. Mother had me copy classic paintings. She bought me books. She dreamed of me going to a fancy art college. My father had a job for me waiting at Gleason's when I graduated. He refused to give me any money for college."

"It all sounds so stressful."

"I enlisted in the Army to get away from it. Mother was devastated. I promised her I would use the GI bill to go to college when I was done."

Sophie let it rest there. Albert watched the open farmlands roll by. There was a world outside his enclave. He was glad to be out in it. It was probably too late, but he had to see this through. He had another cup of coffee then soon regretted it.

"I've gotta stop soon. I drank too much coffee."

Armed with a mocha latte after their brief stop, Sophie got back in the truck.

"No cup holder, obviously," she said.

Albert opened the glove box. "It's still here!"

He clamped a contraption to the dashboard.

"Custom made. Here ya go."

Sophie put her cup in the metal ring.

"You were ahead of your time, Grandpa, in a lot of ways. Tell me some New York stories."

"Things were changing by the time I got there. Before that, Pollock, de Kooning, Rothko, Kline, and a lot of others, plus their wives and/or girlfriends ran around Manhattan like a pack of dogs, humping each other and howling at the moon. Sorry, I shouldn't tell you that. I mostly knew Elaine de Kooning. Bill was a bastard, drunk most of the time, miserable because he was starting to make money. After Pollock died, he was the next big thing. Suddenly the critics and gallery owners loved him. He was selling out as much as Pollock ever did, and he knew it. Funny thing was Pollock couldn't draw a straight line and got rich-- or his wife did after he died. Bill had natural talent but didn't make any money until after Pollock died."

"Sounds like they lived a really free life," Sophie said.

"They confused freedom with irresponsibility. That's why I had to leave. You don't have to be religious to be moral you know. They lived with their choices until they became inconvenient. I couldn't do that."

"Did you regret doing it -- coming back to Rochester?"

"It wasn't anything to regret. It was what had to be done. I chose to get married. It was a consequence of that. I still had to stay authentic and paint. That had consequences too."

"All those years you worked fulltime and made all those paintings. How'd you do it?"

"I didn't spend much time on my family. I became like my father, except I painted instead of going to whatever games were in season. Before I knew it, my wife was dead, then not long after that Bonnie took off and your father went to college. I was alone and could paint all I wanted. I've had enough of this; let's drop it."

They remained quiet for a time. Sophie felt like a small child in the presence of her grandfather with his age and life experience. She again thought about why she -- just a kid really -- was involved with this old man.

Were Mom and Dad totally right? Who am I to declare myself on a mission from God?

Albert was enjoying the drive-in his truck, going down a highway, finally taking a step toward finishing his plan. Soon he would be painting full-time. All his other responsibilities would be gone. No more pressure from his family.

He looked at his map.

"Looks like pretty soon the Thruway heads south. There must be a way to cut across. I'm sick of this highway."

Sophie tapped the phone screen. "Yeah, we get off in two exits. It's almost lunch time."

"We can stop after we get off, maybe find a decent diner."

Soon they exited the Thruway, crossed the Mohawk River, and started through the outskirts of Amsterdam. Not far beyond the city line they saw a roadside diner. It was an all-American mom-and-pop kind of place. They both went for a cheeseburger plate and chocolate shake.

Back in the truck Albert produced a flask and had a couple nips.

"What was that?" Sophie asked.

"Just a little something to settle my stomach."

"Right, and don't think I don't know what's in your coffee too."

"You sure are uptight for a teenager."

"I'm not a teenager, and don't call me uptight. I'm a good girl."

"So, you think running off to Vermont in a rickety truck with your rickety grandfather -- without telling your parents -- is something a good girl would do?"

"I didn't say smart. I said good."

They bantered back and forth. Albert told a few more tales from New York. Sophie tried to enlighten her grandfather with stories about her college friends and what it was like in Chappaqua.

Soon they were into Vermont and the landscape started to become wilder as they entered the Green Mountains. Then beyond Burlington and into the Northeast Kingdom there were stretches of barren land with little towns, few and far between.

"Grandpa, there isn't much out here. I better Google a motel."

"Go ahead, but I'm sure we'll run into one soon."

"I'm not getting stuck in some wilderness flea bag motel. I'm pulling over to look."

"Here's one, but it's still almost an hour to Sunadew from there." Sophie showed Albert her phone.

"The brochure says it's in a remote area. I guess we better stop soon."

They found the small-town motel and checked in. Albert settled in his room for a nap. Sophie forced herself to stay off

Twitter et al for fear of her location getting back to her parents or Jack. She did call Randall with an update.

"That's practically in Canada!" he said. "You'd be stranded if you break down. This is crazy, I shoulda gone with you. I could be there tonight."

Sophie assured him she could handle it, so there was no need for him to saddle his white charger and rescue her, but added, "That really is sweet of you."

He is so adorable, she thought after she hung up.

There weren't many choices of restaurants, so they picked the busiest one. Albert's truck fit right in, and they left it chatting with a mud-covered Jeep. Albert was feeling rested and was animated as he discussed his move to Sunadew.

"I know this is best for everyone," he said. "Everybody gets what they want. I can paint, and I won't be a bother to anyone."

"Grandpa, that's what you just won't understand. You're not a bother. We want to help you and be with you. I feel like I had to bring you here, but I know it's wrong. You should be home where your family can help. I was hoping to be near you and learn from you."

"You don't want to get stuck in Rochester. There's nothing for you there except maybe Randall. He would follow you anywhere, so that isn't an issue either."

"RJ is a friend. I'm talking about you."

"Sophie, I know you care. I do appreciate what you've done for me. You've brought some life back in me. I haven't felt like this in a very long time. But still, I'm old and will be gone soon.

You shouldn't waste any more time on me. I'm doing you a favor -- you and everyone else."

Sophie knew there was nothing she could say to change his mind. She would leave it in God's hands.

Back at the motel, they said good night.

"I haven't looked forward to a morning in many, many years," Albert said. "Tomorrow will be a new day."

Back in her room Sophie prayed for reassurance.

Albert sat on his bed and reviewed the Sunadew brochure and wrote down some questions to ask about cost. He went outside with his flask and a cigarette. He could see the mountains in the distance.

Thirty Two

The next morning came with a cool drizzle. It was a hint that fall came early in these northern mountains. Sophie's phone guided them as they turned onto ever-narrower roads until it suddenly went silent. Sophie felt abandoned. From there on, they only had Albert's map. Eventually they had no choice but to stay on the only road there was. They followed a small river deeper and deeper into a cleft between two mountains. Finally, they came to the end of the road marked by a sign that said SUNADEW. There was a shack, like a guard house, standing at the end of a bridge. A bent-over man leading a large ugly dog came out of the shack.

"You here about movin' in? You Martel?"

"Yes, that's right," Albert said. "I have an appointment."

"Park t'other side of that green building. The office is there."

They crossed the bridge over the river and onto a laneway narrowed by trees and pocked with mud puddles. Sophie drove slowly and turned into a small parking lot. The building seemed to be camouflaged among the brown and green of the forest pressing against it. Albert gathered up a pad of paper and the Sunadew folder.

"Well, let's go get this figured out."

Before they could knock, a woman came to the door. She was dressed in a white shirt, beaded vest, and jeans tucked into rubber boots.

"Good morning, my name is Viola Cunningham. You must be the Martels. Come on in out of the rain."

She appeared to be in her seventies. Her long copper-red hair was still thick, parted down the middle and held back with large black barrettes at her temples. She had light green eyes behind horn-rimmed glasses.

"I'm Albert. This is my granddaughter, Sophie."

"Pleased to meet you both. Sophie, why don't you make yourself at home here? There's a coffee pot on. Albert and I will go in my office and get to know one another."

"I'd like her to stay with me," Albert said. "I want her to hear what you have to say."

"Well, normally we like to meet with just the neighbor. You can fill her in later."

"She'll come with me."

"Well, fine; that's fine. Come on in, Sophie."

Viola led them into a windowless office with knotty pine walls. There was a collection of rustic chairs around a twig-constructed coffee table.

"Let's sit here. We like to be informal and relaxed. I'll get us some coffee."

Sophie looked at the black-and-white group photographs on the walls featuring a handsome man surrounded by young women gazing at him in apparent adoration. There were a few men standing in the back rows.

Viola returned with a tray and three cups of coffee. "Well now, I'll give you our schedule for the day. Right now, I'd like to go over some details not in our literature and try to answer some common questions in advance. Then we'll tour the neighborhood and show you the accommodations. Then we can come back and make the final arrangements. My husband, Clive, will come up for that.

"Clive was a visionary; he had a following in Boston. We all pooled our money for him to manage. In 1969 he bought this camp and brought us here so we could live a true and meaningful life. For a long time, things went great. Then people started to drift away from his teachings. They didn't have the discipline to continue their journey to fulfillment. Gradually, he opened up the community to visitors. Later he saw the need for an alternative to cold and impersonal retirement homes. He developed this idea, and it has worked out well for everyone. He still teaches those that are interested, but I have to admit, there aren't many people willing to give up their selves and follow the true path anymore. There are still several of us early pioneers living here. We enjoy having new neighbors join us. The big difference these days is Clive and I provide everything the neighbors need, so we can all enjoy ourselves every day. Our neighbors don't worry about food, housing, healthcare, or anything else. We still have gardens that anyone can work in, but it's on a volunteer basis now. We also have opportunities to help with building maintenance and groundskeeping for those that want to feel productive and helpful to the community. Of course, we modify the rates of those who choose not to help."

"I'm interested in the art studios," Albert said.

"Oh, that's wonderful. We can take a look at those on our tour. Do you paint?"

"Yes, that's why I'm coming here. I want to be able to paint."

"You will have plenty of time for that along with our community gatherings and the opportunities to be helpful. Shall we go visit the community hall then? We have a nice cart to use. We should be able to meet some neighbors. It's almost coffee break time."

Viola swerved the golf cart around a pile of gravel in the path. There were shovels and rakes leaning against it. They passed four elderly men walking slowly toward a large building at the end of the path.

"Good morning gentlemen. The path is much better. Keep up the good work."

She parked in front of a large log building. There was a covered porch in front with benches and rocking chairs scattered behind a railing.

"This is our main gathering place. It's the dining hall, cocktail lounge, and recreation center. We have pool tables, ping pong, card tables -- things like that. The neighbors love to gather here."

There were rows of long tables with benches and a few chairs. On one side were other chairs arranged around low tables. The walls were lined with faded and fly-specked posters featuring a large portrait of the same man in the photographs at the office. Each had a saying imprinted on the borders.

Give it up. Give it away. Get Freedom.
I know the Way. Follow me.
I made the map. Follow the Path.
Listen. Believe. Follow. Be Free.

Two gray-haired ladies were sitting behind a counter displayed with baked goods.

"This is Nettie and Gloria. They manage the coffee shop and bake all these wonderful goodies. They love being helpful that way. Girls, this is Albert. He's planning on joining our community."

They said hello but avoided eye contact.

In the back to one side was a group of tables and a bar with stools, beyond that a kitchen. Sophie saw some old people cutting vegetables and one sweeping the floor. As they were leaving, groups of men and women were gathering. Some wore paint-splattered clothes. Others took off muddy boots and washed their hands in a large sink by the door. They trudged to the coffee pot then scattered around the tables and hunched over their cups.

Back outside, Sophie saw a covered walkway from where the kitchen was to another long building There was a black van parked near the back.

"What's in that building?" she asked.

“That's our advanced-care facility. It's for people that need extra help. For privacy reasons, we won’t tour that. Our level-one housing is down this way. I can show you what that's like.”

They came to a two-story building. One side had been newly painted to the second story windows.

“We have an open room I can show you. This is one of our double rooms. It's very desirable when one becomes available.”

Viola opened the door to the room. There was a couch and chair with a coffee table on the right. There was a small table in front of a single window straight ahead. Through an open doorway on the left was another room with a bed and dresser.

“As you can see, this is a spacious suite. There is a slight up-charge for this accommodation. Now we'll go over to the studios. I’m sure you're excited to see those facilities.”

They came to a large metal building that curved to the ground. Albert recognized it as a Quonset hut, probably government surplus. They entered through a small side door.

"Ah, there they are, as always. Come and meet our most dedicated artists."

They walked past work benches filled with woven baskets, ceramic cats, and bird houses. In the back of the building there were easels enclosed in cubicles surrounding an open area with a small table. Two women and a man were seated at the table. The man put down his coffee spoon and looked up.

"Well Viola, who do you have here?"

"This is Albert Martel. Al meet Joe, Agnes, and Stella. Mr. Martel is an artist and will be joining us soon."

"Where're you from?" Joe asked.

"New York. How can you work in a place like this? There's not even a window."

Joe laughed. "Oh, we just dabble between coffee breaks and meals. Mostly we sit and gossip. It makes the days go by. You get used to it after a while."

Albert turned to Viola. "Your brochure said I would have a studio of my own and could paint all I wanted. My son was right. This is a scam."

"Now, that's not true," Viola said. "Agnes, tell him. You're happy here, aren't you."

"As happy as anywhere. It doesn't take long to forget why you came, " she replied.

"You all bargained away everything you have," Albert said to the three. "Now you're trapped, and you have to live with your regrets; you'll die with them too. Take me back to my truck."

"But you haven't seen the library, health clinic, or fitness center yet."

"I've seen enough. If I stay, there would be no exit."

Sophie was afraid her grandfather was going to break down in tears as she slowly drove out of the dark valley.

"I saw a bar on the way in," he said. "Stop there."

"Grandpa, I'm sorry that wasn't what you expected."

"Say it and get it over with."

"Say what?"

"Say, I told you so. That's what you're thinking."

“Grandpa I feel bad for you. You couldn’t have known it would be like that.”

“Any idiot would have known. I need to be put away. The bar isn’t far up here. I think it’s called the Bear Town Tavern.”

“Grandpa, drinking isn’t going to help. We’ll find a little diner and have an early lunch instead. Please?”

"No," Albert insisted, "I want to stop here."

When they entered the Bear Town Tavern, two tables of men drinking coffee studied the strangers then went back to their caucus. Albert didn’t want Sophie sitting at the bar, so he took a table next to it. A gangly man with a previously white apron over a green Dickies’ suit came to greet them.

“Coffee?”

‘No," Albert said, "She’ll take a menu. I’ll take a beer and a double whiskey, neat.”

“One menu and one boilermaker.”

The man brought the menu and set the beer and whiskey down.

“Here’s to Bagger. He’s the lucky one between us.” Albert took a sip of whiskey and pulled on the beer.

“Grandpa, you can’t do this. You have to keep going. We’ll figure something out. You can finish your paintings.”

“Knock it off. Don't patronize me. I’m a washed-up old man. You know it -- everybody knows it. I’m going back home. I'll lock the studio for good. Andrew can do what he wants with me. I really don’t care.”

Sophie hurried through her sandwich, hoping he wouldn’t order a third round.

They continued up the road in silence, Sophie saw she still had no bars on the phone. She took a turn that looked familiar. Hopefully, she would climb out of this dead zone.

They started up the narrow winding road, through a forest of oak and maple. The sun was obscured by the canopy arching overhead. As the road steepened, the hard-woods gave way to birch and aspen. They passed a solitary white pine standing tall with craggy branches as a crown. The stumps of its broken limbs reached out like arms against the clouds. Gradually the trees became stunted, their exposed roots clinging to the mountainside, until only ancient, twisted cedars remained in the crevices of lichen-covered rocks. As they came around a corner, the foreground fell away exposing a mountain scene stretching in front of them. Sophie pulled into a small parking area. They both got out of the truck and walked toward a low stone wall that separated the black pavement from the abyss below.

Sophie and Albert were strangers to the outdoors. Most of their lives had been spent in the man-made world. Here was an expanse void of human habitation or marks of man's alterations. The valley before them was formed by steep granite vaults covered with a mosaic of green at the base that gave way to every tone of gray until the summits merged with the sky. The incense of juniper wafted by. Both were speechless as they tried to adjust their eyes to infinity. The atmosphere was filled with multi-colored light from the sun shining through a rose window of clouds. After a few minutes Sophie stepped back a bit.

“I’ve never seen anything like this. It's wonderful, but I don’t like being this close to the edge.”

Albert remained quiet until he turned and said, “Well, my dear, right there is the difference between you and I. You’re afraid you will fall. I’m afraid I will jump."

“Grandpa, how can you say something like that? Don’t you know that would be like a knife in my heart? Your life is precious to me. Don’t you know I love you?”

Albert looked away. “You think you love me, but you just feel sorry for me. You don’t really know me or what I've done in the past.”

Sophie took Albert’s hands and pulled him to face her.

“Grandpa, I love you as you were, as you are, and as you will be. I love you because that's who I am. I promise I'll always love you. I'll take care of you no matter what happens. You can accept that or not, but you can’t change me.”

Albert closed his eyes. He felt faint. His knees buckled, and he had to kneel. Sophie got on her knees also and held him. Gradually he softened and let himself sink into her arms.

He heard his granddaughters' voice, but it seemed distant.

"Grandpa, are you all right?"

He felt like he had jettisoned a weight and was floating away as the mountain shrunk below him. He stayed in Sophie's embrace to keep him tethered until the feeling passed.

"I'm not sure what just happened. Was I gone for long?" he said.

"You've been here with me. I didn't let you go. Let me help you to the truck. You should rest now."

They rode in silence along the shoulder of the mountain. Soon the GPS found them and rerouted them back to a main road. Albert leaned against his rolled-up sport coat and fell asleep.

By mid-afternoon Albert was hungry. They found a diner.

"Dad would love this," Sophie said. "The greasier the better, and it has a buffet"

"They've got prime rib," Albert said.

Sophie ate her chicken marsala with a side of ziti while eyeing a display of desserts. She decided on a piece of white cake with cream frosting. She cut a piece and held it up with her fingers.

"Here Grandpa, do you want some?"

Albert looked at his granddaughter then at the cake.

"Yes... I do."

Thirty Three

Andy awoke. It was Monday morning and a month away from work loomed ahead. Since there had been no forewarning, he had no plans, just a calendar of empty slots. In some odd way this turn of events didn't bother him. He wasn't sure if it was the apathy of depression or something else. Lillian was right; they should get away --someplace new and different. He found her at the kitchen island working at her laptop.

"Well," she said, "I was afraid things were too good to be true."

"What's wrong?" Andy asked.

"I was checking last week's property transactions. That bastard Frank sold his plaza to Douglas Brothers for ten thousand less than I offered him. As greedy as he is, he took less just to spite me. I wondered why he wasn't returning my calls."

"I'm sorry, Lil. I can't believe he's that much of an ass. Maybe they made some kind of side deal."

"You'll never understand. You frat boys don't change -- no women allowed. You want us to stay in our little pink sororities and wait for you to come screw us, then expect a thank you in the morning. I'm going for a run."

"I'm not like that; don't get mad at me," Andy protested.

"Yeah, and how many female partners does your firm have?"

"There's one."

"I rest my case."

Andy thought it better to avoid more of this. *I told her dealing with Frank might come to no good.*

He had some breakfast and went out to talk to the gardener. There wasn't anything to do in the yard. He inspected the patio. It was clean, and there wasn't any grass growing through the pavers. He patrolled the property fence. It was all in good repair. He remembered the driveway culvert had overflowed in the last rainstorm. While he was digging that out Lillian came sprinting up the road. She watched him work until she caught her breath.

"I might get my hair cut. I think I would look more professional. Would you like it if it was shorter?"

Andy knew there was no right answer but gave it a try.

"Maybe a change would be good for you,"

"Why? Do you think I should have cut it years ago?"

"Lillian please, do what you want. I'm sure it'll look nice."

"You're no help. I'm going to bribe Serge to fit me in today. He'll have some ideas."

She got a late-afternoon appointment and had to wait for a matron's perm to set. In addition to the exorbitant cost and tip, Lillian gave the Fifth Avenue expat stylist a hundred in cash and a sincere thank you. He had known exactly what she was looking for.

As she got into her car, Sophie's tone rang.

"Hi, Mom, where are you?"

"Just leaving a hair appointment."

"Did you get a trim?"

"No, you won't believe it. I had it cut short."

"Oh my gosh! Facetime me! Lemme see!"

Lillian switched the call to video and held her phone up while turning her head from side to side so her daughter could get a good look at her new coiffure.

"Mom, that's... It's so gorgeous! Serge, obviously."

"You really like it? It's not too short is it? Do I look old?"

"Mom, you're the most beautiful woman I know. Has Dad seen it?"

"Not yet. I doubt he remembers the last time I had it short."

"I know he'll love it. Anything else new?"

"Actually, there is. Your Dad is taking some time away from work. He's been having a rough time."

"It's because of me, isn't it?"

"I'm not going to lie; you're a big part of it. At least he's dealing with it this time. He seems pretty good."

"Mom, I have something to tell you. Promise you won't go ballistic."

"Nothing ever ends well when you say that. What did you do now?"

"You know how Grandpa wanted to go to Vermont?"

"Don't tell me..."

"I'm home now, we just went up and back. I didn't want to worry you. Things have changed. We really need to talk -- all of us."

"We need to talk about your behavior. You've been so irresponsible. That's what I think has changed. What else has changed?"

"Grandpa isn't going to Vermont. That's all I know right now. We still have to deal with the paintings either way."

"I just don't know what to do with you. Probably we'll be coming up there this week sometime. You need to tell your Dad what you did."

"I know. Can't you break it to him? Then I'll call. I'm fine. Nothing bad happened, so it's no big deal."

"Call him."

"OK."

Lillian found Andy at the grill when she got home.

"You don't have to say anything," she said. "Just get used to it."

"Lil, Baby... that's... you're... it's just incredible! I love it."

"Really, is it too short?"

"It's perfect for you."

"I like it. Kind of a shock though. I haven't changed it in forever."

"I didn't think you could be more beautiful."

"Fiddle dee dee. You stop it now."

After dinner, Andy made an attempt at the pile of papers on his desk. He finished the bills but could not make sense of the investment reports, so he just looked at the totals and set them aside. His phone lit up with Sophie's number. Lillian had said she might call.

"Hi, Daddy."

"Hi, Cookie, how are you today?"

"I'm good. I have some news."

"What's that?"

"Grandpa has decided not to move to Vermont."

"I never thought he would. What changed his mind?"

"Well, we went to look at the place. It was horrible."

"What do you mean, 'you went to look at it?'"

"He and I drove up there on Sunday. Got back this evening."

"Sophie, why are you trying to kill me? I really don't need this right now. You did that without telling us?"

"I didn't want to worry you, and it's done. It went fine."

"Did you rent a car or what?"

"He wanted to go in his truck. He got it all fixed up. You're right; he's sneaky, but it was no problem."

"He risked your life for his craziness. My God, I can't believe it."

"Daddy, it's for the best. Now he wants to stay here in Rochester."

"We're coming up there this week. I thought you had more sense than that. This has to stop."

THIRTY FOUR

On Tuesday morning, Albert was inspecting the progress in the living room. The ceiling was painted. The trim was taped off and the walls patched with spackle. He saw Bonnie's Volvo pull into the driveway.

"Dad, come and sit with me," Bonnie said upon entering. "I have something to tell you."

"The living room looks good. What's wrong?"

"Mr. Bagwell left this side last night. I wanted to tell you in person -- not on the phone."

"I saw him Saturday," Albert said. "I'm not surprised. He was ready. He was a good man; he had a good life. A hard life for a while."

"I know you'll miss him. You guys were good friends."

"We were -- the only one I had."

"His calling hours are tomorrow afternoon. I'll let Andy know. He'll want to come."

"Thanks for telling me. I'm going up to my studio."

Bonnie came toward him. He opened his arms first and accepted her into them. He was getting used to this now.

Albert slowly worked on the portrait of Bagger. He could give it to Eugenia tomorrow. He portrayed him as a younger man but with his wise eyes.

After Andy heard from Bonnie about Mr. Bagwell, he called Lillian.

"I have a showing late today," Lillian told him, "and another one tomorrow morning. After that I'm clear."

"We could leave when you're done in the morning and be there for calling hours."

"I'll come home in a bit and start getting our clothes together then go to the showing. Do you think we'll stay for a while?"

"We could if it works for you," Andy said.

"Alright, Love you. See you in a little while."

"Love you too."

Late Wednesday morning, Andy, Lillian, and Jack were headed west to Rochester. Andy wasn't all displeased that -- for once -- Jack showed some defiance, mumbling about, "I have a job...Gina and I had stuff to do... getting put in the car like a dog and dragged away." Andy tried to mollify him with promises of golf.

Lillian searched Airbnb and other sites to find a place to stay near Rochester for a couple of weeks. There wasn't much available on short notice.

The line was thinning out when Andy, Lillian, and Jack got to the church. Sophie had texted that Albert wanted to go early, so they were already back home. Andy noticed the portrait of Bagger displayed next to the closed casket. It was a wonderful likeness, capturing not only his image but dignity as well. As they consoled the family, Eugenia stopped him in front of the portrait.

"Isn't this special? It was so kind of your father to do it for us. We'll treasure it forever."

Andy was taken aback to think his decrepit father could have done that. "When did he draw that?"

"I guess since Saturday," Eugenia said. "He's so thoughtful."

Andy could not come up with a reply. He thanked Eugenia for all she had done for Albert and how much her father meant to all of them. He shook the hands of Bagger's grandsons and thanked them as well. As he was leaving, Andy was surprised to see Jack Armstrong standing at the end of the line.

"Jack, what are you doing here?" Andy asked.

"The grandsons are in our Scout troop. The Scouts have already been through. I had to wait for someone to sit with Helen."

"I didn't know they were Scouts."

"Oh, sure, they're on their way to Eagle. You promised me a drink sometime. Are you free? I don't have to be back home for a couple hours."

"I just got here, but, yes, I would love to talk. Can you run me home later?"

"Sure."

Andy caught up with Lillian at the door.

"Lil, Jack Armstrong is here. The boys are in his Scout troop. I would love to spend some time with him. Can you find your way to Dad's? Jack will bring me back"

“Sure, I guess. We’ll figure something out for dinner. See you back there.”

Jack waited in line to speak to Bagger's grandsons and the rest of his family. Andy chatted in the sitting room with some of Bagger’s and Albert’s old co-workers until Jack was done.

"How about the Back Door?" Jack suggested.

"That would be fitting, I guess," Andy replied.

Mrs. Beasley had heard the news. She was weepy.

"On the house, guys. I'll miss him. He was a real gentleman."

Jack and Andy took their beers and found a table away from the serious midday drinkers at the bar. Andy inquired about Helen, but Jack shut him down.

“I talk about my problems every day. What’s going on with you? You’re walking around like there’s a bag of rocks hanging 'round your neck.”

“Is it that obvious? I've had some changes. You’re one of the few people who know I have mood problems. Most people just assume I'm a jerk. It’s been rough the last couple of months. I've been up, and now I’m down. Then all this going on with Dad and my daughter. Just to top it off, my law partners voted to force me out for a month, maybe more, so I can’t even go to work.

“That’s a lot all at once.”

“What's funny is I really don’t care about work. I don’t know if it’s a good sign or bad. It’s my daughter and my father that I can’t handle. I’m nearly murderous toward him -- not healthy, I know.”

“Tell me what’s going on.”.

“Like I said last time, Dad is selling his house, which is fine. What isn't good is he convinced Sophie to stay and pack up his barn full of paintings for storage. She won’t go to grad school like we planned. She wouldn’t even go to Paris when I offered. Now he practically abducted her and took her to Vermont in a broken down old truck. She could have been killed.”

“She sounds like a young woman trying find her own way. It seems to me this is because she's spending time with your father. Why is that?"

"That's what Lillian said, it pissed me off then too. Maybe it is, but what does that have to do with anything?"

Jack didn't flinch, "What started it with your father? How long has it been?"

“It's been since the night my mother died.”

"Other people have lost their mothers but don't hate their fathers."

"Not everyone has a father like mine. Let's get out of here."

They said goodbye to Mrs. Beasley.

"Tell Al to stop in. I don't want to lose both of them."

"I'll tell him,” Andy said. “Thanks for the beer.”

Jack slowly drove back to Albert's house. He knew when to let silence do the work. He parked across the street from the driveway. Andy looked at his old basketball hoop. He remembered, on the worst of the nights, shooting jump shots until his legs were trembling. Only then could he collapse in bed and end the day. He turned and looked at his mentor and friend. He saw only patience and compassion.

"What do you want, Jack?"

"Tell me about that night. Tell me what has been between you and your father all these years."

"I've never told the truth to anyone, except Lillian."

Andy felt like he was in a trance. He went back to the night his mother died. The evening had started like most. His mother and father were shouting. His mother becoming more and more hysterical, his father becoming more insulting.

"All you do is sit here and buy crap," his father yelled.

"At least I gave up pretending to be a great artist, not like you. You just hide up there to escape me and your kids," his mother yelled back.

As usual they ended up in the bedroom, shouting, thinking they were sheltering their two children who had nowhere to hide. This night was different. Andy heard his father say, "Don't start with that. You're not going to put us through it again."

His mother was screaming. "I'll do it! I'll do it!"

Suddenly the bedroom door opened. His father wasn't shouting. He was calm. "Then maybe it's the best thing for you -- for us all. If that's your choice, do it. I'm not stopping you again."

"He told Bonnie and me to go to our rooms and stay there. Then he left. He went to his studio."

"Jack, he knew what she was going to do. He left her there and waited for it to happen. He painted while my mother killed herself. He all but shoved the pills down her throat. How am I supposed to forget that? How am I supposed to forgive him?"

Jack put his hand on Andy's shoulder. "Andy, how are you doing with Jesus?"

"I go to church most weeks. We pray every night at dinner. I'm giving a lot of money. I serve on the finance committee."

"I don't mean church. I mean with Jesus. Are you leaning on him? Are you trusting him? Are you letting him carry some of this burden?"

"I feel like there's something keeping me from that."

Jack was silent.

"It's my father isn't it? My anger is keeping Jesus away," Andy said.

"He's here Andrew. You just can't feel Him."

"What do I have to do?"

"What did Jesus do for you?" Jack whispered.

Jack waited.

"I don't think I can make it happen. I've had this anger so long, I'm not sure who I would be without it."

"You can't make it happen at all by yourself," Jack said. "Use this time off you've been given. Take some time alone. Pray; ask God to help you."

"That's not me. I'll try. I'll stay in touch. Thanks, Jack. You're a good friend. "

"I told you years ago to call anytime you needed me. The offer still stands."

The edge of Andy's rage toward his father was dulled. When he came up the driveway everyone was gathered at the picnic table. Albert got up and met him.

"Hello, Father."

"Andrew, I'm sorry I took Sophie to Vermont. There's nothing I can say except that."

"It was a really selfish thing to do. It could have turned out bad. I just can't fathom she would do it without telling us. I'm glad you both got home safe. The place wasn't very good, I take it."

"No, it wasn't good at all. Sophie is a special girl; don't be hard on her. It was my fault."

"I can't stay mad at her. She drives me nuts."

Sophie and Lillian were watching the two men.

"That seems to have gone better than I expected," Sophie said.

"It would be nice if they could call a truce," Lillian said.

"Hopefully I can get a truce with Dad. Here he comes."

Sophie ran to her father and held him tight. "Daddy, I'm so glad you're here. Mom said you might stay for a while?"

"I would like to," Andy said.

"That would be so great. I've missed you so much."

"I'm angry with you. Something terrible could have happened. Plus, you should never take off like that without telling us. I thought you knew that."

"I know I didn't handle it very well. But you taught me to be careful, and I was. You've taught me so many things. Maybe that's why I had the confidence to do it --because you've taught me so well."

"Knock it off. Aren't you getting a little old for that act? Go get me a beer."

For the rest of the day it seemed that a detente had been reached and they all enjoyed being together. They ordered dinner and gathered around the picnic table. Albert talked about Bagger and his days as a plumber. They all let him reminisce until he tired of it and went in the house.

After her family left for the hotel, Sophie went back to her apartment and called Randall.

"How'd it go with your father?" he asked.

"He was fine, he never stays mad for long. I'm used to him."

"More like he's used to you," Randall laughed.

"Whatever could you mean?"

"I mean you have him tied around your finger. You tend to do that, you know?"

"Yeah, but this time he told me grow up. He's never said that before."

"He has a right to be mad, you know. That was a boneheaded thing to do. I was worried about you too."

"That's because you both underestimate me. Anyway, it sounds like Mom, Dad, and Jack are going to stay in the area for a while. Dad is off work for a month. They're looking for a place to stay."

"It might be a little weird, but our cottage is available. Some friends of my Mom's are there now, but they're leaving Friday morning. We rent it a few weeks a year, but it's open until next month some time. It isn't fancy or anything."

"It would be weird, but I can tell them. Are you worried about my Dad?"

"I didn't make a very good first impression."

"Oh, just give him a hug and tell him how great he is. He'll forget all about it," Sophie said with a giggle.

"I doubt that would work for me. Can I see you tomorrow? I could always mow the lawn."

"I'll probably be at Grandpa's. I'll text you after I talk to them about the cottage."

"OK. Good night, Sophie."

"'Night, RJ."

THIRTY FIVE

Thursday morning Sophie met her family at the hotel for breakfast. Lillian was intently working her phone when Sophie sat down.

“I can’t believe it's so busy around here. There are no decent places to rent.”

“As usual, I've solved your problem," Sophie said smugly. "I found a place for you to stay.”

“What another attic?” Andy asked.

“No, a quaint cottage resting on the shore of lovely Canandaigua Lake. There’s boating and swimming available.”

“How do you know about this place?” Lillian asked.

“It belongs to a friend of mine. He said it's available on Friday.”

“What kind of friend?”

“He’s the guy that mows Grandpa’s yard, and he helped a lot getting the basement and living room cleaned out.” She thought it best not to mention he also fixed the truck.

“You mean the weasel I had to practically throw water on when he saw you? That guy?”

“Daddy, that’s not fair. He’s a great guy. His name’s RJ -- Randall. I've been to church with him twice. We’re just friends.”

"You haven't mentioned him before," Lillian said.

"It didn't come up. I mostly see him when he comes to help. Grandpa likes him."

"It wouldn't hurt to look at the place," Lillian said.

"How does a guy like that own a cottage?" Andy asked.

"His family has a farm. I guess it's part of that. I've never been to his house."

"It's probably a shack they rent out for extra money. Let's keep looking; there has to be something around," Andy said.

"He's coming to mow the lawn today. You can talk to him then," Sophie said.

"We can at least do that. I'd like to meet this boy anyway," Lillian said and studied her daughter's reaction.

"Mom, he's a friend. No big deal."

Sophie had a second cup of coffee while her parents went to change. She texted Randall.

Think they want to look at cottage.

K be there 1pm

Better drive car not bike

Got it see you then

K

Randall had been up early to get the Niagaras sprayed in the cool of the morning. After he cleaned the sprayer, he went into the kitchen for coffee. His mother was taking molasses cookies out of the oven.

"Awesome, Mom! These are so good warm. Where's Dad?"

"He was going to mow the headlands in the west vineyard."

"Do you remember that girl I told you about? In Rochester?"

"How could I forget? You talk about her any chance you get."

"Whatever. Her family is visiting and wants to rent a cottage. Could I show them ours?"

"We were hoping to keep it open for a few weeks, but I guess you could. Better check with your dad. He'll be coming down for coffee."

"Fine with me. Maybe get to meet this new girl," his father said. "Don't forget we got a load to get out tonight. Truck's coming at eight."

"I know. I'll be there," Randall said.

Lillian came out of the hotel bathroom. "I love my new cut! I just towel it dry and I'm good to go. But I can fix it fancy too."

"That's nice," Andy said. "I heard back from Don. He and the developer can meet at two today. I'm waiting to hear from Geoff. It will be good to get everyone on the same page."

Lillian muttered, "That's nice," and opened her laptop.

"What'd you say? Are you still looking for a cottage?"

"I didn't say anything to you. I just want to look at listings around here – see what property goes for."

≈

Albert was eating lunch with Sophie when Andy and Lillian arrived. Jack was sullen; this was turning out to be as boring and lame as he thought it would be.

"Dad," Andy said, "the realtor and the other guys are coming to meet at two o'clock. You can let us all know what you're thinking."

"You guys give me a headache. I'll be in my studio."

"Well, then tell me now. What are your thoughts?"

"I guess I'll have to find a place around here somewhere. Doesn't sound like there's any hurry."

"Maybe we'll have a better idea after we meet today."

"I want to take a little walk around the neighborhood," Lillian said. "I'll be back soon."

As Lillian walked back up the driveway, a gray car drove past her and parked in front of the garage. Randall took a breath and got out. He saw Lillian coming toward him. He fought his panic as she reached out her hand.

"You must be Randall, Sophie's friend. I'm Lilly, her mother."

"Nice to meet you Mrs. Martel. I'm here to mow the lawn."

"Sophie said you've been very helpful. We appreciate it. Would you like some something to drink before you get started?"

"No, thank you."

She seemed relaxed, and he felt more at ease. Randall could tell she wanted to say more.

"Randall, I don't want to be forward, but I understand things didn't go well when you met my husband. Is that right?"

“He doesn't have a good impression of me. He felt he had to set me straight about Sophie.”

"May I make a suggestion?”

“Sure... yes Ma’am.”

“My husband values directness and honesty. Your best bet is to talk to him. Say you learned from it and would like to move on. I’m sure you’re intimidated by him, many people are. But mostly, he's a reasonable person.”

“I’ll try. Thank you.”

Randall opened the garage door and was checking the mower's oil and coolant when Andy came in.

“Good afternoon,” Andy said

Hello sir, I’m Randall. We met a few weeks ago.”

“Yes, I remember quite well.”

“May I have a minute of your time?”

“Go ahead.”

“I didn't behave properly that day. I’ve learned from it and would like to move on. I have nothing but respect for Sophie.”

“I understand you've become friends with her.”

“I’d like to think so.”

“Thanks for clearing the air. We'll see how things go. Sophie said your family has a house available to rent.”

“We do. It’s not fancy, just an old cottage, but my dad has taken good care of it. It has a newer kitchen, three bedrooms, one full bath, and what my mom calls 'a powder room.' There’s a dock that’s nice to sit on. I’d be glad to show it to you. If it’s not what you want, that’s fine.”

"We can have a look. I won't hold you up. We can talk later," Andy said

As Andy was leaving, Sophie clattered down the studio stairs.

She's too late to rescue her friend, Andy thought. *I have to admit, he has a good hand-shake, and he looked me in the eye. I probably should cut him some slack.*

Andy walked back to the house. He noticed his father and Lillian sitting on the bench by the lawn. Lillian was patting the old man's back when – to Andy's near disbelief – his father leaned in and hugged her.

Randall was cleaning the mower when Geoff arrived. They chatted for a minute, then Geoff came up on the porch.

"I'll leave you people to decide my fate," Albert said.

Andy thought he detected some humor in his father's voice.

Don arrived with the CEO, Stan Michaels, at 2:20. He shook hands all around. He had the air of a man accustomed to being the last to arrive. The four men walked the perimeter of the property then filed into the kitchen and sat down. Lillian lingered on the porch until suddenly Geoff stood up.

"Lillian, I'll get you a chair from the dining room."

"I can get it; stay there," Lillian said. She pulled a chair up to a corner of the table.

Stan explained that the grant had to be used before the end of the year. The men discussed various options and possible scenarios. They discussed zoning ordinances and variances. They noted the lack of easy access to the property.

Stan offered to ask the state representatives to discuss zoning with the Town Board; especially about how the lack of diverse housing and multi-generational neighborhoods might impact future state aid. However, in the end, he said it was unlikely he would be able to expend many resources on pursuing this property due to the discussed complications and the need to fulfill the grant in a timely manner.

Don discussed their options and again recommended keeping it listed as a single residence. He assured Andy that he would put it on multiple listings and even advise his competitors of the situation. As Stan was making this-meeting-is-over motions, Geoff turned to Lillian.

"Do you have any thoughts?"

Lillian stood up. She towered over the men sitting in the kitchen chairs. All eight eyes were on her.

"Actually, I do. I'm going to buy Albert's property... and the plaza out front. After I have the plaza demolished, I'll form an LLC and transfer the two properties as one to that LLC, thereby making the combined property zoned as mixed use. Then I'll subdivide, leaving the house and garage as a separate lot. After that, if Stan is still interested, I'll offer the remaining three-plus acres to him for his senior housing project. The asking price would reflect the amount of property, the road frontage gained, and current market value."

Geoff looked at Andy. Andy looked at Don. Don looked at Stan. Then they all turned back to Lillian.

"That's brilliant!" Geoff said.

"Dad gets lifetime use, and Sophie can stop working here?" Andy asked.

"That's what I was thinking," Lillian said.

"This really is brilliant. Hopefully Dad will agree to it."

"He already has," Lillian said.

"Maybe we should have asked you earlier," Don said.

"Maybe."

Andy had witnessed plenty of grand-standing power-grabs in his career. This one was spectacular and pulled off by his own wife. He could not have been more proud.

Lillian watched as the men made important-sounding noises and agreed to keep in touch. Then they politely took their leave.

After Don, Stan, and Geoff left, everyone joined Sophie, Jack, and Randall on the porch.

"So, my dear," Andy asked, "how long have you been plotting behind my back?"

"Not long. It started when the deal with Frank fell through."

"What's going on?" Sophie asked.

"If things work out as planned," Lillian said, "Grandpa will be staying here in the house and keep his studio too."

"Oh my gosh! I don't believe it. How'd that happen?"

"I should go," Randall said.

"No, please stay," Lillian said. "We may need your help with some things if you want."

They filled Sophie and Jack in on the details then discussed future plans. The remodel of the house would continue and be expanded throughout.

"This calls for a celebration," Andy said. "Let's go out someplace fun tonight. Randall, can you join us?"

"I can't tonight. I have to load a hay truck later."

"RJ, why does it have to be tonight?" Sophie asked.

"The truckers like to drive at night."

"Can you at least have a beer with us?" Andy asked.

"I can do that – thanks."

After Randall finished his one beer, they made arrangements to look at the cottage on Friday afternoon.

"That kid seems responsible," Andy said after Randall had left.

"He has a thing about hay," Sophie said. "What were you talking about in the garage?"

"You."

"Daddy, did you embarrass him?"

"Hope so. Where should we go tonight? I have to call Bonnie."

Lillian had never known a tension-free time when Andy, Albert, and Bonnie were together. The only minor flareup occurred when Bonnie reminded Andy that she had told him things would work out – that it was "good Karma."

Lillian allowed herself a moment of pride after Andy said, "It didn't just happen. It's Lillian's hard work and brains that's getting it done. You should thank her." And Bonnie did.

That night in the hotel bed Andy asked, "Well Ms. Martel, did you enjoy kicking us in the balls this afternoon?"

"I did, actually."

"It kinda turned me on," Andy whispered

Lillian reached for the light. “Me too.”

Thirty six

On Friday, Andy, Lillian, and the kids took the scenic route to Randall's cottage. When the GPS announced they had arrived at their destination, Andy pulled in front of a barn. They could see most of the way down the narrow lake along the hills to the east. Randall came out of the barn.

"You found it. Did you enjoy the drive?"

"I haven't been out here in years," Andy said. "I'd forgotten how beautiful it is."

"The driveway is just up the road. You can follow me."

He hopped on an ATV and led them down a lane between vineyards that ended in a parking area. They went down a few steps to the house. It was a two-story with a metal roof and white clapboards. Lillian noticed a natural field-stone foundation behind the flower beds. They were met at the door by a tall woman in jeans and a sleeveless green blouse. She had salt-and-pepper hair in a long braid laying over her shoulder. Her deep-set eyes and angular face left no doubt Randall was her son.

"Mom, this is Mr. and Mrs. Martel, Sophie, and Jack."

"It's Lilly and Andy," Lillian said.

"I'm Annie. Welcome. Come on in and take a look around. It isn't much, but we enjoy it here."

Lillian saw it was genuine rustic chic -- what the Westchester crowd unsuccessfully tried to imitate. There were over-stuffed chairs and a big couch in the living room. A farm-house table with benches sat in a room fronted with windows overlooking the lake. The kitchen had butcher-block counter tops and light-green wooden cabinets. There were some open shelves displaying antique china. They toured the bedrooms and baths then went outside and walked down to the lake. Jack's eyes widened when he saw the Jet Ski and two boats at the dock. The beach was partially shaded by a huge willow tree.

"Andy, this is perfect," Lillian said. "Let's take it."

"Fine with me. Jack what do you think?"

"Be OK. Probably no golf courses out here."

"There's one in Naples--Reservoir Creek. Everybody says it's really nice," Randal said.

Andy turned to Annie. "We sure appreciate this. I hope we're not imposing."

"No, not at all. Randall told us what nice people you are. I'm glad it's working out for you."

"I'll get you a check, then we have to go back and get our clothes. We'll be back in a few hours."

"The door'll be open. Make yourself at home."

It didn't take long for the family to settle into lakeside life. Randall gave Jack an informal boater-safety course and cut him loose on the Jet Ski. They went out in the boat, swam, and gathered for cocktails on the dock. Andy had brought his famous omelet pan, so there were breakfasts and brunches featuring his specialty. There were dinners on the patio lit with tiki torches. Lilly enjoyed a change-up in training with long morning swims. Andy explored the lake by solo canoe, sometimes letting the boat drift with the wind. Jack discovered that Reservoir Creek golf course was a links design with challenging holes and spectacular views. He and Andy spent a day dueling up and down the hilly course. Sophie and Randall came and went. She was getting an education on the life of a farmer.

By mid-week the entire family had frequented Naples at the south end of the lake for the shopping and restaurants there. On Thursday, Bonnie brought Albert out for the day. Andy served him steaks, Genesee Cream Ale, and whiskey. After dinner, Andy and Albert sat together on the dock talking; both carefully exploring common ground. Later, Andy guided his father up the steep steps from the dock to the cottage. He closed the car door gently and watched as Bonnie drove away.

By the second Monday, Andy's biggest concern was if the five ducklings and their mother had survived the night under the roots of the willow tree The babies glided out like a pull-toy behind the stately mallard hen. They kept their distance as he launched the canoe for his morning paddle. He was on the lake before the power boats and Jet Skis, sharing it with puttering fishermen. He studied the hills to the east. There was a collection of local history books at the cottage. He had been reading about local Native American lore and could name

Genundawa and Nundawao -- the two hills dominating the eastern horizon. Nundawao – The Great Hill, called South Hill by the locals -- stretched along the lake shore. Genundawa or Bare Hill lay to the north. He watched as the rising sunlight flowed up Genundawa. It wouldn't be a long paddle to its foot on the shore of Vine Valley, the small gap between the two hills. He had learned that the summit of Bare Hill was an ancient ceremonial site and afforded a view down Canandaigua Lake. He paddled back to shore and went to find Lillian.

Lillian watched as Andy came up the steps. She was glad to see he had some spring in his step. *The week has been good for him. This place has been good for him.*

"Hey, Lil, are you up for a little adventure?"

"I have no plans."

"I want to paddle across the lake and hike up that hill over there."

"Wow, that's quite an adventure!"

"We can get three in the canoe. Maybe Jack will go."

"He and Sophie just left. He's helping RJ in the vineyard. He wants to drive a tractor."

"They've become good friends," Andy said. "That RJ knows how to get to us."

"Or, he just might be a nice young man. Have you thought of that?"

"I suppose. Well, do you want to go?"

"We'll need to pack some water and lunch."

"And wine."

With Lillian's strong paddling in the bow, they were able to cut a straight line across the lake. They beached the canoe and asked the lifeguard on duty if they could leave it there. She agreed to keep an eye on it. They stopped in the general store just off the beach to ask directions. They were told if they walked up the road to a green house there was a trail up the hill behind it. The owners of the house would probably let them enter there.

They walked up a steep curving road. They passed a sign marking a prehistoric Indian burial site and continued up the hill. Sure enough, the people at the greenhouse were happy to let them cross their lawn to the trail.

The hill was steep, but the bushes gradually gave way to a mature oak forest where the path was open. It finally leveled off, and they came to a clearing. There was a large mound of charcoal from the signal fire that carried on an autumnal Seneca Indian ceremony. Canandaigua Lake glistened beneath hills shadowed by an armada of clouds sailing from the horizon. At first it seemed silent, but as their hearts slowed down Lillian and Andy noticed crickets chirping, peepers peeping, and birds singing and chattering. There was hammering by woodpeckers and rustling in the bushes.

They found a flat spot and spread out their lunch. Andy opened a bottle of rosé that Randall had suggested and raised a glass to Lillian.

"To us. We have a good life."

"We're blessed."

They chatted about the cottage, Jack, Sophie, and plans for the week, but they both sensed their idle chatter was intruding – disturbing something unseen. They became comfortable in silence. They listened to the sounds of the animal village. They felt the earth beneath them, the warmth of the sunlight, and yielded to the caress of the breeze. There seemed to be a pulse coming through the ground -- like a rhythm from drums softly beating. Andy looked at his wife. Her eyes were closed. Her face was soft. He closed his eyes. He softened his face. His mind stayed blank until he exited time. Then with every breath came a verse of the Lord's Prayer. *Forgive us our trespasses... as we forgive those... who trespass against us.*

Andy prayed, *"Help me. Show me how. Take it from me."*

He felt Lillian looking at him.

"Where were you?" She asked.

"I'm not sure. Did you feel anything weird?"

"It's peaceful here. I was praying. I felt really connected."

"Lillian?"

"Yes?"

"I have to forgive my father."

"Are you ready?"

"Maybe. I'm not sure how to do it."

Jack carefully drove the tractor between the rows of grapes. He was towing a trailer loaded with posts. Randall was walking ahead and stopped at a post that was leaning over.

Sophie had never watched a man work before, to use his body to move something. The task was to replace the broken post. His back rippled; his legs flexed; his arms bulged as he wrestled the old post out of the ground. Then he took a round metal bar and drove it into the soil and made circles to widen the impact. He did this over and over until the shaft was well past halfway into the ground. Then he jammed a sharp new post into the hole and climbed onto the trailer. He lifted a long-handled hammer with an iron head the size of a coffee can. In one smooth movement, he swung it over his head and whacked the top of the post. The sound of the impact made Sophie jump. He hit it several more times then hopped off the trailer. The sweat from the effort outlined his muscles through his tight shirt. The thoughts filling Sophie's mind made her blush.

"Why didn't you put the new post in the hole that was already there?" Jack asked.

"My Grandfather always said, 'Never put a new post in an old hole. It'll just rot.'"

"Is this what you do every day?" Sophie asked.

"No, we do posts in the spring, but sometimes they just break."

"I mean smashing things... pulling things... working like that."

"That's what it takes to grow grapes. Something to think about when you're sipping wine."

Jack confidently drove the tractor back to the barn. Sophie sat next to Randall on the back of the trailer. Their shoulders and legs jostled together as the trailer rolled over the rough ground.

"I've got some other stuff to do today," Randall informed her when they arrived back at the barn. "Can I see you later?"

"Come for dinner tonight. I'll cook."

"I'd like that."

Sophie was worried. It was after one o'clock and her parents were gone and so was the canoe. They hadn't left a note or texted her. The car was in the driveway.

When they glided up to the dock Sophie produced a scene – complete with trembling lower lip and watery eyes.

"I guess we should have left a note," Lillian said.

"Wait a minute," Andy said. "Do you see any hypocrisy here?"

"No, that was different. Mom, I need to talk to you."

"Oh no. Now what?"

"Nothing bad," Sophie said as they walked up to the kitchen.

"I invited RJ for supper. I said I would cook. I kinda got lost in the moment."

"The moment?".

"I just asked him, OK? The only thing I know how to make is lasagna."

"Interestingly, I invited his parents for tonight also."

"Mom, why'd you do that?"

"I saw Annie yesterday. I thought we should. I guess you'll be cooking for your boyfriend and his parents."

"He's not my boyfriend. What am I going to do?"

"I was going to have grilled chicken and a salad. How about you make your sauce and we can have chicken parmesan. Would that be all right?"

"I can make sauce. It's usually good, isn't it?"

"It's always excellent. What kind of moment did you have?"

"You wouldn't understand. I'm going to the roadside stand for tomatoes and stuff."

"I do understand. He's a good-looking man."

"Mom, that's so gross, gaaagh!"

At dinner, Sophie was so nervous she couldn't taste anything. She noticed Randall and Jack both took seconds. Mrs. Johnson was gracious and raved about the fresh basil and garlic Sophie used.

"Nothing like home-grown tomatoes. They're one of the best parts of summer," she said.

During dinner Andy quizzed Randall and Mr. Johnson about grapes and wine production. They discussed the wines they each had brought.

Lillian described their trip up Bare Hill and how peaceful it was there.

"Yes, I believe it's a thin spot," Annie said. "I love going over there."

"What do you mean, a thin spot?" Andy asked

"A thin spot – a place where it's easier to feel God or whatever anyone believes in. Where the boundary between here and the beyond is weak – thin. It's been a sacred place since before the Senecas. There's still a ceremony there every

Labor Day weekend. Native Americans pray, sing, and dance with the locals around a big fire. It's nice.”

After they were done with dinner, Lillian turned to Sophie. “How about you entertain your guests on the dock. I’ll pick up before we have Annie’s dessert. It's supposed to rain, but we should have time.”

Annie insisted on helping and naturally started washing the dishes.

“I remember the first time I cooked for a boyfriend’s family," Annie said. "I guess we all go through it. She did fine. She's so sweet and so lovely. You've done a wonderful job raising her.”

“Thank you, Annie. She’s a handful; I can tell you that. She says Randall is ‘just a friend.' Do you mind telling me what he says?”

“My Randall has had a hard year, but I've never seen him happier, or unhappier, since he met your daughter. I hope he won’t get hurt again like he did last winter, to be honest, Lillian.”

“I see. I’ll try to talk to Sophie. She has the same effect on Andy and me, if that's any help.”

They brought the strawberry shortcake down to the dock. The Martels declared it the best dessert ever.

“Nothing easier in the world to make,” Annie said.

“Annie makes the best shortcake in the county," her husband said. "Nobody makes it like she does. You're right Lilly, there's some lightening to the south. We'll get a storm here before the night is over.”

When they finished their desert, the Johnsons said their good nights and went up the steps with Lillian and Andy.

Finally, Jack got the hint and left Randall and Sophie alone on the dock.

“Dinner was really good,” Randall said.

“I was nervous. I didn’t know your parents were coming. I hope they liked it.”

“They loved it. They really like you too.”

“They’re so nice. I think they got along with my parents.”

“Your father seems more relaxed. He’s an interesting guy.”

“I told you he’d be fine.”

Sophie took Randall's hand, and they sat on the bench. “I've had such a good time this week,” she said. “Seeing what you do and just having fun together.”

"It's been nice seeing you with your family and getting to know you that way," Randall said. “Maybe we have more in common than you think. Family is important to both of us. Isn't that the most important thing?"

“I know what you're saying, but RJ, I have no idea where my life is going. All I know is I don’t want to hurt you.”

“I’m willing to take that chance. Sophie, I care about you… a lot.”

“We better go,” Sophie said.

She leaned against his shoulder.

“I should go,” she said again.

The flashes in the distance became brighter; the booming began to echo off the hills. His arms enveloped her with gentleness, but she felt the strength she had seen in the vineyard. His kiss wasn't an impatient prelude to further advances like the other boys. It was all; it was everything. It seemed to last forever, only to be interrupted by the first heavy rain drops that drummed against her skin. The cadence of the rain picked up. They kissed again then ran laughing, hand-in-hand, up the stairs to shelter.

THIRTY SEVEN

In the morning Sophie could tell her mother wanted to talk. She avoided her or cut her off until she was leaving.

"Mom, I know you want to talk about RJ. I do too but not right now. I need to think. I'm going to stay in Rochester for a couple days. I don't have any answers about anything. It's been great being with everybody. Thanks for everything."

"I understand honey, we'll set aside some time to talk when you're ready."

Actually, she didn't understand. She was only sticking with the plan – Andy's plan. He had said, "We're resting between quarters, just taking it easy. When the time comes, we'll put a full-court press on her." She had decided, *Sophie is safe; she hasn't anything dumb left to do, so let's just enjoy the vacation and face reality later.*

She was looking forward to today. Andy and Jack were going to play golf; Sophie was gone. A long stretch of solitude was awaiting.

Albert was having his after-lunch cordial when he was surprised to see Bagger's Taurus pull into the driveway. Eugenia and Bagger's grandsons got out.

"Good afternoon, Albert," Eugenia said. "Mind if we have a visit?"

"No, come on up. Would you like something to drink?"

"It's kind of you to offer, but we won't disturb you long."

Eugenia sat down heavily, and the identical boys sat together on a bench. Albert still had no idea which one was which. He thought Joshua was the one that talked more, but he couldn't remember.

"The boys here have something they want to ask you, but they're too shy, so they asked me to come along. Joshua, you try now. Tell Mr. Albert what you want."

"Granddad was going to help us, but he got sick," the one in red said.

"Help with what?" Albert asked.

"Our project for Eagle Scout. It has to be done before we turn eighteen, but Granddad couldn't help us."

"Albert," Eugenia said, "these boys have looked up to you for as long as I remember."

"Why would they do that?"

"Because you're a good man, and you were mighty kind to their granddad. Fact is, they want you to help them finish what he started. They don't want nobody else but you to help."

Albert was quiet. He studied the two young boys. Their faces were open, expectant. They were staring at him, biting their lower lips in identical ways.

"What's the project? I'm not sure I'd be any help."

"Benches," the one in blue said.

"Oh Lord, we gonna be here all day if you two don't speak up," Eugenia said. "They're making benches to put around an old folks' home so people have a place to sit outside. Dad had the plans all written down. They both been saving all the money you give 'em for the materials. They don't have enough for all they wanted, but they can get some done at least. They know what they want, but they need some adult help."

"Do you have the plans?" Albert asked.

"Yes, sir," the one in red answered.

"Go get em outta the car," Eugenia ordered. "Go on now!"

Albert inspected the drawings and material list. "You need to bend some pipe and drill holes in it. Was Bagger going to do this?"

"He bit off more than he could chew, it turns out," Eugenia said.

Andy was jubilant when he found Lillian on the deck.

"I take it you won against your son today?" she asked.

"Better than that. We got put in a foursome with a couple a jerks from Boston. They thought they were going to hustle us. We skinned 'em for three hundred bucks. It was fabulous. Best of all they're Red Sox fans."

"Andy, you let Jack play for money? Is that a good thing to do?"

"He was amazing! The more pressure, the better he played. I've never had more fun playing golf. I'm going to make some drinks. Those losers wouldn't go to the bar after we scalped them."

"Gunner, your jock is showing."

Andy was crushing ice when his phone buzzed. It was his father.

"Hello, Dad, what's wrong?"

"Nothing, I called... I called you to ask... I wondered if you would help me. I need some help."

"What's wrong? Should I come right down?"

"No."

"Well, what do you need."

"I want to build some benches."

Oh jeez, Andy thought, *it's finally happened. His mind is slipping.*

"Dad, do you feel alright?"

"I feel fine. I just can't build them by myself. I need your help."

"Why do you need benches?"

"It would be better if I explained in person. Can you come down tomorrow?"

"I was planning on checking on Vivian and Bonnie. I'll be there in the morning. Is Bonnie there now?"

"No, they left. I'll see you in the morning."

Before Andy could say anything more, his father hung up.

THIRTY EIGHT

When Lillian dropped Andy off in the morning, the zero-turn was in front of the garage. Albert had pulled a large metal bench into the middle of the garage floor.

"Good morning, Dad."

"You probably want to know what I'm doing," Albert said, "Here, have a seat." He slid two metal stools from under his work bench.

Albert explained about Bagger's grandsons' Eagle Scout project and showed Andy the plans Bagger had made.

"Dad, do you see any irony in this?"

"I know. I can't change the past, but maybe we can work together and help these kids do what you did. I'm trying to change, Andrew. It's way too late, but I'm trying."

"I have some changes to make too. Maybe this will help. What do we do first?"

"I told Eugenia I would only do it if you agreed to help. Now, I can call her. We have to get the material together. Where's Lillian?"

"She has a meeting with Geoff and Don this morning. She's hoping to get the closing dates set."

Lillian had to park on the street when she got back. Vivian's van was parked in next to the carpet installers' truck. Albert's pickup was in front of the mower. Andy and Albert were in the garage carrying a large contraption to the bench.

"How'd the meeting go?" Andy asked.

"It'll be a couple of weeks or more before any closings. We're on lawyer time now."

"Hey, don't be putting down lawyers."

Lillian went into the house. Vivian and Sophie were sitting at the table.

"I'm done here for now," Vivian said. "When you're ready to do more let me know."

"I'm putting things on hold until we close," Lillian said. "I might do more of a remodel, especially the kitchen. Sorry to take out what you did."

"That's what this place needs. I told the old man that when we started. But that's water under the bridge. Thanks for the work. I'm heading out."

After Vivian left, Lillian asked Sophie if she knew what her father and grandfather were up to.

"They're helping Mr. Bagwell's grandsons do their Eagle Scout project."

"That's bizarre in so many ways. You have no idea. It's a cold today in hell; that's for sure."

"I know. Dad told me about Grandpa not helping him when he was a kid. Grandpa is different now. He really is."

"He does seem to be. Can I take you to lunch?"

"Yeah, that would be nice."

They stopped by the garage. “Ta-ta, we’re off to lunch,” Lillian announced. “You boys are on your own.”

Andy came out. “Can you believe this?”

“Sophie told me about it. I guess miracles do happen.”

Andy laughed. “That would explain it; nothing else does. We’re going to go get the materials. Have a good time.”

Sophie led Lillian to her favorite cafe, as they were waiting for a table Monique approached from inside.

"Monique, it's Sophie. Do you remember me?"

"Of course. I thought you were going to call."

"Mom, this is Monique, she's the director of an art gallery near here."

"Pleased to meet you," Lillian said.

"Your daughter is quite accomplished. You must be very proud of her."

"I am. She was supposed to call you?"

"I was hoping to give her a tour of my gallery."

"I'm so sorry I haven't called. I would love to see it."

"Are you free Friday morning?"

"That would be wonderful, thank-you."

"Stop by. We can talk. Nice to meet you Lillian."

"Likewise. I'm looking forward to hearing about your gallery."

On the way to their table Lillian said. "She seems nice. How did you meet her."

"She's a friend of Derek's, my landlord. He knows a lot of artists and musicians."

"You've really settled in here, haven't you?"

"It does seem like I've been here a while."

"And now you have a young man interested in you. Tell me about RJ."

"What do you want to know?"

"His mother said he got hurt."

"He did. He was going to get married, but the girl broke the engagement last winter."

"And now he's interested in you, obviously."

"Yeah but, like, I told him. I won't be a rebound."

"What did he say?" Lillian asked.

"I don't think he'll give up."

"How do you feel about him?"

Sophie studied the ice cubes in her glass. "I like him Mom. I like him a lot. I wish it was a different time. This just isn't a good time for something like that."

"Like what?"

"You know, getting involved, having a boyfriend, getting serious. I have things I want to do -- travel, get a real job in the city someday. He'll never leave his farm, plus we have nothing in common."

"Sophie, you should always work toward your dreams, but you also have to set priorities -- decide what's really important to you for the long run. There's always a tradeoff."

"What are you saying? What about 'the plan' -- grad school, all that?"

"I'll tell you a story -- the whole story about your dad and me. I was a runner. My sense of worth was measured in tenths of seconds. I pushed myself, and I got faster and faster.

Sometimes I won; sometimes I was runner up. I finally learned being fast wasn't enough. It was all about enduring pain. To win, I had to endure more pain than the runner in front of me. I got good at enduring pain, even the pain of leaving Andy Martel behind to pursue my dream. I told him this just wasn't the right time. I had things I wanted to do.

In my last race before Olympic qualifiers another runner purposely clipped me, and I tore up my knee. I worked hard and got good again but never as good as I was, and it was four years until the next Olympics. I had to make a choice. As bad as that time was, without it, I wouldn't have come back to your father. I would have lost him and never had you and Jack."

"Are you saying women should give up their dreams to get a man?"

"Nothing comes for free, man or woman. Your dad gave up basketball and went to law school hoping that would make me stay. He has never regretted it. Tell me more about RJ."

"He listens to me, and you know how I can go on. He's sweet. He's been so nice to Grandpa, and you saw how he is with his parents. All I know is I like being around him. I think about him all the time. He's someone I could, you know... be with someday."

"It's not like everything has to change if you do get closer to him," Lillian said. "I'm just saying don't close any doors. I'm afraid if you shut out Randall you'll always wonder and compare. If you're attracted to him that should tell you something. We've talked about that; you know how you should behave."

"I didn't expect this from you, Mom."

"I know it's a sudden change. This isn't the advice I would have given you even a month ago. Mrs. Kowalski opened my eyes. You're a young woman now, which means I'm not. I have to face it. I'm praying we can grow together and stay close."

"I thought being a girl was hard. This woman stuff is worse. Are you having dessert?"

Bagger's grandsons were wearing their full Boy Scout regalia to meet with the manager of the metal-supply store. Andy had them rehearse their request for a discount. The boys did well. The manager was patient, and he gave them thirty percent off. They had planned on four benches but had raised only enough money for two. Andy gave them an added donation for all four. Albert bought the boys leather gloves and safety goggles.

Back at the garage they gathered around the bench.

"Your granddad was the best pipe bender in the shop," Albert told the boys. "He had a head for figures. You see all these numbers in the plans? They're the radius of all the curves. See how he plotted out a full-size drawing of the legs on this graph paper? I have to trace it onto wood, then I'll have a template to check against. You can start sanding the burs and edges off the slats and get them ready to paint."

Andy supervised the boys using palm sanders and helped them move the metal slats around. He watched his father deftly trace the curves onto a piece of plywood.

“Andy, you better cut this out. It’s really important to get it right.”

“Dad, I’m not sure I should do it.”

“Just get it close, then rasp to the line. You can do it.”

With that he handed Andy a saber saw and went to watch the boys.

When Lillian and Sophie returned, they saw Andy bent over a piece of wood. His tongue was pressed between his lips in concentration as he worked the rasp. An obviously amused Albert was watching.

“Look at my big strong man,” Lillian said.

“Now, don’t disturb him,” Albert said. “He’s doing a fine job. He can do more than push papers around.”

Andy ignored them both. “There, I think that’s good.”

Albert brought the graph paper over and laid it on the plywood. “Perfect. Nice job. That’s enough for today. I'm late for my nap. See you tomorrow.”

The boys cleaned up and were on their way.

"Sophie, what are you going to do?" Lillian asked.

“I guess I’ll ride back with you. I don’t have anything here until Friday when I go to the gallery.”

"That'll be a nice change for you. Whatever will you do tonight though?"

"Mom, get over it."

On the way she texted RJ.

Coming back to lake take me to dinner tonite?

Sure!!!!

≈

The restaurant was a funky place in Naples -- painted purple and teal on the outside, appointed with vintage chrome and Formica tables.

“Hi RJ,” the hostess said when they entered. “It’s been awhile.”

“Hi, Erin. This is my friend Sophie.”

“Hi Sophie. You know you’re with our sports hero don’t you? We all just worship him.”

“Don’t start ET. Just take us to our table.”

“Do you have female admirers every place you go?” Sophie asked.

“She was a cheerleader. That’s her excuse anyway.”

The waitress came. “Hello RJ, I was afraid you moved away or something. I missed you. Can I show you my specials?”

"Hello Bobbie Jo. No, we can read them on the board. We'll have a bottle of Riesling then order."

"Very good, sir."

“Maybe I should've picked a different place. The food is great here though.”

“I like being seen with a celebrity. I just hope all your girlfriends don’t gang up on me.”

"They've known me forever. They’re just bustin’ my butt. We know everything about everybody. I’m sure they already know all about you by now.”

All during dinner people stopped to say hi to Randall and meet his new girl. They had no privacy at all. Then a band started so they couldn't talk either.

"Do you want to go for a walk?" Randall asked after dinner.

They crossed the street and walked until they came to an ornate old school building.

"That's the school I graduated from."

They walked around back to the playground and sat in the swings. They were the tall swings with long chains.

"We used to see how high we could swing," Randall said, "then jump out. We had a blast."

"You could never move away from here, could you?" Sophie asked.

"For the right reason I might, but it would be hard to do. My great-great grandfather is buried just down the street. Why do you ask that?"

"More of an observation, not really a question. Did you ever kiss a girl on this play-ground?"

"Yeah, I think in fourth grade, why?"

"Don't you think it's about time again?"

"You're the most unpredictable girl I have ever known."

"Get used to it."

THIRTY NINE

Thursday night, after everyone had left the cottage, Lillian and Andy sat on the patio. It was a clear night, a little cool with a breeze rising off the lake. The hills were rolling eastward, exposing the Milky Way.

“I can’t believe two weeks are gone already,” Lillian sighed. “Tomorrow is our last day.”

“It has been great. Manhattan seems like a movie -- not real anymore. Lilly I have something to tell you about that.”

“About work?”

“Yeah. I didn’t ask for a leave. The partners voted to suspend me. I was dropping the ball. They weren’t real clear about what will happen at the end of the month either.”

“Why didn’t you tell me the truth?”

“I didn’t that first night because you were so excited about your business. Then I just didn’t. Now I am.”

“You've been carrying this alone? Why do you do that? Are you worried?”

“That’s part of the problem. I’m really not. I’ll get it together once I’m back. If they take me.”

“After all these years, I still don't totally get you."

“I am what I am. Let's not ruin tonight. We'll work it out. Actually, I wanted to ask you if it’s good with you if I stay and get the boys’ project done. You can go home with Jack. I’ll get a rental car.”

“You definitely should. It’s been good for you and your dad."

“Do you know in all my life, yesterday was the first time my father ever affirmed me? And for cutting a piece of wood. Of all the things I've done, that was the first.”

“He’s doing the best he can, Andy. I don’t get it either. Your Dad has been changed somehow.”

"A lot has changed in the last two weeks. I've done some thinking," Andy said. "Maybe I'm changing too."

On Friday morning Sophie dropped Andy off at the car rental and drove the Lexus directly to the gallery in time for her appointment.

She didn’t have to wait long until Monique met her and started a tour of the gallery. It was a beautiful old building, a work of art in itself. As they visited the exhibitions, for every question Sophie had, Monique had two. She asked about Sophie’s course work, her other interests, her past work experience, and her future plans. After seeing all the exhibits, they went into the work areas and office rooms. Finally, they were back in Monique’s office sitting in front of her desk.

"What do you think? Is it what you expected here in Rochester?" Monique asked.

"It has a fantastic collection, and the exhibits are so innovative and effective. You do a great job."

"You said you didn't have any definite plans right now, is that right?" asked Monique.

"I really don't, not at all. I'll probably end up back at my parents."

"What if you were to find a job here in Rochester?"

"I could look around, but I don't have a lot of time."

Monique got up from the side chair and sat behind her desk.

"Sophie, I'm currently interviewing for an assistant. Would you be interested in looking at the job description and possibly apply for the position? It's all online."

Sophie was so stunned she had to choke back tears. "I had no idea this was a job interview. I would've prepared. I would've dressed more appropriately. I'm sorry."

"I wanted to get to know you as a person, not an applicant. You did fine. You're an impressive woman. Would you consider applying? I can't guarantee anything until we've reviewed all the applicants. I will tell you, you're the only person I've invited for a tour.

"Certainly, I'll apply! I can't believe this is happening."

"I think you have a future in the art world. Of course, to advance you'll need a master's degree. Have you thought about that?"

“I have. I just wanted to take some time before I started on it.”

“There are several excellent programs in the area. Just something to think about.

Monique walked Sophie to the door and shook her hand. “I hope to be hearing from you soon.”

“You will. I'll start the application this afternoon. Thank you so much.”

It was crowded in Albert's garage Friday morning. Eugenia dropped the boys off, then Jack Armstrong stopped by to check on their progress and lend a hand. Albert set Jack and the boys up at the drill press to get the holes in the slats started. He and Andy began adjusting the bending machine.

"I sure wish old Bagger was here,” Albert said. “He could set this up blindfolded. It's a shame he didn't get to finish up with the boys."

"I'm sure he's looking down and happy you're doing it for him," Andy said.

"Just helping them is enough for me. That's all I can do while I'm still here."

"It's nice Jack stopped by," Andy said. "Do you mind him being here?"

"No, he knows the boys better than I do -- maybe knows you better too.”

"Not better, just different.”

Albert was nervous to make the first bend. It had been years since he had last bent pipe. He went slow and checked it more than he had to. Soon all the little tricks came back to him, and eventually the first leg matched the template perfectly. He did one more, then turned the process over to the boys. He watched them carefully and summoned more patience than he thought he had. After a few tweaks, their work matched the template also.

Before they knew it, noon came, and the boys had to leave. Albert had them clean up the shop and put away the tools before he released them back to Eugenia.

"Do you guys want some lunch?" Albert asked after Eugenia drove away. "I can grill some burgers."

The three men busied themselves getting the grill and starting the fire. They waited in the cool of the garage for the fire to burn from blazing youth to useful middle age.

"You've got quite the collection of tools here, Albert," Jack said.

"They've been gathering dust for years. It's been great to get some out again. You seem to know your way around a drill press."

"I've got a wood shop at home, but I don't get down there much anymore. Seems the older I get the less time I have. Course, it takes half the day just to get moving."

"Ain't that the truth."

Andy listened while the two old men made bar talk and sipped their beers. They commiserated on each other's aches and pains. Albert bemoaned the state of today's culture. Jack offered examples of hope like the young Scouts.

Albert got up to dump the charcoal out of the starter chimney. "Still needs to cool down a bit."

"I'll get the meat ready," Andy said.

After Andy left Albert turned to Jack. "Seems to me you've done a lifetime of good working with all those kids. My own included."

"I've gained more than any of them. It's kept me young – on my toes. Your ... Andy didn't need much help, just a place to put his energy."

"I've never thanked you for all you did for him."

"I tried hard not to overstep my bounds. I didn't want to interfere with your family."

"We had some rough times back then. I wasn't much good for Andrew. It was lucky he found you. I'm not used to talking like this."

"I know. It isn't easy for us old-school guys to talk."

"What got you started in Scouts and such?" Albert asked.

"It was a few years after I got back from 'Nam. I needed something positive in my life."

"How long were you over there?"

"I did a tour and a half, early on, when we were still called advisors. Being an advisor didn't keep me from taking a round in the hip. I rode out in a chopper and never went back."

"That must've been rough. I was lucky and joined up between wars -- never left State-side."

"Glad you didn't. I wouldn't wish action on anyone. Saw some bad stuff... had to do some bad stuff."

"That war screwed up a lot of men. How'd you get over it?"

"I had some dark years. Finally, I forgave myself. There was no one else around to do it. Eventually, I found the Church. That helped the most."

"I don't really get forgiveness," Albert said. "What you've done in the past is part of your present and future. You can't change it. You have to accept what happened. Forgiving doesn't change anything."

"It changes the one doing the forgiving. Accepting forgiveness is a big favor to them. It frees them."

"Freedom is what you do with what's been done to you."

"Forgiveness can make the future better," Jack said. "Anger boxes people up in the past. Forgiving releases them from that box so they can move on."

"Jack, I don't take you for a bullshitter. Where you going with this?"

" I'll play my hand. You can walk or put yours on the table. Andrew told me what you did the night his mother died."

"A week ago, I woulda thrown you outta here," Albert said, "but I've changed. Are you saying Andrew wants to forgive me for what I did?"

"He's trying to get to there. You could make it easier for him."

"This has been great," Jack said after lunch. "I did something productive then got to sit around and drink some beers, but now I have to get back home."

"I'll walk you out," Albert said.

Andy watched as the two men who shaped his life walked together. They talked for a while next to Jack's car then did the oddest thing. They straightened up and saluted each other. His father did an about-face and came back to the garage.

"Andrew, can I show you something? Up in the studio?"

Andy followed his father up the stairs. Albert uncovered a painting. "I just finished it. Take a minute to look. You don't have to say anything."

Andy had to lean against the worktable. The light, the silence, the painting took him somewhere -- somewhere deep... and dark. He didn't know the image. He felt he was known by it.

"Who is the woman?" Andy asked.

"Anyone you want her to be," Albert replied.

"Is it Mother?"

"I loved her Andrew. Now I know. I did."

"You've been grieving all these years and didn't know it," Andy said. "You just kept painting."

"This was the only place I could forget-- until these new paintings came to me. Then Sophie appeared. It all seems connected somehow. I'm so sorry for all the lost years."

Andy heard a small, soft voice. "Let it go. Give it to me."

"Andrew, please forgive me." His father's voice startled him.

Forty

After leaving the gallery Sophie rushed back to her grandfather's, but there didn't seem to be anyone around. Finally, she saw her father coming down the stairs cradling a bubble-wrapped painting. He laid it carefully in the car and walked toward Sophie. She was going to run and tell him her news, but something in his face stopped her. He came up on the porch. He reached out and held her in his arms. He looked down. His eyes were red and moist.

"I know what you did. He told me about the mountain in Vermont. He's a different man. I don't understand it but thank you. I have a father."

Sophie went up to the studio. Her grandfather was sitting on the couch. She sat down next to him. He took her hand and looked into her deeply. His eyes were a patinated copy of her father's. As he slowly closed them, he said, "I love you, Sophie."

Andy sat on the bench by his father's lawn and let his emotions ebb. He sensed he had come to a point in the game when the opponent began to fade and their weakness was revealed. Except this time the opponent was in his soul. He noticed some small tree limbs had blown onto the lawn. He gathered them up and added them to the pile of clippings and leaves behind the garage. He met Sophie and Albert coming down from the studio.

"Will you two be alright? I have to get Mom and Jack from the cottage," Sophie said. "I'll meet you back here after we pack and clean up."

"We're fine," Andy said, "I'll stay here for now."

Sophie kissed her two men and left them standing together.

As she walked away Albert said, "That's a special daughter you raised. Do you realize that?"

"Truthfully, I had no idea before all this happened."

"I've had enough thinking for one day," Albert said. "What do you want to do?"

"Let's look through the house and see what needs to be done," Andy replied.

"It could use some more work to make it livable. Bonnie has made a good start."

"How about I call her, and we can see what she has in mind."

When Bonnie drove in she saw her father and brother staring at the roof of the house.

"Hi, what's up?"

"Very funny. We're just looking at how bad the roof is," Andy said. "It needs to be replaced. Dad and I were saying: we need to take a good look and see what kind of shape it's in."

"Might as well start in the basement," Albert said.

Albert lifted the outside door and flipped the switch to light the bare bulbs. It was swept clean. Leaning against the wall were two bicycles.

"I didn't throw those away," he said. "I thought you might have some use for them."

"I remember when we got them. That was a good day," Andy said. "This looks good, let's get upstairs."

They made the climb to the second floor landing. The door on the right was open.

"I sleep in your old room," Albert said. "It's smaller and easier to clean."

"It was a nice room," Bonnie said.

They opened the door on the left. There were sports posters on the wall. The bed was made up and the desk piled with books.

"You never cleaned it out?" Andy asked.

"No, I left it the way you had it," Albert replied.

They moved to the next door on the left. Andy and Bonnie looked at the piles of memories their father had stacked up.

"There's some junk to get rid of," Andy said. "What do you do with stuff like that?"

"Most people just pack it away until they forget about it," Bonnie replied.

"We'll have to go through it sometime," Andy said. "It might even be fun."

At the end of the hall was a final door. "I haven't been in there in a long time," Albert said.

The door was stuck so Andy had to force it open. The shades were drawn giving a dim yellow light. There was a big bed with an uncovered mattress. The walls on one side had shelves of porcelain figurines. The other wall was bare except for a black and white photo of a young couple posed against a city scape.

"Where was that?" Andy asked.

"The top of the Empire State Building," Albert replied.

They became quiet, then turned as one to leave. As they did they brushed against one another. The brush turned to a touch; the touch turned to an embrace. They shared their tears until Albert finally said. "I didn't expect to ever see a day like this. I didn't think I had it in me."

"We have to start where we are and just keep looking forward. I'm willing to try," Andy said.

"It's like a new life," Bonnie said. "I have my family back. It's because of Sophie. You two understand that don't you? Her spirit did this."

"We know," the men answered in unison.

The three sat on the porch and discussed ideas for the house until Sophie, Lillian and Jack arrived.

"Don't you guys look comfortable," Lillian said. "We finished cleaning and packing. We're all set to leave in the morning. I don't suppose you've thought of dinner?"

"Let's eat in. I'll make omelets," Andy said.

Andy prepped the onions, peppers, ham and cheese. He opened the oven and there was his mother's omelet pan; the one he learned on. One by one he served his family until it was just him and his father left. He sat down and listened to the happy chatter around the table.

Above it all he heard, "Good omelet son."

"Thanks, Dad."

ABOUT THE AUTHOR

Paul Mitchell is a retired Nurse Practitioner embarking on his next career with this first novel. He is a native of the Finger Lakes Region of New York State where he lives with his wife, Joan, who is also a retired nurse. They share their hillside homestead with six alpacas that provide fleece for Joan to weave. He is also an accomplished photographer. He enjoys winemaking, history and all things out of doors. His other work can be found on his blog:

http://www.easthillviews.com

CPSIA information can be obtained
at www.ICGtesting.com
Printed in the USA
BVHW090824170722
642199BV00008B/215

9 781087 911670